Summit
Books

Also by Kiran Millwood Hargrave

The Dance Tree

The Mercies

Almost Life

a novel

Kiran Millwood Hargrave

SUMMIT BOOKS
New York   Amsterdam/Antwerp   London   Toronto
Sydney/Melbourne   New Delhi

Summit Books
An Imprint of Simon & Schuster, LLC
1230 Avenue of the Americas
New York, NY 10020

For more than 100 years, Simon & Schuster has championed authors and the stories they create. By respecting the copyright of an author's intellectual property, you enable Simon & Schuster and the author to continue publishing exceptional books for years to come. We thank you for supporting the author's copyright by purchasing an authorized edition of this book.

No amount of this book may be reproduced or stored in any format, nor may it be uploaded to any website, database, language-learning model, or other repository, retrieval, or artificialintellig ence system without express permission. All rights reserved. Inquiries may be directed to Simon & Schuster, 1230 Avenue of the Americas, New York, NY 10020 or permissions@simonandschuster.com.

This book is a work of fiction.An y references to historical events, real people, or real places are used fictitiously . Other names, characters, places, and events are products of the author's imagination, and any resemblance to actual events or places or persons, living or dead, is entirely coincidental.

Copyright © 2026 by Kiran Millwood Hargrave Limited

All rights reserved, including the right to reproduce this book or portions thereof in any form whatsoever. For information, address Simon & Schuster Subsidiary Rights Department, 1230 Avenue of the Americas, New York, NY 10020.

First Summit Books hardcover edition March 2026

SUMMIT BOOKS and colophon are registered trademarks of Simon & Schuster, LLC

Simon & Schuster strongly believes in freedom of expression and stands against censorship in all its forms. For more information, visit BooksBelong.com.

Interior design by Carly Loman

Manufactured in the United States of America

ISBN 978-1-6682-0427-6

for TdF

But that unique sum of things, the experience that I lived, with all its order and its randomness . . . all the things I've talked about, others I have left unspoken—there is no place where it will all live again.

SIMONE DE BEAUVOIR

Part One

1978–1979

Love at first sight is always spoken in the past tense. The scene is perfectly adapted to this temporal phenomenon: distinct, abrupt, framed, it is already a memory (the nature of a photograph is not to represent but to memorialize) . . . this scene has all the magnificence of an accident: I cannot get over having had this good fortune: to meet what matches my desire.

from *A Lover's Discourse* by Roland Barthes

Chapter One

They met on the steps of the Sacré-Cœur beneath a sky of the most fierce and unerring blue, so without variation or hesitation it was as though a painter had brushed cerulean across the horizon, no shade or blight anywhere, yet undeniably a cover up. Or perhaps it was only so blue by contrast to the dome and cupolas of the Sacré-Cœur, which too seemed arranged, virgin white paper cut out and laid across the perfect wash of the sky.

Laure was reading and smoking on the left staircase, her long legs thrust out before her, her prematurely greying hair flipped over and hanging across her narrow face. Erica approached, sweating from the ascent through Montmartre's cobbles in her polyester skirt printed with great bunching florals, rippling and sticking to her thighs. She swears it was the right staircase, remembers turning to her left to look up at the dome pinned against the sky. Smoke in her eyes, an instinctive irritation that did not serve her well in Paris. Each will remember it differently, but on this fact they agree: it was Erica who smiled first, and said—

•

"Bonjour."

Laure did not smile easily at the best of times. She was hungover, and the walk in the July swelter to this reading spot a punishment she was still recovering from, a pilgrimage to atone for the previous night's sins. She hadn't expected to meet an angel at the basilica's steps, only to read and watch people and grouse inwardly at the tourists swarming her city. But when she looked up, this girl was singularly beautiful. Long auburn hair, tanned skin, a hint of Laforêt in the wide set of her eyes, her askance doe demeanour. These judgements Laure made rapidly and without self-awareness. She was adamant she didn't set much store by appearance. Everything about hers was calculated to suggest this, from her man's shirt to her grey trousers, a little short at the ankles. Her hair was lank and stank of beer and smoke, but she was aware of the girl's—the tourist's—nervous expression as she tried again, her accent stronger, more careful, and knew she was experiencing what Michel called Laure's *ravissement*, the strong and slightly terrifying aura Laure exerted as though she were a wolf pinning a prey animal.

"Bonjour."

"Hi."

"Je m'appelle Erica."

Laure raised her eyebrows. "Laure. English?"

"Yes," said the girl, with a slump of disappointment and relief. And then, a flare of defiance: "Française?"

Laure did smile then. "Parisienne."

She did not find tourists charming, and certainly not English ones, but she thought this girl darling. How old was she? Seventeen? Her skin glowed that undeniable golden that came from youth and health, true health from walks outdoors and sleeping well and eating vegetables and not drinking. Laure did none of these things, except walk when she wanted to punish herself. Her particular, slouching thinness came from these frequent atonements and from her father, who ate butter as though it was a sin to leave a scraping in the dish and was rangy as a whippet. Her build bought her a certain kind of cachet—that rapture Michel alluded to—but Laure knew she smoked too much, drank too much, ate too little with colour, or indeed anything that was not bread and butter. Her skin broke out around her bleeds, her jaw rough and bumpy, and her face looked grey in early light.

She propped her glasses onto her chin, an affectation also learned from her father, and looked more squarely at the girl.

"Je suis ravie de vous rencontrer."

"No," said Laure. "You would say, enchanté. Or, ravie."

"Ravie," repeated Erica, her mouth parting to show a kitten-pink tongue, white teeth. Laure ran her own furred tongue over her own furred teeth, took another drag on her roll-up and blew the smoke out in a pointed stream. Erica scrunched up her nose, and Laure knew she was a thought away from coughing and wafting her hand.

"Your accent is too tight. You need to let your words fall."

"Your English is good."

Laure shrugged. *Of course.*

"I am sorry to bother you." Her voice was posh, clipped. Perhaps the formal address suited her better after all. She was sweet.

"It's only I saw you reading, and it's not the sort of thing I would normally do, but it's hot and it's Paris, isn't it?" She gave a silly laugh, and it occurred to Laure that here was a clever girl told it was better to be beautiful than clever.

The girl pulled her bag around to her front, a severe leather satchel in light brown, the sort of thing a schoolboy would carry. Laure watched her struggle with the buckles. There were no creases on the straps—the thing was brand new. A gift? It did not fit with her floaty skirt, the Bardot top—was that cheesecloth?—and in fact none of it fitted. It was a costume, a thing put on to walk around Paris and do things she would never normally do. Her nails were unpainted.

She'd managed to wrestle a book from her bag, a poor reveal too long in the making, but she lifted aloft a copy of *Fragments d'un discours amoureux*, the exact same edition Laure held loosely in her own mauled fingertips, from the Collection *Tel Quel*. Laure's was marked with wine-glass rings across the white background, the image of tense and searching fingertips, the spine cracked and binding perilous, made thicker by her dog-eared pages. Erica's was pristine, as though never opened, though a metro ticket marked a third of the way in.

"And honestly, I thought I was mad. Pretentious, you know, to buy this let alone try to read it in public. I was talked into it by the bookseller. But then I saw you reading here, and smoking, and it made me laugh..." Erica trailed off, realizing she had been insulting, but not realizing Laure loved to be insulted. "Only, I thought if a proper Parisienne were doing it, I could too."

"Which bookshop?" asked Laure, knowing it would be Shakespeare and Co.

"Le Divan."

Laure did not betray a flicker of surprise. "My friend works there."

"Oh! Perhaps she was the one. Dark hair?"

"No. Blonde."

"Ah." Erica dithered. "And I hope you don't mind—" She rummaged in her satchel and pulled out a camera, a boxy Canon AE-1 with a black lens cap. "But I took a photograph from back there, because you do look *very* French. The picture I had in my head, anyway."

Laure did not blink.

"I hope you don't mind," she repeated. "I can destroy the film if you do."

Laure let her gaze trickle down Erica's face to the camera in her hand and back again, knowing she would blush, and she did, deliciously, from her slick collarbones to her round cheeks. She shrugged to show she didn't care, as though she was used to people taking her photograph and telling her they had done so. "First time in France?"

"And Paris! Well, yes of course in Paris. Paris and France. First time anywhere actually, other than England. I've been to London, to the British Museum and the National Gallery, but I knew I couldn't think myself an art lover until I had been to Paris. I've been to the Louvre and the Petit Palais. There's the Pompidou of course, but I go there tomorrow. Today the weather is so good, I thought, why not walk to the Sacré-Cœur, see the church and sit on the grass and see the city from up here. I'm staying on the Rive Gauche, and it was further than I thought, and hotter too."

She fanned herself for emphasis, and the camera strap flapped against her cheek. She blushed even more furiously. Laure wondered what she would look like naked.

Laure smiled perfunctorily, and pushed her glasses back up onto her nose. She meant that to be a dismissal, and was glad when the girl tripped up past her, up the left-hand steps of the Sacré-Cœur, and a little disappointed too, when she lost her scent—girlishly sweet, the sort you would get in a pharmacy—and turned to watch her disappear into the crowd making for the church.

•

Erica collected her skirts in her hand as she moved up the steps against the flow of people, her cheeks hot. She was burned on her shoulders and nose, could feel the skin there stretched and sore. She didn't understand what had happened to her. It was as though she'd left her body and watched another, bolder self walk towards that woman and attempt to talk to her. It was how she'd felt at school, arriving at a conversation already underway, laughing a beat too late and too loudly. She glanced behind her as she entered the cool of the basilica, but she—Laure, a perfect French name—was out of sight. The way she'd looked at her, with such disdain. Erica had felt like a child again.

But she was not a child, she reminded herself, as she took a paper shawl from the stack and covered her tender shoulders. She was eighteen, an adult, travelling abroad with her own money in her pocket. Aside from that woman on the steps, her attempts at French had been greeted with tolerance and sometimes praise, though her dreams of blending in with the students around the Sorbonne were dashed the moment she arrived at Gare du Nord. She had painfully misjudged the style—there were no Bardot tops and bright skirts as *Girl About Town* promised. French women wore leather jackets even in the sun, and turtlenecks, tailored trousers and skirts. Their breasts were small and free under thin knits and shirts, nipples pointed and pert.

Erica shifted her bra strap, feeling sweat soaking the lace. Her own breasts were large and heavy, her nipples indistinct. Her disgust at her own body had been bred into her at school, where the girls would take turns placing pencils under their breasts, praising each other if they fell and retching when they did not. Naked she was too much: too saggy, too expansive, too solid. She did not mind herself in clothes so much, but she felt very self-conscious in her holiday outfit, and wished she'd brought her pleated skirts and work shirts, the tea dresses she'd inherited from her mother and let out at the chest and hips.

But she'd spent all her weekend earnings on these clothes precisely because they were the sort of things she'd never wear. When she'd got the idea into her head a couple of years ago to spend the summer after leaving school in Europe, Paris arrived at her like a flurry of wings, a beating flight of fancy. She'd sold it to her parents on the libraries and galleries, but she envisaged drinking red wine and kissing French men, walking the cobbled streets and lounging in the grounds of the Palace of Versailles, sitting on benches near the Seine, reading Sartre.

Paris was beautiful but faded, the Seine stinking for streets around and the benches beds for drunks and tramps. A single glass of red wine made her stomach bloat and her head spin, and it was too hot for wine anyway. The Palace of Versailles had been bombed by Breton nationalists the month before and would not open this summer. Her sandals chafed and slipped on the cobbles. The pension she booked was dingy, the sheets damp and the walls sweating. The women-only bathroom was shared with Spanish students who laughed when she said hello, and the plughole was always clogged with hairs, and she was sure someone else was using her toothbrush. At least she was not on her period and would not be for her whole stay, thanks to a miracle in a sugar shell taken from the blister pack of pills borrowed from Lucy and swallowed diligently each morning.

But, she told herself, *you are here*. The magic of being somewhere no one knew her was intoxicating. She had found a café on the corner of her street where she could look in four directions and watch the women with their dogs and the men with their bicycles, the students talking intensely or reading and smoking, all of them smoking. She'd been every afternoon, so now the owner started her order without asking, a café au lait like Hemingway and a palmier, and was content to leave her be and let her read and eavesdrop until closing. She loved the hand gestures, the shapes the smoke made in the air as it got dark. She loved the names of the streets: Rue Saint-Sulpice, Rue de Rivoli, Rue Crémieux. She loved the bakeries and the bars, the way the streets wrapped and sprawled and reached for each other, the river.

And as she stepped into the Sacré-Cœur, she loved that too. She had regretted choosing such a hot day to climb the steps, but the immersion into the shaded cool was all the better for it. It smelled of old stone and lit candles and was smaller inside than she'd expected. The benches were flooded with light from the cupola, and she sat on the warm wood and tipped her head back, eyeing the celestial figures of the North Dome, the gold-backed Jesus in Majesty and his attendant angels, more carved into the grey stone, wings stretched wide. She'd spent hours poring over the highly saturated photographs in the library's copy of *Paris on Film*, but they'd blurred the colours into a garish glare. The small squares of the mosaics seemed to glow with light, the interaction of stone and tile creating an oscillation, a ripple that lent breath to the saints' faces, a quiver to the angels' feathers. She sighed, the hairs on her arms standing up. She felt something akin to what those long-ago devout must have felt: transcendence laced with the necessary twinge of fear.

A man sat beside her, a little too close, and Erica stood though she'd have liked to sit longer. She moved away to join the slowly circling crowds and, glancing behind her, saw the man move to where she'd sat. She imagined the warmth she'd left behind meeting his legs. As she read the inscriptions she felt his eyes on her. She dropped a centime in the collection box and lit a votive candle for her grandmother, peered inside the fonts and queued to climb the dome. She'd have preferred to see the crypt, but there was something about the idea of descending while being watched that felt threatening. After five minutes in the queue she changed her mind. She knew it was due to the man's scrutiny, for he had joined the queue too, and now stepped from it to follow her.

It was nothing new, being followed. In King's Lynn it happened sometimes, usually when she was in school uniform, but in Paris it had become a daily occurrence, men of all ages, boys too, openly whistling and making kissy sounds, sitting at her table, or linking arms with her if she let her guard down. She didn't mind too much, and when it made her heart race and her anxiety spike, she remembered her mother's advice to smile smally and shake her head.

This man was insistent though, she could feel it from the moment he'd sat beside her. He was only a few years older, with full lips and thick curly hair, and though he was handsome when he smiled at her, she felt exhausted, already, at what was to come.

"Salut," he said. She smiled at her feet, and tried to move away. He caught her elbow. "Tu es belle."

"Merci," she whispered, and pulled from his grip. The paper shawl ripped and came apart as though doused in water. She crossed her arms over her chest, holding her shoulders, but he was drinking her in, eyes dripping over her.

"Parlons." It is not a question.

"Non, merci."

"Anglaise? English? Hey, cherry, you want to talk to me?"

She walked quickly away from him, could pick out his footfall on the stone behind her. It was all she could do not to run. Not knowing what else to do, she hurried down the right stairs, hoping the woman would still be there. She was, her book held languidly in her hand, a roll-up between her lips, her eyes concealed behind her sunglasses. Erica threw herself down beside her. The woman lowered her glasses to her chin once more, shifted her cigarette to the side of her mouth.

"Back again?"

"Please. I'm sorry." Erica looked around. There was her admirer, coming to a halt on the step beside them. He smiled at the woman, Laure.

"Elle est rapide, ta copine."

Laure said nothing, staring him out. He made to sit down beside Erica but without warning, without changing her expression, Laure barked once, twice. The man laughed uncertainly, but she growled and he hovered in a half crouch. Scenting victory, Laure increased her snarling. People were looking, shaking their heads, but Erica joined in, both of them hissing and growling, and the man said,

"Putain."

And Laure said, "Casse-toi."

And he left.

•

Erica gripped Laure's knee. "That was brilliant."

Laure could see the girl was shaken. Her pallor, her overly bright eyes. She felt the warmth from Erica's hand on her knee, the liquid pooling in her belly. She heard Michel's voice in her mind. *Invétéré*. She had work to do, an essay to write, this book and others to read. But she was bored, so she put her book down, and turned the full force of her gaze on Erica.

"OK?" She placed her hand on top of Erica's. The touch brought Erica's laugh to an abrupt halt, the girl's expression suddenly sober.

"Yes, I'm all right. Thank you. I really am sorry to have troubled you again."

She started to get up and Laure steered her closer instead, so their thighs were touching, Laure's thighbone overshooting Erica's by inches. She liked shorter women. Michel said if she were a man she would be a brute. As it was, she was only a pervert.

"It's fine. I was thinking it was a shame not to see you again. What are you doing now?"

Erica was flustered, blushing again. Laure hoped she didn't play poker.

"I thought I'd read for a while." She pulled the Barthes from her satchel. "Perhaps I could sit with you?" Laure stuffed her own copy into her pocket and stood up, offering her hand.

"It's too hot. Let's get a drink."

After a startled pause, Erica let her pull her to her feet, and Laure abruptly dropped her hand. They walked down the steps, past the green stretches of grass, and from Erica's glances at the people stretched out,

Laure could tell she would rather lie down and rest there. But she followed her down the steps and onto the cobbles, which made Laure feel tenderly towards her. Laure's body was stiff and she pulled her hair across her neck to hide the love bite Hilde had given her the night before. She smiled down at Erica, who was focused on her feet, which were plump and poorly clad in cheap thin sandals.

"Would you like coffee? Wine?"

"Maybe a beer?" ventured Erica, and Laure took her to a small bar on Rue Jean-Baptiste Pigalle she had been to with one of the history students last year. She'd been drunk, and it was darker and dingier in the midday sun than she'd remembered. She ordered them two beers and they sat at a sticky table on cushionless metal chairs outside. Laure took the beer like it was medicine, and Erica sipped.

"Barthes then?" Laure tapped the book in her breast pocket. "What do you think?"

"I'm reading slowly, and I have to look up some of the words," said Erica, "but I think it is so romantic. So beautiful."

Laure laughed into the final swallow of her beer. "Romantic? I don't know what dictionary you are using, but I don't think it is romantic."

"Maybe I am misunderstanding."

Laure didn't care to educate her. "What did you think of the Sacré-Cœur?"

"Beautiful," and then, "It was peaceful. It felt smaller inside, like it wrapped around me. And the light is everywhere, with the gold. It bounces it, doesn't it? The angels, they seem to quiver. It was lovely."

They were weak words. Laure was disappointed, mostly in herself. What had she expected from this tourist? They should have stayed at the steps, read until they were sun drunk and gone back to hers. She could no longer see the path forward, how to navigate this girl into bed before she stopped desiring her. She could leave, but that had the feeling of abandoning a puppy. She smiled perfunctorily.

"Another beer?"

"I'll get it." The girl leapt up and went back inside. Laure got out her tobacco and papers. She heard Erica speaking her godawful French, heard the barman flirting bluntly and badly, Erica's nervous laughter.

What must it be like, to have men everywhere want to fuck you? Laure was convinced it wasn't as fun as those girls made out. Maybe some of them relished it, revelled in seducing men, knew how to turn them on and enjoyed it. Her own allure was made solely for her own sex and she had never questioned it, even as a girl with boys trying to see up her skirt or futilely grabbing her flat chest. None of them did it because they desired her, but out of a sort of calculated curiosity, much as they would squash ants in a line to see what the others would do.

The girls though—that was different. It was as if Laure spoke a language only they understood. She could make them laugh and blush and later, come as they never had before. But that was when she discovered sex could exist for her. For a long time she thought she did not like it, as a concept and certainly not an act. She toyed with becoming a nun, the silence and the clean mountain air and the robes, and the women of course. It all appealed. The first girl Laure kissed told her she was Mama, and Laure Papa, and for a while Laure wondered if this was in fact it, if she was a boy and that was why the sight of the girls in their swimming costumes made her throb, why when she listened to Françoise Hardy she thought of her classmate Sarah Lebroy's freckled collarbones and not, as her friends did, Jean-Pierre from the year above's veined forearms.

It was a relief, then, to come to university and to Paris and discover women fucked women without either party pretending they were men. Laure had not needed to try to find the others—they swarmed to her; something in her essence, her body language, her scent. She settled into her new, expanded life with none of the guilt and unease others experienced—this choice came at a cost, of course. But one she told herself she was happy to pay.

Erica finally emerged with the beers, and two shot glasses balanced between her fingers, at the sight of which Laure lit her cigarette.

"Gin," said Erica, apologetically. "He insisted."

Ah. Free drinks though. That was a benefit that did not come her way often.

•

Laure raised the glass to her and downed the warm gin. Erica followed suit, eyes watering.

"That's disgusting," she gasped, and Laure laughed and agreed. Buoyed by her amusement, Erica asked, "What do you do?"

"Smoke. Speak to strangers."

Erica grinned. This was good. Laure was warming up. Maybe she should brave the bartender again, get them another gin.

"I mean for work."

"I'm studying."

"You're a student?"

Another shrug. *Of course*.

Erica had misjudged her age. She'd thought Laure much older, late twenties at least. She had lines around her mouth, a worldliness in her gaze. "Of what? Oh! Let me guess. English."

"Non."

"French. Literature, I mean."

Laure shook her head, squinting against her own smoke.

"Philosophy."

Laure tipped her hand side to side in a *sort of* gesture. Scenting victory, Erica chewed her thumbnail. It tasted of the clear polish her mother had bought her to stop her chewing her nails.

"Anthropology? Some sort of social science?"

"Art Theory," said Laure, and though she delivered it as a throwaway, Erica read the pride in her voice. It was a chink in her cool that Erica could chisel away at.

"I didn't know you could do a degree in that."

"It's a thesis. I'm studying for my doctorate."

"I'm going to university in September. English."

"Here?"

"No!" Erica was thrilled at the idea. "England. Norfolk."
"Norfolk University?"
"University of East Anglia."
"I don't know it."
Erica absorbed this blow. "Where are you studying?"
"Sorbonne."

Of course. It explained the ease, the obvious intelligence, the belonging. Erica fancied she could pick out the Sorbonne students on sight. They emerged only in the evening, their days spent in libraries or their halls, and swarmed the parks and bars, carrying books, smoking, drinking carafes of wine. Erica's French was not strong enough to understand all she overheard, but it was an eavesdropped mention of Sartre that sent her to the bookshop where she was instead talked into buying *Fragments d'un discours amoureux* from the bookseller who was not Laure's friend, a book only published the year before and already mesmerizing to her. Romantic, she'd said to Laure, and still she felt it. She'd like to know why Laure disagreed, but she didn't want to feel stupid. The gin and the heat were thickening her blood, making her limbs heavy and loose. She liked the feeling, liked sitting on this wonky chair on the hot pavement next to this intimidating and handsome woman. It made her feel more settled by association, almost as though she belonged.

"Alors." Laure clapped her hands together, making her jump. "I must go. It was a pleasure to pass the time with you."

She said it drily, and with a rush of shame Erica realized she had not passed some unspoken test, that after her initial dismissal on the steps she had failed to improve matters. Her mind flicked through every stupid thing she'd said, every graceless action, every immature laugh. Laure was stubbing out her cigarette with deft fingers, licking the end and stowing it in her pocket.

"Yes," said Erica. And without knowing what she was saying, with the impulse that comes with desperation, she said, "May I have one?"

It caught Laure visibly, a yank on a cord.

"A smoke." Erica gestured at the pocket the half-smoked cigarette had disappeared into.

"Sure." Laure took out a small blue tin and a cardboard box. She placed both on the table before Erica, who understood with mute horror she was expected to roll her own. After a moment's hesitation, Erica opened the tobacco tin, peering inside uncertainly.

Laure seemed amused, but she did not embarrass her further. "Allow me." It was an act of unimaginable kindness, Erica thought, that she licked her thumb, pulled a paper from the box and stacked tobacco into it, spiralled up a strip of cardboard into a filter, licked the paper and rolled it tightly. It was a perfect cylinder, a work of art really, and she took it as such, reverently.

"Light?"

Erica had not thought this far ahead. She did not want to actually smoke the thing. She'd only wanted to keep Laure with her a little longer, to linger awhile in her orbit.

"Non, merci."

"Rien."

There was nothing left to keep her. Erica smiled, looking as though being left was of no consequence. But she felt more alone as Laure walked away than she had been before they met.

Laure turned, and the light was brilliant on her face, short, downy hairs on her cheeks, her eyes a deep-water grey. She saw Erica was staring at her, and gave a goofy smile, performative and true. She called,

"There's a reading, tomorrow at Le Divan."

"OK," called Erica, too loudly, so relieved not to be saying goodbye for ever.

"Eight o'clock." Laure raised her hand in a salute, and was gone.

Le Divan was in the sixth, at the corner of the Rue de l'Abbaye and the Rue Bonaparte, barely twenty minutes from Erica's pension, but there was too much to do to spend a leisurely day getting ready. She rushed her time at the newly opened Centre Pompidou, though it was to be the centrepiece of her Parisian experience and the ticket was expensive, merely glancing at the Jasper Johns and the Gerhard Richters, and returned instead to the treacherous cobbles of Montmartre to seek out the second-hand clothing shop she had spotted the day before. She could not, would not, turn up to the reading in paisley. The shop smelled bad, body odour and smoke, and most of the racks held clothes more suited to the bin or Laure's build than Erica, but she found a mustard dress, only slightly stained, of thin knit that clung nicely to her hips and breasts, highlighting her waist with a silver coin belt. Though cheap, it cost double her day's budget, but she figured there might be food at the reading, and if there was not, she could do with skipping some meals.

She did not have time to wash it, so when she got back to her horrid little room she sprayed the dress with Charlie Blue and heaved open the flaking window to let it air in the sluggish breeze. Then she went to the damp bathroom and locked the door, selecting the sharpest of the razors lined up on the windowsill, and shaved her underarms and legs, contorting herself to reach even the midpoint of her calves, then took cream that smelled of roses and rubbed it into her stinging skin. She didn't bother to wash away the stubble in the sink—let the laughing girls see how it felt. The bathroom was home to the pension's sole mirror, and she checked her face, thought perhaps she felt a spot coming beneath her lip, but with her mother's voice in her head resisted picking at it. With some lipstick, it wouldn't show.

Outside, one of the Spanish girls was waiting, wearing only her underwear.

"Bonsoir."

The Spanish girl clucked her tongue in reply, shouldering past her and shutting the door hard. Erica returned to the room and checked the clock. Five thirty. The day was passing very slowly. Why was she so anxious, as though waiting to sit an entrance exam? Perhaps because this was a scene from one of her fantasies, an invitation to a book reading in Paris. An invitation extended by a quintessentially French woman, someone so utterly unlike her.

She sniffed experimentally at the dress, could still smell the smoke layered under artificial jasmine, the slight voluptuousness of fat from the vents of the café below. She took it down and shook it out.

"A great find," the shopkeeper had insisted. "Very style."

The stain was more noticeable in the strip light of the bedroom and she turned it off. She could still make it out—it looked like coffee, billowing across the right hip, but the reading did not start until eight. There would be bodies pressed together. She shivered in delight. Maybe she would meet a man there, handsome and intense with hair like James Taylor, one of Laure's friends from the Sorbonne. She could go to UEA with a boyfriend, Marc or Luc from Paris. She imagined them writing to each other, calling one another from the hall's telephones, twirling the cord around her finger and laughing at his jokes.

Her stomach rumbled. She was so hungry. In the basement there was a communal kitchen with a small fridge and a toaster full of mouldy crumbs. She had not paid extra for the use of it but there was no lock on the door—perhaps she could go down and see what there was. But there were bumps on her inner thighs where they chafed, and her hand had looked so fat beneath Laure's elegant fingers, her leg double the other woman's width. Better to be hungry.

She took out the Barthes and her Collins English–French dictionary, and opened it to her marked page: *désréalité*. She preferred reading in public where self-consciousness forced her to abandon the dictionary and simply read. She didn't understand everything, or even most individual words, but in the flow of letting her eyes move as they did when reading English she gained more meaning, and when she did understand a word, she found the context it offered lapping like a ripple both forwards and backwards across the surrounding sentences. But alone, she was more diligent, feeling a duty to stop every time she didn't know something, looking it up in her pocket-sized dictionary, sometimes making a note in the back so she could string several unknown words together and form a transliteration of sorts. When she got home she'd buy the translation, and see how much she got correct.

Feeling restless, she set aside the book. The hands of the clock had barely moved. She turned to the blank pages at the back of the dictionary. They were meant for notes but Erica used them for writing. Erica had always written, and started taking it more seriously a couple of years ago after her English teacher praised her re-writing of Rudyard Kipling's "If." She'd kept a painstaking diary ever since—*the unexamined life* and all that—but had left it behind at home as it was too cumbersome. This trip she'd settled for using these limited pages, precious space that made her more mindful of what was important to put down.

It was filling up with little vignettes, about the woman who gave her dog coffee from her saucer at the café, or the man who followed her for half an hour before she finally lost him by turning into a library and darting amid the stacks. She had an idea of turning them into short stories eventually, though the form was not one she especially enjoyed. All her favourite writers were masters of it, so she should be too. Today, there was only one person she wanted to write about. In her mind's eye, she moved towards the Sacré-Cœur, and noticed the woman on the steps for the first time. *Through the camera lens, she looked like an angel, or a wraith—*

When she next looked at the clock the room was dim. She hadn't turned on the light again and didn't realize her eyes were straining. The clock said seven thirty. Erica threw the books aside and reclasped her bra, hooked her knickers out of her bum and then kicked them off, putting on a clean pair instead. She pulled on the dress, which felt tighter than it had in the shop though that was impossible, she hadn't eaten after all, and pulled the coin belt a notch snugger as punishment. Using the shiny metal of her lipstick as a mirror, she traced her lips in a blush pink, lined her eyes and applied blush to her cheeks and exposed clavicles, and brushed out her hair. It fell to her waist in gentle waves, the one part of her she liked without qualification.

She had no bag but her satchel, so she put her book and lipstick inside, counted out enough money for a drink and rolled up her emergency fifty-franc note and slipped it inside her bra. For good luck, she tucked the cigarette Laure had rolled for her in there too.

She had looked up the route to the bookshop in her city map, so she put that in her bag and locked her door and walked down the stairs and out of the pension as she was taught, confident but unshowy, looking like she knew exactly where she was going.

•

Laure was nervous and she didn't know why. She'd met Pauline that afternoon, her husband away and her daughter with the nanny, and they'd fucked slowly, Pauline licking Laure's ankles and kissing the backs of her knees as she worked her with her fingers, Laure sinking into the thick mattress and clean white sheets and trying to come. She couldn't, and so they switched and she made Pauline sweat all over her lovely fresh sheets. Someone would change them before her husband came home.

They'd recently stopped talking after, and Pauline would not let her smoke in the apartment, so Laure was left with the hum of her elusive orgasm and the chatter of her brain while Pauline dozed in her arms. She knew, as she dressed, their affair was coming to an end. It was never exclusive, even outside Pauline's marriage she slept with other women and men, but still they saw each other every week and Laure knew her body now. She knew her likes and her dislikes, her mild kink for wrists and ankles, connective joints where she could tongue tendon and bone and flesh. Laure had a theory this was because during her daughter's birth the baby got stuck and her wrist fractured when they pulled her out, but Pauline did not like this theory.

"I am not your dissertation," she said. "There doesn't have to be a construct behind everything."

But Pauline was wrong, and this was another reason their passion was fading. She was too unimaginative, too uncurious about the world. She didn't even ask about Laure's love bite. Her walls were lined with books but they were unread, large glossy photo books and hardbacks of classics. It was window-dressing, just as Pauline's sensuality was. She was not an imaginative lover either, and did not pursue Laure or her own pleasure with any genuine intent. She had sex the same way Laure ate: as a necessity. Maintenance.

Their affair had begun last winter, when Laure had been invited to the

Président's dinner as one of their prized students. Pauline's husband sat on the board and had been there too, but mainly stayed outside smoking, as had Laure. He had introduced Laure to Pauline, mentioned possible patronage. This never materialized but Laure briefly fell into their circle, coming to a couple of dinners. Pauline kissed her in their hallway after their third encounter, tasting of Périgord pudding and vermouth. She was Laure's first married lover but was herself a practised cheat. It had been exciting, arousing even, but the novelty was gone and, Laure had to admit to herself, so was her desire.

She kissed Pauline perfunctorily in the hallway where it had begun, and hoped it would be the last time. As she lit up on the pavement outside the gorgeous Belle-Époque building, Laure wondered again how exactly people fell in love. Desire felt easy, and so did its leaving, but however did someone become as entangled in another person's soul as they did in each other's bodies? Everything she read made her convinced it was exactly what Pauline protested against: a construct, an inorganic forcing of matters, a word that could be filled and emptied endlessly of meaning but was too often bound to one set of values. She loved her friends, and sometimes fucked them too, but she could not imagine binding to them for ever. It was not a condition of her sexuality, for Hilde had loved her ex-girlfriend and claimed now to love Laure, and Marie and Agnès slept with no one else and had lived quite happily in the same small garret in Montparnasse since first term. They even called themselves unmarried marrieds, and wore bracelets threaded with each other's hair. But they were Classicists, traditionalists by nature.

She had half an hour to reach Le Divan, ample time but not enough to shower at the YMCA or to return to her squat to change. She could have showered at Pauline's, could finish her cigarette and knock and wash in Pauline's marble bathroom with her clean towels and perfumed soap. But she did not want to go back. Onwards, now.

She had a new old book in her pocket, bought from a bouquiniste yesterday, a hardcover of Maupassant's *Pierre et Jean* she did not need, but that leapt out at her because of the colour of the binding, sky blue as the backdrop to the Sacré-Cœur. They'd had a *Madame Bovary* in the same handsome livery, but she'd felt that too on the nose. She would find a bench near the bookshop and read awhile to ensure she was not there early. Not that she'd care how that would look, but she was used to being late and did not want to get a reputation.

•

Erica was early, and no one was there yet. The booksellers were still setting up, pulling out benches and unfolding chairs. She resisted the urge to help, and instead sat in the café next door, sucking in her stomach to stop the coin belt vanishing between her tummy rolls, and drank a black coffee because it was the cheapest thing on the menu. The caffeine made her jittery almost instantly, but she finished it anyway, even the black sludge at the bottom of the cup, and tried to read. But it was Thursday night, traditionally a student night, and even out of term time here they came, the students in their uniforms of black jackets and slacks, blazers and pencil skirts. Erica was soon too busy watching to even pretend to read, and Le Divan quickly filled and spilled onto the pavement, the spare chair at her table commandeered by a couple, the girl sitting on the boy's lap and kissing him like a cat lapping from a bowl of milk. Erica did her best not to stare, and at eight thirty decided to try and get inside the bookshop for the reading.

 She moved through the crowd that wrapped around the corner plot. The glass windows were smeared with condensation from within and blocked by bodies leaning against them without, and so she could not see inside to tell if the reading had actually started. Of course, she was not there for the reading, but it was a pretence she was willing to commit to in order to stave off any potential disappointment at neither Laure nor her future French boyfriend being there.

 The benches and chairs were full, but everyone was talking very loudly with no sign of reverent hush or a readiness for paying attention. People had glasses of wine from somewhere, and Erica saw the till point was cleared of books and leaflets and laid out with glasses and bottles of wine. She fought her way to it.

"Vin blanc, s'il vous plaît."

"Non."

Erica flushed, wondering if she was about to be asked for her age, but the bookseller gestured at the bottles and said,

"No fridge. Only red."

Knowing it was a bad idea, she paid for a glass and carried it carefully to the edge of the room, where there was a gap to stand against the bookshelves and look out over the milieu, frequently checking the door. She set down her satchel and fanned herself with her free hand. There was not even room to turn and examine the books. The air was thick and getting thicker, and she slid a hand behind her to pluck the fabric of her dress away from her back. There was no sign of an order to proceedings, and she wished someone in charge would begin, give the evening structure. If Laure wasn't coming, Erica would need a distraction.

She finished her wine and bought another, finding her spot taken when she tried to return. Forced to strike out into the crush, she drank her wine down to a manageable level and battled her way back outside. As she stepped through the doorway she half tripped over a bag, tumbling into clean air. Someone caught her elbow, causing her to sling her wine in a crescent moon over the pavement before her. She felt wine splatter over her chest.

"Shit!"

The hand on her elbow held firm and set her back on her feet as hoots of laughter rose from the crowd behind her. Cheeks flaming, she looked up and saw a man grinning apologetically down at her.

"Pardon. It was you or the wine."

"Merci," she said, though she wasn't feeling especially grateful. Behind him, she caught sight of a familiar tall frame. Laure, in a camel trench coat. She raised her eyebrows—a greeting? An admonishment? She must have brushed right past her. Erica wished the pavement would open and swallow her, or a van come and flatten her into the Paris cobbles. She watched a woman, short and slim, lean into Laure and say something, smirking. Laure shrugged the woman off and looked at Erica, jerking her head slightly in invitation. Erica went gratefully, like a beaten dog, dabbing helplessly at the red wine on her chest.

"Here." Laure pulled a balled handkerchief from her pocket and offered it to her. Erica felt like she might cry, but she smiled with all her teeth and wiped away the wine. Laure waved away the soiled handkerchief and introduced her friends.

"Françoise, Barbara, Michel, Christophe, Léa, Hilde, Claude, Agnès, et Marie."

Erica waggled her fingers and immediately wanted to die. "You work here," she told Marie, and the angular, crop-haired blonde nodded. She had large green eyes and looked like Jeanne d'Arc by way of a poet. Her fingers were tightly laced into Agnès', a round-faced Black woman, and if Erica had any doubt about what they were to each other, Marie kissed Agnès' neck before disappearing inside for more drinks.

"Where are you from?" asked Michel, a bearded man of extraordinary beauty.

"England."

"England!" Michel clapped his hands in delight. "London?"

"King's Lynn. It's a town, in Norfolk." Erica wished she had something to do with her hands. She tapped the empty glass with her nails. "Are you studying here?"

"We are all students."

"Classics," nodded Agnès.

"History."

"Anthropology."

"Girls," said Claude with a wink.

"We all study those," said Françoise.

"Almost all," said Léa and Michel in unison, before bursting into laughter.

Hilde and Laure were the only two who had not spoken. Hilde was pretty, with a snub nose, a ringer for Lulu, but she looked miserable, her blue eyes rimmed with red. Laure hadn't looked at Erica since inviting her over, and Erica thought she felt a tension between the women, as though they'd just been fighting. Marie emerged from the shop with two bottles of wine and a clutch of glasses, and the others cheered. She passed out the glasses and poured, Erica gratefully accepting a refill.

"Careful," said Claude jokingly, as Erica took a hasty sip.

Marie rolled her eyes as Agnès nuzzled back into her hair. "Ignore him, he's a child."

"I'm older than you!"

"Your brain is ageing slower than your body."

"They are brother and sister," said Michel conspiratorially.

"Your English is so good," said Erica, feeling slightly dazzled. "All of you. Do you learn at school?"

"Of course. But we read, we listen to music."

"I love Kate Bush," said Léa, fluffing up her fine blonde hair.

"Me too," said Erica, though she didn't own a single record.

"Diana Ross!" shouted Michel, and broke into "Love Hangover," swinging his hips and pursing his lips. When he was done their circle applauded, though a shout of "Tapette!" caused Michel to glare over his shoulder.

"Do you like Kate Bush?" Erica asked Laure, trying to gain a foothold in the conversation.

Hilde laughed nastily. "Quelle andouille."

"Quoi?" asked Erica.

Hilde rattled off a string of words Erica didn't understand, but Marie tutted and Agnès nudged her gently. Laure seemed unaffected by any of it, her hands busy rolling. It was beginning to look more like a crutch than an art form, and Erica felt irritated by her lack of engagement. But as though she'd read her mind, Laure licked along the paper, sealed the roll-up, and said,

"Joni Mitchell. I'm devout."

"Ah oui," spat Hilde. "Le grand amour."

"Casse-toi," said Laure, without temper.

Hilde yanked away from Agnès and pushed inside. Erica watched her go and saw that in the shop people were still, the noise level dropped.

The reading must have started, but no one outside seemed interested in going in. In the lull, Erica heard a loud male voice speaking in rhythmic, impassioned French, the clicking of fingers as applause.

"Are you studying?" said Léa.

"Yes. No. Soon. In September I start university."

"What's your research?"

"No, sorry. Undergrad. English."

"Ah, you're a schoolgirl," said Françoise, but without the spite Hilde displayed.

"I'm eighteen," said Erica, feeling the hateful blush bloom across her chest again. "Nineteen in March."

"We don't mind how old you are," said Christophe kindly. "Michel is ancient. A thousand years old."

"Vingt-neuf," said Michel. "Experienced."

Christophe purred. Erica thrilled at their company. She had never met homosexuals in the flesh before. She took another swig of red wine.

"My mother saw Joni Mitchell at the Royal Festival Hall."

"Vraiment?" Laure blew out a blue stream of smoke, and Erica realized it was dark, the sky bruised navy and the light from the bookshop painting everything in gold and shadow.

"Yes. She said it was the best night of her life."

"Cool," said Laure, and Léa and Françoise echoed her. Erica felt she'd been blessed.

"There are some good bands on at UEA. My uni. I'm hoping she might come. Joni, not my mum." Erica crossed her fingers and held them up. Françoise laughed, and Erica felt her blessing evaporate under Laure's frown at the superstitious gesture.

"Allez," said Barbara. "J'ai mal aux pieds."

"Oui." Laure threw her smoke down and shoved her hands in her pockets.

"Hilde?" said Agnès uncertainly.

"Quitte-la."

Barbara linked her arm through Laure's and Léa took Erica's.

"Lover's tiff," she said. "Hilde is jealous. Has Laure told you about her socialite?"

"No," said Erica.

"She didn't tell Hilde either. The socialite is some rich man's bored wife, a practised slut." Léa didn't sound judgemental, more admiring.

Erica nodded sagely, deliciously scandalized. It made perfect sense Laure would have multiple lovers, multiple women lovers. She was handsome, like a beautiful boy. Like Björn Andrésen. Briefly, Erica imagined holding her hand, as Agnès held Marie's, and then giggled at her absurdity.

"What's funny?" asked Léa, smiling too. Her eyes were hazy, unfocused, and Erica realized she was on something.

"Rien."

"Tu parles français?"

"Un peu."

Léa was a far kinder conversant than Laure, and pretty in an unthreatening way. They walked on arm in arm as Léa explained to her, in simple, slow French, that for months Laure had been sleeping with an older woman, a mother no less, in her twelfth arrondissement pre-war apartment, that her husband was a prominent sponsor of the university and they strongly suspected knew about his wife's affairs and got off on them. That sex with his wife was fine, but if he learned Laure was a paid-up member of the Communist Party he would probably have her killed. Erica did not know if she was meant to take this literally.

"Et Hilde?"

"Ah."

Hilde, she learned, had been involved with a girlfriend for many years, and now was on a rebound with Laure, but had convinced herself she was in love with her and was growing increasingly jealous of Laure's other lovers and frustrated with her lack of commitment.

"But it is because Hilde is still in love with Carolina. The ex. So many threads, and Laure is the knot. But you must not let that put you off."

Realizing Léa's meaning, Erica shook her head. "No, no, we are just friends."

That was not entirely the right word. Acquaintances? Laure had invited her here and not even bothered to speak a full sentence to her.

"You're straight? Claude will be pleased."

Erica looked over her shoulder. Claude grinned and gave a sardonic wave. He was cute, she decided. Not James Taylor or Björn Andrésen, but cute. He'd do. *Straight.* What else would she be?

"Where are we going?" she said, thinking to ask for the first time.

"Barbara's. Her parents live in the fourteenth, but they're never there."

Erica pulled up short. "My bag!" She'd forgotten it at the bookshop.

"What?"

"I left it behind."

"It'll be gone," said Léa. "None of us bothers with a bag."

"What's wrong?" Laure had stopped too, and turned to look at them, frowning.

"I left my bag behind." Erica felt panicky. Her room key was in there, and she could not afford the fee Madame Allard had mentioned if she lost it. And her dictionary with its notes, her book, her map. "I have to at least see if it's still there."

"It won't be," shrugged Laure. "But I'll come with you."

She let go of Barbara's arm, who exchanged a weighty glance with Michel. Erica followed her, feeling the group's eyes on her back.

"Behave, little sister!" called Michel, in English so Erica knew she was meant to understand.

"Is Michel your brother?"

"Non."

Erica looked back. The group were joined each to each—a hand around a shoulder or a waist, Michel linking little fingers with Barbara. A stab of longing in Erica's chest, to have such ease with another person, let alone several. Maybe that was waiting for her at university. Someone, many people, who would help her slough off her unremarkable girlhood and change her life. Maybe others who wanted to write—or at least people she could say that to openly without them laughing.

"Thank you for coming with me," she said, and Laure nodded. She looked tired, purple shadows under her eyes, her cheekbones stark. She raised her cigarette to her lips, and in its flare Erica noticed a bleeding hangnail.

"How was the Pompidou."

"Incredible," said Erica, remembering her visit as though in fast forward, zipping through the galleries, up the escalators, turning her back on the views of Paris and leaving early to buy this dress. "I thought I would find the building ugly, but it is an eruption, isn't it?"

"Eruption." Laure's mouth turned down at the sides. "I think it is vile. But I see that."

"Have you been?"

"Not yet. It only just opened. Will you go to L'Orangerie?"

"It wasn't on my list. Should I?"

Laure halted abruptly. "Definitely. *Les Nymphéas* are so excruciatingly beautiful. They swallow you down."

She was more animated than Erica had ever seen her. "Perhaps we could go together?"

Laure looked down at her, and without Erica realizing what was about to happen, Laure kissed her, full on the mouth. It was sudden, and quick, and Laure drew back with her eyes open, checking Erica's reaction. A hundred thoughts raced through Erica's mind and then stopped, replaced by a sort of high-pitched white noise. She had the taste of tobacco on her lips, a humming warmth. The spot beneath her lower lip throbbed as blood rushed to her face. *Straight.* What else. Without thinking, she reached to kiss Laure again, and the woman laughed and turned her head, snaking her arm around Erica's shoulders. "Not here."

•

Laure could read Erica like a book. Her bewilderment, her arousal. She could also tell she had never kissed a woman before, did not know the rules of engagement. The first kiss had been daring, a second would have been stupid. The streets were busy, and their first graze of lips easily missed, but it would not do to risk being seen by the wrong sort of person. But it was conclusive, and for the first time since seeing Erica, Laure knew the matter was settled, and she could relax into the rest of the evening.

Erica began to talk non-stop, about the Pompidou, about Paris, about her pension, and though the arm around her was meant to reassure her, Laure could tell she was more nervous than ever. They reached Le Divan, which was as busy as when they'd left it half an hour before. Erica disappeared inside to search for her hideous satchel and Laure drifted into conversation with a politics and philosophy student she knew from undergraduate days and hadn't realized was still in Paris. As they exchanged updates, she saw Hilde inside, staring out at her with a manic intensity. God but she was sexy when she was angry, which she always seemed to be—if not at Laure then at her parents, or her ex, or the state of the world. Laure ignored her, and as she knew she would, a moment later Hilde was beside her.

"You piece of shit," she said. "Why are you like this? You know I would die for you."

"You're a fool, Hilde," said Laure, as the politics and philosophy acquaintance slipped tactfully away. "Don't make a scene."

"Don't make a scene," she spat. "What about your little fat tart? Spilling her wine, spilling out of her dress."

"She's not my tart. She's nothing to do with me." Up until ten minutes ago, it had been the truth.

"You invited her here."

"I mentioned it to her. She likes reading."

"Everyone likes reading. You are such a slut, Laure. You should have been born a man."

"But then you would not want to fuck me."

"Go to hell."

"Gladly," she said, and went to intercept Erica. Hilde shouted after her, as together they walked away once more from the bookshop. "Bitch!"

Erica at least knew better than to look back. Laure asked, "Your bag is gone?"

"Yes," she said, and there was a definite wobble in her voice.

"Did you lose much?"

"My books, my key."

"There are more books, spare keys."

"I can't afford it."

That surprised Laure. The girl was clearly well off, spending her summer here instead of working.

"Your money?"

"I have some in my room. Enough, but not to replace what's gone."

"It'll come around," said Laure, slinging her arm back around Erica. "Shall we go to Barbara's?"

"Yes," said Erica eagerly, and then, seeming to realize she was being offered another option, "If you want to?"

"For a bit," said Laure.

There was music filling the stairwell when they arrived at Barbara's parents' place.

"The Bee Gees!" exclaimed Erica. "I love them!"

"Michel does too," said Laure repressively. Now they were in the relative privacy of the apartment block, she allowed her hand to drift lower, to the small of Erica's back. It was curved like an Arp, no hard edges anywhere. Erica jolted but then leaned into Laure's touch and Laure turned her smoothly, pressing her against the wall. Laure's leg went between Erica's and they kissed, Erica ready this time, her mouth opening, her hot tongue finding Laure's.

"There you are." Léa was on the landing above, grinning down at them. "Come on, I need you to settle an argument, Laure."

She held out her hand to Erica, who giggled breathlessly and climbed up to meet her. Laure followed into the dark and smoky apartment, shrugging off her coat and closing the door behind. She did not know how the neighbours tolerated the noise, but they had never once, according to Barbara, complained.

The apartment was not large, and could have fitted inside Pauline's drawing room. It was split into several small rooms, more wall than space, but their group was crammed into the kitchen, Michel and Françoise dancing in the only floorspace, and the others arranged on the counter and chairs, candles lit and placed on top of the fridge. Léa had pulled Erica onto a chair with her, and Barbara poured two more glasses of wine.

"What's the debate?" asked Laure over the noise, leaning against the table and accepting her glass.

"*India Song*," said Agnès. She was smoking, though she didn't usually. Everyone was, Laure realized, even Erica accepting puffs of Léa's joint, which Laure hoped she realized was cannabis. Something in the air, infecting them all tonight. Laure liked to think it was her. Michel said she was not the bellwether for their group, but the weather itself.

"Trash," said Barbara dismissively, and then, mindful of Erica, repeated herself in English. "Trash. It's self-absorbed, shallow, narcissistic, colonialist trash."

"The characters are self-absorbed and colonialist," said Léa. "The film shows them to be and so is not." Léa turned to Laure, who was focused on the deep valley of Erica's cleavage. "What do you think?"

"I think you are both correct."

Barbara threw up her hands in exasperation. "We should never have asked the post-structuralist."

"*Student* of post-structuralism." Laure refilled her glass. "Now you mention it, didn't Duras say herself in an interview the meaning to the images came after? So if the director herself had no hold on a fixed point, why should you, or you, Léa."

"Fine, so we are both correct. But what do you think?" said Léa. "You loved it when we went together."

"I didn't love it. It revolted me, and it amazed me."

"That's a contradiction."

"It's a truth. Both things fit, and they cannot sit together. You have to break it all apart."

"I'm too high for this," said Claude, swinging his legs against the cabinets.

"Me too," said Léa, resting her head on Erica's shoulder. She was a good foil for Erica, wispy and blonde next to Erica's luxuriant darkness. Erica was sitting quite still and smiling, taking brief puffs of the spliff she was clearly not inhaling. Laure wondered about giving her a brief précis of the discussion, for in their temper they'd all switched back to French, but she seemed content, the dear. Let her not trouble herself.

The record ended and Barbara left to change it while Michel and Françoise continued shimmying to the silence until Christophe pulled Michel in to him with his legs and wrapped them around his waist. Michel freed himself and leaned over to Laure and asked,

"Did you see Hilde?"

"Mm."

"You should let her go, you know."

"I am not holding her."

"Make her hate you, at least."

"I'm doing my best."

Michel snorted. "You forget I know you, sorcière. And this one?" He meant Erica.

"She's only here for the summer."

"Mm."

•

Erica was listening very hard. She wished she could mark her place in the conversation, as she did in her books, and reference her dictionary. She thought sadly of her lost Collins, a gift from her father on her sixteenth birthday, when she first started saving for Paris. It was the first and only gift he'd given her that made her think he understood her. She had years of notes, novel ideas, lines for poems she never got around to writing, and observations from her trip, all gone. But this night was tumbling her along, and with the same feeling one might get white-water rafting, she was terrified and exhilarated.

She could sense Laure beside her, her cool energy, the burning coal at the centre of it. A cord, binding them. Erica had thought about kissing girls before, practised on Lydia's hand before dances and given each other love bites. Once she had rolled back and forth with Rosie on Rosie's parents' bed, fully clothed. It was make-believe, play-pretend.

But this was different. Desire had steam-rollered her the moment Laure kissed her briefly in the street. She wanted the woman in ways she didn't wholly understand the mechanics of, knowing only the in and out of the two boys she had slept with at school. What did this mean? *Straight*, Léa had said. Was she fully aware until this evening, in a room full of not-straight people, that there was another possibility? Her parents had never mentioned it. They'd never mentioned sex at all. She didn't see anyone else naked until the changing rooms before swimming at school, and then she'd only focused on how other girls' ribcages showed, how their hips were narrow and their breasts high and neat.

She felt like the whole room could sense her arousal, as though she was giving off a scent. She drank more wine to quiet the sensation, but it only made her feel heavier and more languid. She tried to concentrate on the conversation, but it had drifted on. They all spoke so *fast*. She was sure English people did not speak so fast.

She took another toke, careful not to inhale, and when the music started again it was something French she didn't know, but she got to her feet with Léa anyway, swaying her hips and remembering to suck in her stomach. Laure did not dance but Erica felt they danced together anyway, every motion a call and response. Claude moved close on a slow, shmaltzy tune and she enjoyed using him, imagining his hands as Laure's. Though she hadn't inhaled, she felt high, the room thick with smoke and the candles burning low. Claude was singing along to the song, his breath tickling her ear. He had a nice voice, and she told him so.

"Merci, belle. You like Claude François?" She thought he was talking about himself in the third person. His hard-on was pressing into her thigh. She wondered how to excuse herself as he went on, "He died you know. This year, electrocuted in his bath."

"No, he was fixing a lightbulb," said Laure. She was suddenly at Erica's back, as tall as Claude, and she gently and firmly extracted Erica from his grip. "Allez."

Erica nodded, her whole body seeming to vibrate with want. The others were pairing off, she saw. Michel and Christophe were kissing passionately, as were Barbara and Françoise. Marie and Agnès were gone, though Erica hadn't noticed them leave, and as Laure led Erica from the smoky kitchen she saw Claude shrug and close in on Léa, who had been dancing alone.

"Is she—" started Erica, but Laure cut her off.

"They've done it before."

"But should we—"

Laure stopped her words with a kiss. Erica moaned and let herself go limp, like a kitten bitten on the neck by its mother. She could not believe she was kissing a woman, but if she let herself forget and thought just of the kiss, it was so good she allowed the implications not to trouble her, as natural as letting her hand tangle in Laure's hair, pull her tighter into her body. Now was not the time for thoughts. She felt Laure's hand slip between her legs and press her just so, and wondered if she really was going to let this happen here—yes, the answer was yes—but then Laure stopped kissing her and said, "Come on."

It was very dark outside, purplish traffic fumes obscuring the stars. Erica felt breathless, sobered by the night air, and knew if Laure kissed her again she would not, could not, want to stop. But was it so bad? Here, under the glowing, lovely Paris pollution, she did not think it could be. Laure walked fast on her long legs, and Erica had to scurry to keep up. As they left the residential neighbourhood and crossed the fifth, the black sprawl of the Jardin du Luxembourg spread away like a vast sea to their left. It was ringed with a high gate but there were shadows everywhere, the surrounding buildings imperious and mute. Erica pulled on Laure's hand, a question—*here?* She did not know if she could wait much longer for whatever was about to happen. But Laure shook her head and hurried her on, through busier streets and quieter ones, past cat-calling men and tramps asleep on benches, the closed-up boxes of the bouquinistes, across the Pont de la Tournelle and the shining Seine, the rarefied silence of Île Saint-Louis and Pont de Marie, into the heart of Le Marais.

At last, after what must have been an hour, Laure pulled a set of keys from her coat and unlocked a gate, slipping through into an unlit cobbled courtyard littered with broken furniture, and stopping before a barricaded door. Laure unlocked two padlocks and slid across a bolt, gesturing Erica inside. She only hesitated a moment, knowing if Laure were a man she would have run screaming. Instead she went inside and stood in the dark while Laure closed and locked the door behind her, and led her up a flight of what sounded like metal steps, through a final locked door, and then clicked open her lighter.

"Welcome," said Laure, dropping her hand. Erica stood as though in a night forest, listening for rustling, for clues. Laure lit candles that poured small pools of light onto a table littered with bottles and ashtrays and books. It smelled bad in here, stale, but then Laure was offering her a beer and putting on a record. "Crimson and Clover" seeped from the player, scratchy and seductive. As Erica's eyes adjusted to the gloom, she saw Laure covering a battered leather sofa with a sheepskin. Her shirtsleeves were pushed up and her forearms glowed in the candlelight, pale and luminous as a Vermeer, and Erica thought how this song would always be this moment for her, Laure lit just so, and a squat in Paris, and unbearable desire. Erica set down her undrunk beer on a cluttered sideboard and went to her.

Laure straightened as she approached and regarded Erica with the same cool challenge she'd first looked at her with. Her collarbones were sharp enough to cut. Erica placed her tongue into the hollow of one and licked it, tasting salt. Laure did not move. She was letting Erica take the lead. Erica understood it was another test, and this time, she was determined not to fail.

•

Laure woke from a sleep better than any she'd had in months. Years maybe, since she was a girl in her childhood bedroom with the iron bedstead and broken-springed mattress. Light was leaking in through the unlined curtain, and it was cold, as it always was first thing in her apartment no matter the weather.

Apartment was an optimistic word—Laure had been squatting here since its previous inhabitant, Anita, a Maoist she'd had a brief fling and then a long friendship with, moved back to Uruguay. It was an ex-joinery, and the air still smelled of sawdust. The sofa was Anita's as was all the furniture, the smoke-stained curtains, the mugs. Laure's only additions were the books and an unframed print of the album cover of *Blue*, tacked up over the boarded-up fireplace. Laure had taken the board down briefly when she first took over the apartment, and quickly understood why Anita had kept it blocked. If it was not pigeon shit dropping down it, it was pigeons themselves, sometimes dead but worse and more often, half dead. She hated having to break their poor little necks. Vegetarian was a dirty word in her father's house, even here in Paris among her student friends, but even if she could afford it Laure doubted she would eat meat.

Laure shivered. She was completely naked, the sheepskin meagre shelter and the sofa's flaking leather sticking to her side. She peeled herself upright and looked around. Erica was gone. Laure felt a swooping sensation: relief and disappointment. The same mix she had felt on the steps of the Sacré-Cœur. Erica had been an eager lover, not experienced but inspired, and perhaps because her expectations had been low Laure had come under her tongue harder than she ever had with Pauline, or even Hilde. Erica's own orgasm was something Laure had to coax out of her with patient repetition. She was, as so many first-timers were, guarded about her own pleasure, at first not wanting Laure to go down on her. But when she did come she was more beautiful than ever, that blush all over her body just as Laure had imagined, her thighs soft and dimpled, her belly loose and velvet.

They had stayed up and talked after, the post-coital radiance softening Laure as it sometimes did, laying her bare in a way that always surprised her most of all. She'd talked about Michel and Marie, her first friends in the city, how Michel had bought all her food for the first few months until her funding came in. Laure had promised to take Erica sightseeing, to Père-Lachaise and the catacombs, to see the Monets at L'Orangerie.

She pulled on a jumper and her underwear, found mismatched woollen socks and began the arduous task of making coffee. She'd skip-dived a coffee grinder and bought a cafetière from Bastille market, mended the hairline crack at its lip with electrical tape. She was just boiling water in a pan when Erica emerged at the far end of the room, through the door that led to the grim Turkish toilet Laure never braved, looking traumatized. Laure let her gaze slide over the glug jug propped upside down to dry on the windowsill, deciding not to mention she used that when caught short.

What Laure said was, "Yes, it's bad. At least you wore your shoes." But what she thought was, *I am so happy to see you.*

•

When she eventually found it, Erica thought she would vomit at the sight of the toilet. It was a hole in the ground, splattered with all manner of things. But the thought of throwing up and coming face to face with that hell hole made her determined not to, so she clamped her mouth shut and pissed holding her nose, and got out as fast as she could.

The magic of the previous night and early hours of the morning were fading in the face of the squalor Laure lived in. The building seemed mostly deserted, an old factory of some kind, winches hanging from the ceiling and a pleasant herbal smell once she was out from under the fetid cloche of Laure's room. But some of the doors she tried led onto other dwellings, unlocked and full of sleeping figures. She only glimpsed inside before hastily closing them, noting that they were similarly shabby, but none were so sordid as Laure's. It had taken Erica a full minute to cross the cluttered floorboards, covered in bottles and piles of dirty laundry, ashtrays and glasses that appeared to be stolen from a variety of local bars, the heels of bread and mouldy butter scrapings on plates, coasters, and sometimes pamphlets. It looked no better on her return, and Laure showed no sign of embarrassment as she picked her way back to the sofa across the scattered islands of floorboard, pulling the sheepskin over herself as in her haste for the bathroom she had not replaced her bra.

"You don't use that?" she asked, at last.

"Of course not. I go to the café across the street."

"And when it is closed?"

Laure shrugged. "I hold it."

"That's not good for you, you know," said Erica. "Gives you infections."

Laure offered her coffee. It was burnt and strong but Erica drank a whole cup, knowing that even if she'd been offered milk it would be taking her life in her hands to accept.

"Where do you wash these?" she asked, unable to stop herself.

"Down the hall. There's plumbing, a sink, a shower. Only for us women."

"There are other women living here?" Erica had seen only men.

"Three of us. But the men are fine too. They don't use the toilet either."

"Someone does."

"It is a bit different from your pension?"

"Yes," said Erica, realizing what she'd taken for the poverty of her accommodation was only basic. She knew she was being rude but the lack of sleep and the shock of the room in daylight had forced it from her.

"We are not all in Paris only for our summers." Laure did not sound offended. In fact, she seemed a little amused.

"Of course. It's expensive, to live here?"

"Expensive to live," said Laure. "But I am barely here. I am at the library, or class, or the community café Michel runs, or at Marie and Agnès'. It's somewhere to sleep."

"And sleep with people?"

Laure laughed shortly. "I must admit I am usually at theirs."

"I'm honoured."

"Tant pis." Laure raised her cup. "You did lose your key."

Erica groaned and fell back on the sofa. "I'd almost forgotten. I have to pay for a new key."

"Do you have enough?"

Erica fumbled on the floor for her bra. Her emergency fifty francs were nowhere to be seen. "I had a note somewhere. It must have fallen out when we . . ."

She felt her easiness vanish, her brief feeling of superiority fade. She felt the furious blush again, the traitorous blood rushing to her face.

"Fucked?" offered Laure.

"Do you have to use that word?"

"Made love?" smirked Laure, and Erica hated her a little bit, as much for her teasing as for how good she looked, even in this foul room with dark circles like gouges under her eyes, her hair lank with grease. She began rolling another cigarette, and Erica saw her nails were bitten, and tinged yellow with tobacco.

"Slept together."

"Ah, you like a euphemism."

"Where do you learn your English?" Erica shook her head. "Honestly? All of you speak it so well."

"Joni Mitchell." Laure jabbed her thumb at the tacked-up poster. "Books. Films. It's the language of the oppressor but the oppressor has good music."

"Oppressor?" Erica snorted, feeling oddly defensive. "We fought with you in the War."

"You are not an imperialist, are you?"

"Let me guess—you are a pacifist."

"Aren't we all? But no, I believe war is sometimes a necessity. But it should be fought between soldiers, not civilians. Did you know two million civilians died from war-related causes in your colony of India alone?"

Erica blinked. She had not known this. "What about your colonies?"

"Six hundred thousand," said Laure. "And double that in French Indochina."

"So why are we the oppressors?"

"Come on. You and les Ricains run culture, or think you do. You export all your books and films and import none of ours. You think yourself superior because we all speak your language, but it is because it's been forced into our mouths and you think yourself above learning ours."

"I tried to speak French to you," Erica said, her cheeks hot.

"It was so bad," said Laure, lighting up. "It hurt my ears."

Now Erica hated her simply because she was rude. More than that, she was being cruel. Erica knew girls like her, knew they thrived off reaction, but she could not help it. She stood up and snatched her bra from the floor, kicking aside detritus, trying to find her fifty-franc note. She wanted to get out of here, take a hot shower and forget she'd ever met this horrid, grimy woman.

"Mais non," said Laure. "I'm teasing."

Erica ignored her. The red wine sick feeling that had risen in the toilet was growing again, and she refused to throw up in front of Laure. But she needed her fifty francs. In the room at the pension she had her allowance for food, for museums and occasional metros, but the new key would wipe her out.

"What are you looking for?"

"My fifty francs," said Erica.

Laure leant forward, clenching her cigarette between her teeth, and joined in sifting through the mess on her floor. Erica moved aside a bottle of red wine that spilt its dregs over her foot.

"Ugh! How do you live like this!"

"Very well thank you," said Laure, unconcerned. "Voilà."

She held up the crumpled note and Erica snatched it off her. "Merci."

Bundling her bra under her arm, because she did not want to undress in front of Laure, she stomped over the heaps to the door.

"Attends," said Laure. She pushed herself off the sofa and scooped her keys off the table, and walked deliberately slowly to Erica. She was completely naked, and flashes of the early morning reared at Erica: Laure's long, deft fingers between her legs, inside her, the perfect pressure and rhythm, her long, boyish body pressing into her, all hip bones and ribs. Her beautiful pink nipple, like a nut in her mouth.

Laure smirked as though she knew exactly what Erica was thinking. She bent down and scooped a shirt off a heap, pulling it over her head. It was unbuttoned to her breastbone and Erica could see the points of her nipples through the fabric. Her clitoris throbbed and she hated Laure all the more. The woman stood over her, her hips slung forward like a man. How did she smell so good, when she also smelt of cigarettes and stale wine and sex? There was a scent to her, like sap or honey. Erica had found it on her hair, along her collarbones, inside her. "I have to come down with you, unlock the padlocks."

Erica gave a tight nod, trying to ignore how her stomach swooped at the contact between their bodies, Erica's hand on the door handle and Laure's over it, their hips touching. She knew she was going to have to kiss her, though her mouth tasted vile. She had to touch her, to feel her against her. She tried to resist it, and with a defiant jut of her chin she said, "The French invaded Britain, you know. You colonized us."

Laure laughed, and dropped her keys.

·

Their lovemaking was faster this time, no savouring each other. Laure pulled Erica's hair, Erica bit her nipple. They knew what worked for each other, and both wanted to get to the point, the release. Erica was louder this time, freer, and it was pleasurable to learn her abilities were not beginner's luck. She was a good lover, instinctive, as Laure herself was. They were both sweating when Erica came, quivering and dropping against Laure, her warm breasts pressed against her, her gorgeous weight pinning her down. Oh but she was a *woman*, with her soft belly and full ass, her hip bones hidden like buried treasure, striking like gold bars against Laure's own. Laure reached to turn Erica's mouth up to hers, but Erica burrowed her face in deeper to her shoulder, taking her weight on her elbows.

"Don't. I stink."

"I don't care."

"I do." Erica pushed up, clutching her discarded dress to herself and turning away to fasten her bra.

"I have seen you naked," said Laure, amused, propping herself up on her elbows. "Up close."

"Don't," said Erica, and from her voice alone Laure knew she was blushing. "I'm gross."

"Excuse me?"

Erica said nothing, pulling the dress over her head and turning to look down at her. "I do know I'm fat."

"And?"

"You're meant to say I'm not fat!"

"I don't care. I like it."

"How can you like it?"

"Your breasts, your ass. I like them. I like your body."

Erica was studying her face. She seemed genuinely shocked.

"I saw that girl you slept with."

"Hilde?"

"She's beautiful. Slim."

"She is," Laure shrugged. "You are beautiful too."

Erica snorted and pulled on her knickers. Laure followed her lead and got dressed too, pulling on slacks and a shirt. "You must know you are. I've seen all the men look at you."

"Men look at anything."

"And women?"

"I hadn't thought about it before."

Laure retrieved her half-smoked cigarette, her lighter, keys, some loose change. "You should." She unlocked the door. "Shall we get a drink?"

"It's the morning."

"Bof." Laure locked the door behind them and led the way through the warren of the squat, unlocking and locking, and finally barricading the outside door. When she turned to the cluttered courtyard, Erica was chewing her thumbnail.

"I'm not . . . you know."

"Quoi?"

Erica gestured at her.

Laure fought an instinctive desire to close her arms over her body. She stood straighter instead. "A lesbian?"

Erica blushed. Laure brushed past her, leading the way to the gate onto the street. Her chest hurt suddenly. Too much wine, that was all. Too many cigarettes. She rubbed her breastbone. Erica was hanging back. She looked stricken.

"It's OK," Laure said over her shoulder. "You aren't the first tourist I've fucked. Sorry, *slept with*."

Erica winced. Good. She unlocked the gate and bowed Erica through.

Chapter Two

After the coffees, to which Erica refused the addition of whisky, Laure offered to walk her back to her pension. She found she needed to atone, for Erica perhaps and the grubby way she made her feel, and the day was clear and fine, not so punishingly hot as the past few. It was natural to link arms, though Laure could tell Erica was fighting some internal battle from the way her arm was stiff, her elbow angled to keep distance between their bodies. Laure would not admit even to herself she was hurt by it, but she was unsurprised. She knew it was Erica's first time. She had been many women's first time. Some were indeed tourists, trying it out.

But she had lied to Erica, and more so Erica was lying to herself. She was not a tourist, it was clear from everything from the way she kissed her to the way she looked at her. She was, if not a lesbian, then a traveller between, like Agnès, who had loved men before and threatened, when she and Marie fought, to do so again some day. But Laure would not be the one to tell her that pretending you were not a thing you were would wreck everything. Let her find out for herself.

They reached the pension, a post-war construction of depressingly rigid design, though perhaps Erica liked it, admiring as she did the Pompidou.

"Would you mind coming in? Explaining about the key?" Erica addressed this to Laure's left ear, grudgingly.

Madame Allard was a whiskery, canny woman, who Laure could tell disliked her on sight. Erica waited on the front steps while she told her about the missing satchel, the lost key, and could tell the woman was inflating the cost of the replacement by the second. She named an impossible price, a stupid price.

"You must be joking?" said Laure.

"Do I look like I am joking?"

She did not.

"She wants forty francs," Laure told Erica, who paled. She had never seen someone whose feelings were so obvious, as though her skin were a pellucid surface.

"You're kidding?"

"I'm afraid not."

Erica groaned and dropped her head into her hands. "I'll have to go home. I can't afford to stay."

"She's ripping you off." Laure was disappointed in Erica. She accepted defeat so readily. "Look, do you want to stay here?"

"It was the cheapest place I could find."

Laure looked at her, calculating. This was not her problem, and she was well within her rights to leave the girl to it. But something stopped her, the same sensation that had made her turn back on the Rue Jean-Baptiste Pigalle to tell Erica about the reading. She would blame the good sex, but she hadn't so much as kissed her then. It was an impulse, an instinct. She didn't trust it, but she couldn't resist it, either.

"I know somewhere."

"Where?" said Erica, and then, "No, don't tell me. Even if I could find somewhere, I couldn't afford food or the metro, nothing. I'll only just have enough to change my ticket home."

Laure felt the same irritation at her weakness, her surrender, but also a twist of something else. She refused to dwell on it, knew she did not want Erica to go home. Not yet.

"When were you meant to go?"

"Not until August."

Laure stood up and held out her hand to her. "Allez."

"Where?"

"We'll fetch your things from the room."
"I still have to pay her."
"Follow my lead."

•

Erica listened as Laure argued with Madame Allard. From what she could understand, she was telling her she had to open the room, because Erica's money was inside. She felt tearful, exhausted, sore. She wanted to go to sleep but needed to prepare for her walk to the bus station. Maybe Laure would help her carry her bags. God, the humiliation. Thank goodness she knew no one in Paris.

At last Madame Allard threw up her hands, Laure seemingly haranguing her into submission. She took a set of keys from behind the desk and led the way up the flights of stairs to the fourth floor. When she turned onto the landing Laure leant over and whispered in her ear.

"Pack fast, all right? Leave what you can."
"What? Why?"
"And get ready to run."
"Laure—"

"Vite," said Madame Allard impatiently, unlocking the door and standing back. Erica went inside and Laure bundled past her, throwing open her suitcase and chucking clothes into it.

"What are you doing?" said Erica, at the same time as Madame Allard asked the same in French, shrilly. The old woman gripped Erica by the shoulders and shook her, asking what they were doing, were they thieves, was this woman a prostitute, was she being robbed.

But Erica shook free and joined Laure, grabbing her toothbrush and make-up case and throwing them into the suitcase just before Laure snapped it shut and, yelling at Erica to keep up, burst past Madame Allard and ran down the stairs, the suitcase held shut in her arms.

Madame Allard was frozen against the wall where she'd fallen, and Erica stuttered out a "Je suis désolée," before pelting after Laure.

Madame Allard recovered herself. "Trou du cul! Salope! Chienne!"

Erica broke out through the heavy front door in time to see Laure disappearing onto Rue Claude Bernard. Underwear and skirts were scattered along the pavement, and Erica picked them up as she ran, too out of breath to call after Laure. She turned the corner and was pulled into an alley that stank of piss. Laure was panting too, the suitcase dropped in a tumble at her feet.

"Merde!" she panted, holding her ribs. Erica dropped her collected clothes onto the split suitcase, not caring how filthy the ground was. Laure began to laugh, both of them gasping for breath, Erica feeling like she might wet herself. The moment one of them stopped, the other would set them off again. A woman walking on the main road peered in at them and said something chastising, which only made them laugh harder.

"Stop, please!" Erica begged, crossing her legs. "Stop, stop, stop."

She regained herself, wheezing, hands on her knees. Through the stabbing pain of a stitch she gasped, "What if she calls the police?"

Laure huffed, swallowed, and managed, "Do you owe her money?"

"Only for the key. I was paid up until the end of the week."

"You saw, she has loads of spares. She was cheating you. Did you get your money?"

Erica nudged the make-up bag with her foot. "Yes. Oh God! What do I do now?"

Laure was looking at her, and Erica recognized desire in her face.

"No," she said firmly. "Come on, help me pick this up. I need a shower, to brush my teeth. Where did you say I could stay?"

"With me."

Erica paused in the act of zipping her case. Her heart, still pounding from her escape, began to race again. "Pardon?"

"You heard."

Erica could not go and stay in that dump. More than that, she could not go and stay with Laure. She could not trust herself not to sleep with Laure again, and then, what would that mean?

Laure spoke again before she could answer. "It's no matter to me."

This, perversely, decided Erica.

"I could stay with you," said Erica, finishing her zip. "If you're asking."

"I'm not asking."

"You don't want me to stay with you?"

Erica looked up at her from under her lashes, as she had hours earlier, from between Laure's legs. Laure's pupils visibly dilated, and Erica felt a curious calm come over her. She understood she had power here. She realized she had never felt powerful before. "As you insist, I will. But first, a shower. Not in your hovel."

"There's a YMCA nearby."

"Good." Though she did not know where they were going, Erica led the way.

•

Laure had never lived with anyone before aside from her parents and briefly Michel, never shared a space and a room. She was an only child and happy to be, and she'd instantly regretted her invitation to Erica. But Erica, it turned out, was also an only child, and though she was less happy in her own company she knew how to be silent, to sit with her own thoughts and not have to fill every gap with chatter. Her early loquaciousness must have been nerves, and it charmed Laure to think of it.

The first few days were a little strange, both of them uncertain about their arrangement. Erica kept offering to leave, until Laure wished she would. On the very first night Laure escaped for a drink to steel herself, sitting in the café across from her squat and practising in her head how she would convince Erica to go. One drink became two, then three, then she spotted Sarah, a fellow art theorist, and they talked until it was dark and the world tilted slightly when Laure stood up.

The room was lit with candles when she returned, and there was the smell of lemons and vinegar. She could see Erica lying on the sofa, a book in her hand. Laure halted at the threshold, sniffing the air.

"You cleaned."

"You can't expect me to live like this. You can't expect *you* to live like this."

Laure walked slowly inside. The floor's expanse stretched out like a dark sea, little pools of candlelight showing clear surfaces, bare floorboards. Empty bottles were assembled next to the door, bags of rubbish tied next to them. Her clean clothes were folded and lined along the wall, and the dirty ones were massed in towering heaps, sorted into whites and colours ready for the laverie. Plates were cleaned and dried, stacked on the small table that served as a kitchen counter, the corkscrew next to them, her three forks and two knives arranged neatly. Corks—dozens of them—were amassed on the windowsill, and the glug jug was full of water, a half-drunk glass beside it. Laure wondered how to tell her. Instead she said,

"I don't want a wife."

Erica let out an empty laugh. She stood up and set down the book, *Claudine à l'école*, marked with a roll-up, not dog-eared or splayed as Laure would have left it. Erica walked towards her. She was dressed in one of Laure's shirts, which had been her father's. It strained across her chest and hips. She looked effortlessly beautiful, her thick dark hair swept back off her face and held by a blue handkerchief. Laure's blue handkerchief, still stained with red wine. Laure readied herself for a kiss, Erica's tongue on her neck, but Erica only took the keys from Laure's hand.

"I'm hungry," she said. "Coming?"

"Yes. But first, about that jug . . ."

After that, she went about her business as usual, meeting Léa in the Jardin du Luxembourg, going to Marie and Agnès' for dinner, browsing in bookshops and drinking, paying deference to her thesis by spending an afternoon in the library or writing in Michel's community café. The only difference, aside from not seeing Pauline, Hilde, or any of the others, was that Erica came too, everywhere, and it surprised Laure how easy it was to spend time with her. Her friends liked her, Michel especially, sitting patiently with her speaking French, swapping poetry recommendations: Jacques Prévert for Edwin Morgan, Arthur Rimbaud for Denise Riley.

"She's a rare one," he told Laure. "Don't mess it up."

Erica liked the same things Laure liked: books and walking, Paris and art. She was even interested, or did a good job of pretending, when Laure got on her high horse about the pavements of the city, mercilessly hacked back to widen the roads in the days when Paris was run by a motoring lobby.

"But surely that's illegal!" Erica had gasped, and Laure felt a thrill that she was to be the one to open Erica's eyes to the corruption of everything, the deep rot that sat at the heart of government.

Through Erica Laure felt she was discovering her adopted city anew, not only the narrow roads but the white stone of the mansions, the light on hand-polished doorknobs, the dog shit and the beautiful people. The history, which Laure had long absorbed and intellectualized but now appeared fresh and pulsing: revolutions and love affairs, blood and lust. Of course history was made and changed in Paris. They went together to the Père-Lachaise and Erica pulled a button off her shirt to put on Gertrude Stein's grave. Laure was amazed she knew *Tender Buttons* but not that Gertrude Stein had loved a woman. She did not want to be the lesbian prophet to this girl, but she could not help herself. Laure took her to see the commemorative plaque at 27 Rue de Fleurus, and bought her a copy of Alice B. Toklas' cookbook from a bouquiniste.

"Not that you'll be able to make a thing in my apartment."

"Not that I would want to," said Erica, but Laure could tell by her face she was moved. Laure felt a stirring of unease. Perhaps she should not have made such a gesture. She remembered how, as a child, she would beg her father to let her feed the stray cats that collected on the tin roof of their disused barn.

"You'll only encourage them," he said. "What if one day you aren't here to feed them, what then? They'll starve. Let them fend for themselves." And when she pointed out some of them were only kittens, barely open-eyed, he shrugged. "Those that can't survive shouldn't."

If something in her soul rebelled against this notion, voiced by their neighbour's son Yves, she learnt to tamp it down, to think logically, as her father did. Logically, she should not have given Erica a gift, something she could attach meaning to. But then, she should not have invited her to stay, should not have kissed her, should not continue to kiss her every possible moment, to worship her body with her mouth and her fingers, to in turn let her pull from her moans of pleasure and whispered confidences. As with the cats, when it came to Erica there was a divide between her soul and her logic, and she refused to look at it squarely. Laure was in the grip of something she did not understand, and as with all things she did not understand she preferred to believe it below her notice.

Michel was keen to disabuse her of this illusion. "You like her," he said, after a week of their suspiciously smooth cohabitation.

"She's all right."

"No, you *like her* like her. You're going around with her. Going steady."

Laure snorted. "She's staying with me. It's not easy to see other people."

"You would if you wanted to. And you don't want to."

"Shut up."

"No need to get snappy. I thought you liked truth. Or is it only your version of the truth?"

The real truth was, Laure thought her version of the truth was the only true one. Not that others' views didn't matter, but they were so often simply *wrong*. It was an embarrassing state of affairs for a student of post-structuralism, but for all her theses and debates, people tended to ask her to be the definitive voice on a matter, and that had mingled with her inherited pig-headedness to add a rigidity, a fixedness that sat at the core of her being and lent her not only *ravissement* but a dangerous certainty in her correctness.

"It's OK," said Michel, and they looked over at where Marie, Agnès and Erica were kneeling by the record player, arguing over what to listen to next. "We like her too."

He slipped his arm around Laure, armpit hair tickling Laure's bare shoulder. She was wearing a sleeveless top she'd forgotten existed, it had spent so long in a pile on the floor. They'd taken five trips to the laverie on Rue du Petit Musc, and three more to the bins of the Café Louis Philippe, commodious enough to hold months' worth of bottles.

She liked Erica. Of course she did. But she didn't *like* like her. And she didn't, couldn't love her. She'd never loved anyone, let alone an English girl she'd known for barely a month. But then, what were those moments? The ones that came increasingly and not only in unguarded times in bed or drunk, when she felt in her chest a piercing sort of pain that was equal part pleasure. It was not love—if Laure were to feel love it would not be in such clichéd terms. And she would not love someone so young, not only in years but experience too. Someone who might only be trying things out, having a summer experience with a woman. A tourist.

But this, the more reasoned voice in Laure's mind told her, was her own prejudice speaking. Erica was young in many ways, but she was also surprising, interesting, and brave. The latter trait didn't so much dawn on Laure but launch itself at all of them when, on a muggy Wednesday, they allowed themselves to be talked into going to Parade by Michel. It was not Laure's habit to go to lesbian bars, let alone gay bars—the drinks were too expensive, the crowd older and more set in their preferences—but she could tell Erica was curious. The bar itself was fine, the music too loud and too American, but she enjoyed watching Erica dance with Michel through the fug of smoke as she mooched beside the door with Agnès. Marie had refused to come. She had a bad feeling, she said, in one of her witchy moods, but clearly it was not so grave as to stop her friends going. But when Laure's eye was caught by the group of men outside, clad in long coats despite the heat, she knew Marie had been right.

Later Laure told herself it happened too fast for her to do anything, but in truth it all happened very slowly. So slowly, she had time to note the coats were ugly, too large. Functional, made for concealment. The men drew out long, dull lengths of metal as though to a command, yet none of them spoke. This too she remembered. That as three of them began swinging indiscriminately at the groups outside, and four made for the doorway inside which she and Agnès still stood, an eighth—she even had time enough to count them—smashing the blacked-out glass window with a sharp *crack*, they did not shout, or scream, or hurl abuse. On their faces there was a cold kind of fury, hatred drawn from a cool, deep well.

One shouldered inside, past Laure, his baton catching Agnès on the elbow and sending her spinning to the floor. Laure crouched over Agnès and pulled her to her feet, anticipating the stampede for the door. Maybe this was when the screams started, but Laure's ears could only hear the wet thwacks of the batons as the men met the crowd, drew back their arms again and again, the music still playing as the DJ abandoned his record player, Gal Costa's soprano floating over the panic.

She was being forced against the broken glass pane, shards grinding under her shoes. She couldn't see Erica, or Michel. She tried to make Agnès go outside without her, but her friend was hysterical, clinging to her, and the rush for the door shoved them into an excruciating bottleneck. Laure's feet left the floor at one point, and when she found it again she trod on something soft, human. Suddenly she and Agnès were spun out into the street where the baton men left outside had lost their upper hand, set upon by the crowds. They ran, but not before one lit a rag in the mouth of a glass bottle and threw it through the broken window. The screams inside reached a higher pitch, and for a moment Laure thought it was all about to explode, the whole world about to blow to pieces around her. But the Molotov cocktail missed the curtains, falling with an ineffectual smash to the concrete floor. In the flare of light she thought she saw Michel, the tall broad shape of him. Agnès was still hanging off her, whimpering, but Laure guided her gently across the road, where people had thrown open their doors and were passing out water and cloths to those bleeding.

"Where are the gendarmerie?" said a weeping woman, and Laure did not tell her the men in coats could have been police, that the police would not help them. She'd never been in an attack before, and the whole scene took on the sheen of unreality, even when Laure realized she was bleeding herself, her nose leaking, filling her mouth with metal. She peeled Agnès' shaking fingers off her wrist.

"Don't," pleaded Agnès, but Laure passed her over to a woman wielding a wet towel and hurried back to the bar. It was a crisis of two halves now, the outside lulling into that state of shock after atrocity, while inside there were maybe a dozen people scattered on the floor, a few groaning, others unconscious, the small fire glinting off pools of blood. Most of the assailants had fled, and in the corner beside the abandoned DJ decks stood Erica, her hair plastered to one side of her face, and a man with a baton raised before her. Her hand was outstretched in entreaty, and her face completely calm as she spoke rapidly. Laure ran to her and saw that she was shielding a man, his face a sheet of red and pale, bleeding heavily from a gash above his eye. In the attacker's hesitation was the implicit threat of violence, his eyes raking over Erica's disarrayed clothing, and Laure felt a swell of hatred so fierce that if she'd had a weapon herself she would have used it. Instead she approached warily, seeing Erica notice her and hold her at bay with the merest twitch of her eyebrow.

"Let's go outside," she was saying in French. "We can talk."

"You are a fag?"

"I'm a woman," she said. "Come outside, talk to me."

Behind her, Laure felt pressure, feared the crunch of metal on her skull, but it was a hand, pushing her aside, and three people—a woman and two men—launched themselves at the attacker. They span him, almost balletic, and the baton was wrenched from his hand. In the destabilizing glow of the fire and the disco lights, he looked young and fearful, a boy.

Laure darted for Erica, who in turn pulled on the cowering man's elbow, and they ran from the bar, Erica's hand in her own making Laure's heart feel like a pinball, loose and wild in her body. Outside the bloodied man was swept off into a doorway to be tended to, and Laure suddenly realized it was Michel. She began to shake, her teeth chattering, and Erica wrapped her arms around her, their hearts ricocheting together.

They left before the gendarmerie arrived, walking fast away at the first distant sound of sirens, and Laure felt what she did not often feel in her safe corners of Paris: hunted. After they delivered Agnès home to Marie, she and Erica took Michel home. He seemed lucid, but the gash above his eye was still seeping. They changed the dressing and while he called Christophe, Laure and Erica bathed together, washing each other's backs. The three of them slept in his double bed, arms tight around each other, Laure pressed in hard between the two people she loved—yes, *loved*—most in the world.

•

The following Sunday, Laure and Erica went to Marché d'Aligre, that glorious, grimy sprawl of a market, and picked up an enormous unravelling rug of dubious origin. The seller claimed it was Moroccan, but was happy to take next to nothing for it, and together they struggled laughing along Rue d'Aligre until Michel spotted them through the window of Commune Libre d'Aligre and summoned several friends to help them carry it the three kilometres to Laure's apartment.

As they wound through the concrete and cobbled streets, Erica took a photograph of them all, the rug held aloft on their shoulders, Laure and Michel at the fore, looking like something from *Death in the Jungle*, a fabric python defeated in their arms.

Once they reached Laure's squat, the group stayed to watch the great unrolling, and Michel went across the street to buy wine. They sat and smoked, Erica passing on the roll-up every time it reached her, and listening to an earnest young man in a tatty bowler hat explain, in halting English, the origins of the proletariat. Really, she was doing her best to eavesdrop on Laure, who was talking intensely with a broad and handsome Black woman called Evelyne. What she had gathered so far was that Evelyne had known a man called Henri Curiel, had been with him the day before he was assassinated. Laure seemed fascinated by her. Their heads went closer and closer together, and Erica forgot to pretend to listen anymore. Then Laure put her arm around Evelyne, and Evelyne dropped her head onto her shoulder, and it was like a crossbow bolt to the gut.

Erica lurched to her feet, across the newly laid rug, and into the stairwell, clinging onto the railing. She had drunk too much. It was a feature of her time with Laure and her friends, and she still hadn't built up anything like the tolerance the rest of them seemed to have. She sat down hard on the top step. Her chest ached. She had noticed Evelyne as soon as Michel had rallied his friends, knew Laure would gravitate to her. And there it was, the proof she'd been steeling herself against. It was almost a relief to see them sitting close, talking so intensely.

The awful scene at Parade had caused a minor crisis for Erica, realizing she was now allied with a way of life and a people who were despised. It was the first moment she'd felt true shame, and shame heaped upon shame for this sensation, and she'd thought, seriously, of leaving. But she had not left, and here were her thanks.

But maybe this was good. Confirmation of what she had expected—that Laure did not care for her, at least not as she cared for Laure. She could begin the process of soothing her heart, putting all the pieces of herself back together. Perhaps Evelyne and Laure would sleep together, and Laure would think it was no big deal. Should Erica? She did not know the rules by which lesbians lived—Laure had many lovers, like a man in a novel. Of course she wouldn't stop just because she had met Erica. Who did Erica think she was?

"There you are."

Laure sat down next to her so their thighs were touching, and Erica moved away.

"What's up?" Laure had brought her papers and tobacco with her, was already rolling. Erica ground her teeth in frustration. Could she not, just once, have a conversation without doing something else?

"Nothing. Just needed some air."

"You must be the only person in the world who has stayed so long in Paris and still doesn't smoke."

"I smoke. Sometimes." The truth was, she never inhaled. She still had the roll-up Laure had made for her, found during the clean-up, tucked flat into her passport.

"It was a compliment."

Erica felt something bubbling up in her throat. Nausea? Tears?

"You know, your compliments are never that nice."

"Non?"

"Non."

Laure licked the roll-up and stuck it behind her ear. Erica could smell her citrus soap on her. They showered at the YMCA every day, went to the launderette every week. The apartment no longer stank of smoke, the glug jug had been replaced by a bowl they scrubbed out after every use. They'd thrown out the sheets on her bed and Erica found a job lot at a second-hand shop down the road, had washed and dried them and had them pressed as a gift. Laure had told her she did not want a wife but she did not seem to mind a maid.

"You look very beautiful tonight."

Erica laughed hollowly. "It's not a compliment if you have to ask."

"You didn't ask. Look, if this is about Evelyne—"

"It's not," said Erica, too fast.

"OK." Laure fetched the roll-up from her ear and passed it back and forth between her fingers. "She knew someone I admired. A man called Henri Curiel. He was a comrade, a good man. He was shot by Fascists in May."

Erica felt miserable. How could she compete with a Communist? "I'm sorry."

"I did not know him. But Evelyne did. We were only talking about him, his good work."

"You don't have to explain."

"No?"

Erica shook her head, feeling stupid as well as sad. "You never promised me anything."

But even as Erica said it, she felt it to be a lie. Wasn't everything a promise between them now?

"I know," said Laure, but she put aside her cigarette anyway, and kissed her deeply.

The next weekend they went to L'Orangerie, Erica using Léa's student card to get in for free. Until now she'd only seen outside, the glittering glass and metal worked between like a sketch, a confection of light. As they walked along the Rive Droite, it was as if they both understood why they'd waited a month to take this trip together, as though by taking Erica to see her favourite paintings, Laure was letting her into some sacred part of herself. The museum had been due to close for renovation for weeks, and Laure was worried if they waited much longer Erica would not see the paintings before she left.

They were quiet, intensely so, and suddenly shy of each other, Erica apologizing for bumping hips, Laure careful to blow her smoke away from Erica's face. It was as if they were on a pilgrimage, apart and united. But as they crossed into the ordered expanse of the Jardin des Tuileries, Laure took Erica's hand, and Erica felt herself melt against her lover, breathe more easily. It felt so good to walk beside her, to hold her cool long fingers.

Perhaps it was because she had never been in love before, but Erica felt herself more fragile, thinner-skinned, as though everything from noise to light could permeate her more easily. Walking through these bright gardens, with families playing around the trees, the sculptures, and elderly couples on the green metal benches that scattered the pathways, she felt it to be almost unbearably beautiful. That she was in love with Laure was something she accepted without scrutiny or resistance: it was simply fact. And since their kiss on the stairway last week, she'd all but accepted her feelings were returned. The last of her defences, weak as they were, had tumbled, and she was laid bare to it all. To Paris, to Laure, to this perfect summer. Even red wine had begun to agree with her, and she and Laure had got into the habit of sharing a bottle and a baguette from the boulangerie on Rue Tiron for lunch before heading out for the day, and then on to a bar or a reading. In the early hours, Michel and Christophe would often peel off to a dance club; now Parade was closed it would be Arcadie or La Pergola, but the women preferred to stay in. Instead they would go back to Barbara's or Marie and Agnès', or even, in its new sanitary guise, Laure and Erica's. Laure and Erica's—that was what Léa once called it, and Laure had not corrected her. Erica had held onto this moment ever since.

Yet there was still no easy word for what they were to each other. Françoise would tease Laure and call Erica her *femme*, and Laure a *Jules*. Laure reacted violently to these terms.

"We're not in the sixties now, Françoise. We are women who love women, that is enough."

This too stuck in Erica's heart like a shining needle, exquisitely sharp. She knew Laure likely meant love as sleeping together, or in opposition to loving men, but what if? What if she did not? Labels did matter to Laure for all her rejection of Françoise's teasing, Erica knew. She cared she was a student of the Sorbonne, a lesbian, an art theorist, a smoker and a Communist. So why would she not label what Erica was to her?

They approached L'Orangerie, a colonnade of sandy stone encasing the glasshouses that gave it its name. The gardens were busy, but soon the tourists would be heading for the cafés for a pick-me-up, or their hotels to change for dinner. Erica watched them, with their guidebooks and boxy cameras, and felt herself apart from them, though her own camera was slung over her shoulder. She felt she belonged, with Laure beside her, and with this came a sense of superiority she enjoyed for its novelty.

There was no queue, and they pushed against the current of people leaving, swimming upstream until they reached a grand staircase. Laure pulled Erica to a halt and turned her to face her. She placed her hands on her shoulders.

"Don't speak when we get inside. Just walk to the centre, next to the bench, and stand. Pivot on the spot. Look."

Laure's face was deadly serious, and Erica felt a giggle pushing at her throat, but she swallowed it. She nodded, and Laure took Erica's camera from her shoulder and slung it over her own.

"And no photos. Not until you've seen."

Unable to help it, Erica saluted, and immediately regretted it. Laure looked tense, and Erica forced herself to be serious. "Sorry. Yes. I understand."

She followed Laure into the gallery.

The room was oval, painted white. Light flooded in from skylights, and Erica's immediate impression was of expansiveness, of a space beyond the limits of the walls. The paintings were arranged along the curved edges, the colours washing in and out of their frames. Remembering Laure's instructions, Erica walked to the centre of the room, and turned back to face one of the canvases.

It showed a lake or a pond, a body of water distinct from a river by its stillness. The colour was something like purple, something like blue, an undeniably uncertain light, that indigo-dawn she sometimes saw brushing the sky as she and Laure stumbled home drunk. But more than that it was pink, and navy, and lilac, the colours of the marshes at Burnham Overy Staithe at the tipping point of night and day. Homesickness crashed over her, for the wide flat skies of Norfolk and for her parents. Her parents. What would they think of this, of her?

But then the feeling drifted away. She felt herself slip deeper into the painting, or was it flowing out to meet her? She could almost feel a breeze stir the willows, the cool of her drying hair a suck of breath on her nape. Impossible to believe these were not real, impossible to forget that they weren't. As she turned slowly to take in the next one—a brightening of the sky's reflection, a yellow sluice that was in fact green and black and brown—she understood that Monet had been a man in love. He too had felt light pass through his skin, into his bones, seen the glow that sat inside everything. He understood the hunger for the present moment, and in his work here held those transitions still, or almost still, quivering between light and dark, true night and true day, the crossing of a threshold, pinned in place.

Erica thought then of her own moments between: the hesitation before approaching Laure on the steps, before kissing her, before kneeling to press her face between her legs. She loved those hinge moments, before desire tipped into fulfilment, and felt that same satisfaction here: the moment after sunset, the moment before a new day, the waterlilies hovering in the act of unfurling. Even the colours were flickering, unfixed. Clouds of water made clouds of water. Lily pads heavy green-black, the water pushing back on gravity. The sky's reflection, deep as it was high.

The room emptied out by degrees, but Erica didn't notice. She was wrapped up in the paintings, and Laure was wrapped up in her. She watched the light on Erica's face change and felt at once absolute peace, and abject terror. She wished she could roll a cigarette, busy her hands, but instead she sat on them, on the bench in the oval room, and watched Erica watch the season turn of the paintings. She despised the chocolate-box reputation Monet had gained, the smash-and-grab ownership that commodification had exercised over these masterpieces, the simple loveliness they'd been reduced to. To Laure, these paintings were about death. Death as a condition of life. The darkness that underlay everything, even the purest light. The reflection of the sky, the trees, as above so below.

It always took Laure time to sink into them, whereas she could see Erica was instantly transported. The instructions to look, to see, had been as much to herself as Erica. It took time to clear the theories from her head, every lecture she'd been to on modernism and Impressionism crowding in, shouting, every line in a book underlined flashing before her eyes. She looked and looked. *Not everything is a construct, Laure.* Pauline was as right as she was wrong, and here, in front of *Les Nymphéas*, Laure understood this fully. Once she waded through the context, she was simply there, in a moment in time and space, before these images, just as Monet had been, standing in his garden in Giverny, the light fading alongside his sight. She looked and looked, and began to see. Mark after mark after mark. Paint as a poetic sign, a sign capable of signifying multitudes. Paint as two sides of a multisided signifier. *Hush.* She quietened her mind like a bolting horse. *Look.*

The water lapped at her face. The light shifted across the canvas, across the trees, through the garden, through the canvas. As Erica moved in her periphery, Laure felt the tug of the string between them, felt it spiral its tendrils towards the paintings too, so they were all entangled here. She knew she would remember this feeling for ever, and that it would be nothing like the feeling itself, only her memory of it. It was unbearable to her that soon L'Orangerie would close, the paintings moved into storage for the renovation, and Erica would be gone.

Erica crossed to stand in front of her, at the core of *Les Nuages*. Her head was tilted, her arms extended behind her, her fingers interlinked. She looked a bit like Degas's *La Petite Danseuse*, her foot struck out, the awkward clasp of her hands. Her hair tumbled down her back in waves, still damp from the shower. Laure acted almost unconsciously, lifting Erica's camera to her eye, and taking a picture. The snap of the shutter jolted Erica visibly, and she spun around, her hands reflexively flying apart.

"Sorry," said Laure, instantly remorseful. "Sorry."

She stood up and opened her arms. The room was empty of people, and full of them and the gathered light of Monet's garden at Giverny. Erica smiled and went to her, blinking dazedly as though just waking.

"Wow." She leant her forehead against Laure's chin. Laure breathed in, smelling the artificial sharpness of her shampoo, the talcum softness of her skin beneath. Their hands brushed, their little fingers intertwining.

There was the clearing of a throat, and they broke apart. A stern man in a suit was waving them out. Erica, an eager schoolgirl at heart, apologized and hurried out, but Laure took her time, slinging the camera across her chest. Ignoring the tutting attendant, she turned slowly in the room, trying to drink in enough to sustain her until next time. The light, the colours, the marks built with patient and loving repetition. There was a lesson here, if she could only be alive to it. Then she followed Erica out into the garden.

The days passed so sweetly Laure almost forgot they would soon end. She understood why Paris was famous for lovers, a city full of shadowed corners and exquisite light, even the texture of the buildings seductive, moving from rough to smooth, new to worn. But then August was almost spent, and the date on Erica's ticket approached, and Laure did not once ask her to stay. Instead they made love, they talked, they read aloud with their heads in each other's laps. They walked around Le Marais and across the bridges, and ate fresh nectarines from Rousillon sliced and sandwiched in Tomme de Chèvre sitting in the Jardin du Luxembourg. They went into the catacombs through an unofficial tunnel Claude told them about, and kissed in the dark against the shelves of bones. They tried to sneak aboard a bus to Giverny because they'd spent their money on beer, and were chased off by the irate conductor. Laure claimed she didn't want to go there anyway, that the paintings were enough, the gardens sad and abandoned, but in truth she'd have loved to see Erica among the willows, overgrown but still lovely, show her the place Monet so adored.

They walked to the Gare d'Orsay, which was to become a museum and was currently a squat where artists and poets slept on abandoned platforms and in the stripped-out hotel rooms that once sold for hundreds of francs a night. They tried to work out how to get in, called up to the flags and banners unfurled from the windows—soyez réalistes, demandez l'impossible; pouvoir À l'imagination; je jouis dans les pavés—but no one answered. Erica knew better than to ask to go to the Eiffel Tower, but Laure took her anyway, and they circled its base, sharing a strawberry ice cream and sneering at the tourists queuing to climb it. Laure's appetite was better than it had been in years, and she did not know if it was chocolate or Erica's ministrations that eased her cramps during her monthly bleed. She was ravenous, for sex, for bread, for cheese and for pastries. They went to the showing of *India Song* at the Paris and she conceded that yes, Léa, she liked it. Léa high-fived Erica in celebration.

She also liked being a guide, taking Erica to private museums to see odd artifacts, to experimental theatre at community cafés, back to the Pompidou to deride the architecture. Most of all she liked learning Erica, what made her laugh, her favourite colours, her favourite positions, her favourite books. They exchanged second-hand copies of *One Hundred Years of Solitude* (Erica's favourite), and *La Religieuse* (the book Laure thought would most amuse Erica). Neither said I love you, Je t'aime, but it was love building surely between them, though there were depths of themselves kept concealed. Both avoided talking about what came before, what was to come next, and so all Laure knew was that Erica was from a small town in Norfolk, and her parents were still alive. Erica knew even less about her, and Laure was glad to keep it that way. It was better to be in the present, to know and worship each other in this moment. If she loved Erica as she was here, now, she could be hers fully. Forget the past, which she could never claim. Forget the future—they talked not at all about Erica's approaching departure. It was impossible that two months ago they had not existed in each other's worlds, and now everything was changed. Laure was in love, and everything tasted better. She felt herself being redrawn in the écorché style, flayed and soothed, remoulded. She understood at last Barthes' *lunatic chores*, the joy she took in brushing Erica's hair, peeling and de-pithing her oranges. *What love lays bare in me is energy*, and she felt galvanized in a way she hadn't since first moving to Paris, talking about a better world with Michel. She wanted to make the world just so for Erica, to maintain for ever the perfect bubble of their happiness.

In the final week of being together, they were lying intertwined in the warm patch on the new-old rug dressed only in their underwear, Laure reading *On Photography* and Erica rapt by *Nana*, gasping and asking Laure if Zola really wrote that, used that word. And then, so lightly Laure did not at once understand, did not have time to brace herself for the conversation to come—

"I start university next week."

Laure sat up, sending Erica rolling off her with a short laugh. "Yes?"

"Yes." Erica's hair was fanned out around her face, and she had slung an arm over her eyes to block the sun. "I'm excited. Nervous. How did you find it, coming here?"

Laure shrugged. She could feel herself closing down, and though she knew she should not she reached for her tobacco, her papers. "Fine."

Erica laughed again, a bit too brightly. "Fine? I'm giddy about going to Norwich! If I were in Paris—"

"Why not?" Laure stayed intent on her hands, letting her hair form a curtain to hide her face. She sensed Erica stiffen.

"What?"

"Why not study here? There are universities. English courses."

"Oh." Erica rolled onto her side, the soft curve of her belly spreading onto the woven fabric, the creamy dip of her waist accentuated by the rise of her hip. "I mean . . ."

Laure could tell without looking she was blushing. "You think the French can't teach English?"

"I'm not actually that interested in English."

Laure did look up then, paused in the act of spreading the tobacco. "What?"

"I mean, I am, and I'm excited, but I'm really interested in what's after that. There's a master's course at UEA, and I thought studying there before might help my chances."

"What's that?" Something in Erica's face made her heart sink. "You're not going to do engineering or something, are you?"

"English to engineering?" Erica laughed. "Why would that be so bad?"

"I have never met an engineering student I liked."

"You're ridiculous," said Erica, reaching out and tucking Laure's hair behind her ear.

"What is this magical course then?"

"Creative writing."

Laure snorted.

"Creative writing," said Erica, louder. "It's a new course. I probably won't get in but . . ." She crossed her fingers. God, but Laure hated that gesture.

"But what do you learn?"

"How to write. Books. Novels." Erica was frowning at her, as though she was being deliberately stupid, but Laure was genuinely incredulous.

"You're going to pay someone to teach you how to write? You could just write."

"You pay someone to teach you how to think."

"I learn what people thought in the past in order to form new thoughts."

"And I will learn what people used to write so I can write my own."

"That's just reading." Laure tapped the Zola in Erica's hand. "You can do that for free, if you use a library."

Erica let out a huff, and sat up, reaching past Laure to pull the sheepskin from the sofa and cover herself with it. Laure knew this was a bad sign, that for Erica clothes were armour, that she only felt truly comfortable naked when she was at her most relaxed.

"This is why I didn't tell you. I knew you'd make fun."

"I'm sorry, but do you think Zola did creative writing? Did Dumas? Did Camus, or Hugo?"

"For a feminist, you set a lot of store by male writers."

Laure refused to be thrown off course. "De Beauvoir? Colette? Duras?"

"I thought you thought Duras was a narcissist."

"A narcissist who can write."

"And I can't?"

Laure held up her hands in mock-surrender. "I don't know. I didn't even know you did write until a minute ago."

"Well, I do. And I used a sample on my application for the English degree, and it got me in."

"Good for you." Erica let out an exasperated cry and made to stand up, but Laure gripped her wrist. "I mean it! Congratulations."

"The problem with you is I don't know when you're making fun and when you're serious."

"I am always both," said Laure, drawing Erica towards her and kissing her wrist, her elbow, her neck, her lips. Laure loved how easily she could calm Erica, far more easily than she could herself. They kissed awhile before Erica drew back with the dazed look Laure recalled from L'Orangerie.

"I have a gift for you. I was going to give it to you tomorrow night, our last night—"

Laure stopped her words with another kiss. She didn't think she could bear to hear her say it. "I don't need anything."

"It's only small. Here."

From behind her suitcase she pulled a cardboard tube. Laure took it with a feeling of misgiving. "What is it?"

"It's a present," smiled Erica. "Open it."

Laure pulled from the tube a scrolled poster. She knew what it was already, had known the moment she'd seen the tube. She unfurled it to show a cheaply printed reproduction of *Matin*, blurrily photographed and oddly cropped. Erica was beaming at her.

"Voilà!"

A flare of anger, so sudden it was like a static shock. This girl knew nothing about her. She had been play-acting all this time, pretending to listen. Erica hadn't even told her until this moment she wanted to be a writer. Did they know each other at all?

"Don't you like it? The walls are so bare in here, and it was so special being there with you—"

"Exactly. It was special. So why would I want this piece of crap?"

Erica blinked. "Sorry?"

"You should be." Laure dropped the poster to the floor, where it refurled itself with a shushing sound. "It offends me to look at this."

"You must be joking—"

"No, you must be. This rubbish, this tat, this, this . . ." Laure searched for the words, but for the first time she felt the limits of her English, something lost in translation. "This is what is wrong with tourists. They come and they take photographs, they buy their key rings and their postcards, and then that becomes the version they remember. Not the aura, the energy of the real thing. All they are left with is an impression of an impression. Something palatable and digestible and toothless. When you know the paintings are nothing like that. Seeing those paintings with you, it was nothing like this."

She kicked the roll of paper. None of what she had just said mattered. All she wanted to say, to howl, was *Stay. Don't leave me with only memories.*

Erica flinched. "You really think I'm stupid? Of course this isn't the painting. I thought it would be something nice, to remember me by."

"I don't want this. I don't want nice. I can remember how you smell, how you taste, how you look at me right now. I don't want *stuff*. It makes the absence of the real thing worse. How do you say?" She knocked her chest with her fist.

"Hollow."

"Oui. Hollow."

Erica stood up, letting the sheepskin drop. Laure could tell she was shaken, upset by her outburst, but she pressed her warm body against Laure's and kissed her. "You are a terrible snob, Laure."

Laure laughed to hide the fact she might cry. Hadn't she just asked Erica to stay? Or had Laure imagined that, saying aloud what she had asked a hundred times in her mind?

"I'll miss you," insisted Erica.

"Mm."

"Will you miss me?"

"I had a life here before you. I have a life."

"I know that." Erica sounded hurt, and Laure was glad. "Will you visit me?"

"Will you want me to?"

"Of course." Erica frowned, drawing away. Laure felt her absence as though her own skin had been peeled away. "Why would you ask that?"

"You aren't a lesbian, remember?"

Erica blushed deeper. "No, but . . ."

Laure snatched up her lighter. What did she mean, no? Wasn't she here, half-naked in Laure's apartment, with Laure's taste still in her mouth?

"I mean . . . I don't know. Do you . . . are we . . ."

But it was as if Laure were on a rope, crawling along a dark tunnel. All this time she thought she was getting closer to the light, but there was nothing ahead of her. The rope yanked and she was falling backwards, the weeks of bliss racing past, coming undone, erupting in flames. Her skin itched all over. She lit her cigarette. Lately her lungs had felt sore, her throat raw as she inhaled, but she desired the discomfort now, with the same urgency she used to press her shoulder into the bare nail when she listened to her father cry, or walked miles on no sleep and too much wine.

"No," she said. "We aren't."

The air in the room was stifling. Laure couldn't breathe, so she dragged harder on her cigarette.

"Laure . . ."

"I need a drink. Want anything?"

"It's the morning—"

"So?"

"I'm all right, thank you."

Laure nodded and pulled on trousers, a shirt. Without another word, she left, her mouth full of bitter smoke.

•

Erica didn't follow her. She sat beneath the sheepskin, sunlight sticky on her back, and tried to sort through her racing thoughts. She looked around the apartment, at the ornate wooden chairs they'd rescued from the skip at Gare d'Orsay, the records they'd bought together in Bastille. Hadn't Laure, only minutes ago, asked her to stay in Paris? It was what Erica had been hoping for, dreaming of, fantasizing about. Spending for ever in this summer with Laure and her friends—their friends—suspended in this haven they'd created together. Laure had offered her this vision, and Erica had swatted it aside, even picked a fight. She knew Laure would laugh at her desire to study creative writing, that was another matter. Erica had wanted to change the subject. Why?

Because it isn't real. It can't be. A voice, perhaps her mother's, gave brutal, clear voice to the feeling that had shadowed Erica through every moment since she'd kissed Laure. At first she'd thought it was fear, but now she realized it was worse than that. Shame. The idea of telling her parents she was staying in Paris to live in a squat with a lover was unthinkable, the idea of telling them it was a woman laughable. She loved Laure. She was not a fool and could admit that. And her parents were not religious, not bigots, but they were also from King's Lynn. If gay people lived there, they kept themselves to themselves, lived quietly. She knew she could not live how Laure and her friends lived, at the edges of things, even in Paris. Their bars raided, their friends beaten. She didn't want to exist like that. She wanted to get married, to have children. She wanted to write novels, but she was not Gertrude Stein or Virginia Woolf, someone extraordinary or content to struggle with unhappiness. She wanted simple joy, simple happiness, simple love. And loving Laure would not be simple.

No. She would get on the coach in two days' time. If it made her a coward, or a traitor, or a tourist, so be it. Laure had made it clear she would be all right without her. She had her life here, and Erica had a life waiting for her, one she had not yet made. She was left with the bare facts of the matter: she would leave, and her heart would be broken. She let her tears come with a sense of surrender, succumbing to a hurt that was unavoidable.

Laure came home hours later with a bottle of vodka, another of cheap champagne, and a cake from the boulangerie on Rue Tiron, covered in strawberries.

"Are we celebrating?" said Erica, tartly. She had long since stopped crying, but sadness weighed heavily on her. She already missed Laure, though she stood just in front of her.

Laure shook her head slowly. "We are getting drunk."

She set the cake down between them and opened the champagne. They took turns swigging from the bottle, eating the cake from the box with forks and then their fingers, and then from each other's fingers. As they ate, Erica recited to herself a poem she'd read in a book since swapped with Michel for Verlaine's *Parallèlement*. It was about strawberries, and lovers, and not hurrying the feast for the one to come. She'd remembered it as sexy, but now the first lines repeated in her head like a hymn: *There were never strawberries / like the ones we had / that sultry afternoon*, and she understood for the first time the past tense of it, the longing for what is passed. The fumbling for something that is gone and cannot come again. A memory made sweeter for the fact it is a memory. That was what she meant by the poster—for it to be a trigger, a portal, a way back. She wanted to tell Laure this, to frame the thought in words before champagne made it elusive, but Laure was looking at her in that way, and so she set aside her fork and filled her mouth with champagne, feeling the bubbles break against Laure's and her tongues, and it was easier, after all, not to speak.

•

On Erica's last evening, Léa insisted they throw her a goodbye party. Laure wanted to refuse outright, but Erica seemed enthused by the idea, and so she chose instead to brood on this, wondering why Erica did not want to spend the night with her alone. She point-blank rebuffed the idea of having it at her apartment. The idea of not being able to leave when she wanted to filled her with dread, so Léa said she would handle it.

They ended up at Barbara's, where Léa had fixed awful-tasting Bloody Marys and bought little gristly steak pies and, in keeping with the British theme, insisted they play only music by British people: the Beatles and Elton John and Queen. Claude picked a fight because he wanted to include Van Morrison, and Marie told him this was an imperialist action as he was Northern Irish, and there was a lot of banging of the table. Erica, though, was in her element. She drank and danced and laughed, took tokes of Léa's spliff and flirted with everyone. Laure watched her move through the room as though she were a stranger and saw she would love university. She would fall in love there and forget all about her. It was enough to make her breath stick in her throat.

Then "Catch the Wind" by Donovan came on, and Erica stopped dancing. She turned to Laure, focusing her full attention on her for the first time, it felt to Laure, all night. She took Laure's hand and pulled her to her feet.

"Laure doesn't dance," said Marie.

"I know," said Erica, and she wrapped her arms around Laure's neck like she was at her first school disco, and they swayed together, the room melting away. Laure rested her cheek against Erica's hair, pulling her in closer, as close as she could. When the song finished, she looked up to see the others pressed against the kitchen counter, watching them sadly.

"Ah, Laure," said Michel, and Léa burst into tears.

That night they did not do anything but kiss. They didn't talk about the future or reminisce about the past months. They didn't laugh together about Léa weeping, or lament how awful the Bloody Marys were, or cry about their parting. They lay in each other's arms, and kissed until their lips were sore and the sun was rising, and the day had come, as it always must.

Laure walked Erica through the early morning streets, not smoking, not speaking, Erica's suitcase in one hand and her hand in the other. The coach station was full of goodbyes, and Laure tried to remind herself that to wish to possess another person was bourgeois, and that, like de Beauvoir, she must live her ideals. And besides, theirs was only one farewell, only one parting. Thousands, millions of people said goodbye every day, under worse and harder circumstances. Billions of people had survived first love, and its attendant heartbreak.

As they stood beside the bus, Erica began to babble. "You will write? You have the address? And I can write to you at Marie's? You'll tell me if she moves? I can always send them to Michel at the café if needs be. And I'll visit you, just as soon as I can. And you come to Norwich, there's a gallery there now, just opened this year—the Salisbury Centre. Or the Sainsbury Centre. I know it's not Paris but Norfolk is beautiful, I think you'll like it, there are even fewer hills than Paris."

She ran out of breath, and Laure felt no need to respond. They had discussed all this. It was all agreed. But Laure felt insulted at the idea of being pen pals. What would there be to say, about a life not lived together?

"I'd best board." Erica looked up at her, and Laure knew she wanted to kiss her, but there were too many people around. Her eyes were such a beautiful brown, her skin tanned from their walks outside, her lips bruised from their kisses. Laure wanted to bite her, to mark her, to give her some signifier or brand that she was hers, hers first and fuck ideals. They embraced, Erica gripping hard, Laure already in the act of letting go. Erica's shoulders were shaking, and she took deep, trembling breaths. When they drew apart, her eyes were full of tears.

"Take care," said Laure formally. "Be good."

Erica smiled. "Ravie."

There was a lump in Laure's throat, like a chunk of apple. "Ravie."

Erica kissed her, very light and very quick, just below her left ear. She took her suitcase and climbed aboard, reappearing in a window above where Laure stood. Laure wanted to walk away, but she couldn't. God but it *hurt*. It was agony. In her mind she saw Erica as she had been on the steps of the Sacré-Cœur, waving Barthes under Laure's nose. Laure had been reading "The Ghost Ship," from *errance*: *How does a love end?—Then it does end?*

It was ending. Erica was waving, like the schoolgirl she so recently was. The coach began to move, and Laure resisted the urge to run alongside like a dog. She waved until Erica was out of sight, and the coach gone, and took out her tobacco. *The love which is over and done with passes into another world like a ship into space, lights no longer winking.* The place where Erica had last kissed her burned like a brand. Her hands were shaking too much to roll. Laure threw down the tin, which bounced off the pavement and onto the road. She bent in half, hands pressed hard over her face, and shouted into the red dark.

Chapter Three

Erica had meant to write. She started, many times, but what to say? Laure had made clear she hated facsimiles, and Erica was so busy in those first few weeks at university she couldn't summon the energy for anything more complex than a straightforward account of her days. Then, when she was mired in studies and social events, it felt almost cruel to send a list of all the ways she was glad to be here, and all the things she loved about UEA. The grounds, with their lake and trees, the Ziggurats, the Sainsbury Centre full of wooden sculpture and gilt-framed paintings. The town that could have felt a city if she'd come straight from King's Lynn, but as it was, was no match for Paris. She loved it anyway, cheap beer and bookshops, cinemas showing *Grease* six times a day, back-to-back. She'd been three times and was certain Laure would not have seen it.

She thought of Laure, all the time. She had Laure's voice in her head when she listened to pop records, saw cheesy films, drank Black Tower and kissed men. To each of these things, she knew Laure would react the same way: with an insouciance that hid deep disappointment and judgement. It was that voice that stopped her writing to her altogether—all those inane observations, prosaisms. She realized over those first months in Norwich that she had spent all her time with Laure feeling stupid, but that this was not so much Laure's failing as her own. In arrears, she decided to attempt to abandon this tendency, quieting the self-flagellating, punitive voice in her head by contributing in lectures, reading every book with full attention, writing her essays over and over with a rigour unmatched by her peers. She gave to her studies the deep thought and attention she failed to give her letters, and in the end her work felt like the best way to honour the impact Laure had had on her.

But she was not a hermit wedded to the library, though she loved it there with its yellow-tinged strip lights and rollable stacks, its open, industrial hush. For Laure had also unlocked something else in her: desire. Erica had learnt more about her body in those two months with Laure than she had in all her years before, and now she felt awake to pleasure, ravenous for it. She cooked for herself, pasta with fresh tomatoes instead of canned. She bought bath oil smelling of roses and rubbed it into her skin after showers. She touched herself, and let men touch her. Though there were openly gay men and women at UEA, they closed ranks early in the term, like the drama society or the Dungeons & Dragons gamers. So Erica contented herself with men. Her first was a geographer on the next floor down, a red-haired gawky type with a beautiful smile and gentle hands. She could tell she surprised him with her attentions, and as he looked up at her while she rode him in his single bed, his roommate locked out, she saw the awe on his face and felt the power she'd sometimes, but not often, felt with Laure.

It was an undeniable and guilty relief to discover she still desired men. She loved the graceless contradictions of their bad teeth and soft lips, their stubble and their velvet earlobes, their veined forearms and urgent arousal. It was a cliché, but she loved how simple the mechanics of their gratification were, how she did not have to anxiously watch their face to know if what she was doing was good or not, that the pleasure they in turn gave her was blunt and undemanding. She taught more than one boy how to touch a woman, how to use his tongue. Léa and Agnès had often derided their male lovers, but now Erica suspected they had not bothered to give them much of a chance.

By the end of the first term, she'd begun sleeping exclusively with a different geography student, a tall, skinny blond boy called Robert. If she sometimes closed her eyes and thought of Laure when he went down on her, twining her fingers through his shoulder-length hair, or wrapped her arm around his ribcage, angling her hand so it touched only hairless, smooth skin, or breathed in the smell of roll-ups on his neck, it was a harmless fantasy. She did not love Robert, but she liked him, he was interesting and kind, though bad in bed. He called himself a feminist, and they shared half-baked and passionate opinions about politics. They went to see Fairport Convention together in the LCR, and when they played "One More Chance" Erica began to cry, and Robert knew not to ask questions, only wrapping his long arms around her and swaying, his smoky hair tickling Erica's nose and making her cry harder. In short, he was a good man, good enough to quieten Erica's unacknowledged fear that she should never have left Paris.

At the start of 1979, the year still fresh, Erica decided she would try, once more, to write Laure a letter.

She'd spent the festive season at home with her parents, and then, on a whim and at the suggestion of Robert, he, she and a group largely composed of the foreign students who could not get home for Christmas took a draughty, mice-ridden barn that had been converted into a bunk house a quarter of a mile from the north Norfolk coast to see in the new year. It was on the estate of a large stately home, and Erica strongly suspected it was part of some tax evasion, for the conversion was halfhearted and depressing. There was an outhouse, and the kitchen was sparser than Laure's.

It didn't matter though, because the beach was the most beautiful in the area, a seemingly endless expanse of pale golden sand that rose into sand dunes fifty feet high and edged with swaying grasses that looked soft and were sharp enough to cut. The tide washed in around them along channels filled with samphire and sea lavender, making islands of the dunes and creating a perfect mirror for the pine forest that edged the beach. The wind howled along the flats but the dunes protected this little bay within a bay, and they spent whole days there, dragging their sleeping bags with them, getting high around a bonfire and listening to one or other of the men agonizingly fingerpick their way through Dylan or Cohen, drinking local beer they bought in gallon kegs from the brewery and eating pints of prawns caught fresh from the boats in the town down the road. She and Robert cycled there each morning and bought bread and beer, fish and potatoes to wrap in foil for the bonfire. It was often so windy the bikes skidded from under them on the ice, and at night Robert kissed the bruises on her hips and thighs.

"I love you," he'd say, and it was easier, sometimes, in the effort of the bad sex, to say it back.

The foreign students made Erica reflect on how she must have been in Paris. They observed everything, from the burnt jacket potatoes to the newspaper toilet paper, through the lens of quaint novelty, though the Greek students drew the line at getting in the freezing sea. The northern Spanish and Danish students had no such qualms, and on New Year's Day Erica plunged naked and screaming into the North Sea waves, holding tight to Robert's hand and both of them pretending not to look at Esme's breasts.

Erica had been here many times, but never without her parents, and never in the dead centre of winter. It was a new sort of freedom, different from Paris because it was ownership over a place she knew, had grown up in and returned to as an adult. When she came home for the final few days of holiday before term started, she felt oddly benevolent towards her parents, who had been an irritation over Christmas, as though it was she who was the parent and they the well-meaning but needy toddlers. It was in this spirit she decided she was ready, at last, to write a letter she would actually send.

5 January 1979

Dear Laure,

I'm writing to you from home, my childhood bedroom. It feels like that now, no longer my bedroom, but a place of the past. "I have put away childish things"—isn't that from the Bible? My parents bought me a portable typewriter for Christmas and I am still getting used to the smaller keys. Please forgive any misspellings.

I hope you would be proud of what I have become these past four months. Or perhaps I was already in the act of becoming, during our time together. Whatever the case, I know I owe you so much for your friendship and care for me last summer. I cherish those memories, and enclose the photograph you took of me in L'Orangerie in the hope you will hold it close, as I keep the photograph I took of you on the steps of Sacré-Cœur. You are currently a bookmark for "Sadler's Birthday," by Rose Tremain. Have you heard of her? She studied at UEA.

I'm realizing this letter sounds like a goodbye. I'll go no further before saying it is, and it isn't. It is in that I feel myself changed these past months. I don't know why you haven't written to me, but I hope it is for the same reason I didn't write to you before now: life rushing on, not knowing what to say, or rather how to put into words what I want to say. But maybe you have not thought of me at all. So I think I must say goodbye to the version of myself who would worry about all that, and absolve you—if you'll allow it—of any guilt over not writing.

And now, an invitation. I saw in 1979 next to the sea, and so loved it I've decided to celebrate my birthday this year at the same place. I'm going to be 19 on the 15th of March, and it falls on a reading week. We're going to rent the same place from the 10th–17th. If you'd like to come, I'd like you to—Michel if he can, and Léa too, if she likes (I do not know how to add an accent on this keyboard, so will add it in by hand). My address at halls is on the envelope. When's your birthday, by the way? It feels weird not to know.

Let me know, and XXXXXXXXXXX I miss you. I hope you'll come.

Bisous,
Erica

•

The letter sat, unopened, on Laure's lap. She had watched it like a wild animal since she'd fetched it, trembling, from Marie's.

"You should open it here," Marie had urged her. "In case it's bad news."

But that was all the more reason to return to her room to read it. In deference to Erica, she cleared the sofa and its circumference of books and tissues, dirty clothes and bottles. It was nowhere near as messy as the day she'd brought Erica there, but still she felt Erica's judgement as she surveyed the clutter, watched the dust motes floating in the pale winter light. Her breath clouded in the room, and she kept her coat on, slipped beneath the sheepskin to open the envelope.

She read it once and then rolled a cigarette, used her lighter to light it and a candle. She looked a long time at the photograph, at Erica caught in the act of turning. She knew it was towards her, but she felt like she was moving away. Laure traced the curve of her plump cheek, the smear of dark eyelashes, her long, long hair.

She held the letter up to the flame and read it again, as though there might be a hidden meaning, a layer written in invisible ink. She scrutinized the xxx'd out text, and found nothing she wanted there. She lifted the paper to her nose and sniffed it, as though she might find Erica's perfume, but even the smell of ink had faded. The fact it was typed was damning enough. Not even a signature, or a line of kisses. Aside from the accent on Léa's name, the photograph, perhaps Erica's spit on the envelope flap, it was impersonal as a bill.

"Shit," she whispered to herself. "Shit."

She let the letter drop, and fell into a pit.

It was not far to fall. Laure had not felt right for months, not since the moment Erica left. There was a gap, a rip in the fabric of things. *The bed's too big, the frying pan's too wide.* She felt a lot of things more deeply now, the divide her father had imposed between brain and soul all those years before narrowing to nothing, Erica's absence tunnelling through her and leaving behind spaces for unwelcome and useless emotion to rush in.

Her friends did their best of course—they were never better than in a crisis. Léa showed up with a bag of pills the first night Erica left.

"Come on," she said, holding a glass of water and indicating for Laure to stick out her tongue. "If you cannot forget her, you may as well forget everything for a while."

The Quaaludes got Laure out of her house and to a dyke bar, where Léa had massed the troops, and while they danced on sticky floors Laure let a shaggy-haired, whippet-thin girl kiss her and snake her body around hers. She went back to her place and fingered her, the drugs making everything from time to her tongue elastic. She woke the next day in the courtyard of her building, bruises all over her arms. For a moment, she'd forgotten—but remembering was like death. She didn't bother to go upstairs, but went straight to the café for a beer.

Every time she saw Marie or Michel, she'd ask if a letter had arrived. At first it was too soon, then there were postal strikes throughout autumn, and then, as November arrived, it started to feel too late. In response, Laure threw herself into a faithful routine of self-medication. It was not so different from the life she'd lived before Erica, except now morning drinks were the rule, not the exception. She would no longer reward herself for a good day in the library with a drink, but took a hip flask of vodka with her, coming to like the burn as it hit her throat under the reading lights. Habitual drinking suited her so well she wondered why she hadn't thought of it before. Her father, after all, had been mired in a cycle of drinking and repentance from the day of her mother's leaving, so she knew all the tricks. It was bred into her, an inheritance. She stopped calling home altogether, a rare enough occurrence as it was. Phone calls were the last tether to her previous existence in that dull farmland outside Rouen—to sever it was only the final act of an intention set when she first moved to Paris, that her father would never know she was a lesbian. Her life would be what it was, cleaved, and she had decided not to mind. The alcohol helped.

She paid for this need by taking on extra teaching, and to her dismay discovered she was good at it. Worse, she enjoyed it. She was allowed to set her own assignments and had budget for field trips, so she took her undergraduates to the Pompidou to see Kandinsky's *Avec l'arc noir*, and then the Louvre, sat them in front of *Le Radeau de la Méduse* and drew a line between these two paintings, explaining how both were trailblazers, masters of composition, how they could direct your eye like music, and all the time thinking of Erica saying, *For a feminist, you set a lot of store by male writers*. In answer, on the next trip she took them to see Dora Maar's photographic collages and Hilma af Klint's paintings, imagined Erica smirking, and that night, as every night, drank herself into a stupor.

Michel was first to recognize she was in trouble, of course. A heavy drinker himself, he selflessly arranged trips to the cinema instead of bars, walks in the park instead of readings at the café. He even tried to implement a no alcohol rule at the café, but it was laughed out of the room.

"You're too precious for this, Laure," he'd tell her, watching her with her hip flask. "You look like a bouseuse. You're brilliant, and young, and you must not waste it."

"You're too sentimental. And a hypocrite."

"Of course," he shrugged. "But isn't it love to want for others what you cannot have?"

"Sobriety? You don't want that, surely."

"I want health. And I am too cock-blind to seek it with any meaning. But it's not too late for you."

"No, I can't stand cocks."

He clucked his tongue and linked his arm through hers. It was December, awful and cold and dark. Breath spiralled from his mouth, and Laure admired his profile, like Titian's *Man with Glove*, his straight nose, full mouth, the scar above his left eyebrow from the attack at Parade. A lovely face, a face she loved. But she could not stop for love, when that was what had got her into this mess in the first place.

"To you, things seem so bleak," he said. "But all over the world, beautiful things are happening. In London you know, they are opening a bookshop, only for gay literature. I read about it in *Gay News*. On

Marchmont Street, right in the middle of London! One day I'll go. You know what they are calling it, little sister? Gay's the Word. Like the Ivor Novello musical!" He clapped his hands in glee, and burst into song. "Everything reminds me of you!"

Laure allowed him a small smile. "You are a walking cliché."

"Says you. Though I prefer archetype. We are ourselves, and that is beautiful." He pulled her even tighter in to him. "It will be all right, Laure. More than. It will all be beautiful."

But even the word summoned Erica for Laure, just as music did, or every painting she admired, or the sparse sun falling on bare trees, the silver thread of current in the river. She hated how sentimental she had become, layers, whole striations of skin peeled away so she discovered she was no better than a left lover in a pop song, mooning about. In Paris, of all places, for god's sake. She *was* a cliché, and Laure despised cliché.

"Please, Michel. Can we go to a bar now? I'm freezing my ass off."

He kissed her forehead, his nose cold against her hairline. "I love you, little sister. Don't forget it."

"So prove it. Buy me a drink."

They spent the afternoon in a dive on Rue Tiquetonne, drinking themselves out of melancholy and into it again, and Michel told her he was in love with Christophe and so understood better than she knew how it felt to be abandoned. Laure, in her drunken haze, realized none of them could be saved, and this cheered her a little.

Barbara tried next, with slightly more success. Laure turned up to her parents' place already drunk at two in the afternoon, and Barbara ripped up their tickets for that evening's showing of *The Marriage of Maria Braun* and instead ran Laure a bath. She made her drink glass upon glass of water, and sat beside her on the closed toilet lid and said,

"Laure, this must stop. I know you are sad, but you think you are the first to be heartbroken?"

Laure started to protest, but her words were trapped by hiccups.

"You are heartbroken, and the sooner you accept that the better. God knows we've all been waiting for it. But a tourist, Laure?" Barbara smiled sadly. "I'm teasing. We all loved her. But she was a child. She barely knew what she wanted, other than you. It's over, but that doesn't mean everything is over."

"It does," wailed Laure, in a voice so unlike her own it frightened her. "I miss her. I loved her and she left me."

"You sound like Hilde. Or Anita. Or me, back in the day."

Laure looked up at her through her tears. Barbara's clear blue eyes blinked back at her. "Barbara. I didn't . . . I'm . . ."

"Oh God, don't try to apologize now. And don't worry, I don't love you anymore. Not like that. But it took me years to get here, and yet I still managed to be your friend, to watch you with other women, even help clear up the messes you made. I managed not to kill myself in the process." And then, as though she could read Laure's mind, "And don't think my pain wasn't real, or as bad as yours. It is the condition of the heartbroken to believe no one has felt as they have, ever in the history of the world. It's an affront to feel otherwise, I know, but the sooner you accept that for every lover there is someone suffering, the sooner you'll heal. And drinking will only keep you sunk in yourself. You need to look outside, and realize you aren't special. You aren't alone."

Barbara reached out and wiped away Laure's tears. Laure caught her hand and kissed it. When Barbara didn't pull away, she licked her wrist, and Barbara laughed softly.

"Ah, Laure. You can't fuck your way out of this, I'm afraid."

Barbara was right, about the drinking as well as the sex. Laure managed to cut down on the former, but the latter came too easily to her. Hilde came running back after they spent New Year's Eve at the same party, and one of her ex-students approached her at a reading in Le Divan early in January. Her ego needed it, whatever Barbara said. But it didn't help. The only thing that did, was time.

In the coming weeks, with that strange invigoration a new year imparts to even the most cynical, Laure slowly began to rebuild the divide between her soul and her head. She made great strides in her thesis, ate at least one green thing a day, began calling her father once a week. He didn't ask what had prompted the abrupt cessation or recommencement of this contact, only if she had heard of Ayatollah Khomeini and how come no one told him he was in France until he'd gone. She started to spend more and more time with the ex-student, Annie, and stopped waiting for a letter.

So when Agnès told her one had come, addressed to her and bearing the profile of Queen Elizabeth II, she felt elation, and utter dread. And here it was, everything she feared: the jovial tone, the outright offer of friendship, the complete lack of anything true or meaningful, no acknowledgement of what those two months had been at all. Friendship. Friendship! The word was like a vice, squeezing all breath and hope out of her. Laure saw what a waste of time her efforts of the new year had been. Erica didn't love her anymore, and nothing mattered.

She began missing classes, deadlines, readings and parties. She began using the piss bowl for other things too, and showered only when she went out to buy more supplies. She still saw Annie, but when she went to Hilde drunk and unwashed, Hilde refused to sleep with her.

"You're screwed, Laure," she said from her threshold, seeming to Laure like St Peter at the gates or Cerberus. The flatmates who hated her were listening, Laure was sure. "And I'm sick of trying to unscrew you."

Laure giggled. "You wish."

"Grow up, Laure."

After a few weeks' languishing post-letter, Laure stopped bothering to leave her apartment. Annie brought her cigarettes and beer, and food too. She offered to clean her apartment, but Laure said no. Michel came most days too, holding his nose and taking her laundry. She wished he would leave her alone, and told him so, but he didn't. But he also didn't try to stop her drinking, or make her leave the squat. He still kissed her on the forehead goodbye, and sang as he dropped off her clean washing, but there was something distracted in his manner. She registered this somewhere in the back of her mournful, beer-soaked mind, but she couldn't haul herself out of her inner monologue to ask what was going on.

This descent yawned on for a month, the first days of spring arriving through the filthy windows, before the next intervention. This time, it was Marie who came to try and fix her. Marie, the second friend she made in Paris, the closest thing Laure had to a sister, and the only one of them who had known long-term love.

"This has gone on long enough," she said, schoolteacher stern, standing over Laure, who was lying on the floor, rolling a cigarette. She looked so neat in her jumper and skirt, her favourite suede boots. Laure had missed her but didn't think now was the time to say. She'd missed Agnès' birthday party too and thought maybe Marie was here to kick up a fuss about that but instead she was gesturing at Laure as if to say *what a waste of skin*.

"It's fine. I got the time off teaching."

"So who's paying for all that?" She glared at the bottles.

"Annie."

"Little orphan Annie, is it? Enabling fool. Is this still about the letter?"

"I don't want to talk about it."

"Show me."

Laure didn't want to, and even more she didn't want Marie to see where she kept it, but after a pause she pulled the paper out from under her limp pillow.

"What are you going to do?" Marie asked, after reading the letter.

"Drink."

"Great plan," said Marie drily. "And then? Are you going to go to England?"

"Of course not."

"Maybe you should. Get it out of your system."

"What? Go to the beach and play happy families? Watch her with some boy, and pretend I am fine with being an experiment, a summer fling?"

"What if she is with a woman? Would that be worse?"

Laure lay back on the floor, the cold leaching through the gaps in the boards, her breath dancing in the air. She blew out smoke, then breath, then smoke, then breath, watched how the smoke hovered and the breath cut it apart. She heard Marie's question and let it trickle into her brain, felt the beginnings of an extraordinary pain, and pushed it away.

There was a creak as Marie got down on the floor beside her. She reached across and took the roll-up from Laure, and as she smoked, she held Laure's hand.

"What's going on? Is it just Erica?"

The pain spiked again. Laure sat up and swigged a mouthful of beer.

"Is it your dad?"

"Non. He's fine." Or he had been when she last called a few weeks ago.

"Then? You're in trouble, Laure. We can all see it."

"I'm fine."

"Talk to me." Marie sat up too, and passed her the cigarette. "I know you tried to sleep with Barbara last year."

"I was just grateful."

"I'm a little offended you aren't trying to sleep with me."

"If Agnès were here it would be a different matter."

Marie punched her lightly on the arm. "You can't stay like this. Stuck on her."

"I'm not. I was with Annie just last night."

Marie took the cigarette again. Laure hadn't seen her smoke in years, but she remembered now how it was a habit of hers to smoke right down to the filter, as though her fingers were made of nickel. "You like her?"

"Sure."

"Of course you do. She looks at you like you are God. Have you realized she doesn't talk around you, only listens? It is like Erica at the beginning, before she found her voice."

"She talks." But the moment Marie said it, Laure knew it was true. "And?"

"And she's not your equal. Hilde gave you a good fight, Pauline was stupid but she was old, rich. You loved Erica. You need to be with someone who has power over you, one way or another. You'll only use them otherwise."

"I'm not 'with' Annie."

"Mm."

Laure stood up. Her head throbbed, and she fetched another beer from the windowsill. She'd made the switch from vodka because it made her hands shake, and from wine because she could keep drinking beer throughout the day without feeling too drunk, just a nice gentle buzz, like winding down a river. "Are you here to lecture me about Annie, or Erica?"

"I'm here to tell you I'm worried about you. And I think you should be worried about you too."

Laure wished Marie would leave. Because she was unravelling, slowly, the protective web Laure had wrapped around the crux of the matter, the thing sticking like a thorn at the heart of her hurt. It was about Erica, the fact Laure had fallen in love for the first time and was now grieving the end of that love. But she was also grieving her former self who had been, if not happy, then content. Erica had shone a new light on everything, and now Laure found she was discontented with her aloneness, which now felt lonely; with her room, which now felt grimy; with her work, which now felt like lip service to the ideals Laure wished she could uphold—why *were* all her favourite artists men?—and even with Paris, which once held all she'd needed. Even her orgasms felt emptier, not so much a release as a moment of forgetfulness that faded as soon as it began.

In short, Laure felt like a failure in all the ways that she used to feel proud. And despite this, if Erica came back she would forget it all. Erica was the ailment, and the only cure. In the meantime, or for ever, all she had was her teaching, her *ravissement*, her drinking.

She did not share any of this with Marie. She knew what she would say: much the same as Barbara had said, though in kinder words. That she was being self-indulgent. That she was reaping what she had sowed. That she should move on. So she only said,

"You don't need to worry. I'm eating, I'm working on my thesis. I'm fine."

"And you aren't going to England?"

Laure opened the beer. The click and hiss of the tab and the bubbles lifted her spirits. "I would rather drink piss."

"You basically are," said Marie, indicating the can. "What is that? Can't Annie afford Jenlain at least?"

Laure snorted. "You aren't worried about my drinking?"

"Of course I am. Aren't you?"

Laure swigged again.

"Are you going to write back?"

"No."

"I know you already have the letter drafted."

"I'm not going to write back."

Marie smiled sadly. She got to her feet, and kissed Laure's cheeks. "When you do, take a breath. When things are set down they are not easily taken away."

She paused at the door, her hand on the bolt. "And Laure? Take a shower. Annie is too cunt-drunk to tell you, but you stink."

Hi Erica,

Go fuck yourself.

Erica,

Who even celebrates their birthday anymore? Total bourgeois narcissism.

Erica,

I wish you'd come back. I can't think without you. Do you still love me?

14 March 1979

Dear Erica,

It was nice to get your letter. It has been busy here, I've been studying, teaching. No hard feelings. Glad you're happy. I have teaching this week so can't come to your birthday, sorry. Léa has a new boyfriend and they are saving to move to Valencia, so she can't afford to come. Thanks for the invite though. My birthday is the 27th July.

Laure

•

5 April 1979

Dear Laure,

Glad there are no hard feelings. I was sorry not to see you, but I'll come to Paris for your birthday? There's a Tàpies exhibition on at Galerie Maeght (do you know it?) and Léger at Berggruen on that month so I was going to come anyway. Let me know if you'll be in town. Excuse the postcard, but I knew it was going to be a short message! Do you like Leonora Carrington? The Sainsbury Centre has a couple of her paintings and I'm obsessed.

Bisous,
Erica xxx

Erica read her message back three times. She had written it out already on a plain piece of paper and made edits, trying to balance the tone. It was a pack of lies of course. She had cried after reading Laure's letter, which was waiting in her pigeon hole when she returned to university. It was so cold, so formal.

But in the weeks and then months of waiting for a response, Erica had realized some things. Firstly, that she missed Laure, and didn't want to never see her again. Secondly, that she thought they could be friends, and that if she needed to make the effort to make this happen, she would. And thirdly, that she was in love.

Not with Robert. He had fallen by the wayside early in January, as though the new year trip, lovely as it was, had purged her of her desire for him. Her new lover was a history of art student called Donna, who she'd met at the picket in front of the LCR in support of university porters. She'd fancied her on sight, a rangy, butch woman with cropped brown hair, shouting through a megaphone. It was not the overwhelming desire she'd felt for Laure, the instant, bone-deep admiration, but it was more comforting for it, like something she could, if need be, tame. They'd bonded over their disappointment at the cancellation of Richard Thompson's solo gig, but agreed it was for the greater good. They'd talked on about music, and Erica mentioned none too casually that her ex-girlfriend was obsessed with Joni Mitchell. Donna had looked her up and down and said, "You're gay?"

"Sort of," was the best Erica could offer.

"Didn't you date that geography student?"

Erica felt thrilled Donna knew this about her. For the first time, she said aloud, "I like both." And then, to make Donna laugh, "Art historians and geographers."

Donna was initially wary, but Erica bided her time and made sure she was everywhere Donna was. Learning she was an organizer at SWP, Erica joined too, putting herself in her path at meetings, and a couple of weeks later they slept together. They'd been inseparable since. Donna lent her *Realism* by Linda Nochlin, and *Loving Her* by Anne Shockley, and in return Erica offered *Nana* by Émile Zola, and an English translation of Barthes' *A Lover's Discourse*. They read concertinaed in Donna's bed, and when Donna asked why she only read books by men Erica felt a hollow stab of victory.

Donna took her to see Leonora Carrington's *The Old Maids* and *The Pomps of the Subsoil* at the Sainsbury Centre, and talked about her treatment of domesticity and the occult. All the time, Erica was wondering what Laure would make of it. For Erica's birthday, Donna bought her a poster of *The Old Maids*, and Erica laughed so hard she nearly cried. At Donna's suggestion, she cancelled her group birthday trip and instead they went walking the north Norfolk coast, camping in the pine forests and getting sand everywhere, returning to university chafed and sunburnt, Erica nursing what she suspected was trench foot, but happy. If she thought about what could have been, if Laure had said yes, and come to Norfolk, and they'd walked along the miles of sand and walked hand in hand into the ocean, and slept beside each other in the bunk house, then she could easily swat these what-ifs aside.

So Erica was shocked to find how desperately sad Laure's letter made her. All the feelings of inadequacy and longing rushed in at her, and she'd fled to Donna, not explaining, only kissing her, undressing her. She needed to obliterate the insecurity that threatened to overwhelm her.

"That was . . ." Donna had gasped, collapsing back on her flattened pillow. "You are . . ."

Erica kissed her again, and felt her self-doubt recede.

She still hadn't told Donna about the letter. She hadn't told anyone: not her friends from the course, or Rosie, her childhood friend who was the only person she'd talked to in any detail about Laure. There was no need—it was bland as skimmed milk. Her response was similarly nothing for Donna to worry about. Donna thought it was good to be on speaking terms with your exes, that enmity was a patriarchal demand made by heterosexual relationships.

"It's pitting women against each other, it's about ownership," she explained. "Imposing hierarchy on people. It's imperialist."

"Yeah," said Erica, but she was not sure she understood, and if she did, she didn't agree. Of course there were hierarchies. Donna's exes were her exes for a reason, and Donna was with Erica now. Did she not therefore implicitly like Erica more than her exes? Fine to still be friends, but why wouldn't she put Erica above them? Erica had met one of them, a square-jawed fellow art history student called Jill, and thought her plain enough not to be threatening. Now that thought *was* misogynistic.

She also knew Donna wouldn't mind her exchanging letters with Laure, and that if she did, she could easily soothe her. The not-telling was the issue, but one easily put aside. The question of Paris was what she wrestled with for days after posting her reply—she ran through all the scenarios in her mind. Arriving at the coach station with Donna beside her, Laure standing on the pavement, just as when she'd left her. Arriving at the coach station with Donna beside her, and no Laure. No Donna, and Laure there to meet her. No Donna, and no Laure.

Erica shuddered at the last possibility. Better, she decided, to have Donna there.

"Do you want to come to Paris with me?" They were lying by the lake on a bright, chill day in May. It had rained all week, the miserable weather coinciding with exam prep, and as Erica sat staring out at the pounding rain with a practise paper open on her desk, she felt such a sense of melancholy it scared her. At the first sign of sun, the students flooded out onto the waterlogged grounds as though it were high summer. Donna and Erica lay on the outskirts of a group of Donna's friends, Jill among them.

Donna spoke to the sky. "When?"

"When term ends. We could catch the train to Portsmouth, get the ferry to Le Havre."

"Sure." Donna said it casually, but she squeezed Erica's hand. Erica felt a mix of elation and guilt, though she wasn't sure why.

"Hey Don, you coming to Rachel Sweet next week?" Jill was shielding her eyes and frowning over at them. Erica got the distinct feeling Jill didn't like her, but she didn't flatter herself to think she was jealous. She'd overheard her asking Donna "What's Erica's deal?" in reference to Robert, and saying she was "half-lesbian at best" and Donna should be careful. This needled Erica, and emphasized the feeling she had whenever she hung out with Donna's crowd that they didn't feel she belonged. She'd never felt that way in Paris, with Léa and Barbara and Agnès.

"I would," said Donna. "But I'm saving for Paris."

"You're going to Paris? When?"

"End of term."

"How come?"

Donna squeezed Erica's hand again. "Yeah, why?"

"There're some exhibitions. And I have friends there."

"Oh yes," said Jill drily. "You never mentioned it before."

No one laughed, but the others exchanged looks. Erica flushed. She hadn't talked about it *so* much.

"Yes, well." She stood up, brushing damp grass off her jeans. Donna got up too, and Jill rolled her eyes.

"Yeah, run along, Don."

"Jill!"

"Donna." They stared each other out, and Erica started to walk away.

"Hold up," said Donna. She fell into step alongside Erica, slipping her hand into her back pocket. "Ignore her, she's stressed about exams."

"You can go to Rachel Sweet if you want. You don't have to come to Paris." Erica's lungs felt horribly tight.

"I know. Do you want me to come?"

"I asked, didn't I?"

"Why are you picking a fight?"

"Because your friends are horrid."

"OK. Hey, stop. Are you all right?"

Erica's boots were sliding around on the mud, and she unwillingly slowed down. Her breath was coming small and wheezing.

"Erica? Are you all right?"

Erica let Donna guide her to a bench, and sat with her head between her knees. Resentfully, she listened to Donna as she counted her breaths in and out for her. Gradually, her breath came more easily.

"Better? What was that?"

"Nothing," said Erica, light-headed. "I don't know."

"You should see a doctor." Donna was peering into her face, and Erica felt an inconvenient stab of affection.

"What's Jill's problem?" she said, returning to the attack.

"She just doesn't know you."

"It's not like I haven't tried."

"You haven't."

Erica stood up, skidding and nearly falling. She still felt dizzy, her breath ragged. Donna guided her gently back down. "I have! I come to all your meetings, I went to Angie's godawful poetry reading. I even let Jill take her shitty books out on my library card!"

"See this is the problem. You think it's a favour, like you're blessing them with your presence."

"I don't—"

"It's fine. But maybe lighten up on them. I don't need you to come to the meetings. I can tell you're not a socialist."

"I am—"

"Erica. You're a market socialist at best."

Erica didn't know what that meant.

"And that's OK. We don't have to believe the same stuff. We don't have to like the same people, or have the same friends. Do you even know who Rachel Sweet is?"

"No."

"She's the woman on the poster on my wall."

"Oh. The one who looks like me?"

Donna laughed. "Yeah. But she was there first."

Erica felt a swell of remorse. "I'm sorry."

"For what?"

"Not knowing who Rachel Sweet is."

Donna threw up her hands. She was still laughing, but there was exasperation in her voice. "I don't mind. I mind that you dismiss people, how they feel."

"I don't!"

"You're dismissing my feelings right now!"

Erica had never heard Donna shout except on a picket line before. But more than how she said it, she was shaken by what she was saying. It was the sort of accusation Erica would have levelled at Laure, had she the backbone when they were together. "I don't mean to. I'm sorry. But I don't know why you're defending Jill."

"I'm not." Donna's shoulders slumped. "You're not listening."

She turned and started to walk back to the group. Erica wanted to call after her, to kick mud at her, to go and push Jill in the lake. But instead she regained her breath, then trudged to the LCR, and bought two tickets to see Rachel Sweet on the fifth of May.

Chapter Four

Laure chewed on her hangnail, tasting blood. The hands on Barbara's watch, visible if Laure shifted just so, pointed to ten past three. It was June and over the last month the heat had built to an almost unbearable pitch, and all of them—Michel, Agnès, Barbara and Laure—were crowded into the shade of the lindens in Place des Vosges. Léa had peeled away three hours before to meet Erica off her bus, and should have been back by now. No, not only Erica. Erica and Donna.

Donna. It was a stupid name. Léa had spoken to Erica on the telephone and, briefly, to Donna, said she sounded nice. Laure had considered inviting Annie, but she had spent the past few weeks trying to slowly peel away from her, and the simple satisfaction of meeting Erica's lover with her own beside her wasn't enough to convince her it was worth the undoing of that work.

"Laure, you OK?" Michel squinted up at her. His trousers were rolled up so his white calves were in the sunshine, his head in Agnès' lap.

"Yes."

Barbara put aside her book and pushed up onto her elbows. "You don't look OK."

"Thanks a lot."

"Leave her alone, Barbara," said Agnès. "At least she bathed."

"Are you my friends or what?" snapped Laure. "Shit, I'm going."

"Don't be silly," said Barbara, catching hold of her wrist. "We're teasing. Joking. Remember jokes, Laure? You used to make them too sometimes."

Laure huffed and flopped back onto the grass. She could tell Barbara was silently urging Michel to step in. She, Marie and Agnès were the advance guard lately, Michel the cannon sent in when they were out of ideas. Laure knew she was worrying them, scaring them all, but she didn't have the energy to reassure anyone. She sometimes wondered if it would be better for them all if she simply disappeared. Michel reached out and stroked her hair. "It's going to be all right. It might be fun."

"I don't get why she's coming. I didn't invite her. I don't even like my birthday. And how can she afford it? I bet she was lying about her parents being poor."

"They're bank tellers, not bouseux," said Agnès. "It's not so expensive to get to England, you know."

"She does know," said Barbara. "She thought about going in March."

"Shit, Barbara. I'm going to stop telling you things."

"I wish you would."

Laure's blood felt hot as her skin. She stood up. "I'm going—no, I'm serious. You guys are assholes."

But just then she heard her name, Léa's voice. Her heart sank, but she turned around and saw Léa urging on a couple behind her. There she was. She was wearing jeans and a cobalt-blue V-neck, her hair in a long plait over her shoulder, a backpack the size of her torso slung over the other. She looked tired, radiant: tanned, her curves more pronounced, at ease in herself. She saw Laure and smiled, and Laure felt like she'd been punched. The force of the feeling was stronger than she could ever have prepared for. She wanted to run, but her legs were liquid. Damn Barbara, forcing her not to have a drink before this. She felt light-headed and nauseous, shaky. She reached instinctively for her cigarettes, and replaced them instantly.

Beside Erica walked a tall, slight woman with slicked-back black hair, looking like Michèle Carvel in *Adam est . . . Ève*. Their hands were linked loosely, with the ease of an established couple. Laure's heart was knocking about somewhere near her knees. Barbara laid a steadying hand on her hip as Agnès and Michel ran forward to hug Erica.

"Traitors," she muttered.

Barbara pushed her gently forward. "Come on, Laure. You can do this."

"I feel like shit."

"You look great. No, really. You look beautiful, Laure. Not that you care about that stuff." Barbara squeezed her elbow. "Let's go."

Erica detached herself from Michel, and without a hint of awkwardness, threw herself at Laure. "I missed you!"

Laure returned the hug, and everything from last summer rushed in at her: every kiss, every fuck, every embrace. Erica felt so good, soft and yielding, and under her perfume—no longer that overly sweet girlish scent but something woody and rich—she smelt exactly the same. *I missed you*. She pulled away.

"Hey, Erica. How was the journey?"

"Long. The crossing was so windy, I thought I would be sick."

"I actually was sick," said the Carvel-alike. "Hi, I'm Donna."

They shook hands, ridiculously formal, and the others laughed. Donna grinned too. "I'm not a hugger either."

"I'm sure Erica has changed that."

"For sure. It's like dating the octopus from *Tentacles*."

Laure snorted, and heard Léa whisper to Erica, "I see what you mean."

It was impossible to deny. Donna was cool. She bonded with Léa over bad horror films, and Michel over her namesake Donna Summer, and Marie over the SWP. Even Laure had to admit that, for an undergraduate, her art history knowledge was not totally inane. But none of this helped the fact that seeing her kiss Erica, or dance pressed against her, or walk along the streets of Le Marais holding her hand, was like a blunt bread knife sawing through Laure's chest that even her three-beers-before-breakfast couldn't soothe. Would it be easier if Donna were hateable? Laure asked herself this question for the hundredth time as they sat crowded onto the roof of Marie and Agnès' new apartment, and Léa and Barbara walked towards her with a birthday cake lit with twenty-four cigarettes.

"So wasteful!" Laure shouted over the singing, snatching up five and stuffing them all into her mouth.

Barbara hooted and clapped. "A joke! Laure is doing a joke!"

When they'd passed out one to everyone who wanted them and returned the others, snuffed, to the packet, Léa took the birthday cake downstairs, the others following like gannets. Laure gestured she would follow and stayed smoking on the roof, looking out over the lights of the fifth, interspersed by the dark inland sea of the Jardin des Plantes. It was a Haussmannian building, the roof slickly sloped, and Laure thought of diving into the darkness, the ground opening to receive her.

"Laure?"

She jolted, and nearly lost her balance, but a firm hand gripped her by the shirt and held her steady.

•

"Jesus Christ!" Erica yelped, still clutching Laure's shirt. "What were you doing so close to the edge?"

"You're the one sneaking up on me."

"I didn't sneak up on you." Erica felt herself reddening, was grateful for the darkness, punctured only by Laure's cigarette. "Sorry, though. Are you OK?"

Laure took a shaky drag. "You still don't smoke?"

"No. I'm asthmatic."

"I didn't know that."

"Nor did I, till last month. Had an attack. High pollen count." And fighting with Donna, but she didn't want to bring her into it.

"Merde. Are you all right?" There was genuine concern on Laure's face, and Erica felt a thrill of relief. Laure looked thinner, her hair braided with even more grey, eyes deeply shadowed, but she was still the sexiest person Erica had ever seen. In fact, her vulnerability enhanced her appeal. Everything, from the slouch of her shoulders and the uninvested way she held her cigarette to how the tip of her ear poked through her hair, seemed calculated to arouse in Erica memories of last summer. All the things she had tried so hard to forget.

"Fine, I have an inhaler now." She patted her pocket. "But I thought it was best to stay in the fresh air while they smoke downstairs."

"Ah." Laure looked away. Was that disappointment? If it was, did that mean she had hoped Erica was here to speak to her alone?

"Do you want me to . . ." Laure mimed putting out her cigarette.

"No, it's fine."

Erica came to stand beside her. The night was blessedly cool beneath the clear sky. The week had been obscenely hot, and she and Donna were staying in a hostel with no external windows. They hadn't so much as kissed in bed since arriving, stripping down to their underwear and lying starfished on their separate bunks. Erica thought of last summer, how Laure would lick the sweat from her thighs. She shuddered.

"Cold?"

"No. The view is amazing. How did they afford this place?"

"Agnès' grandmother died, left her money."

"She owns it?"

"Mm."

"Wow." Erica wished she'd brought a drink up with her. She didn't know what to do with her hands. She pushed them into her pockets. "Are you still on Rue Charlot?"

"Mm."

Erica sensed Laure tense beside her. The sounds of Paris seemed to drop away, and Erica knew Laure was, like her, remembering the room where they had come to learn and love each other. How had she been able to stay there? Erica had only survived their parting by being somewhere else, with new people, new lovers. And here was Laure, still in Paris, surrounded by the same friends, in the same room they'd shared for two exquisite months. Erica hadn't even met a girlfriend this week. Did that mean Laure still loved her, or rather that her time with Erica had meant nothing to her, and so it didn't hurt to stay where they had been together?

"You said you're teaching. How is it?"

"Good. I like it."

"I bet you're good at it. You taught me a lot. I mean, about art." But Laure was smiling, that neat, small smile she remembered so well. "And other things I suppose."

Laure looked at her then, and Erica felt an answering throb between her legs. "Donna's nice."

Nice. That word again—she thought of Laure's letter. Erica broke her gaze and sat down on the sloping roof. Laure stayed standing, looking Byronic with her shoulder-length hair and bare forearms. Erica could smell the booze on her, and even that felt romantic.

"She is."

"I'm happy for you."

"Are you?" Erica looked up at her, but Laure's face was shadowed.

"Of course."

"Are you with anyone?"

Laure snorted. Erica took that as a no.

"It's so good to see you, Laure. You know . . ." She hesitated. "I kept that cigarette you rolled for me."

"What cigarette?"

"Never mind. I just mean, I really did miss you."

"So you keep saying."

"What does that mean?"

"I'm not interested in fighting with you, Erica."

Erica's chest felt tight. She wondered if she was, in fact, suffering the effects of Laure's smoke. "I don't want to fight. I want to be friends."

"I don't want to be your friend." Laure looked down at her, the cut of her cheekbones agonizing. Erica could see the points of her nipples through the thin cotton of her shirt.

"Why not?"

Laure stubbed out her cigarette and launched the butt into the night. "Don't play dumb, Erica. It doesn't suit you."

Before Erica could gather her thoughts, Laure turned her back on her, and disappeared inside.

For the rest of the week. Laure was barely around, leaving Léa and the others to do the hosting with Laure joining them only in the evenings. Though she was as articulate as ever Erica smelt booze on her breath whenever she got close enough.

"Is Laure drinking?" she asked Léa, as she watched Laure across the table at a bar on Rue de Lappe, sinking her fourth beer in under an hour.

"Obviously."

"No, I mean, is she drinking too much?"

Michel cut in. "Laure always drinks too much."

"I mean—"

"We know what you mean." Michel lowered his voice further, so Donna, sitting on Erica's other side, wouldn't hear. "It's not your problem, Erica. Leave it to her friends."

"I am her friend."

"Non. You are the girl who broke her heart."

Erica felt hot. She leaned over to Donna and told her she was going to the loo, and then slid off the high stool, pulling a reluctant Michel along with her. Shutting them in the stinking cubicle, with a door so thin it was no quieter in here than outside, she turned to glare at Michel under the blue light.

"She broke my heart too, you know."

"You seem to be doing fine."

"I wasn't, for ages."

Michel cupped her cheek. "And I'm sorry for you. But you got to leave. She was the one who was left."

"She could have asked me to stay."

"Didn't she?"

Erica opened and closed her mouth like a fish. The walls were covered in graffiti, and over Michel's shoulder she read, *Lisez moins, vivez plus. Le sacré, voilà l'ennemi. Chaque Baiser Lesbien Est Une REVOLUTION.* "Not really."

"I understand you have suffered. But Laure, she *is* suffering. She's only been showering this week because you're here. She's been a mess."

"She could have come to my birthday, or written to me. She could have told me how she felt."

Erica knew what she sounded like: a petulant child. But the sugar in her vodka grenadines was making her anxious, and she longed for Michel to see her point of view, to take her side, to stop looking at her like she was a disappointment.

"What do you want, Erica?" said Michel, as someone started to pound on the door. "You want her to tell you she still loves you, as if that wasn't obvious? You want her to kiss you, in front of your girlfriend? Follow you to where, Norfolk, and have no one but you?"

Erica flushed. She didn't want that, did she? So why was her overwhelming feeling one of relief at Michel's confirmation that Laure still loved her? That she still had a stake in Laure's life, her heart. It was cruel, awfully cruel, but Erica felt a sort of triumph. Erica was sure she was a good person, but she was starting to think she perhaps was not very moral.

"It would be the same for me, in Paris."

"Charmant." Michel unlocked the door, and bundled past the queuing women.

"Michel!" Erica forced after him, but there was no sign of Michel at the table, and Laure was gone too. Barbara and Marie had their heads close together, and as Erica approached she saw Léa shrug at Donna.

"Erica!" Donna spotted her and stood up, coming towards her, brow furrowed. "What's up with Michel? He just grabbed Laure and left."

Erica looked at the exit, and thought she saw Laure's tall frame pushing through the mill of smokers outside. Shrugging off Donna's hand, she hurried after, ignoring Barbara's exasperated call of "Ça va?" Though a few people were smoking indoors, most had used the warm night as an opportunity to get some air and flirt. Erica felt her lungs start to itch as she scanned the crowd, spotting Michel dragging Laure after him down the Rue de Lappe.

"Wait!" she called, and ran after them. Michel looked over her shoulder and from the sneer of his mouth she knew he was swearing, but he didn't break his stride. Laure, though, pulled up short.

Erica caught up to them. Her chest was hurting now, and she scrambled for her inhaler.

"Ça va, Erica?" Laure's voice was soft, concerned, and she felt her hand on her shoulder, moving to rub her back.

"On y va," said Michel. "Voilà, la butch."

"Erica?" Donna's voice now, but Erica was fighting panic. Breaths were becoming harder, bright stars starting to pop in front of her eyes. "Where's your inhaler?"

She felt Donna's hand in her pocket, Laure's on her back. She leant into Laure, trying to pull her scent into her lungs.

"Allez," insisted Michel.

"Attend!" snapped Laure, and Erica felt the burr of her voice through her chest, felt her ribs against her breasts.

"Here." Donna was pressing her inhaler into her hand, but Erica's grip felt weak. The inhaler was put into her mouth and depressed, the cold vapour metallic on her tongue.

"Breathe," said Donna.

"Breathe," said Laure, and Erica breathed, feeling the iron band around her lungs loosen. She began to cry, and Laure held her, properly, for the first time since she'd arrived.

"Imbécile," said Michel. "Elle se fout, et tu tombes dans le panneau."

"Are you OK, Erica?" Laure started to pull away and Erica clung on tighter. She knew Donna was right there, that she was making a scene, being cruel, but she couldn't help it. She just wanted Laure to hold her awhile longer.

Rough, ragged fingernails scrabbled at her hands, breaking their grip. Michel yanked her away and wheeled her around to face him.

"Viens, on se casse." His face was livid, and Erica shrank away.

"Michel . . ." started Laure, but Michel had a firm hold of her hand and, without another word, disappeared around the corner of Rue de Charonne. Erica watched them go, and wished she had a friend like that, someone to pull her away, slap her even, tell her to stop all this. She felt entirely alone, and beastly for feeling that way when Donna stood, as always, right beside her.

"What's going on?" Léa appeared behind Donna, but neither of them answered her.

"What just happened?" Donna's voice was wary and, knowing it was hateful, knowing it made her the worst sort of hypocrite, Erica turned to her, and let her take her in her arms.

•

Laure had never seen Michel so angry. All of them had their rages, but not Michel, not like this. He pulled her on, ignoring her enquiries and attempts to stop, and only halted when the dark channel of Canal Saint-Martin opened up before them. Michel threw himself against the railing, panting, hitting the metal with his palms. Laure kept a careful distance.

"Michel?"

"She's a bitch, Laure."

"What happened?"

Michel turned to face her, slumping against the railing. "She's a bitch, or she's a child, or she's both. She doesn't deserve you."

"I don't care about her like that anymore."

"No? Is that why you're missing deadlines, never leaving your house—"

"I'm out right now."

"Because *she's* here! And don't get me started on the drinking."

"You can talk."

"I might be drunk, but I don't need a six pack to get me out of bed in the mornings. You're not eating, not sleeping properly. You're going to kill yourself, Laure. Is that what you want? To die over the tourist?"

"She's clearly not a tourist."

"So she has a new girlfriend. But she doesn't belong here. She's hurt you too much."

"We hurt each other," said Laure, though she didn't know why she was defending Erica. Hadn't she, in her most savage moments, wanted to hear exactly this? So why did it sting this sharply? The water glittered slickly behind Michel, and Laure felt an urge to leap, as she had on the roof of Marie and Agnès', into the filthy depths and never come up.

"She doesn't know what she wants," said Michel. "She wants everything. Barbara has been saying it since you met."

"Barbara's jealous," said Laure spitefully. "Because I love Erica and I never loved her."

Michel looked at her sadly. "Maybe. But we all love you, and it's because of that I think you shouldn't see her anymore."

"She wasn't faking. She does have asthma."

Michel shrugged. "So that's one thing she's not pretending about. I'm not saying she didn't love you. Maybe she still does. But it's toxic. She's insecure, it's obvious."

"You like her."

"I love her. I'll never forget what she did in Parade, protecting me. But not as much as I love you. She's going to hurt everyone around her unless she understands what she actually wants. But I'm sick of talking about her. Laure, you need help."

Laure groaned. "God, Michel. Is this another intervention?"

"Yes. I gave you time, I let the others have a go. But I knew I couldn't leave it to Barbara or Marie. They're too soft on you. What does Marie call it? Your *ravissement*."

"You came up with that."

"Well, it doesn't work on me."

"I don't trust you gays."

Michel looked hard at her, and Laure had the sensation of the ground, so long slanted, slowly returning to level. She didn't want it. She didn't want him to right her.

"Claude goes to a meeting for people drinking themselves to death."

"So *dramatic*."

"Alcoholics."

"We don't do that in France."

"No." Michel smiled sadly. "But you've always been special, Laure. I think you should go."

"You drank with me, tonight. We were drinking together."

"I didn't understand. I thought I did, but I didn't. Not until this week, with Erica here. I see it now. You can't get out, can you? I thought you were just being lazy, or you just needed time, but you're stuck and she isn't going to come back and get you."

Laure crouched beside the barrier, her arms around her legs. She felt the muscles in her back stretching, her spine clicking. She needed another drink. Michel ducked down beside her, his cologne fresh, his arm strong. "You're in trouble, little sister," he said into her hair. "You need to stop drinking."

Beneath the beautiful, thick cushion of alcohol, Laure felt a spiralling sense of relief. It felt good to have someone tell her, in plain words, that it was not normal to feel like this, as though existence were a barefoot walk along a razor, a slow and excruciating crawl towards death. That she could not be expected to live this way for ever. But fuck, she did not want to change. She did not want to move on.

"I don't," she said, and she was crying. "I'm fine. I'm fine."

"It's time, little sister. Put her behind you now. Leave it in the past."

Michel hugged her, and though she wanted to push him away, she thought now of her father. How she'd seen her father do it, time and again over the years, sweep aside the bottles, empty the wine rack, pour gin down the drain. What was it he always said? That there were good days, days they could not yet imagine, still to come. Michel said it could be beautiful, and maybe this was what her father meant, as he wiped the splashes of red wine from the sides of the sink. That it was all possible. That this could be the first day of the rest of their lives.

Part Two

1981–1983

Am I in love?—yes, since I am waiting. The other one never waits. Sometimes I want to play the part of the one who doesn't wait; I try to busy myself elsewhere, to arrive late; but I always lose at this game. Whatever I do, I find myself there, with nothing to do, punctual, even ahead of time. The lover's fatal identity is precisely this: I am the one who waits.

from *A Lover's Discourse* by Roland Barthes

Chapter Five

"What the fuck is this reading list?"

Erica snorted. Emma was staring, incredulous, at the reams of paper they'd been given upon arriving to register for their MAs. Emma was taking critical theory, Erica creative writing, and it was only when the administrator clearly hadn't known the creative writing course was running that year that Erica understood how select her "selective course" was. Four of them on the entire thing, and she had not yet met any of the others.

"Mine's not bad," she said, flicking through the papers. "Look, *The Bloody Chamber*, *The Lost Steps*, *The French Lieutenant's Woman*—"

"You don't like Fowles, do you?" Emma stared at her in mock-horror. "I thought you had taste."

"Fowles is a good writer. Doesn't mean I like *him*."

"So you think we can separate art and artist?"

"Emma, classes don't start till tomorrow, and all I want to focus on is getting as drunk as possible between now and then."

"Spoilsport." Emma linked her arm through Erica's. They'd met the previous night in their halls on Fifer's Lane, and had decided they were best friends almost on sight. Emma had chosen to forgo the traditional first night pub crawl from Artichoke's to Zac's in order to arrange her books and cover every inch of her magnolia-painted walls with posters and postcards, and that had cemented it for Erica.

"I *love* marginalia!" Erica announced, as they got steadily drunker and more sugar-high on cider, and Erica scrawled *marginalia over magnolia* onto their arms in biro. She'd arrived in Z Block the week before in order to take some extra shifts at the SU, and done exactly the same in her room. She enjoyed spotting crossovers in their taste: Bruce Springsteen brooding alongside a poster of the original cover of *Mrs Dalloway*, postcards from the Sainsbury Centre tacked up next to a torn-out advert from a magazine featuring *Gabrielle d'Estrées et une de ses sœurs*. The sight of it sent an unhappy jolt of memory through Erica's body. She'd seen it for the first time with Donna on that ill-fated trip to Paris, and when she'd tried to make a nipple joke Donna had burst into tears.

"Why won't you just say you still love her?" she'd begged. It was only two years ago, but Erica had been so much younger then, so much crueller, and she had kept Donna tethered to her through a heady mix of genuine affection and desperate manipulation. Now it made her sick to think of it, how awful she'd been that Paris trip, not only to Donna but to everyone, and for the next few months Donna and she had struggled through, barely sleeping together, fighting constantly. But their relationship was doomed after Michel's outburst. Doomed from the outset, really, because with hindsight Erica knew she had still been in the grips of heartache over Laure. Laure. Erica could think of her now, even say her name, without the attendant pang of longing, of regret.

After Donna there had been only men, and that seemed to make it easier. She managed to mend her friendship with Michel through a series of long, heartfelt letters that went mostly unanswered before the breakthrough of a birthday card this year. The holy grail of a phone call came after graduation from her bachelor's, and he'd even invited her to Paris that summer, but Erica had to save. She had a small maintenance grant, but money was going to be tight. She didn't care: she was doing it, the course she'd long dreamed of, the first solid step towards becoming a novelist, and it only added to the experience to be living in penury.

The condition of this truce was never to mention or ask about Laure. She had not attempted to contact Laure directly, and probably never would, though any mention of Paris would inspire nostalgia. She had to resist writing to her when nationalization of the banks was announced—surely they would be celebrating at the community café—and even the news a cannibal had killed and eaten a man there in the summer led to a pleasurable afternoon in bed with herself and her memories. Maybe she was not as over it as she hoped.

"Have you been to Paris?" she'd asked, tapping the nipple-tweakers, and Emma shook her head.

"I *dream* of Paris. Stein! De Beauvoir! Hemingway! Have you?"

Remembering this exchange, Erica nudged her new best friend. "Talking of problematic male authors, aren't you the one who went mad for Hemingway yesterday?"

"Hush," Emma giggled. "He's my one weakness. My other favourites are morally unimpeachable."

Impossible, thought Erica. She knew, now, that no one was one thing. At twenty-one, and armed with this knowledge, Erica felt herself at last to be an adult. She had survived heartbreak, slept with men and women, held picket lines, hitchhiked, read many of the classics on the reading list, and now was an MA student on the best—the only—creative writing course in the country. The future spread out like a field of wildflowers before her, vivid with possible beauty. Her writing sample had been praised as "visceral and urgent" by the course leader, the revered Malcolm Bradbury, and Erica was already imagining those words on her first book cover. She'd be in a roomful of people who would challenge her, push her, make her a better writer—if not on the creative writing element, then she had Emma to look forward to when they joined in the critical classes.

But all that began tomorrow. Now, there was a group of MA students of different English disciplines meeting at the Adam and Eve, and she intended to make a good first impression.

The pub was steamy with condensation. It was pouring with rain and Emma and Erica arrived drenched, propping their bikes against the empty outside tables. Erica made straight for the toilets, checking her lipstick in the mirror, wiping away mascara where it had run. She was only glad she hadn't been talked into a perm by Rosie, who assured her it would suit her. She took her hair out of its plait—it was past her bum, now—and finger-combed it. It would dry nicely.

Emma was already in the thick of it. The students had secured a corner table, benches along two sides and chairs along the other. The table was full of empties—they had clearly been here a long time. Erica tamped down her nerves and approached, smiling brightly. "Hello."

Emma pulled her in. "Erica! This is Erica. Come sit, move up, Joe. Erica this is Joe, he's doing literature, this is Lydia, Nicholas, Paul, Kim, they're all on my critical theory course, and—sorry, I've forgotten your name."

"Didn't tell you yet," smiled the man opposite Emma, occupying the seat next to where Erica was standing. "Anthony. Ant."

"Don't you think that's *hilarious*," said Lydia, a little too loudly. "Look at the size of him!"

Erica tried to get the measure of him, but it was hard to tell when he was sitting down. His shoulders were broad, his hair dark and swept back off tanned skin. She took the vacant chair beside him. "Hi."

"Hi." He smiled, and Erica felt a stirring of interest. He wasn't the most handsome of them—Nicholas was a dead ringer for Billy Dee Williams—but he had warm brown eyes and nice teeth, a bland southern accent.

"Ant's like you," said Emma. "Writer."

"Creative writing MA student," said Ant. "You?"

"Same," said Erica with relief. "Did you hear, there's only four of us?"

"Usually three," said Ant, draining his glass. "Bradbury's hard to impress."

"We must be *brilliant*," grinned Erica.

"The finest minds of our generation. God help us all. You want a drink?"

"I can get it. Emma?" Erica gestured *pint* at her friend and Emma nodded and mouthed thanks, before returning to her conversation with Joe.

"I'll do a round," said Ant, standing up with her. He was tall, but it was more the breadth of him. He must be a rugby player, Erica thought, with a stab of misgiving. He certainly didn't look like a writer.

They joined the three-deep queue for the bar. "What do you write?" he asked.

"Novels," she said. "Well, I haven't yet, but that's what I want to write. Some poetry, short stories, essays, you know. You?"

"Short stories."

"You been published?"

He ducked his head, and Erica found it charming that he clearly wasn't being faux-modest. He really did look shy about it. "A bit."

"A bit? More than once?" Erica laughed, but her imposter syndrome lurched to the surface.

"*Books and Bookmen*, before it went under. And *Granta*."

"Wow," she said, thinking of her typewriter and box files, the childish joy she took in typesetting her essays as though they were in a magazine. Erica hadn't heard of either of the ones Ant had mentioned, but mentally filed the names to search out in the library later.

"What critical module are you taking?" he asked.

"The postmodern novel."

"I think we're all taking that. I mean, Malcolm Bradbury! Did he interview you?"

"Yes."

"Jealous. I got Samuel Haines. What was Bradbury like?"

"Intimidating. Brilliant." In truth, he'd been amiable, even sweet, but she wanted to tell Ant what he wanted to hear.

"I can't wait to meet him. I can't wait to get started on this whole thing. The group seems cool." He glanced back, where Lydia was none too subtly draping herself over Nicholas, and Emma and Joe remained locked in conversation. She hoped it wouldn't turn into the sort of night where everyone peeled off in couples. Though she called dibs on Ant if it did.

Ant ordered nine pints of Carling without asking her what she wanted, and though she hated Carling Erica found it weirdly gratifying. Her lovers since Donna had been almost performatively deferential, and sometimes Erica just wanted one of them to make a decision. She tried not to notice that Ant's wallet was a brown leather type, expensive-looking and lined with notes, the shiny corner of what could be a condom packet poking from above a photograph.

"That your family?"

"Oh." He blushed, and pushed the shiny corner down. Definitely a condom. "Yeah. My mum, my dad, my sisters."

"They're pretty."

"Lawyers. Viola's working on the contempt of court act."

"Cool," said Erica, wondering if she was meant to know what this was and marvelling at the name Viola.

Balancing the pints between them, they resumed their seats, and started new conversations, Ant with Kim, and Erica with Nicholas. He was on the critical course, but he wanted to be a playwright and adapt novels.

"Why didn't you apply for the creative writing course?"

"More to fall back on," said Nicholas, and then, hastily, "though if I were braver, I'd have applied. It's amazing you got in."

"It's OK, my parents don't get it at all. They wish I'd done the critical course. Do you want to adapt your own novels?"

"No." He grimaced. "That would be weird."

They were all, it turned out, writers. Lydia was a poet, who'd had two poems placed in a local poetry competition, "but it was judged by Tony Harrison" to which Nicholas and Ant "ooo"ed and Erica stored the name in her head alongside the magazines Ant mentioned, to look up later.

She wondered why they hadn't applied for the Creative Writing MA, if all of them, like Nicholas, thought it too specialized. Erica had been so tunnel-vision about it, she hadn't considered this angle. Or maybe, like Laure, they didn't think it was something worth being taught. The idea it was all a waste of time was something she'd bundled to the back of her brain. She was here, and she was proud of that.

During their third round, Emma got out her creased reading list, placed it on the beer-soaked table and invited dissection.

"I mean, men much?" Emma said, rapping the damp paper. "It's 1981, we have women writers now."

"Don't you think that's an over-simplification?" said Nicholas. "Maybe they just chose what was best."

"Best according to who?" said Emma, clearly spoiling for a fight. "The creative writing list at least has Angela Carter and Iris Murdoch."

"There's Austen," said Nicholas, pointing. "And Woolf."

"God, Woolf." Emma rolled her eyes. "The woman writer for people who hate women writers."

Erica sat back, grinning. Emma was going to eat Nicholas alive.

"Have you read many?" Ant said, leaning over.

Erica, who had just taken a sip of lager, shrugged. "A few."

"That means yes," he grinned. His incisors were oddly sharp, like a wolf or a vampire.

Erica held her hands up in mock-surrender. "You got me. I'm a swot."

"Me too. What's that say?" He pointed at the biro still on her arm. "*Marginalia over magnolia.* Ha! I like that."

She felt, through the fuzz of her tipsiness, the sharp certainty she liked him. She smiled a little hazily up at him, and he grinned back.

"Did you do your undergrad here?" he said.

"Mm-hm."

"You'll have to show me around."

She let her leg drift to touch his. "Where did you go?"

"Cambridge."

"Ah."

He looked embarrassed, his ears reddening. "Yeah, that's the correct reaction. I'm a reformed law student. Got a term into my conversion course and thought—there has *got* to be more to life than this. I don't think my father will ever forgive me."

"I think my father thinks I've made this course up."

"Ha! Snap. 'Why do you need to study writing? Can't you just write?'"

Erica smiled, but the words catapulted her back to the squat on Rue Charlot. "I'm sure he'll get over it. He must be proud you're published."

"Oh, it's all a giant waste of time to him. And money. I think he thinks real literature hasn't existed since Shakespeare. Or at least Dickens. Never mind he reads Agatha Christie at a rate of knots. When I wrote my first poem and showed him, he asked if I was a poof." Ant caught himself. "Not that there's anything wrong with that. But I'm not."

"Good to know," said Erica, squashing her unease.

Ant sighed. "But he could have pulled rank and stopped me coming at all, so I guess I should be grateful."

"Ah, you're a daddy's boy?"

"Absolutely."

"Now this sounds interesting," said Emma, leaning over. "Who's the daddy?"

There was nothing stopping them sleeping together, and perhaps this is why it took so long. There was certainly no competition in their class. The other two students were an older man, at least thirty-five, who lived off campus with his family, and a narrow-faced gay man called Gerald. They sat around a large table, the tutor with their essays or stories spread out in front of them, discussing why they used this turn of phrase, if speech marks were redundant, if the novel was, as Barthes and Tom Wolfe claimed, indeed dead. But most of all, more than style and plot, character and perspective, they talked about ideas, and Erica felt her mind stretching as though it were a muscle. Her writing, which until then was something she approached as precious and fragile, became fair game, every choice probed, her sentences broken down and smeared out on annotated handouts as though across slides for a microscope, examined and analysed. She learnt her weakness for pathetic fallacy and dream sequences, latched onto framing devices for a time and then let them go. She re-read her favourite books as a writer, turning the perfect first lines of *One Hundred Years of Solitude* and *The Haunting of Hill House* over and over in her head, looking for the joins. When she thought of Laure now it was because she wanted to show her what she was learning, how you could teach writing because look, see how much better her writing was? But of course, Laure had never read anything she wrote because Erica hadn't shared that part of herself with her.

She shared it, all of it, with Ant. She, Emma, Ant and Nicholas would regularly read each other's work outside class, and it became steadily harder for Erica to distinguish between her liking for Ant, and her love for his work. His was not her usual taste: witty and dark, more Amis than Rushdie—Erica was newly obsessed with *Midnight's Children*—but there was a vulnerability to his writing that lifted it out of imitation and into art. He was working on a novel, about a chef who becomes obsessed with his sous chef, shades of *The Collector* and *The Sea, The Sea* with a merciless humour all his own. He was brilliant, and everyone agreed that if anyone was going to be published, it would be him.

Being published, it became apparent, was the aim of everyone on the course. No matter how many times their tutors emphasized that this course had transferable skills, preparing them for a career in anything from copywriting to editing, and that the world needed more readers, not writers, and that rushing to be published was like trying to run a marathon before ever going for a jog, all any of them could talk about was who knew which agent, and what publisher they would not, under any circumstances, accept a contract from.

That it was all fantasy, that it was a possibility that none of them would be published, let alone win the Booker or the James Tait Black, that the odds were stacked against them, was an unspoken terror that shadowed every conversation. Erica felt the spectre of failure perpetually on her shoulder. It made her writing feel weighted with expectation, and sometimes she forgot that she loved it, and instead wondered whether she simply liked the *idea* of writing, and the sound her typewriter made when she got into a flow.

Ant, though, was her champion. *This*, he'd write in the margins of the typed pages, *is beautiful*, or *Ha*. And, best of all: *!!* He spoke about her stories as though they were real, proper literature, worthy of dissection and discussion. That a writer she so admired admired her work was heady and intense, like a long draught of the whisky she initially pretended to like to impress him, and then came to savour.

His effect on her was not lessened by the hours they spent together, mostly in class or with the critical students, but sometimes alone. They'd take their typewriters—both of them addicted to the clack of the keys—to the library or the lake, and write as though they were racing each other, elbows clashing, but neither wanting to move away from the other. No one had been in the lake that year, after a boy drowned in the summer, and there surrounded it a melancholic, macabre appeal, like a misty moor. They'd all—the old married man, Gerald, Ant and Erica—written about this drowning for one assignment or another, though Erica was the only one who'd been on campus when it happened, and hadn't seen it. But she'd witnessed the aftermath, and if she felt a carrion crow queasiness about drawing, verbatim, on the traumatized exclamations of those who had seen him slip below the water, she batted it aside in the name of art. Ant's story turned into the boy staging his own death, and if he could take those sorts of liberties without qualms, Erica could surely tell the truth.

Most times Erica would touch herself she'd think of Ant, and always these scenarios began with an offer letter from Macdonald & Jane's or Picador or Jonathan Cape for her as yet unconceived novel. Her running through generic scenery to find Ant and him, dressed in a linen suit like someone from *Brideshead Revisited*, sweeping her off her feet and kissing her, undressing her, pressing her down with his broad, long body. The intercourse itself faded to black, and then, sometimes, there would be a woman's hands between her legs, bitten-nailed and smoke-stained, long, grey-streaked hair catching between Erica's fingers.

Ant and Erica's abstinence was a mystery to everyone, not least Erica herself. The MA students were either married or patently unmarried, but by the end of first term most everyone had slept with everyone—as Emma said, there was fuck all else to do but fuck. It was incestuous, Lydia sleeping with Nicholas and then Nicholas with Emma, who previously dated Joe for a time before it turned out he was engaged to his childhood sweetheart, who came up on weekends from Birmingham and unironically dressed like it was the 1950s. Kim was utterly uninterested in anyone her own age and involved with the forty-something manager of the Odeon in town. Paul was gay, and loyal as a Labrador to a succession of awful men, which led to many a heartbreak and late-night cry fest in Emma's or Erica's room, even over ferret-jawed Gerald.

Emma was constantly urging Erica to make a move.

"Come on, it's not like you don't have the opportunity. All those cosy late-night writing sessions."

But the truth was, Erica didn't mind the suspense. It felt like kismet, meant, some master plot moving them slowly into position, waiting for the second act to begin. The knowledge it was inevitable didn't change the fact she was a little scared. Ant had become, entirely by accident, her best friend, and Erica didn't want to mess it up. She also didn't want to end up in his novel. But as the weeks roamed on, and their connection grew, she knew that when the time came and he made his move, she would be powerless to resist.

While she waited, Erica saw a few men, but it never went further than a one-night stand, and if Ant dated, it never entered the circle of gossip that linked them all. Erica preferred to think he was saving himself for her, but most likely he had something the rest of them lacked: discretion.

This was never clearer than when, at the end of their first term, Emma and Erica received in their pigeon holes the most elegant invitations either of them had ever seen.

Thick, cream card engraved with black calligraphic writing, inviting them to Anthony R. W. Cowper-Gray's twenty-fifth birthday party on New Year's Eve at his family home in St George's Hill, Weybridge,

Surrey. At the bottom, a homage to J. R. R. Tolkien's infamous party invitation sign off:

**Carriages at midnight Ambulances at 2am
Wheelbarrows at 5am Hearses at daybreak**

It was like a posh wedding invitation. On the back, written in Ant's now-familiar cramped hand: *Welcome to stay afterwards, let's make a trip of it.* Erica looked over at Emma's invitation, and with a mix of relief and disappointment saw hers bore the same handwritten addendum. Though the wallet had been an early hint otherwise, Erica had thought he was like the rest of them, with his disapproving parents and worn-out typewriter and student discount card. But here it was, spelled out on luxury paper stock. Two-middle-names-double-barrelled-surname clear. Stay-over-no-mention-of-sleeping-bags obvious. *Anthony R. W. Cowper-Gray.* She didn't even know his middle names. *Rich Writer. Really Wealthy.*

Emma looked up at her, grinning with delighted astonishment.

"Bloody hell. He's minted!"

Just how minted became apparent the moment they stepped off the train at Weybridge Station. Joe was visiting family in Berwick-upon-Tweed, Kim and her Odeon manager were holed up in Norwich, and Paul had to work in his parents' shop for the holidays, making them promise to take pictures and steal any personalized stationery on sight. So it was Nicholas and Emma, recently exclusive and extremely in love, and Erica their awkward third wheel who made the journey from the fenlands of Norfolk to the genteelly green-circled towns of Surrey.

They'd looked up St George's Hill on a map, and saw it was largely unlabelled, its extent marked in an unbroken line, like a country's border. They'd assumed they would walk to Anthony's family home—Abbeydore House—as the station exit abutted the entrance to St George's Hill, but when they arrived and milled for a moment, uncertain, outside the station, a sleek black car pulled up, and Anthony got out. Erica, Emma and Nick were bundled up in fleeces and jackets, but Ant wore only a well-cut blue shirt that brought out his tan, the fade of ski goggles around his brown eyes. Erica's knees actually went a little weak at the sight of him.

"A Bentley?" Nicholas whooped and embraced Ant. "You serious?"

"We were going to walk," said Emma, awestruck. "But this is much better."

"Visitors can't walk onto the estate," said Ant with a rueful grin. "Security."

He glanced at Erica for the first time, quickly, as though checking she was still there.

"It's good to see you all."

"Paul is *gutted*," said Nicholas gleefully. "Wait till he hears about the Bentley!"

They piled in, their rucksacks looking tragic in the deep, spotless boot. The seats were cream leather and Erica sat tensed in the front, worried she was going to moult poor all over it. She gazed straight ahead, as though interested in anything except Ant, but in truth her heart had started racing the moment he climbed out of the ridiculous car and waved. She was worried he could hear it, knocking around her chest like a ricocheting bullet. Though they had sat so many times together, closer than this, touching even, there was something about the two weeks apart that had amplified her desire. Watching endless television in her parents' orange-wallpapered sitting room, she'd wonder what Ant was doing right now. *Anthony R. W. Cowper-Gray.* Probably not sitting in total silence as the audience laughter on *The Two Ronnies* erupted from the TV, eating dry chicken and stodgy cauliflower cheese from his lap "as a treat." Probably not counting down the hours until his father fell asleep in his chair and his mother went defeated to the kitchen to tidy up. That was usually Erica's cue to steal a bottle of Stone's Ginger Wine and drink it in her bedroom.

It wasn't her parents' fault. They had tried, asking her about the course, buying her *Noble House* by James Clavell because the shop assistant at WH Smith said it was the biggest book of the year. Erica had tried too, to begin with. Her mother had been delighted with her Lady Diana Spencer weds Prince Charles commemoration plate, and her father with his ergonomic garden trowel. But they were just so—there was no other way to put it—*provincial*. Recently it had begun to bother her there were so few books on the bookshelves, only the family Bible passed down by her father's side, her mother's childhood Georgette Heyers, and endless Yellow Pages, which didn't count. Books were cheap, so it wasn't money that was the problem, it was uninterest, and Erica was coming to think a lack of curiosity about the world the gravest of crimes. It was no wonder she had spent her first adult summer in Paris, cut her holidays at home short with work or trips with friends. She had nothing in common with people who thought Salman Rushdie was an exotic fish dish, who existed so apart from all that was happening out there, where Erica lived. She loved them of course, but in a tolerant way, as though she was doing them a favour.

It was a relief, always, to leave them behind. When she got on the train to King's Cross, it was with the giddy sense of escape. She would not have a life like that—working in a bank or office, thinking prawn cocktail was foreign food, and watching *Last of the Summer Wine* unironically. No, she would live a life of meaning, and adventure. Hadn't she already? Donna, Robert. Laure. An undergraduate degree, and now a postgraduate. A life of books and beauty and success. Not money, not necessarily, but she could be persuaded.

This resolution reverberated in her brain as they glided through a pair of automated gates and onto tarmac so smooth it was as though the car were on a travelator. The interior of the car was lush and hushed, like the foyer of an expensive hotel, and as Ant drove them along the gently undulating road, Emma and Nicholas giggled like schoolchildren, pointing at the high stone walls, the screens of trees, the names of the out-of-sight but no doubt enormous houses like places in storybooks: *Bodvean, Brambletyre, White Knight's Cottage*. Beneath her anticipation, Erica felt a stirring of unease. She didn't belong here, with her

Woolies jewellery and British Home Stores jeans. She worried these surroundings, this car, would show her up as shabby where at UEA she had seemed bohemian and charming. This feeling grew as they turned up a long gravelled drive, the stones beneath the car's wheels barely audible. At the end of the drive stood the largest house Erica had ever seen. The lower half was painted white, and a wisteria, bare and grey-trunked, wound over an arched doorway. The upper half was timbered with rusty brown planks of wood, lending it a romantic bent that made it no less imposing.

"Shit," said Nicholas. "*Shit*."

Perhaps, she thought, as Emma shrieked, *I imagined it all*. The glances, the electricity when they touched. The way his face softened when he looked at her. The way he laughed at her feeble jokes, and read every book she lent him. Surely no one who lived here could want her. Ant came to a gentle halt outside the black door with its shiny brass knocker. Branded vans were ranged in the driveway, SALTERS SEAFOOD LUXURY CATERERS and FOUR SEASONS MARQUEES, assumedly in preparation for the party that night. The others bundled out of the car and Erica sat, frozen a moment, in the front seat. What was she doing here? It felt like a fantasy coming apart in her hands. Why hadn't she worn new clothes, put on make-up?

"Erica!" Emma knocked on the window, almost entirely muffled by the glass. "Come on!"

Behind her, the front door opened and Ant and Nicholas carried the bags into a brightly lit hallway. Reluctantly, she opened the car door and climbed out. Emma linked Erica's arm through hers.

"This is going to be *fun*," she whispered.

The hallway could have fitted her parents' entire sitting room inside. It was stone-flagged and laid with beautiful rugs, and Erica thought of Laure, Michel and his friends carrying the old, unravelling, flea-ridden carpet down the Rue Charlot. She went to take off her shoes and Ant said,

"It's fine. The floors are cold. Do you want some slippers?"

The thought of shuffling around in borrowed slippers felt awful, so she shook her head. She guessed bringing dirt in didn't matter if you had a cleaner. Which they must, for this place. A whole army of them.

"Leave your bags there," said Ant, pointing at the foot of the stairs. "Emma, Nick, you guys are in the pool house, but I'll fix you a drink first. What do you want?"

"Got any Dom Pérignon?" chanced Emma.

"That's for tonight," said Ant, and none of them were sure if he was joking.

"Tea please," said Erica, and they followed him through the hallway and into a large kitchen that backed onto a conservatory. Through the glass Erica saw the sweep of a lawn interrupted by a marquee draped in an Arabian-style pale silk that rippled in the brisk winter breeze. Beyond it, disappearing behind a high hedge, was the chain-link fence of a tennis court—she could see the white lines—and to the right, the unnatural blue of a swimming pool cover, pulling on its tethers in the wind.

"I know what you're thinking," said Ant's voice close to her ear, making her jump. "Why didn't we just set up the marquee on the tennis court?"

Erica tried to arrange her face into a neutral expression, but when she turned around Ant's face was alight with silent laughter. She laughed, with relief as much as anything.

"I know it's ridiculous," he said. "Do you still like me?"

"Of course."

He pulled her into a hug, a proper one. She'd missed his voice, his smell, and when they drew back she saw in his face the same recognition, affirmation that what they shared was not imagined, but something true.

The day took on a feeling of promise, so charged and strong she'd not felt anything like it for years. Anything like it since Laure had kissed her in that grimy stairwell outside Barbara's parents' flat. They were shown their rooms, Emma and Nicholas in the pool house, which was the size of a small flat complete with kitchen, bathroom and a double bed. Erica came to poke around, but she had a room in the main house, in the east wing. It was the loveliest room she had ever seen, with a double height ceiling sloping into the eaves and a sleek white-pebbled gas fire burning neat blue flames. The bed was huge and four-posted, draped with gauzy material. It was painted white, all white, with a white bouclé rug and a white bouclé pouf in front of a dressing table with three mirrors angled to the light. She'd caught Emma's eye in it and Emma had winked.

Erica couldn't believe some people actually lived like this. Not as a treat, or a holiday, but came home to freestanding bathtubs and grounds and lit fires, like something from a regency novel. Erica's idea of wealth had been relatively modest, she saw that now: a detached house with a bathroom on the upper floor, custom bookshelves, good speakers for the record player. But this was like a different planet.

Ant was busy with party preparations, so he told them to make themselves at home.

"Drinks at six," he said, checking his watch. "Is anyone hungry?"

They all shook their heads, Erica remembering the flakes of pastry down her top from the sausage roll she'd bought at London Waterloo.

"Well, if you change your mind, help yourself from the fridge."

Emma and Nicholas peeled off to their pool house and Erica retreated back to her white haven. She ran a bath in her ensuite, pouring liberal amounts of rose oil from the small blue glass bottle on the bath caddy. It was the same sort she used herself, and she wondered and then dismissed the idea this was a deliberate detail. She lay soaking in the tub for over an hour, reading a second-hand paperback of *Voyage in the Dark*. Beside her, her tea cooled and developed a skin that stuck to her lip. The two dresses she'd brought were hung on silk-padded hangers she'd found in the large wardrobe and hung off the back of the bathroom door to steam. She didn't want to have to ask for an iron, or indeed anything in this house, in case Ant produced a maid from somewhere and Erica would never be able to forget.

She'd agonized over what to wear. For many years, her mustard dress bought in Paris that fateful summer had sufficed for any more formal occasion where cleavage was not an issue. It was so vintage the style had eventually come back into fashion, and she'd even stitched appliqué bows to hide the wine stains, and shoulder pads to balance her hips. But for some reason, she felt almost superstitious about wearing it around Ant. As though some romantic doom had penetrated the fabric, poisoning the possible future she hoped for with him. Still, there was very little else she felt as confident in, so she had brought it with her. She regarded it through the mist of the steamed-up room, and it was like peering back in time to that first evening with Laure, when she had never kissed a woman and never been in love. Noticing for the first time that Laure only smiled with her mouth closed to hide her wonky front tooth, slanted at an angle against the other as though turning its back. Erica would come to adore that tooth, for she only saw it when Laure was too lost in ecstasy to be self-conscious, her chin thrown back, her white neck exposed, the red red depth of her mouth.

Erica moved her hands from her thighs and placed them deliberately, chastely onto the lip of the tub. Not here, in Ant's house.

The other dress was black, low-necked mock wrap-style, in a slinky material she was certain had been created in a lab and would catch fire the moment it so much as saw a candle. Though it was tight and daringly cut, it was the safe option. She knew she looked good in the yellow, but it was dangerous both in what it represented and evoked. *No*, she thought, *the black*. Tonight was a night for new beginnings.

She climbed out and wrapped herself in a fluffy white towel that felt like a cloud against her slick skin. She put another on the cotton sheets so she wouldn't mark them, and lay down naked on the bed to let the oil sink in, enjoying the cold air of the room and the warmth of her body, the smell of the fire. She'd shaved in the bath and her legs were smooth, her pubic hair shaped into a neat triangle. She didn't really believe anything would happen, here in Ant's family home. They'd waited so long, another few days wouldn't hurt. But it made her feel better to know she was prepared.

She tried not to reflect on what it meant that her desire was something she could manage, something she could control. It was never like that with Laure. When she needed her, it was agony to wait, and if it had been safe she'd have not thought twice about pulling her down to the stinking underbellies of bridges crossing the Seine, or into rubbish-strewn alleys. But she'd been young, a child practically. She'd grown so much the past three years, and perhaps being able to control herself was nothing more than maturity, her prefrontal cortex inching towards completion.

She put on her new bra, a push up Emma swore by from British Home Stores. It had rather more success on Emma's smaller chest, but still when Erica pulled the dress on she appreciated the way it closed the gap between her breasts. She brushed out her hair, flipping it over her head the way Laure used to do to expose one ear, the side of her neck. It always made Erica want to nibble her earlobe, and she hoped it would have the same effect on Ant.

Checking the carriage clock on the mantelpiece, Erica applied her mascara, blush and lipstick, grateful she wasn't approaching her period, when angry red lumps she couldn't resist picking rose along her jawline. She stood in front of the full-length mirror in the corner of the room, and spun, looking from as many angles as possible. *Not bad*. A thrill in her belly, at the thought of what might lie ahead. Then, taking a deep breath and rolling back her shoulders, she picked up her black heels and left the bedroom, padding along the thick carpet and down the polished wooden stairs. At the bottom, she slipped her feet into the shoes, a brutally pointed affair with a kitten heel, but they made her legs look longer.

She had just straightened up and was checking her breasts hadn't escaped, when a woman's voice said,

"They've not gone anywhere, don't worry." Erica jumped, yanking her finger out from under her armpit, and felt her face redden. A tall, elegant woman dressed in a crushed satin wine-coloured trouser suit was smiling at her from the doorway of the kitchen. "You must be Erica."

And this could only be Ant's mother. Even if she hadn't seen the photograph in his wallet, she was almost as tall as him, with the same wavy brown hair, though hers was worn in a shoulder-length bob. She was very trim, and her eyes were a fierce blue, clever and amused.

"Sorry, Mrs Cowper-Gray," gasped Erica. "I just—"

"Call me Elizabeth, please." She extended a cool hand. Erica took it, feeling frumpy and constricted, all her confidence evaporating in the presence of this effortlessly lovely woman.

"Ant is in the garden. Some school friends arrived early. Would you like to join them?"

Erica's stomach flipped. Seeming to read the uncertainty on her face, Elizabeth gripped her below the elbow.

"Let's have a champagne first. French courage."

She steered her into the kitchen, where a flurry of people in catering whites had commandeered the various surfaces. Through the glass of the conservatory Erica saw the early evening was staved off by candles in hurricane lamps lining the path to the marquee. It looked like a bridge across dark water, the safe harbour of the fancy tent at the end, fluttering like a flag.

Elizabeth retrieved a bottle of champagne from the fridge and opened it with practised efficiency. Ant hadn't been kidding about the Dom Pérignon. Erica could taste the money. It was nothing like the cheap champagne she and Laure drank on their last night, or the warm sparkling wine she'd sipped from a paper cup after her graduation, which had managed to be both too sweet and too sour.

This was cold, and dry, and the clink of the crystal against her teeth set a bell ringing in her head. She had never tasted anything so good.

"Ant tells me you're a writer, the best on the course."

Erica coughed, laughing and wincing as bubbles escaped up her nose. "Ant's the best writer. He's brilliant."

Elizabeth smiled, and the lines beside her eyes spread like origami ripples. "I know. I think even his father knows, or he'd never have let him do it. The Cowper-Grays have been barristers and judges going back to the Conquest almost. But he's written since he was a little boy, and before that he told us stories. Oh he was a wonderful liar! You'd believe him if he told you it was raining lemonade. And always his nose in a book—

another tragedy for James, who despite being a man of the law wanted to be a professional rugby player. Difference is, his father never let him follow his dream. What do your parents think?"

"They don't," and then, knowing that sounded harsher even than she'd meant it to, "I mean, they don't read. So I don't think they understand why I write."

"Mm. Why do you?"

The question caught Erica off guard.

"Maybe that's a hard one," said Elizabeth, rescuing her. "How about, what do you write?"

"Novels. I haven't yet, but I'm working on it. The course tells us to focus on the craft and the stories will come."

"Not useful if you need to make a living though."

"No," said Erica, thinking how much lower the stakes were for Ant. He could have a whole wing of this house to write in. She knew she was never going to move back to her parents' semi-detached in King's Lynn, but whatever awaited her would certainly be no more spacious—perhaps a room in a boarding house by the sea. She would walk in the mornings, swim when it was warm, return to her lodgings and work part time in a library or a bookshop or as a typist. She'd have her whole evenings to write, and it wouldn't matter if she was exhausted, because when her book got a deal she would give up work and write full time.

Writing full time. The mystique of it was blinding, and very far away from what she was capable of now. There were her writing sessions with Ant, but often she was so distracted by his arm against hers or his face across from her she wrote clichéd rubbish at best, gibberish at worst. Ant, meanwhile, was on track to complete his first draft by the end of second term.

"Sorry?"

Elizabeth had asked her something, and Erica had missed it. Elizabeth smiled again. "Ah yes, you are a writer. Always in your own world. Well, have a top up and get out there. Ant will be so glad to see you."

"He collected me from the station."

"Yes," twinkled Elizabeth. "I meant dressed like that. You look wonderful."

The compliment mingled with the champagne to make Erica strike out across the grass with purpose. It was bitterly cold, the night sky gritty with stars. She twice nearly turned her ankle on the gravel of the path, but there was no one to see and she composed herself before walking into the marquee.

It was lit with fairy lights, strung in abundance overhead and down the silken walls. Sofas and large cushions were strewn around the edges, arranged about low tables. It smelt of roses, and Erica saw basins of water filled with floating petals set either side of the entrance; next to them stood tall electric heaters. The water rippled with the bass of Depeche Mode. Beside the black-tied DJ was a bar, stocked better than any in Norwich, and this was where the early arrivals were thronged. They were mostly male, though a couple of very slim blonde girls in scoop-backed dresses were sipping from martini glasses at the centre of the bar, the nubs of their spines distinct. Their faces were beautiful and very well made-up. They put her in mind of harpies.

Ant stood a little off centre, dressed in a nicely tailored powder-blue jacket, pushed up to show his tanned forearms, loose-cut chinos and suede loafers, looking like he'd stepped out of an edition of *i-D*. A similarly broad-shouldered man stood beside him with his arm slung around Ant's neck. As Erica got closer, she heard him entreating Ant to take a shot.

"Come on! It's past six."

"I don't want to get ahead of myself."

"Booo!" The man roused the others to join in, booing until Ant took the shot of vodka. He turned to grimace and caught sight of Erica. He looked slightly dazed, and instead of shying away, Erica strutted towards him, feeling like Sandy. *How about it, Stud?*

"Hi," she said.

"Hi," he said.

"Who's this?" his friend asked, grinning unfocusedly. He was wearing a suit, and looked like he'd come from a mid-level office job.

"Erica, this is Mark, and you mustn't believe a word he tells you."

Mark held a hand to his chest, mock offended. His yellow silk tie shone in the golden light. "I am irreproachable."

"Incorrigible more like. Mark and I were at school together."

"And university, and on the law course, until he buggered off to play Byron in the arse-end of nowhere with a bunch of normal-for-Norfolks."

Ant groaned and rubbed his face. "Erica is on my writing MA."

"Ah, sorry," said Mark, not sounding very sorry.

"That's all right," said Erica, "though I must say your stereo-types are very outdated. We only sleep with the sexy cousins."

Mark brayed, sending a warm breath of vodka into Erica's face. "She's fun! Hear that, Margie? Some girls can give as good as they get."

One of the expensively thin women flicked them an irritated look. "If that's what you like, go ahead."

"My ball-and-chain," stage-whispered Mark. "Can't take a joke."

"If you ever made one maybe I'd laugh." Margie held out a bony hand to Erica. "Thank God you're here. It was turning into a cock-fest."

"There are more girls coming," said Ant defensively.

"We don't doubt *that*, Tony." And then, to Erica, "Are you one of Tony's girls?"

"I'm his friend," said Erica, her cheeks flushing.

"Oh, we're all *friends*," said the other woman. "Great friends, aren't we, Tony?"

"Would you like a drink?" asked Ant, gesturing at the bartender.

"Though come to think of it," said the second woman, louder now, "friends don't get too busy to answer your calls all of a sudden, do they?"

"Patricia," said Margie. "Shall we have a smoke?"

"Why not," said Patricia, her voice a little too high. Erica realized she was already drunk, unsteady on her vertiginous heels. Though with that amount of body fat a sniff of a martini would probably finish you. "Coming, Tony?"

"I gave up," he said tightly.

"You find that so easy, don't you."

"Come on, Patricia," said Mark bracingly, pushing her gently ahead of him with Margie holding her elbow.

"You promised me," muttered Ant.

"I know I know. Don't worry, she won't cause a scene."

The bartender was standing waiting for Erica's order, and in the face of so many suits and unable to think of a single other drink, she asked for a martini.

"Vodka or gin? Wet or dry? Dirty or with a twist?" asked the bartender briskly, scooping ice into a shaker. Erica dithered before choosing a combination at random. Ant turned back to the bar, leaning onto the rail and groaning.

"Happy birthday," said Erica, and he laughed hollowly.

"Thank you. Thank you for coming."

"Of course. Are you all right?"

"Fine, fine. It's just this was my mother's doing. She loves a party, and she's never forgiven me for making her miss New Year's Eve 1956. Every year she insists on all this," he gestured around them, "and invites all the same crowd. Patricia included."

"She's your ex?"

"Don't hold that against me." He swigged from his beer. "Point is, it's not really a party for me."

"Oh," said Erica. "You really do this every year?"

"Yup."

"Wow."

"It's like being stuck in a time loop. But this year should be good."

"How come?"

"Because you're here."

She looked at him. She could smell his familiar cologne, earthy and mellow. She wanted to kiss him, desperately. His lips twitched, as though he knew exactly what she was thinking.

"Erica!" Emma's voice pierced the swelling bubble of tension. Erica turned to see her teetering in ankle boots and a skin-tight pencil dress, hanging off Nicholas, gorgeous as ever in a pea-green suit. Some of the men at the bar sniggered, but Ant went to hug them both as the bartender slid Erica's martini over to her. It was cloudy, with an olive lolling around the bottom.

"Vodka martini, dry and dirty," he reminded her. She looked at him for the first time. He was cute. She took an experimental sip. It tasted like seawater, but in a good way. "Like it?"

"Yeah, thanks."

"Anything you need," he grinned, and went to serve one of Ant's other school friends.

"This is *mad*," said Emma when she reached her. "What is that?"

"A martini."

Emma sipped and grimaced. "Ew. No. Vodka cranberry please," she called to the bartender, and then, *sotto voce*, "I'm sore as anything, we've been at it non-stop."

"I thought Nicholas looked happy."

"Oh, I love this song!"

Emma began to swing her hips to "Don't You Want Me Baby." The school friends smirked, clearly the types to wait until they were drunk before dancing, but with champagne and vodka martini in her veins, Erica thought *fuck 'em*. She took Emma's hand and pulled her onto the dance floor. When "Let's Groove" followed, Nicholas joined them, and Ant was not far behind.

For the next two hours they hardly left the dance floor, apart from to get more drinks to slop over their feet or for Ant to be greeted by another friend. Erica had never seen Ant dance before, only nod seriously to bands at the LCR, but she was delighted at how he moved, confident and sexy, swinging her around the floor, which filled steadily until at eight o'clock the caterers arrived with platters of seafood: crabs and lobster and oysters and smoked salmon on little discs called blinis, and salads and for the seafood averse, sliced steak coated in peppercorn sauce. Erica was talked into trying her first oyster, and like the martini found it strange and a little disgusting but also delicious.

"They're from Brancaster," offered the caterer, when she returned with Ant for another, and Erica laughed because she'd travelled all the way to the alien world of Surrey to eat an oyster caught not twenty miles from her home town.

Oysters though, it turned out, were not adequate lining for two glasses of champagne, two martinis and a vodka shot. As the opening strains of "Lay All Your Love on Me" by ABBA rang out, she began to feel distinctly sick. Detaching herself from Emma and ignoring Ant's questioning shout, she hurried out of the back of the tent. A seating area had been set up, with large fire pits and more cushions strewn with blankets. Blessedly, the siren call of ABBA had drawn almost everyone inside, apart from a couple kissing passionately on a blanket.

Erica stumbled out of the light cast by the fire pits, searching for a bush or tree to hide in, but a large, firm hand caught her wrist.

"Hi," said Ant. He was drunk too by now, smiling unfocusedly down at her. Erica swallowed the rising tide of vomit and tried to smile.

"Hi."

"You are so beautiful." He looked like he might be about to cry. "God, Erica. You are the most beautiful woman I've ever seen."

Erica thought of Patricia with a stab of triumph, swiftly extinguished by another wave of nausea.

"I was going to wait until midnight," said Ant softly, his words slurring slightly. "But I don't think I can."

"For what?" she managed.

He moved closer, and Erica's stomach clenched in panic. Oh God it was actually about to happen. Anthony Really Wealthy Cowper-Gray was about to kiss her. The butterflies in her stomach felt more like kamikaze pilots. He guided Erica to a large cushion, her whole body tingling with anticipation. But instead of pressing his own large, firm body against hers, he drew away.

"Wait here," he said. "I'll be right back."

Erica stifled her squeak of dismay. She arranged herself alluringly on the cushion, her limbs clumsy and heavy with drink, and after she watched him disappear into the tent she leant over the velvet tassels and vomited neatly into the shadows behind.

She collapsed back onto the cushion. She was so, so drunk. The stars were spiralling overhead, her head lolling. She needed to sober up, and tried to sit straighter but the cushion was too enveloping. She hoped Ant had gone for champagne and it would take away the foul taste in her mouth. She'd forgotten she'd been sick but now she remembered. She scraped her tongue against her top teeth, panicking.

Maybe she had time to swill her mouth out in one of the bathrooms. Elizabeth seemed the sort of hostess who'd have fancy mouthwash by every porcelain sink. She struggled to her feet, heels sinking into the grass, and peeked inside the tent. The disco lights made everything slow then fast, strobing and making her head spin worse than ever. Emma and Nick were kissing passionately at the edge of the dance floor, Ant's awful friends were shoving each other in time to "Another Brick in the Wall." Where *was* he?

And then she saw him by the bar, discernible by his height, his breadth, his profile. The turn of his head, his jaw lit just so by the lights, the glint of his white teeth as he smiled. Smiled down, and an arm reached up, encircling his neck. And Erica watched as he craned down to the lithe form of Patricia, who was hanging off him, whispering into his ear. Was that her tongue, probing his earlobe?

"Fuck," she said, to no one but herself. She moved away from the music, the lights. She followed the gravel path, making for the enormous house, lit like a spaceship in the dark.

Her heels chafed and ankles rocked on the stones, and she stumbled off to the side, collapsing onto the wet grass to remove her shoes, fumbling the buckles, but they were so small and fiddly and *God* she felt so miserable. She groaned and lay back, breath smoking into the frigid air.

Of course. Of *course*. Who did she think she was, in these shoes, this bra, this dress. It was all make-believe. If she hadn't drunk so much, if it wasn't New Year's Eve, if she wasn't so broke she'd borrowed money for the train from Emma, she'd call a cab and leave that moment. But at least she had a room to herself. She would get up early, go before anyone else was up. She would vanish, never to be seen again, and Ant would regret every day he ever chose the harpy.

Erica's teeth chattered. Who was she kidding. Patricia fitted perfectly here. Erica was too large, too common—she was lying on the manicured lawn for pete's sake. But she couldn't move, not for anything. Her eyes closed, just for a moment, the world turning perceptibly beneath her as she lay, pinned in place, under the stars.

Something had crawled into her mouth—a small mouse perhaps—and was now determinedly decomposing on her tongue. There was no other explanation for how foul it tasted, how furry her teeth felt. Erica cracked open an eyelid and winced at the light leaking through a small gap in the curtains. Whoever had closed them must hate her, not to have hermetically sealed the day out. It certainly hadn't been her. Her memories clawed to the surface and snapped at her eyeballs like vicious terrapins. She hadn't made the house, let alone midnight. She remembered hearing fireworks, like gunshots, but she was already under the bedsheets, holding on for dear life. It was like being in the midst of a cannon battle on a choppy sea.

Who *had* put her to bed? *Please God, let it be Emma.* But she checked under the covers, slowly, every movement sending shooting pains through her skull, and saw she was fully clothed. She felt her legs. Still in tights. She groaned. The signs weren't good. Emma would have had no qualms about undressing her—they'd done it for each other many times. And she certainly would have thought to remove her tights, the waistband of which was now cutting into her belly. She slid them down and kicked them off the side of the bed. Her legs were already beginning to stubble. The feeling moved her inexplicably to tears. The passage of time. The leaning of everything towards chaos. The damn fucking *entropy* of things. Life, death, it was all here in the determined regrowth of her coarse black leg hair. Perhaps there was a short story in that? *Each pore a neat eruption, a forging of the new.* Was she going to be sick again?

Then she saw a glass of water next to the bed, a bottle of paracetamols set beside it. That, too, made her want to cry. Stupid hangover. Or was she still drunk?

Erica heaved herself, feeling much like a seal flobbling its way up a sandbank, towards the water and pills. The cracking of the foil reverberated through her skull. She took two and swallowed, with great difficulty and much gagging, for her mouth was so dry it seemed to absorb the water on contact. Collapsing back on the pillows, she tried to sort through the reptilian slipperiness of her memories. She remembered dancing, so much dancing. Ant's body close to hers during "Every Little Thing She Does Is Magic," Emma falling over and being helped up by Mark, and then one of the harpies—Maude? Maggie?—the one that was Mark's girlfriend—wife?—screeching and yanking him away. Nicholas and Emma laughing it off, dancing closer, and Ant pulling her against him. Oysters. Another martini. Mark returning with shots. Patricia, shaking her slender hips towards Ant. And then—

Oh God. Oh. God. Her, abandoned on the pouf. Patricia wrapping her arm around Ant's neck.

Erica wanted to cry. Instead she ran to the bathroom and retched bile into the toilet. Her throat was raw and her stomach empty. She crawled on the cold tiles and turned the taps, resting her forehead on the cool floor while she waited for the bath to fill. It felt so good against her prickly, sweating skin.

She woke and for the second time, she was on a rocking ship, sea spray coating her face. Someone was hammering on the bathroom door and . . . Jesus Christ, had she wet herself? No. The entire floor was wet. Erica yelped and scrambled for the taps. The bath was overflowing, the water rushing off the tiled area onto the whitewashed floorboards.

"Erica! I'm coming in!"

Ant burst in through the unlocked door, and they stared at each other a moment before he turned the brass taps off.

"Erica," he said feebly. He was pale and dark shadows sat under his eyes, and he had never looked so handsome. "I thought you were dead."

I wish I was dead. What did she look like? Last night's make-up smeared over her face and spread by the water leaking from the bath, her breasts in disarray, her belly free of the control tights. She felt utterly wretched.

"Sorry," he said, backing out. "I thought you might have fallen asleep in the bath. The water was leaking into the drawing room."

"I'm so sorry," said Erica, her voice coming out several octaves lower. "I fell asleep."

"It's all right. Do you . . . do you need help?"

Erica's instinct was to say no. But she couldn't think where to start. Her mind was sore and mortified. "Yes."

Ant leapt into action as though trained for it. He spread towels on the floor and emptied a third of the water from the bath. Then, without embarrassment or hesitation, he helped Erica to her feet and sat her on the closed toilet lid. He fetched her more water, returning as she was struggling with her dress, trying to get it over her head.

"I'm covering my eyes," he said. "Do you want me to get Emma?"

Erica shook her head, then remembered he had closed his eyes, and, feeling as pathetic as she sounded, said, "Help."

He helped her manoeuvre the dress over her head. She fumbled with the bra strap, and he reached around and unclasped it with such practised ease it almost made her laugh. She kicked off her underwear and he supported her into the bath, his proximity almost intoxicating enough to make her forget how awful all this was. That the first time Ant was seeing her naked, she was hungover, her body lined all over from sleeping in her clothes, her face in god-knows-what-state. That it didn't matter anyway, because he had probably kissed Patricia last night, probably slept with her. She sank into the bath.

"Do you want anything?" he asked the door. "Tea?"

"No," said Erica, desperate for him to leave her to her humiliation.

"I'll wait outside, all right? In case you fall asleep again."

"It's all right—" she began.

"Or I can get Emma. But I'm not leaving you alone in here."

"Fine."

"I'll stay?"

"Fine."

He closed the door softly.

Erica lowered herself under the bubbles and screamed into the water. What the actual *fuck*. She was going to have to leave the course, leave England. Move to a shepherd's hut in the wilds of the Highlands, or Snowdonia. She was never, ever, going to be able to recover from this.

She stayed in the bathtub longer than was polite, but she couldn't bear to get out and face Ant. Slowly, the pain in her head receded as the water and pills took effect, but the shame and disappointment grew. She refilled her glass from the cold tap of the bath, and drank the slightly stale-tasting water.

She scrubbed her face, her body, the rose scent comforting. Her fingers were starting to pucker before she got out and wrapped herself in a fresh towel from the seemingly endless supply.

"I'm out," she called. "Thank you."

"That's OK. Are you feeling better?"

"Much." Physically. Mentally, her inner critic was just getting started. She brushed her teeth twice, swilling with the mouthwash left thoughtfully on the sink. She braced herself and looked at her face in the mirror.

It was not as bad as she'd feared. Her eyes were puffy and bloodshot, and she'd burst a smattering of blood vessels beneath her left eye, which looked like a fading bruise. But her skin was almost attractively pale, and her lips looked full and pink. She thought she heard the creak of a floorboard, the soft closing of a door. He was gone. She breathed out, and walked out of the bathroom.

"Oh."

Ant was still there, sitting on the bed. "Sorry. I'll go."

"Don't."

He looked like a lost little boy. Erica came and sat next to him, pulling the towel down over her thighs. He was wearing nylon shorts, and she could smell his sweat.

"Shit," she said. "Have you been *running*?"

"Yeah."

"Shit."

"I have to, when I'm trying to work something out."

Erica knew she was expected to ask, and obliged. "What were you working out?"

"You."

"Ah." She leaned slightly against him, felt a throb of want as the hairs of his legs brushed her calves. "And?"

"Well." He put his arm behind him, so he could angle his body towards hers. "I think I've been a fool."

That was not the answer she'd been expecting. "Oh?"

"Yeah. Wasting all this time."

"Oh." Erica wanted to cry. Did he mean their time together had been time wasted? Had he, after putting her to bed—she was sure it had been him—gone and fetched Patricia, and bedded her in his Egyptian cotton sheets? Hell, he'd probably proposed.

"I should have just told you, straight away."

"What?"

"Erica." He turned his head so his mouth was inches from her bare shoulder. His voice was practically a whisper, a growl. "Isn't it obvious?"

He shifted his weight, and bit, very lightly, the base of her neck. She felt herself soften, pool into liquid, and, dimly, remembered another bite of her throat that made her melt.

"Wait," she said, determined not to be even more of a fool. "What about Patricia?"

He drew back with such obvious surprise on his face she already knew how mistaken she'd been. "What?"

"You were together, at the bar."

"She was putting it on me. I'm not interested."

"Oh." She looked into his eyes. "So you aren't in love with her?"

"Erica. Do I really have to spell it out." He laid her softly back on the bed, and parted the towel. He kissed down her body, her breasts, her stomach, her thighs. He knelt between her legs and put her thighs over his shoulders. His tongue found her centre, and pushed. He worked his fingers inside her, his tongue on her, until she begged for him.

"I don't have a condom," he rasped.

"Pull out."

"You sure? I don't think . . ."

"No more thinking."

She pulled him on top of her, and as he moved inside her, hard and rhythmic and perfect, so perfect, he kissed her mouth and her ear, whispered into her hair. "God, Erica. Erica, God. I love you. I love you."

And for the first time in her life, Erica said it back, out loud, and meant it.

Chapter Six

It felt like surfacing from a deep pond: the first day Laure woke up sober, and did not immediately want to jump from the nearest high building. The depression that had stalked her for months, years—now, she counted them, one, two, three, four . . . could it really be four years since Erica had left for the last time?—thrown off like a heavy shawl. She lay very still, as though moving would reawaken the beast, alert it to the kernel of happiness she felt beneath her breastbone, right under the place Gabrielle's hand was resting.

Gabrielle was still asleep, her arms flung out like a child's, her full lips slightly ajar, the wash of her dyed auburn hair spread out over the pillow like an aura, or a halo.

Laure had never met anyone who slept so deeply, so beautifully. She looked like a painting—what was that awful Leighton she used to teach? *Cymon and Iphigenia*. She'd seen it only in facsimile, used it in contrast to Giorgione's *Dresden Venus* to illustrate her point about eroticism and cliché. And these were words that suited Gabrielle: she was beautiful to the point of cliché. Aquiline nose, rosebud mouth, thick lashes fringing deep blue eyes, her wrinkles only serving to highlight the incredible softness of her skin, like rose petals—that Laure had fallen in love with the first femme woman she'd dated since Erica had not escaped her notice.

Laure shifted, very slowly, and slid out from under Gabrielle's hand. Her fingers curled and she let out a little sigh, turning over and tucking her hand beneath her chin, the lines around her eyes crosshatched by the creases from her pillow. She would sleep for another hour yet. Gabrielle used to be the one who rose first, but lately Laure had been waking with the sun, and spending an hour on their small concrete balcony overlooking the Rue de Saintonge. It was only a street east of her old squat on Rue Charlot, but it felt like a different world. A new build with automatic doors, an elevator, neighbours who worked as teachers and nurses, and lived in identical flats arranged along long corridors. Radiators. Bedframes. Lightbulbs and running water. Laure had finally arrived in the new decade, leaving so much behind. Aesthetically it was a disaster, but it was clean, and safe, and Gabrielle was here.

Fellow recovering alcoholics, they had met last year, in late autumn 1982, at a meeting in a community hall in the twelfth, chosen by Laure because it was still walking distance from her squat, but somewhere she was unlikely to meet anyone she knew. Attending the Michel-mandated meetings with Claude had been too inhibiting, and somehow seeing him fall off the wagon, or he her, felt more dispiriting when she was there to witness his taciturn refusal to speak in meetings. She also came to feel, though it was not openly acknowledged, that Claude somehow held her responsible for his sobriety, as though she had become his keeper and not a fellow lost soul. It was clearly not a short road for either of them, coming on three years since Michel took Laure to her first meeting, and Laure needed yet another fresh start.

The new group was based on an American programme, and run by a woman from Missouri who pronounced *bonjour* as *bongjower*. She'd dispensed with the religious aspects of the programme, but still Laure did not enjoy the performatively confessional structure, how often everyone cried, the vegetarian spring rolls served with sweet chilli sauce as their "snack included" every week.

She stayed only for the woman, a lot older than her, who sat at the front at every meeting, and nodded earnestly as she listened to each sob story, each denial, each revelation. All seemed to touch her equally, this blue-eyed woman, who once wore her auburn hair tied back, revealing a multitude of piercings in her pointed, almost elfin ears. Laure never missed a meeting after seeing her. At Laure's eighth meeting, the first of the new year, the woman stood to share her story.

"My name is Gabrielle, and I'm an alcoholic."

She talked about a father who left, a mother who drank, taking a sip of an almost empty beer in her early teens, drinking whole cans, then wine, then a move to the city, and vodka, gin, whisky, a failed marriage. She was an artist, she said, without embarrassment, and her hands would shake if she didn't drink, and if she couldn't paint she couldn't think, couldn't breathe, so she had to drink to think, to breathe. To live.

Laure sat, rapt. It was an almost mirror image of her own story, husband aside: the absent parent, the early first drink, the acceleration into alcohol as a daily need, a daily pleasure, a daily chore.

"In the end . . ." Gabrielle shrugged, her hands spread out before her. Large hands, almost mannish, out of step with the rest of her. Completely captivating. "I decided if I must stop breathing awhile in order to be free, this is what I must do. I take photographs now."

She was five hundred and eighty-six days sober.

"Why do you still come to meetings?" asked Laure afterwards, approaching her beside the tepid, slightly damp spring rolls.

"Because I will never not want to drink. I come to remind myself of all the reasons not to."

"You come to stare at the animals, still caged?"

The wrinkle between her brows deepened as she frowned. She was easily fifty, and beautiful. "Of course not. I come to remind myself not to slip back between the bars."

Laure was hooked on Gabrielle. All it took was a passing mention of an ex-girlfriend for Laure to ask her out for coffee the next day, a Saturday. Michel was delighted to hear about it. "Finally, the pervert is back!" he said down the line, Laure calling from the box in the street and reversing the charges to the café. But it did not feel like a return to her old ways. For one thing, it was to be the first time Laure hadn't drunk on a date. She drank before, of course, and walked to the agreed café on Rue

Jeanne d'Arc in the freezing January air, eating an apple to cleanse her breath—a trick she'd picked up from Claude. Gabrielle took one look at her when she arrived and said,

"You're drunk."

"No."

"You've drunk. I can see it."

She stood up and though her expression didn't change, there emanated from her some deep fury, almost mythical in its power. "Goodbye, Laure."

"What? Where are you going?"

But Gabrielle had walked out of the café and away without another word. Laure slumped at the table and lit a cigarette, ordered a beer. Later, she checked her reflection in the dank, spotted mirror of the café toilet, and wondered how Gabrielle had known on sight. She looked no different than usual. But then, she couldn't remember the last time she saw herself sober. Maybe it was even that summer four years ago with Erica, when they had stayed in bed too late to get more wine, and she had faced Erica to the dark window, and watched their reflections as she touched her.

"The pervert is no longer a young woman," she lamented to Michel on their phone call. "But a sad old man left in a café alone."

"Nonsense," said Michel. "You are a beautiful old man. Try again."

"Maybe."

"You can tell me of your triumph tomorrow morning—is ten all right?"

She agreed and rang off, deciding her pride could take another knock. At least, it was worth the risk.

So, the next meeting, she approached Gabrielle once more. "I'm sorry," she said.

"I can't be with someone who isn't at least trying," said Gabrielle. "I value myself too much for that. And you should too."

Cowed, Laure agreed, and convinced her to come for another go. The same café, the same time.

"If you don't drink between now and tomorrow, I will come."

"How do you know I won't have drunk?"

Gabrielle smiled, all the lines around her eyes crinkling. She was older than Laure first thought, her hair grey at the roots. She went home with Laure after the meeting, and they fucked softly, Gabrielle making little mewling sounds, and falling asleep with her arm across Laure's chest, holding her close. The immediate afterglow of pleasure made sleep easy, but Laure woke in the early hours, feeling sick and panicky, and reached automatically for the bottle of vodka beside the mattress.

Gabrielle woke, and propped herself up on her elbow, watching her in the glow from the streetlight through the curtains. Laure wanted to be defiant, to swig from the bottle, as though she'd had what she wanted from Gabrielle, and now could do as she liked. But she had not had what she wanted, only a taste. She wanted more, she wanted all of it. She set the bottle down, and went back to bed.

In the morning Laure woke in a pool of sweat, Gabrielle stirring beside her, and someone knocking on the door. Laure felt ghastly, and was tempted to ignore it, but somewhere in her aching brain she registered it was Saturday, and Michel was coming round. She dragged on last night's shirt and knickers and padded to the door, her body tender all over. She felt like she'd been hit by a car. She was gagging for a drink. She unlocked the bolts and Michel, invisible behind a pile of books, tumbled inside.

"Fuck, I thought my arms were about to come out of their sockets! I'm going to get a key cut, I've been knocking for ages—well, kicking, my hands are full as you can see."

He let the pile of books drop onto the sofa and collapsed down beside them, before registering that Laure was not alone. He sat up, staring at the mattress marooned in the middle of the floor.

"Ah, sorry, sorry! Who are you?"

"Gabrielle." She was propped up on her elbow, her left breast exposed, nipple dark against her white skin. Her expression was unmistakeably hostile. Laure fought an inappropriate urge to laugh.

"This is Gabrielle. And this is Michel," she said, and then added, "my best friend."

If she thought this would wipe the glare from Gabrielle's face, she was wrong. Laure felt a sluice of cold sweat surge over her skin. She really needed a drink.

"Enchanted," said Michel, looking from Gabrielle to Laure with a crooked brow. She knew it was not the nudity that had him rattled but Gabrielle's rudeness. "Do you want to do this later?"

He gestured at the books. Laure had asked him to bring any books with colour plates from the café, so she could use them with her students to explore collage and Mallarmé's *A Roll of the Dice*. The café frequently had donations from bouquinistes and bookshops looking to clear stock, obscure or outdated titles, and barely anyone read most of them. Michel was doing her a favour, and she wished she could summon the energy to be grateful, but all she could think about was how desperate she was for a drink, and Gabrielle's mood was making the air hard to breathe.

"I don't know. It's fine. Can you just leave them here?"

Michel looked at her, hard. It was a long journey from the café, the closest metro line closed for renovations. They hadn't seen each other for more than a week, only talking on the phone, and he would be expecting a catch up.

"I can," he said slowly.

"I'll see you at Marie and Agnès' on Wednesday?"

He stood up, frowning now. He looked again between Laure and Gabrielle, and Gabrielle sat up to wrap her arms around her knees, the blanket sliding off to reveal her chest fully.

"Is everything OK, Laure?"

"Fine," she said, but as she said it, her stomach gave a twist and she turned to the piss bowl and vomited neatly into it.

"Laure!" Michel was by her side in a moment, his cologne too strong in her nostrils, his hand too warm on her back. "What's happening, are you sick?"

"She's detoxing." Gabrielle's voice came from Laure's other side, and through her watering eyes she saw Michel's battered leather boots, Gabrielle's neatly painted toenails and the white cloud of her pubic hair.

Her hand slid over Laure's shoulder blades, cool and firm, and there was a moment when both of their hands were on her, before Michel moved his away.

"I've never seen her like this."

"She's detoxed before?"

"Yes, a few times."

"Clearly not for long. Why did you let her drink again? It's not safe to keep doing it."

"Excuse me?" Michel sounded astonished. Laure tried to speak but all she could do was retch ineffectually into the bowl.

"It could kill her."

"I know," said Michel, in his dangerous voice, the one Laure had only heard him use while fighting with Christophe, or that night with Erica. "Sorry, who are you again?"

"Gabri—"

"Because I'm her best friend, and I've been looking after her for years."

"Not very well."

Laure made a mew of protest, but now her head was swelling with a headache so monstrous she wanted to cry.

"Laure? Are you going to let this woman talk like this?"

"Michel," said Laure weakly, into her vomit, "please."

"I think you should go," said Gabrielle.

"Go?" From the arrangement of their feet, Laure saw they were squaring up to each other. "I don't know you. Why would I leave my friend with some one-night stand?"

"I'm her sponsor," said Gabrielle. "I'm the best person to help her through this. You clearly can't."

With an almighty effort, Laure pushed herself upright, her head spinning, throbbing fit to burst. "Please stop."

"I think *you* should leave," said Michel, moving to put his arm around Laure, but the smell of his cologne made her stomach convulse and she pushed away from him, spinning back to face the bowl.

"Laure," said Gabrielle, her blessedly cool hand back on the nape of her neck. "Do you want me to go?"

She just wanted one of them to make the aching stop, to pass her a beer. She made a sound that was not yes or no but *please stop talking*.

"This is ridiculous," said Michel. "Just leave."

"No. She needs me. Don't you, Laure?"

And because fear was steadily mounting alongside pain, Laure nodded smally, the movement sending waves of agony down her neck and back.

"Then I'll stay too." There was the creak of sofa springs as Michel threw himself back down.

"I think it's best Laure's left with someone who understands." Gabrielle guided Laure onto the single chair and placed the bowl in her lap, still rubbing her neck.

"Until she can tell me to, I'm not leaving. I don't know you and I don't trust you."

"What?"

"You heard. Her sponsor? This is wildly unethical."

Laure blinked up at the scene, scanning the floor around her for the nearest bottle. Michel was sitting clench-jawed on the sofa, staring up at Gabrielle, who had moved to stand over him, hands on hips, Michel's eyes level with her pubic hair.

"Michel," she said weakly. "It's OK."

"You want me to go?"

She wanted to sleep. "I'll see you on Wednesday."

With a look of utter disdain Michel pushed himself up off the sofa once more, dislodging some of the hardbacks, which fell with clunks that seemed like gunshots to Laure's sore head. He slammed the door and she whimpered, cradling her head in her hands.

"It's all right," said Gabrielle, softly. "It's all right. You're safe. This will pass. It will pass."

Laure clung to those words, for the next days were a nightmare. Sweats, shakes, the unbearable, pressing sensation of impending doom. There was no quieting it, the rumble of danger, of death that stalked her. Wednesday came and went, and if Michel or Marie came to ask after her, Laure was incapable of noticing anything outside of her own pain, and soon she lost track of the days. At one point a kind of paralysis settled on the left side of her body, as though it had floated away and was no longer part of her. She felt it was the press of an angel, or a demon, some spirit engaged in a struggle for her very soul. When her arm was returned to her, weak and tingling, she believed she might well die, begged Gabrielle for a drink, and when Gabrielle silently passed her the bottle, she'd push it angrily back at her, and beg her to pour it down the drain.

"You do it," Gabrielle replied, and of course Laure could not. And so the cycle would repeat, Laure despairing and raging, furious with Gabrielle for holding her hostage like this, furious with herself for being so weak as to be reduced to this wailing, frightened child, the same child who cowered in the shadow of her father's armchair, finishing his drinks, waiting for maman to come home.

Stupid Freud. Stupid American meetings, tracing everything to the root. But Laure knew that this was where the wrongness started, the badness. Fathers left all the time, but mothers? She must have done something awful to disrupt the natural order of things and drive her mother away. Even now, as an adult, knowing her father in all his difficulties and complexities, she still blamed herself and not her parents.

That Gabrielle had the same blue eyes as the very first woman who left her was not a thought she lingered on, and nor was their age difference. Nor did she comment on the stretch marks on Gabrielle's breasts, her belly, the same marks her married lover Pauline had had from pregnancy and breastfeeding. Pauline had hated them, spent her husband's money on serums and lotions that smelt good and made not a jot of difference, but Gabrielle wore hers matter-of-factly, without explanation.

Sobriety, sold as a promised land, was the worst thing she'd ever lived through. After the nausea and the headaches came a crushing tension in her temples and jaw, a rigor that pills wouldn't touch. Her heart raced as though she was sprinting even when she was only lying down, and spiders crawled along the inside of her skin. She couldn't bear to be touched, and Gabrielle would sleep on the sofa while Laure rocked and shook, sleepless, in the bed. Every morning, Gabrielle would strip the sweat-soaked bedsheets and put on fresh ones, walk them both to the laverie and feed coins into the machines. Laure would sit on the long metal bench with her head in her hands, and though Gabrielle urged her to leave and lie down in the park, Laure felt it was a just punishment to sit amidst the racket, the tumbling colours of other people's clothes like the tangled insides of her own head.

That she could not have survived without Gabrielle was not in question. Though it was a thankless task, the woman didn't leave her side though Laure often railed at her, or screamed in her sleep. In the haze of her terror and pain, she asked for Michel, for Marie, for Barbara, perhaps once for Erica. But none of them, after that scene with Michel, came. Gabrielle stroked her hair, told her she was here, she was going nowhere. When Laure was able, Gabrielle transferred her to her own rented apartment on Rue de Saintonge. It was small and clean, and smelt strongly of bleach, but Laure was grateful for the running water when, after a near-two-year absence, her period returned with a vengeance. Gabrielle ran her a bath and murmured comforting words.

"It won't be like this for ever. You're safe. It will pass."

Laure lay awake at night, listening to the rapid gallop of her heartbeat, repeating this phrase to herself. The second week she fevered so hot Gabrielle filled the bathtub with cold water and helped her into it. Laure walked beneath the willows at Giverny, small leaves like thorns that caught in her eyes. She sank and rose and sank, and when the fever broke she cried in relief that she was still alive.

Gradually, the emergency of withdrawal receded, but what remained was almost worse. A hollowness, the perpetual sense of something missing. Laure became aware of her bones beneath her skin, the fragility of her skeleton, the workings of her living body.

She pored over books, some Gabrielle's, others Gabrielle brought from the squat for her, about Goya, Picasso, Bosch—those who knew the torment of a body at war with itself—searching for recognition, but found none. Frida Kahlo, there had been a tortured soul, but her work had never spoken to Laure. *For a feminist, you set a lot of store by male writers.* Now why was Erica back in her head? Erica could not have saved Laure like Gabrielle did. But in the American alcoholics' meetings, it was important to make amends, and as Laure's sobriety held for a month, two months, three, she felt she wanted to. To Erica, though what exactly she'd done wrong she was unsure. She only had the sense of needing her forgiveness.

But first, there were the others. She wrote letters to Pauline, to Hilde, to Barbara. She wanted to call Michel, but Gabrielle dissuaded her, saying it was better to write, to give him her address and see if he wanted to reinitiate contact.

"Of course he will," said Laure, and Gabrielle looked at her sadly.

"It is different now, Laure. You told me how he drinks, they all drink."

"They're not alcoholics though."

"Hm, maybe, but they don't understand what it is to be sober. It is a religion, almost, something you must devote yourself to. Or maybe it is like leaving a cult. It is hard to be around people still drinking, who don't know how to have a difficult conversation without a drink in their hand."

Laure opened her mouth to defend her friends, to defend the way of life that so recently she was a part of, but nothing Gabrielle said was wrong. She swallowed, frowning down at the stack of paper Gabrielle had bought her.

"You will be like a mirror to them now, and many of them won't like what they see. It's challenging. They have not walked through fire as you have. You will find only sober people understand. So many of my former friends fell away when I finally chose myself." Gabrielle took her hand. "It's all right, Laure. Maybe I'm wrong. But you must set everything down plainly, clearly, so they can make the decision for themselves."

Laure was sure Gabrielle was wrong. She did not know Michel, what Laure had put him through before, how he had always stayed her staunchest support: sending him to collect her clothes from irate exlovers' apartments, never paying him the rent she promised him for the first months in Paris, all the late phone calls from telephone boxes on unfamiliar streets, asking him to pick her up. She apologized for these things in her letter, and for disappearing the past few months. She thanked him for his friendship, and hoped he would accept her apologies and the new path she was on. Writing this felt mildly ridiculous—of course Michel would accept her however she came. He was the person who taught her what true acceptance, kindred recognition, looked like.

She put Gabrielle's address and phone number at the bottom of each letter, and Gabrielle posted them for her. She knew she should write to her father to apologize for her complete abandonment of him, but she was emotionally spent. Erica was out of the question—what to say to her? If she'd had any idea, it was lost to her now. Instead she wrote to the Sorbonne, asking for her job back. She assumed she had been fired after not showing up for four months, but they had been chronically understaffed. Even if she had to apply for other jobs Gabrielle had reassured Laure that she would support her.

What exactly Gabrielle did was still hazy to Laure. The box room of her apartment was a darkroom, with lines strung across the ceiling and the scent of vinegar in the stop baths. When Laure was out of the miasma of her detox, she asked Gabrielle to show her her work, but Gabrielle was coy about it.

"I'm between projects," she'd say, "I never look at my old work. Besides, most of it is sold." There was one photograph of hers in the bathroom: a woman's spread legs, a mushroom between her labia, the stalk presumably extending into her vagina. It was in black and white, but for the mushroom, which was hand-painted in a pale peachy pink. Laure liked it, the slightly threatening eroticism of it, but attempts to engage Gabrielle in conversation about it were dead ends.

"I think I'm moving away from photography," she said. "I might even work towards a career in somatic healing. It helped me a lot, after my marriage."

How a photographer who did not take photographs earned enough to keep an apartment in a clean building on the nicer side of Le Marais was a question Laure did not know how to approach. While Gabrielle was mostly calm, almost trancelike as she moved through the daily inconveniences of life, when something really upset her she presented an impenetrable sort of anger, the deep black anger of someone capable of awful things, and she hated to be questioned on topics she didn't want to discuss. Laure wasn't scared of her, she knew Gabrielle would never hurt her, but she didn't want to incite her rage. And perhaps the money came from her ex-husband. To probe at it would be painful, unkind. Besides, Laure didn't have the energy to question her good fortune, with melancholy tethered to her ankles like manacles.

That Michel hadn't banged down the door once he knew where she was only added to her gloom.

"I think I should call Michel. Or Marie," she said, a few days into April and a few weeks past sending the letters. She'd had nothing except a reply from the Sorbonne, offering a couple of classes. She'd not responded. Whatever sharpness sobriety may have gifted her was dulled by her depression, and the thought of those bright, interested faces looking at her made her exhausted. But not seeing her friends was like living with too much gravity.

"When you're feeling a bit stronger," soothed Gabrielle. "And besides, they have our address. Why don't they come here?"

The worst thoughts rushed at her then. *Because they're glad I'm not around. Because I've caused nothing but trouble.* Her certainty while writing the letters felt far away. Maybe Gabrielle was right, and they wanted to leave her behind? Laure allowed herself to be persuaded to wait, much as she allowed herself to be persuaded into sex with Gabrielle, even though her libido remained absent. She performed the motions, and still enjoyed giving Gabrielle pleasure. She had done so much for Laure, the least Laure could do was offer her this. At some point, surely her sensation, her cravings would return.

So when Laure woke without the grinding weight of the depression she'd felt for years, she took it as a sign. She walked out onto the bright balcony and thought, *Yes. Today can be the day.* It was the day before her twenty-ninth birthday. She would call Michel, and ask him to go for a walk in Parc des Buttes Chaumont, his favourite, so he would know she meant business. And it would be good to walk again: she had not gone further than the laverie in months. How had her world shrunk so small? And he would forgive her, and he and Gabrielle could begin again—they all could. And then tomorrow—

She felt a slight thrill of panic. What was there to *do* on a birthday but drink? Thank god for Gabrielle, her love, her steadiness. She would help her navigate it all.

Laure went inside and put a pan of water on to boil, then lifted down their two cafetières. The smell of the coffee brought Gabrielle walking tousled through the door. Laure loved how her body looked, its folds and wrinkles, its marks and scars. She'd always had a terror of death, but getting older looked all right, a body growing into its stories. But still when she tried to translate her admiration for Gabrielle's looks into something sexual, there was nothing. She still felt numb in that regard, as though alcohol, in its dimming of everything else, had heightened her sex drive and, now everything else was dialling up, that faded away.

"Morning," she smiled, and Gabrielle came and nuzzled her neck.

"Good morning, my love. What great thoughts has your day brought you so far?"

"I think today I might call Michel."

Gabrielle's hands tightened on her waist. "Really?"

Laure tried to turn to face her but Gabrielle held her steady, pressed against the counter. Laure set down the coffee cups, pushing gently back against Gabrielle and also against the creeping discomfort that had nothing to do with the Formica edge pressing into her pubic bone. She peeled Gabrielle's hands from her sides and slid away. Gabrielle's face was closed, her nostrils flaring.

"It's been months. Six months. I've not missed a birthday with Michel since I moved to Paris. He'll want to hear from me."

Slowly, Gabrielle shook her head. Her eyes filled with tears. "My love, don't you see? He knows where you are. He has our address, our number. I thought you'd let go of this."

"He's my best friend, Gabi. I want to call him."

Gabrielle cupped her cheek with her hand. "I understand. Truly, I do. But I don't want to see you hurt. You've been hurting so badly, for so long."

"I feel better." Gabrielle looked at her doubtfully. "No, listen. This morning, I woke up and looked at you and it was like the colour was back. I feel lighter, can't you see it?"

"I do, I see it. But love, shouldn't we wait? At least to see if it holds?"

"I want to call Michel. I miss him."

Gabrielle nodded, and gestured at the phone. Laure took it from its cradle, feeling self-conscious but unable to ask Gabrielle to leave. She began to dial Michel's number when a small, soft sob came from behind her. She turned in time to see Gabrielle cover her face with her hands, and start for the bathroom.

"Hey." Laure replaced the receiver and hurried to catch her before she closed the door. "What's wrong?"

"Nothing," said Gabrielle, forcing a smile. "Sorry, it's nothing."

"Tell me. I know Michel will love you, you got off on the wrong foot."

"It's not that," she snapped, before her face creased into anguish. "I just had something planned today, as your birthday gift. But you should call Michel, of course you should."

"Oh." Laure felt caught. She wanted to hear Michel's voice, see his beautiful face, but Gabrielle looked distraught. "What?"

"A surprise," she said. "It's OK. We don't have to. It's your birthday and you should spend it as you choose."

She kissed Laure chastely on the lips before gently closing the door. Laure stood with her forehead pressed to the painted wood. She thought she heard Gabrielle crying quietly, trying not to be heard. Laure looked at the phone, silent in its cradle. It never rang, for either of them. For the first time, Laure understood Gabrielle was lonely. What was one more day, or even two? Gabrielle was right—Michel knew how to find her. Perhaps she could have the best of both worlds, spend today with Gabi and then tomorrow Michel would call her. She knocked, softly, to be let in.

The hotel was one of the oldest in Paris, a hushed, tucked-away boutique off the Rue Christine. It being so close to the Sorbonne, Laure had walked past it many times but never noticed it—the discreet brass plaque, the closed wooden door the size of a cathedral's. Even if she had spotted it, it was clearly not the sort of place for her. But Gabrielle led her confidently under the archway, through the courtyard filled with people drinking and smoking, and into the plush lobby. Their footsteps clacked on the marble floor, the sound instantly swallowed by the velvet sofas and thick curtains partitioning the reception from the breakfast area behind. Laure's skin itched. She had not been in such rich surrounds since Pauline's, and now she didn't have the cushion of drink to help her ignore her distaste.

Gabrielle was wearing a burgundy fitted dress with a matching belt in a style Laure had never seen her in. She looked buttoned up, elegant, Grace Kelly in her middle age. They could be mistaken for mother and daughter—the thought flashed at Laure as she regarded them in the gilt-framed mirror behind the reception desk. She did not know Gabrielle's exact age, but she must be in her late fifties, and maybe this was why the receptionist did not react when Gabrielle approached her.

"One room for one night," said Gabrielle, and then, to Laure, "Why don't you sit down while I sort this."

Laure did as she was told, quashing her surprise and slight unease that this hadn't been so planned that Gabrielle had made a reservation in advance. *Don't be ungrateful.* But as she sat in a Louis XVI armchair and was offered a glass of champagne or iced water, she wondered what exactly Gabrielle was playing at. This was obviously not what Laure would have chosen to do for her birthday. They might not have discussed their ages or Gabrielle's profession, but their politics seemed to be in complete alignment. She'd spotted the rack rates on the gateway, and they were obscene. She should stop Gabrielle now, ask her if they could go for a walk and a coffee in the Jardin du Luxembourg instead. But Gabrielle was handing over a credit card, and then turning to her smiling, reaching for her hand and tucking it under her own.

"Come," she said gleefully. "We have a suite."

They had no luggage, but the porter accompanied them in the small lift to the second floor and opened the door for them, showing them in turn the living room, the bathroom and separate toilet, the double doors leading to the bedroom and a second bathroom, and a whole room with floor-to-ceiling mirrors he slid aside to show them wardrobes for their non-existent luggage. Gabrielle gave him a note and he left with a deferential bow of the head.

"Well?" said Gabrielle, looking at her triumphantly. "Isn't it beautiful?"

Laure looked around her. It was beautiful, and grotesque.

"It used to be a monastery. Well, it was built over the ruins of a monastery, thirteenth century, founded by Saint Louis."

Her eyes had that overly bright quality they sometimes took on. She was trying very hard, and Laure tried to look interested. "Wow. Have you stayed here before?"

"No, I saw it in a magazine, years ago. It looked so beautiful, and I always wanted to come. But I never had the right excuse." She pulled Laure into her and smiled up into her face. "Are you happy, my love?"

"Yes." But Laure was fighting the urge to cry. She felt her fragile, precious happiness fading like light on chill water. Why could she not tell the truth? Who was this timid, agreeable woman unable to speak her mind? She would be twenty-nine tomorrow, and she'd never felt so much like a child. But Gabrielle seemed unable to read her mood, and kissed her passionately, unbuttoning Laure's shirt. Laure let herself detach from her body, and stared up at the white-painted ceiling as Gabrielle stripped her, waiting her turn to give her what she wanted.

When it was over, Gabrielle sprang up, sweaty and energized, and announced she would run them a bath. Laure rolled over, a dull ache in the pit of her belly. The sadness was washing in, and she felt helpless to stop it. On the dresser opposite, level with her eyeline, sat a champagne bucket, the gold-foiled neck of a bottle protruding, two glasses crossed at the stem, a small card folded beside. *Bonne anniversaire!* in neat cursive. Whoever had put them there must have worked fast, running up some back stairs to beat them in the lift, melting away before the porter led them to their door. Invisible people, not to be seen. Laure wished, as she had so many times before, she could disappear. She eyed the champagne, imagined the cold bright burst of it—that would be one way to vanish. Her mouth watered, and she rolled the other way. The telephone, white to match the sheets, the ceiling, the gauzy curtains, sat on the bedside table. A possibility. An unanswered question.

She could just hear Gabrielle singing over the gush of the tap, "La Vie En Rose," one of her favourites. She kept her radio tuned to news or classic French stations. Laure couldn't remember the last time she'd heard a Joni Mitchell song. *I was a free man in Paris, I felt unfettered and alive. Nobody was calling me up for favours, no one's future to decide.* With a surge of certainty, she picked up the phone, pressed the button for an outside call, and dialled Michel's number.

With each pause, each ring, she felt her blood run more electric, jumping through her wrists, making her hands tremble. But the line rang out. Refusing this anticlimax, Laure pressed the switch hook and redialled, this time the community café. It was a Tuesday, and he was usually off on Tuesday, but it had been nearly six months since she'd seen him, an extraordinary amount of time, and maybe he'd changed his hours.

The phone was answered by an unfamiliar woman, who paused so long when she asked for Michel that Laure readied herself for disappointment. But she must have instantly passed over the phone, for suddenly, gorgeously, the next voice she heard was Michel's.

"Hello?"

Laure immediately started crying. She tried to speak but her throat was tight.

"Hello?" repeated Michel. "Who is this please? Do you need help?"

Laure tried to say, "It's me," but it came out as a squeak. Michel went so quiet she'd have thought he'd hung up if there hadn't been the background noise of the café. And then he said, as though her name were a miracle, "Laure?"

"Yes," she managed.

A muffled scream. "Laure?"

"Yes, it's me."

"Oh fuck. Fuck! Where have you *been*, Laure? I thought you were dead!"

"What do you mean?"

Michel's voice was trembling. He sounded angry, on the verge of tears. "How dare you vanish like that? Where are you?"

"I don't understand." Laure swallowed hard, trying to regain control of her breathing. "I'm at a hotel right now, but I was at Gabrielle's all that time. I barely left."

"Gabrielle's? The nudist? How was I meant to know where that was? And what hotel? Are you all right?"

"I'm fine." But Laure felt like she was stumbling away from the scene of some awful disaster, head bloodied, ears ringing. Through her confusion, she registered the sound of running water had stopped, alongside Gabrielle's singing. "Michel, I have to go."

"Wait, what hotel, Laure? Where are you?"

"I'll call you back—"

The bathroom door opened, and Gabrielle stood in the doorway, her smile falling as soon as she saw the receiver in Laure's hand. Laure had been about to drop it back onto its cradle, but instead she found herself gripping it tighter, seized by a sudden, instinctive fear. "Michel? I'm at the Hotel Chris—"

But Gabrielle had moved swiftly to the bedside table and depressed the switch hook. The dial tone hummed in Laure's ear. Both of them looked at the phone, as though neither could believe what had just happened. Then Gabrielle sat down on the bed, and Laure dropped the receiver onto the duvet, scrambling back and away.

"Laure," said Gabrielle gently, as though soothing a wild animal. "What's happened?"

Laure stared at her. She knew, had known since the moment she'd heard Michel's voice. He had not abandoned her. But she could not, just yet, believe Gabrielle had betrayed her.

"You tell me."

"Who was that?"

"You heard. It was Michel."

"Ah. I thought you were going to wait?"

"I changed my mind."

It was absurd, but Laure felt herself delaying the moment of direct confrontation.

"OK. Well, can we get back to our day now?" Gabrielle was watching her closely. Her scrutiny made Laure's skin crawl.

"I need to leave," said Laure, sliding out from the sheets and pulling on her trousers.

"Leave?" Gabrielle let out a hollow laugh. "What are you talking about?"

"Where are the letters, Gabi?" She held up a hand to forestall the denial. "Don't play dumb. The letters I sent for my friends."

A long pause. Laure pulled her shirt on and began to button it, turning to face Gabrielle. There was no remorse, only that shrewd calculation. At last she said, "It was for your own good. They weren't good for you. They were letting you drink yourself to death."

"They sent me to the meetings. They knew I needed help—"

"But none of them were willing to put their lives on hold for you, were they?"

"They did, many times. But none of them made me their prisoner."

"Prisoner?" Gabrielle walked around the bed until she stood before Laure. "Where was the lock on the door? The shackles?"

"You made me feel I had nowhere else to go!"

"You didn't want to go! You love me!"

"Maybe." Yes, she did love Gabrielle. But there was something else, the instinct of a prey animal, the instinct of the woman she used to be. Clarity. How had she been so foolish? She looked directly into Gabrielle's doll-blue eyes. "And I hate you too."

Gabrielle's face didn't crumple. She didn't even flinch. She absorbed the blow with nothing more than a smirk. "No, you don't."

"I hate you for making me feel all I had was you. For touching me when I didn't want to be touched—"

"What does that mean?"

"You know I don't want sex. You know and still you touch me, make me touch you."

"Oh, that is just like your generation. You regret a fuck and it's rape. Ever heard of the boy who cried wolf?"

"My generation?" Laure shook her head in disbelief. "I'm not a child, Gabi. And I know what you've done, even if you don't. I'm going."

"Where will you go?"

"Back to my life!"

Gabrielle snatched the bottle of champagne from the cooler. She held it out to Laure. "Go on then, drink yourself to death."

They squared up to each other. Beneath the swallowing current of her anger, there were deeper, treacherous understandings, things Laure could not yet allow herself to name. Even now, she thought about staying, just so she would not have to face them. But this urge was what decided her.

"I'm leaving." She moved past Gabrielle and into the living room, scooping up her shoes. "Goodbye, Gabi."

"Laure?" Gabrielle stood in the doorway. Her voice, her stance, had changed again, become submissive, wheedling. How had Laure not noticed this behaviour before? "Can we not forget all this? Can we not go home, and be together?"

Disgusted as she was, an exhausted part of Laure longed to agree. When Erica left she read and re-read *Fragments d'un discours amoureux*, searching for solace, for meaning. What she found was recognition, an altogether less comfortable sensation. She returned, over and again, to "Affirmation": (*Someone tells me: this kind of love is not viable. But how can you evaluate viability? Why is the viable a Good Thing? Why is it better to last than to burn?*).

These lines chased themselves around her head. They could burn together. She imagined going back to her stinking squat without alcohol to convince her the way she lived was fine. Going to her friends, one by one, and explaining where she had been. The humiliation, the pity. Going begging to the university for another chance, her last last chance. What reason would she give this time?

Gabrielle opened her arms to her. She was not a Good Thing. Her love was conditional on control. But did it matter? Laure could let herself be kept, be looked after. She would not have to work, she had somewhere to live, someone to visit galleries with. At twenty-nine she would be married, if she were straight. Why not vanish into companionship as so many others did? As for the betrayals, she herself had been forgiven enough times to extend the same, if she must.

But even as this fantasy comforted and horrified her, she saw the bottle in Gabrielle's hand. It was not love, however twisted, that made her do that.

"Goodbye, Gabi," repeated Laure, as calmly as she could. Gabrielle suddenly threw the bottle. Laure ducked, and it hit the door behind her, one of the frosted panels exploding into shards raining down on her like gravel.

Barefoot, she fled, taking the stairs and running through the plush hallway, only noticing as her soles slapped against the marble she was bleeding, slipping, ignoring the stares, the alarmed shout from the receptionist. And then she was out in the bright July sunshine on a dirty Paris street, terrified and elated, pausing only to slip her shoes onto her stinging feet before running, lungs bursting, towards Rue d'Aligre, and Michel.

Chapter Seven

Laure woke at the same point in the journey home she always did, just as the bus broke Rouen's outer boundary. She lifted her head from Michel's shoulder. Past his snoring profile flashed the familiar grey buildings, the legacy of Allied bombing a uniformity that was likely the origin of Laure's dislike of concrete. She drew her focus back to her friend's face. He had lost weight, his cheekbones pressing like stretcher bars under the beautiful canvas of his skin. She hoped worry for her was not the cause of his diminishment, but when she thought of how she'd have felt if he'd disappeared as she had, she thought it likely.

She'd arrived at the café yesterday afternoon, wincing on her cut feet, to find him pacing inside, calling a succession of hotels and describing her in hysterical tones. He'd thrown the receiver down and she watched it swing on its cord as he gripped her to him and cried.

"I'm so angry with you. You stupid girl. Where have you been?"

When he'd calmed down, his colleagues cleared a table and they'd sat by the grimy window. She told him the story about Gabrielle in all its ugly, radiant detail. Michel kept crying, a steady stream of sniffling and sighing, and when Laure was done he said, "Why didn't you call me?"

"What?" Laure frowned at the sky outside the window. "I told you, I wrote you the letter. I thought you didn't want—"

"You could have tried harder. You could have come to me, I would have helped you."

"I know. I know. I can't explain, Michel. She made me feel like you weren't good for me, or that I wasn't good for you. I don't know."

One of the volunteers, a new boy called Alim, brought each of them a bowl of stew. The blackboard announced it was Tabakh Roho, and the smell of spices filled the air. Laure felt already that her senses were unfurling, leaf by leaf, towards sensation again.

Finally, he said, "What will you do now?"

Laure knew she wouldn't feel safe at the squat anymore. The hatred on Gabrielle's face, the thrown bottle—she didn't want to be anywhere she could find her. And besides, she was moving on now. If she could get her job back, she would be able to get a deposit on an apartment saved. Start her sober life.

"Stay with us," said Michel.

"Us?"

"Ah." He smiled weakly through his tears. "Christophe finally came to his senses."

Laure gasped, leaning across the steaming bowls to grip his hand. "Michel, I'm so happy for you." A heavy pang in her chest. "I missed so much."

"There's time. But listen, there's something I need to tell you."

His face was grave, and she noticed for the first time how loosely his favourite sage-green shirt hung, how hollow his cheeks were. She waited.

"Your father called the Sorbonne, left his number. They called me, since I was the contact on your contract. He's sick, Laure. His liver. He wouldn't tell me much, but I think you should see him. Maybe it would be good to leave Paris for a while anyway."

Laure absorbed this information, felt it seeping into her marrow. The first, needling threat of pain. Liver, of course. She took a shaky mouthful of stew. Her father's hands shaking as he poured another drink. She hadn't seen him for half a decade.

She was grateful Michel had insisted on coming with her. They'd retreated to his flat, and he'd helped her remove the glass from her feet, washed the wounds with vodka and bandaged them. The smell of the coarse alcohol made Laure's mouth water, and Michel removed the bottle as soon as its work was done. They'd called Marie and Agnès, Barbara, Claude and Léa. All of them overjoyed to hear her voice, all of them furious. Then she'd called her father, and he'd not reacted to the news she was coming, but nor did he try to put her off, which she knew meant he was desperate for her to come. A tender sort of melancholy overwhelmed her as she hung up the phone. At least there was time to make amends. And though she would never voice this, even to herself, it felt useful to have a legitimate grief to mask her mourning for the end of Gabrielle's and her relationship. She knew it would be weeks, months before she came to terms with what had happened, that in time Michel and the others would become demanding of more detail. But for now, she could focus on her father.

Michel woke as the bus drew to a jerky halt at the terminus. Bus stations were singularly depressing anyway, but they always reminded Laure of Erica leaving, and Michel sensed a downturn in her already bleak mood.

"Come," he said. "A coffee, for courage. My treat, birthday girl."

Everything had been his treat. Laure had nothing but the clothes on her back, and even if she'd returned to the squat before they'd left, there was no money there. She would be starting from scratch when she returned to Paris. They drank two cups of burnt coffee each at the café attached to the bus shelter, waiting for the service to Bois-d'Ennebourg to be announced.

"So this is Rouen," said Michel, looking around at the perspiring concrete.

"This is the new part," said Laure, feeling oddly defensive. "The old town is that way. We could go there if you like."

"Maybe later," said Michel, amused. "You are the mistress of procrastination."

"I'm here, aren't I?"

"You are. Thank God." Michel took her hand and squeezed. An older woman at the next table smiled indulgently. The bus was announced, and

Michel picked up his carrier bag. He'd insisted on bringing food from home for her father. "We can't turn up empty-handed."

"He'd prefer a bottle," Laure had said.

"I think his doctors might have something to say about that."

They boarded, and Laure felt a rush of something powerful and hopeful. Nostalgia maybe, excitement even, at seeing her father. Their relationship was not easy, but she loved him. It was only this love that was driving her to transgress the divide between her two lives so spectacularly. She squeezed Michel's hand as the concrete fell away and the fields sprang up, as though he was the one needing comfort.

They left the bus and Laure wished Gabrielle's version of sobriety didn't include cigarettes. She craved one worse than she had in weeks. Michel took her hand as they walked through the flat fields. Sweat stung the cuts in the soles of her feet. The sun was at its height overhead and their palms were sweating too, but Laure drank in the contact while she could.

The approach to the old farmhouse was long. The fields were crowded with flax, its lilac-blue blooms in full song, the air sonorous with their particular scent, earthy and fresh, an echo of the petals' colours shading into the sky. Her father would scoff at the tourists hurrying through Normandy on their coaches to reach the fabled lavender fields of Provence.

"Why don't they open their eyes? Can't they see the flax is every bit as lovely? Not that I want them here, trampling about, but at least it would make those Provence elites miserable."

She could conjure him at any time, his intonation, his balding head and tufty ears, the narrow body, the crooked teeth she shared. So when she knocked at the door, and a stranger answered, it took her a moment to understand it was her father. He was stooped and his skin had a yellowish tinge in the unforgiving sunlight. He squinted into the light flooding behind them, his glasses propped on his chin.

"Papa? It's me."

"Laure?" His eyes were hazy. He had become an old man. Laure felt like Rip Van Winkle, waking that morning to find her father aged a hundred years. Or was he Rip Van Winkle? She couldn't remember the story properly. She couldn't remember when she'd last read a book at all that wasn't about tortured artists, or one of Gabrielle's self-help tomes.

"Yes. I said I was coming."

"I know, my memory is fine, thanks. Who's that?"

"My friend Michel. The one who called you while I was away."

Michel swept forward. "A pleasure, Mr Boutin." He kissed him on both sunken cheeks. Laure grimaced. She should have briefed him better. Her father grimaced too.

"How are you feeling, Papa?"

"I'm fine, absolutely fine. I thought you'd decided to let me die in peace."

Laure laughed, trying to take it as a joke. "Are you going to invite us in, Papa?"

Her father grumbled and stood aside. Inside was hazy with smoke, the smell of food gone bad. As she walked past him, her father smelled too: stale beer, stale smoke, stale breath. He was still drinking, of course.

Her father walked with an unfamiliar shuffling gait to his usual chair. He turned to sit and reached for the Gitanes smouldering in its tin ashtray. The tableau might as well not have changed since she was last here five years ago.

"Are your legs hurting?"

"Everything is hurting." He picked up his cigarette. "I'm old."

"You're fifty-eight, Papa."

"My father died when he was forty-two."

"I know."

"Plenty more at eighteen." He waved his cigarette out at the fields, meaning *in the war*.

"I know." Laure smiled awkwardly at Michel, who was looking at her with an encouraging expression. She knew he was not a judgemental person, but what could he think of this place? Smoke-stained ceiling, sagging with rot. The curtains drawn at every time of day, the kitchen, glimpsed through the ajar door, a health hazard—

Laure caught herself. But of course Michel would not flinch at these surrounds. Hadn't she lived like this until Gabrielle stole her away? Seeing it now was like an electric shock to her soul. The table was covered in books, as it always was, more piled beside her father's armchair. She squinted to read the title of the topmost volume, butterflied open. Alain-Fournier's *Le Grand Meaulnes*, a favourite of his.

"Would you like something to drink?" Laure asked Michel.

"Didn't you bring your own bottle?" groused her father.

"Laure is sober," said Michel, and Laure wanted the swollen floorboards to swallow her up.

"Is she now." Her father's gaze took on a gimlet-eyed sharpness, and Laure saw he was not as decrepit as he was trying to appear. "Following in the fool's footsteps, are we?"

"Do you want anything, Papa?"

"Beer."

"I won't fetch you a beer."

"You may as well go back to Paris right now if you're going to be a puritan."

"I don't think it's puritanical to not fetch the man with liver failure a beer."

"Spoilsport."

Michel snorted at their exchange, and her father looked at him with renewed interest. Did he think they were lovers?

Laure walked into the kitchen, opened the fridge. Inside, a mouldy block of cheese, packs of butter, some sort of medicated gel and a bottle of milk. Laure opened the foil cap and sniffed experimentally. Off.

"Is there anything I can get you, Mr Boutin?" she heard Michel say.

"I'm not dead yet."

"Have you lived here long?"

"Since I was born. My mother birthed me on that hearth rug."

"Goodness."

Laure went back into the room. Michel had stepped quickly off "that hearth rug," and dithered next to the sofa. Her father returned his excoriating gaze to her. "You're limping."

"Hurt my foot. Both feet, actually."

"How?"

Laure ducked the question, reaching for Michel's plastic bag of offerings.

"Shall I?" she asked, holding up an orange, and her father grunted. With the scent of the fruit came this: her father would peel her an orange every day they had them, leave it whole and perfect outside on the newel post for her to eat on the way to the bus stop to school. She'd forgotten that. Forgotten until she felt the pith clag beneath her fingernails, but now she remembered waking to an empty house, her father already at his job as a labourer on the neighbouring farms and later, when it was found he was better with the books than a brush hook, as their clerk. Her father could have been anything—she knew that as a child, his voracious reading habit matched only by drinking. But now she felt it, the wasted potential. The house seemed to sag with it. She handed him the orange and he nodded his thanks. She offered one to Michel, who shook his head as her father began peeling apart the segments and popping one into his mouth, all the time eyeing her keenly. Behind his stoop, he was sharp as ever.

"So. Twenty-nine."

It took Laure a moment to realize he was referencing her age. He'd never been one for birthdays. "Yes."

"And what are you doing at the moment? The Sorbonne said you'd left."

"I'm not sure yet," said Laure, aware of Michel sitting very still and unobtrusively on the sofa opposite. She wanted to sit beside him, unpin herself from the skewer of her father's focus, but as ever, it was impossible.

"So what. Are you keeping her?" This at Michel, who sat up straight. She wondered if her father reminded Michel of his own. Her father was nothing like that monster, who'd beaten Michel so badly his collarbone still ached in cold weather, and thrown him out when he'd discovered he was gay. Coming out was a fraught discussion in their circles, and everyone had a war story. Barbara's parents wept over the lack of grandchildren. Marie's had disowned her. Agnès' didn't know. Michel's mother still came to see him in Paris, bearing gifts of homemade jam and fruit cakes, but his father said he was good as dead to him.

Now, standing over her father, the smell of oranges in her nostrils and smoke from the smouldering Gitanes in her eyes, Laure wondered why she had never told him. He would not beat her. And if he threw her out, she had Michel with her. With the same charge of reckless certainty she'd felt leaving Gabi, she said,

"Michel's a friend. But I was being kept, for a while, by a woman."

A sharp inhale from Michel, but Laure, intent on her father's face, wondered if he hadn't heard her. "Papa? I said—"

"I heard you." His tone was neutral, and he put another segment of orange in his mouth, chewed deliberately.

"We were together," she said. "The woman and I. We were . . ." Why did she feel so afraid of the word. "Lovers."

Her father swallowed. "And now?"

"No," said Laure, still uncertain if he understood. "We aren't together any more. But I still . . . I only like, only love, women."

"I understand, Laure," said her father impatiently. "You're a lesbian. What, did you come all this way to tell me?"

"No," she said. Whatever reaction, she hadn't expected irritation. "I didn't expect to tell you."

"I knew there was something," said her father. His posture, his face, hadn't changed. He was still intent on his orange. "You were always so . . ." He tilted his hand side to side as if to imply imbalance, a listing ship. "Why didn't you tell me before now?"

Laure exchanged a glance with Michel, who was mute, gripping the arm of the sofa. "I don't know how to answer that question."

"Then let me try." Her father popped another piece of orange into his mouth and swallowed. "You thought that despite my never attending church I believed sinners such as yourself belonged in the seventh circle of hell. Though, are lesbians sodomites? Actually," he said, waving his remaining orange at her, "don't answer that. That despite me pressing into your hands the works of Flaubert, Foucault and de Beauvoir, I did not know that such people existed? Or maybe you thought that because I live here, in the house I was born in, that I am a small-minded, provincial bigot who simply could not tolerate such deviance?"

He sounded furious. Laure could do no more than stare at him. He looked up at her and she saw that, to her surprise, his eyes were brimming with tears.

"Or, and this is the one I cannot abide, you thought that if you told me I would hate you, or laugh at you, or decide that I didn't want such a thing for a daughter. Is that it, Lolo? You think there was a version of this conversation that ended with me not loving you any more?"

A lump was filling Laure's throat. She felt like she was dreaming. She never would have given him the chance to say such things, to let him into her life this way. Because the truth was she had thought all these things, and worse. She had wanted to leave her father behind. To shrug off the dirty house and the endless fields and be someone new. But she had hauled her mess with her and worse, abandoned her father in the process.

"Papa—"

"If you are going to apologize, please don't." He ate the remaining slice of orange, jaw working violently as though the fruit had mortally offended him. But the temper passed as a flash of lightning, his gaze rolling onto Michel. "And you? Are you a queer too?"

"We prefer gay," said Michel, smiling weakly. He had tears in his eyes too, and Laure knew he was thinking of his own father. How different this was. How lucky she was.

"And why wouldn't you." Her father looked back at her. "Sober then?"

"So far."

"Good. Keep it up. There's nothing you're missing, I can promise you." He turned briskly back to Michel, who was wiping his eyes. "Are you sober too?"

"No."

Her father pushed effortfully to his feet, and Laure understood he meant to fetch beers.

"I wonder if—"

"Ach, and please don't be someone who preaches. Let people make their mistakes."

"It's only because I care—"

"I know. I know you do, Lolo."

He went into the kitchen. *Do you mind?* mouthed Michel, and Laure shook her head, dazed. The lump in her throat refusing to budge. What did she feel? Guilt, and gratitude, and regret. Something else, too big to name. Her father came back with two beers, and a bottle of Orangina so dusty Laure wouldn't've been surprised if it was from her childhood.

"Thank you," she said.

He grunted, settling down in his chair again. "Now, tell me. What happened with this woman who was keeping you?"

At some point in the early evening, her father dozed off in his chair. Michel was already asleep, three beers down and curled up on the sofa. He'd been silent most of the evening, and barely eaten when Laure and her father ransacked the carrier bag he'd brought. She and her father had continued talking, a little about his illness but mainly about the books they'd read recently, local gossip about the village, the municipal election results. And then they sank into a comfortable silence, and his eyes closed, his face going slack.

Laure sat watching the two men for a long time, until the sun started to set and the sky darkened over the fields of flax. A bizarre sight, unthinkable really: her father and Michel in the same room. She wondered what was up with Michel—it was not like him to not have an appetite.

She stood up, took her father's ashtray from the pile of books and emptied it into the bin, ensuring every last cinder was extinguished. She felt wrung out, exhausted, and yet calm. There was something about this house that did this to her. She sometimes mistook it for boredom, but now she stood in the silent gloom of the kitchen and did not long for the noise of traffic, or singing drunks, or any of the sounds of the city. She was content to stand here, in her body, sober and alone.

Laure made herself a cup of tea, pouring out the off milk. She could fetch some from the farm next door, if they still kept cows. Yves' family were gone, she didn't know where, and now wished she'd thought to ask before so long had passed. She sipped the strong brew. The tea at Gabrielle's was as weak as her coffee. She guessed she wouldn't see her cafetière again, or any of her clothes. But that was no loss, a small price to pay. Gabrielle hadn't allowed her to go to her squat herself to fetch anything, claiming she needed to focus on her sobriety, not fall back on distractions. Gabrielle had decided what clothes to bring, what books Laure was allowed. How had Laure been so foolish? She watched the light shift. She felt there would be time, now. To make amends. To breathe. She added sugar to her cup.

Mr and Mrs Steven D. Parker
request the honour of your presence
at the wedding of their daughter
Erica Mary
to
Anthony Richard William Cowper-Gray
son of Mr and Mrs A. G. W. Cowper-Gray
on Friday, the twenty-seventh day of July
Nineteen hundred and eighty-four
at three in the afternoon
St. Mary's Church, Weybridge
Reception following
Abbeydore House
St. George's Hill
coaches provided

Abbeydore House
St George's Hill

5 August 1983

Dear Laure,

I am nervous about sending this, which is why I think it's the right thing to do. Nervous that you will laugh at me for getting married. Nervous that you will roll your eyes at Ant's name, and this invitation. Nervous that you will hate me for inviting you at all, and nervous you will be angry the wedding is on your birthday (see above regarding date). Your 30th!

However, it was impossible for me when planning the guest list, to leave your, Michel, and Léa's names off. I know we left things as bad as they could possibly be, and you may well still hate me, or not think anything at all about me, but aside from all the other things, you were one of the best friends I've ever had. I'm hopeful that perhaps we could be friends again or, failing that, forgive each other. If that doesn't sound too grand.

I think you will love Ant. Perhaps Léa or Michel has told you, but we met on the Creative Writing MA and he has since been published. His debut novel "Gargantuan" has been very well reviewed by the Sunday Times. The original title was "Gargantua," after the Daumier lithograph, as it deals with themes of obsession and consumption, but the marketing team didn't bite. It could be worse—one more "commercial" suggestion thrown around was "Yes, Chef," and upon the editor's view it perhaps wasn't literary enough, the alteration was "Oui, Chef." We can laugh about it now.

How about you? Are you still teaching at the Sorbonne? Just writing that gives me goosebumps. I suppose I should address this to Dr Boutin, as Léa told me you were awarded your doctorate with no corrections. She is very discreet when we talk on the phone, and bats away most of my questions, but she did share that with me.

I do ask questions though, Laure. I know I was a vain, cruel child, but I have grown a lot these past five years, and I hope if you let me I could become a good friend to you.

I hope you are happy, and healthy, and that you will consider coming to England for the wedding. You, Michel and Léa are most welcome to stay at Ant's family home—we are here while we decide where to settle and there are almost as many spare rooms as this family has names. Weybridge is only a half an hour by train from London, and the National Gallery has recently acquired "The Avenue, Sydenham" by Camille Pissarro, which may tempt you even if canapé-sized portions of roast dinner and the sight of me sweating in yards of white lace doesn't (I am wearing a Cowper-Gray family heirloom, and no one in this family seems to have had hips).

This letter is going on, and I only set out to write a small entreaty. But I still don't know when to stop—that hasn't changed.

Love,
Erica x

20 August 1983

Dear Erica,

It was good to hear from you, if a little unexpected. Up front I will say: I am sorry, but I can't attend your wedding. I recently repaired my relationship with my father (perhaps Léa has told you he is ill? But defying all expectations and still alive. He has dark humour about it, and it has rubbed off on me) and we have agreed to spend my 30th birthday together in Monet's gardens at Giverny (did you know it is now open to the public? We tried to go this year, but you have to book in advance). I know Michel has let you know he can't make it as his health has been bad, but Léa can be our emissary (she is convinced you are marrying into royalty and all her Republican principles have evaporated).

I am happy for you, and Anthony Richard William Cowper-Gray. Seriously, congratulations. And congratulations on the Creative Writing MA—what are you working on?

Thank you for your congratulations on my doctorate. It was a rocky path, but the principals at the Sorbonne have been good to take me back. I'm certain Pauline had an influence somewhere. It's a long story, but I am happy, and healthy. I've been sober for the best part of a year now. And if I'm honest, I'm glad you're in touch. I've missed you too.

I'm currently staying at Marie and Agnès' (both of us are spare-room squatters it seems?), so if you would like to call me there, we can catch up properly.

With affection,
Laure

Part Three

1985

I encounter millions of bodies in my life; of these millions, I may desire some hundreds; but of these hundreds, I love only one.

from *A Lover's Discourse* by Roland Barthes

Chapter Eight

Erica pulled the desk in front of the window, dust motes thick in the sunlit air. She'd viewed better apartments, bright, high-ceilinged, picture-perfect, but she'd have had to borrow more money from Ant. Her allowance was embarrassing enough as it was. This would do. It had a bed, a window, a desk, a bath. All she needed. To choose one of those other apartments would have been akin to defeat, a mimicry of where she'd been the past eighteen months. And Ant had insisted she not go for the most basic—this had air conditioning, a welcome luxury in Parisian summer heat.

She sat down in the rickety chair and placed her hands on the worn wood of the desk. She was here. She had followed an idea through. What's more, she was here alone. For the first three months or so of their marriage, following Ant on tour had felt like an enormous adventure. Instead of a honeymoon, they'd set off for a six-week publicity trail for *Excavations*, his second novel, a trip which took them from a tiny, beautiful bookshop in Land's End to a sold-out appearance at the Edinburgh Festival. She'd basked in his reflected glory, revelling in the audience's indulgent laughter and rapturous applause, toes curling with glee whenever he mentioned her, and how she was his first, and best, editor.

Then they were off to Germany and Spain, where *Gargantuan* had just been released in translation, and even through the stilted flow of a translator his answers were received with reverence. Whenever she was asked what she did, which was not too often, she said she was a writer as well, working on her first novel. She must have promised half a dozen publishers she'd send it as soon as it was ready. In truth, it was hard to focus on her novel, a novella really. She envisaged it as something small and perfect, like Kate Chopin's *The Awakening*, something that needed breath, pauses, silence. The problem was, beyond wanting it to be a love story that also commented on social issues, Erica had been unable to pin down a protagonist, or much of a plot. Ant made the suggestion early on that she should write about Laure, but she dismissed it out of hand. There was no chance she would expose herself that way. His second suggestion galled her even more.

"Magical realism then," he said. "You love the South Americans, *Midnight's Children*. Why are you trying to write this tight little world?"

"It's not tight, it's restrained," and then, because discussing her non-existent book with a successful author, even if he was her husband, was demoralizing, "and I don't want to talk about it right now."

"Right now" became "ever," and Ant eventually stopped asking.

With the winter came discontent, and she began to resent the constant travelling, how Ant seemed to dictate to an invisible amanuensis even at dinner parties, and how increasingly she felt surplus to requirements not only at events but afterwards too. Ant was exhausted when they eventually reached their lovely and anonymous hotel rooms, and they made love less and less. She'd lie awake, his warm weight beside her, and toy with the idea of going down to the hotel bar, ordering a glass of wine, writing notes or perhaps even an opening to her novel. *Passing Rain*, that was her working title. Neat, classy, enticing. But she never did, only lying in the inevitably orange light seeping in through the gaps in the curtains until sleep eventually overwhelmed her.

She knew Ant would not resent any decision she made about going with him or staying at home, but this made it harder to be selfish. He was living his dream—her dream—and his happiness carried her for a while. But as the trip to Spain and Germany was chased by an invitation to America, both of them started to fade. She'd never been to New York, but she couldn't face it.

"I won't come this time. I need to knuckle down. Focus," she said, with an edge to her voice that was aimed squarely at herself. He'd accepted her decision with the requisite balance of disappointment and understanding, and she'd gone back to Abbeydore House, ostensibly to write. Ant's father was working on a case in the Cayman Islands, so it was just Elizabeth and Erica knocking around the enormous house with the winter "skeleton staff," the housekeeper Rachel and the cook Maria.

Elizabeth arranged a study for her, with a working fireplace, a view of the lawn and swimming pool. The walls were lined with books and Elizabeth didn't bother her until their traditional six o'clock gin and tonic, but still focus did not come. In the end, she spent most of her time reading, which, she reassured herself, was much the same thing as writing.

She read *Life & Times* by J. M. Coetzee, and *North and South* by Mrs Gaskell, re-read *Candide* and *The Ravishing of Lol Stein*, though she drew the line at *A Lover's Discourse*. She and Laure were on friendly though distant terms—Laure had sent a card for the wedding, and when Erica heard from Léa that Laure's father died in September the previous year, she sent a note of condolence and a long letter. She'd not heard from Laure since, nor spoken to Léa since that call, when she'd also learned Michel's illness was getting more serious, though no one seemed to know what was wrong with him. Her summer in Paris felt like a parallel universe, her tethers to that time and place fraying. Sometimes she looked upon herself not even in that detached way anyone looks at their younger self, but as an utter stranger. Would that stranger be living in her mother-in-law's west wing, procrastinating?

Ant came back from New York just before Christmas, hollow-eyed and pale, bearing gifts of perfume for his mother, and frothy lace underwear for Erica. He managed to talk his mother out of her traditional New Year's Eve birthday party for him, and took Erica to the soft launch of a beautiful hotel in Oxfordshire. They ate tiny plates of perfect food and smoked cigars at midnight before going to bed, Erica in her confection of green lace and satin, tasting of smoke, drunk but feeling solid and found under Ant's warm hands.

The next morning, the first day of 1985, they walked in the beautiful gardens, spiderwebs strung frosted between high woody stalks of lavender. Erica could tell Ant was working up the nerve to tell her something, and in her hungover paranoia she sprang to the worst conclusion.

"I missed you so badly," he said. "It's a bad place to be lonely. There's so much to do, to see. I went to a party nearly every night. Everyone talking, all the time. Saying nothing."

Ant was about to tell her he'd met someone. She imagined a Joan Didion figure, forbidding and cool and published.

"It made me think about what was important. It made me realize what matters to me." Ant stopped and turned her to face him. She braced herself. "Erica, do you want to have a baby with me? We could start trying this year. Today, even."

Erica's brain skittered. She blinked slowly up at him, the white sky bright around his head. They'd talked about children, having them someday, but Erica thought she'd have written her book, maybe two.

"That was a joke," said Ant, scanning her face nervously. "But maybe this year?"

She opened her mouth without knowing what to say, but was saved by Ant hurrying on. "I know you hate the tours and I'm not expecting you to come on more, but I'm going to France in the summer, and Paris in September for the Rentrée. Maybe we could meet there, drink too much red wine and eat too much rare steak, and when we come back . . ." He linked his fingers through hers. "We could start trying."

Paris. To go back to Paris with Ant—what would that feel like? To go back to Paris with Ant, knowing it was a . . . a what? A last hurrah? His fingers were rough in hers, and she imagined softness, the smell of talcum powder, and something in her body gave an involuntary tug of want. That's all it took, that momentary stirring of something primitive, to decide this momentous thing. She nodded, fast, before she could second-guess herself. Yes to Paris, yes to the baby. Yes to the next step.

"Yes?" He bent down and kissed her, blotting out the sky. As the kiss deepened, Erica imagined returning to the study in Abbeydore House, to her sheets changed for her once a week and G&Ts with Elizabeth. She wouldn't, couldn't, go back. It was too comfortable. She was stagnant there. An idea stuck in the back of her mind, a writing retreat in Paris, a novel growing in the Parisian summer heat, and when Ant drew back and said, "I'm so in love with you," the words felt as they used to: full of immense promise, unending possibility.

She'd spent the first four months of the new year in the Abbeydore House study, plotting, researching, reading. Ant was meant to be toying with ideas for his third novel, but most of his days were taken up with interviews and calls with film or TV agents, and in the evenings they'd both join Elizabeth and Henry for gin and tonics, the ritual made special again because it was limited. Soon these days would be behind them. Elizabeth tried to talk her out of Paris, especially after the cinema bombing in March, but Erica was resolved. She would have her writing time in Paris and then they would return and start looking for their own home.

She and Ant lay awake late into the night, and talked about where they would live, what sort of house they wanted to buy, where would be best for the children. Any mention of these impossible creatures evoked a sense of vertigo and longing for Erica. She would write her book, they would buy a house, have a baby. After Paris, the next phase would be in motion, as it should be.

If occasionally her fear grew louder than her excitement, her certainty increased when, as they celebrated her birthday at Maggie Jones with Nick and Emma, Emma declined Ant's offer of wine.

"I'm pregnant," she said, and between her and Nick passed a look of such tenderness, Erica felt an overwhelming rush of jealousy.

"Congratulations," she said, standing to hug her friends, catching Ant's eye and finding in his gaze reassurance. Soon enough, it would be them.

In May, Ant set off for the UK festival circuit, and Erica packed up her typewriter, books and clothes, and caught a flight to Paris. Ant had insisted on paying for her to fly, though she drew the line at first class. It was already a pointlessly short flight, and excruciatingly expensive. She imagined what the other passengers thought of her, with her patterned dress and typewriter case—perhaps they thought she was a famous author on her way to book events in the French capital. She let herself live this fantasy on the short flight, pretending to make notes while actually eavesdropping on the couple behind her. Erica hadn't read or spoken French for half a decade, but she was pleased how much she understood of their discussion about Christine's troubled son and his new school. She tested herself with the taxi driver, the woman letting the apartment in the seventeenth, and neither of them scoffed or replied in English. She'd chosen this part of Paris because it was quiet, residential, with good markets and parks nearby. This is what she told herself. But it was also an area that held no connection to Laure. She'd not told her she was here. Nor Michel, or Léa. Erica was here to work, and must stay focused. Must begin.

Now she pulled her typewriter out of its case and set it on the desk. Next to it, she ranged the books she hoped would by osmosis make *Passing Rain* everything she wanted it to be. Then she sat down. The chair was hard, and she stood again almost immediately, went searching for a cushion. She returned with a pillow, settled, and stared out of the window at the bright Paris sunlight. *Passing Rain* by Erica Cowper-Gray . . . no. She would not want to be accused of hanging on to Ant's coattails. *Passing Rain* by Erica Parker. She stared at the blank sheet of paper wound into the typewriter's grip. Then she wrote:

PASSING RAIN

by

E. M. Parker

She smiled at it. Yes. The balance looked good on the paper. She cast around for the first sentence. She'd played a lot the past four months, deciding her characters' names, the plot they would move through. She had her pitch down pat: *Three brothers return to their childhood home to sit beside their father's deathbed. Past loves and old grievances surface as outside, it won't stop raining*. The one thing she'd not decided on was her opening line. Her fingers held poised above the keys, their tips humming with anticipation. She placed them back onto the desk. The sun was warm through the glass. She rummaged in her bag for her sunglasses. A child shouted outside, the unmistakeable bounce of a ball against a door. Erica's stomach rumbled. She stood and slung her bag over her shoulder. She'd fetch supplies, and then she could begin in earnest.

•

The news Erica was back in Paris was like a blow to Laure's sternum. Perhaps it was a mistake, and Agnès had not actually sighted her in the local supermarket, wearing a button-down shirt dress and enormous sunglasses, smelling a tomato. But these details made her certain it was Erica: the large sunglasses, the smelling of fruit, touching it with her bare hands.

"The tourist didn't even wear plastic gloves," sneered Agnès.

"Didn't you speak to her?" Laure asked. She was standing in her office in the Sorbonne's Faculté des Lettres building, overlooking the Square de la Sorbonne. Agnès never called her at work, and when the switchboard put her through Laure had been sure it was about Michel, though Wednesdays were Barbara's days with him. She'd stood to take it, clenched against bad news, but she did not feel uncomplicated relief when Agnès told her the true reason for her call.

"No. I was passing, and . . . I don't know. I wasn't sure until I was further on and looked back, you know? And I didn't know if you'd want me to talk to her."

"Why would I care if you talked to her? We're friends now."

"Oh please, Laure. Did you know she was here? Exactly."

"Friendly, then. Was Ant with her?"

"Her husband? Not that I saw. But the ring was awful. A big clunky rock."

Agnès had firmly taken Michel's dim view of Erica, and run with it long after Michel and Erica patched up their relationship.

"What are you going to do?" said Agnès.

"Nothing. She's not here to see me." Saying it aloud did not make it less painful. If she had reason to go to England, she would have told Erica. There was no reason not to: they'd put aside their past, and she was married now.

"Well, hopefully she'll be gone soon. Have you heard from Barbara today?"

"No."

"Good, us neither. You're going tomorrow?"

"Of course."

"Can you ask if he liked the soup? I can make more for Saturday."

They rang off, and just before Agnès put down the phone Laure heard Marie in the background asking, "What did she say?" She rolled her eyes and sat down in her chair, back to the window. Marie was especially flappy about her since she'd re-emerged into their lives after the Gabrielle debacle two years ago, and even when Michel's illness began to draw the others' focus, Marie remained cautious and deferential to her, watching her as though for signs of erosion. But she did not need to worry. Laure's sobriety had held firm through the aftermath of the break up with Gabrielle, and even her father's death. Her final image of him yellowed as old paper against the pristine hospital sheets only added to her resolve.

Michel was the greatest test. Even before he and Christophe broke up, he became quieter, and began losing weight. The weight loss accelerated after Christophe moved out, but it was not only heartbreak. He was terribly thin now, consumptive almost, and in the last year he'd become prone to fevers and rashes, some so short-lived it was pointless to see a doctor. For the past month he'd been so lethargic he couldn't work, and so they'd developed a rota of care. Barbara was in charge of calling the doctor every week, hassling for more tests, and Laure took Thursdays and Sundays with him, taking him shopping when he had the energy, reading to him or listening to music if not. Christophe had moved on with a man he met at work, but he visited every Monday until recently. Sundays were spent trimming Michel's beard and nails so he'd look his best for his former lover, and still the one great love of his life.

"How do I look?" he'd ask, and Laure would say, "Right nice and pretty." And he'd reply, "Right nice and pretty?" in mock outrage—lines from *Jezebel*, a favourite film of Michel's that Laure found a bit silly. They'd been to see a re-release of it together, not long after they returned from Bois-d'Ennebourg the first time. A trip to the cinema felt impossible now. The lights made Michel's head ache, and they couldn't even turn his records up as loud any more. In the absence of medical answers, Agnès and Marie made increasingly green soups and bought powders and pills from their local health food shop. Michel was good-humoured about it, but Laure could tell he was scared. What would he make of Erica being back in Paris? She eyed her telephone, the stack of papers beside it she was meant to be marking. She picked up the receiver and dialled Michel's number.

"Hello?" He always sounded like he was whispering nowadays. She could hear a record on in the background, something male and croony.

"Hi."

"Hi, little sister." She could hear the smile in his voice, and smiled too. She always felt twitchy on Wednesdays, it being the longest she'd go without seeing him. "Aren't you at work today?"

"Yes, but Agnès doesn't care. She just called me at the office."

Michel groaned. "Oh god, if it's about that awful soup—"

"Ha! No. It's . . ." She hesitated, feeling silly to have disturbed him. "Is Barbara there?"

"She's gone to the laundromat. What's happened?"

"Nothing. Agnès just saw Erica in Prisunic."

"I'm sorry?"

"Yes. On Rue de Batignolles."

"Your Erica?"

"Yes. Not mine, but yes, Erica." *The tourist.* "Did you know she was coming?"

"No. Maybe Léa?"

"Yes."

A pause. "How do you feel?"

"Fine," she said automatically. "You?"

"Laure."

"I don't know. It's a shock, maybe?"

"Mm." Michel coughed away from the receiver.

"That doesn't sound so good."

"Don't. Barbara already called the doctor. It's just a sore throat. Are you going to see her?"

"No. I don't know where she is staying or anything. She's probably here for a romantic break with her husband."

"Ah. The double-barrel. Do you want to talk about it?"

"No," said Laure, though that was why she called. "I'll see you tomorrow."

She put down the receiver and tried to focus on her papers, essays from her second-year students on Art and Morality. Earnest answer after earnest answer. Erica, guileless and open-faced as she listened to them discuss Duras in Barbara's apartment. Her breasts white, pressed against each other in that yellow dress. Seven years, almost to the month, since they met on the Montmartre steps. Laure tapped her fingers on her desk, then pushed her chair out. A walk to clear her head, reset. Ready herself for the similes to come.

That evening Laure ended up bringing most of her work home with her. Nine months ago she'd taken a small, bright bedsit on Rue Bréa, genteel and quiet, only a short walk to work through the Jardin du Luxembourg. Life in this sleepy microclimate had shown her predilection for mess had not only been a condition of her alcoholism. At least she managed to clean the clothes that lived in piles on chairs, and there were no bottles ranged like missiles amidst the books. She'd outgrown her snobbery about posters and prints, so the room was a riot of colour, the rug she and Erica had bought taking up most of the floor, notebooks of lesson plans on every surface. Aside from that and her record player, she'd not brought much from the squat with her. There was not the space, in the bedsit or in her head.

She kicked off her boots and turned on the radio, a habit she'd learned from her time living with Gabrielle, though her choice of station was different. She was less comfortable with silence since becoming sober, and lately spent most of her evenings alone. She'd not slept with anyone since Gabrielle, too busy with work and then her father, and now work and Michel, to put any effort in. She was happy to wait. Gabrielle had been a line in the sand: she would not sleepwalk into another calamity.

She made a cup of ginger tea, opened the window doors to let in the fresh May evening, and sat to mark the papers. The radio was playing hits: Jeanne Mas, Indochine—bland, rootless music of no consequence to her. Finally that Joan Jett cover of "Crimson and Clover" had fallen off rotation on all the popular stations and Erica and that summer had drifted safely away, more and more distant, so safely she'd assumed even further contact would have no impact.

But she felt on edge, knowing Erica was in the same city, shopping at the same supermarket Laure visited with Marie and Agnès. If she was shopping, surely she was staying awhile? She could easily afford restaurants for a shorter stay, her husband being rich. And staying in an apartment, somewhere with a place to cook, to slice those sweet-smelling tomatoes and dress them with oil, basil, garlic. Laure pressed her hands to her face, forgetting she held her pen.

"Shit." She checked her face in the bathroom mirror, a black line across the side of her nose. She licked her finger and rubbed it off, then splashed her face with water from the sink. She sighed, giving in to her nagging impulse, and called Léa.

"Hello?"

"Léa, it's Laure."

"Did Erica call you too?"

Laure took a beat. "No."

"But you know she's in Paris? She just called me, the sneaky bitch."

"Yes. Agnès saw her earlier."

"She's here to write her novel." Léa sounded good-naturedly sceptical. "I thought she'd have warned me, I'm going to Valencia next week. We're going for a drink, want to come? That café on Place Saint-Germain-des-Prés, so you can have your tea."

"Very kind." Laure's heart was racing. "Now?"

"At six. I'm sure she'd love to see you."

"I don't know . . ."

"Oh, come on, Laure, of course she will."

"Is her husband coming too?"

"No, he's on tour somewhere or other."

Erica was in Paris alone. Writing her novel. Laure fought an urge to laugh, though it did not come from somewhere unkind.

"Six, yes?"

"Café des Deux Magots. I know, but once a tourist! Bisous."

It was a bad idea, but all the reasons it was a bad idea were too exposing and incompatible with the progress Laure felt she'd made to acknowledge. She changed her shirt and brushed her hair, deciding she was overthinking whether to wear perfume or not, and spraying it on her wrists and neck. She'd never bothered with scent before getting sober, but now it felt like part of her armour. She'd not think twice about wearing it to meet Léa alone. She checked her watch, her father's. He'd left her this watch, his books, the house. She'd still not got round to listing it. She stroked the worn leather strap—even drawn tight it was loose on her. *OK, Papa, wish me luck.*

Deux Magots had, like many once illustrious literary cafés, traded too hard off its history and become somewhere Parisians avoided, left to the tourist crowd. Laure couldn't remember ever going there, but it was only twenty minutes from her apartment. She walked with her hands thrust into her trouser pockets, fingers worrying at an old receipt. She could pass a day, maybe two, without wanting alcohol, but not a day went by when she didn't crave a cigarette. How much better this walk would feel if she could roll and then smoke one, keeping her hands busy and her nerves steady.

Léa had secured a table outside. She stubbed out her cigarette, waved and rose to kiss Laure on both cheeks, Laure inhaling the smoke on her breath like a crazy person. She needed to calm down.

"Does she know I'm coming?" Laure asked, after they'd ordered their drinks.

"No, she'd have left by the time we spoke. She's in the seventeenth—ah, but you know that." Laure must have paled because Léa squeezed her hand. "Stop worrying! She'll be so glad to see you, she asked after you on the phone."

Laure nodded, forcing herself not to ask for details. She was glad when her tea arrived, and she could focus on pouring the water, adding honey, a sprig of mint. Léa took a long slug of her white wine and then set the glass down heavily on the table, squealing and jumping up.

"There you are!" Laure looked up and saw Erica crossing the road towards them. She was wearing the large sunglasses, a blue and white striped dress. Her skin was pale and her lips very pink. The fabric stretched over her thighs, showing the shape of her hips, her belly. She carried a chain strap leather handbag. She looked put together, expensive. Laure's body felt like slow sand, trickling through the choke point of an hourglass—slipping backwards, beyond her control. She saw Erica see her, noted the slight hesitation in her step, the red tinge sweep across her collarbones before Léa wrapped her in a tight embrace.

They broke apart, and Laure stood up, knocking the table with her thighs and sending ginger-infused hot water across the table. *Shit.* She wiped it with disintegrating paper napkins, the watch face winking at her. *Thanks a lot, Papa.*

•

Erica had imagined this moment a thousand times, yet she still felt entirely unprepared. At first she thought Laure a mirage, the work of her imagination—but no. She was moving out from behind the table, wet napkins in hand, and smiling her small, restrained smile. Erica's heart gave a pathetic leap. They hugged, and Erica felt like she'd forgotten how to hug.

"Ravie," she said on impulse, and Laure's smile became more guarded still. *Fuckssake Erica.* "Hi. This is a lovely surprise."

"See?" Léa elbowed her way between them and regained her seat, motioning to the waiter. "What're you drinking?"

Erica eyed their drinks. Laure was still sober, then. She wondered if she'd mind her drinking wine too, and as though she'd read her mind Laure said, "Go ahead." Her voice was the same. Of course it was, it had not been so long. Seven years since their summer—nothing to a lifetime. Laure's hair was even greyer, cut short to skim her shoulders. It made her neck look longer, her face more angular. When they embraced she'd smelled unfamiliar and exciting: no smoke lingered in her clothes, and her perfume was strong and earthy.

Erica ordered white wine, and Léa amended it to a bottle they could share. It was good to see her too. She was still with the man from Valencia, doing long distance while she waited for a job offer to come through. Her skin was tanned, blonde highlights in her hair from Spanish sun. They both looked good. Getting older suited them. She tugged self-consciously at her dress. It was a tad too tight, not what she'd have chosen for a first re-encounter with an ex-lover.

"How's the apartment?" asked Léa. "Seventeenth, yes? You're near Agnès and Marie's new place."

"Really?" Erica felt Laure looking at her, tried to act like it didn't bother her. "When did they move?"

"Last year. Wanted to be somewhere quieter. Old marrieds, those two. No offence."

Erica looked down at the ring on her finger, a family heirloom from Elizabeth. A large emerald nestled in diamonds on the thick gold band that had to be made larger to fit her finger. It was not to her taste, but she understood marrying Ant meant marrying his family too. Her sense at the wedding was her parents were glad to have handed her over: they left before the first dance.

"The wedding was beautiful," said Léa. "I told Laure all about the dress, the cake."

Laure nodded. "It sounded lovely. Sorry I couldn't be there."

"No, I understand. I'm so sorry about your father."

Laure sat up a little straighter, and Erica could almost sense her effort not to pull away from the topic. "I had some good time with him. It was good, in the end. Between us."

Erica nodded, and the waiter set down a glass and wine cooler on the table, leaving Léa to pour for them both. She held up her glass in a toast.

"To you being back in Paris! And to your book. You'll have to tell us about it."

"Santé," said Laure, and they echoed her, clinking teacup against glasses. Erica hoped that would be the last mention of her book, but Laure went on, "Tell us about the book. What's it called?"

"*Passing Rain*," said Erica, second-guessing the title even as she said it. Oh god. Did it sound too much like pissing rain? She gave them her pitch, and Laure nodded, seeming genuinely interested.

"So it is about the inheritance?"

"Yes, and no. The inheritance beyond money, the house. His approval, I suppose, his legacy. I'm thinking he might be an artist, or a collector, and his sons involved in the art world." Erica took another gulp of wine. It sounded very thin suddenly.

"If you want to talk art, you have a lecturer of the Sorbonne at your disposal," said Léa, faux grand. Laure waved her bow away.

"But of course, if I can help . . ." The offer dangled in the air. Erica's cheeks felt hot. She hoped Laure didn't think the art angle was about her, though everything she knew about art came from either Laure or Donna. Mainly Laure. She remembered standing in front of *Le Radeau de La Méduse* as Laure talked her through the angles, the twin opposing narratives read from dark to light, from hope to despair. The linger of her finger against her wrist. Their embrace after *Les Nymphéas*, Erica feeling the atoms of her body charged, rearranged. She realized she hadn't replied.

"Thank you. How is Michel?" she asked, clumsily moving them on. Laure slumped once more.

"Not good. I'm sure it's a blood disorder, but they've run a hundred tests. He's tired all the time, to his bones."

"Thin too," said Léa. "And did Barbara tell you? He's coughing again."

"Oui," said Laure. "I spoke to him earlier."

"Do you think he'd be up for a visit?" Laure and Léa exchanged a look, and Erica wished she'd not asked.

"I can ask him tomorrow," said Laure. "How long will you be here?"

"A few months. Ant's coming in September, for the Rentrée Littéraire." Erica tried to read any change to her expression at the mention of Ant, but none came.

"That's a long time," said Léa. "I thought you said a few weeks! Magnifique, you'll be here when I'm back from Valencia."

"I'm seeing it as a last chance to be strict with myself, finish the book." *Start the book.*

"Last chance before what?" Léa lit another cigarette.

There was no way Erica was going to mention children in front of Laure. "The rest of life, I suppose."

"And what do you have planned for your time here?" asked Laure.

"Writing, mainly. See some art of course. Eat. Speaking of which, shall we have dinner?" She was starving. She'd not eaten anything since a tomato salad hours ago. She'd felt paralysed by choice at the supermarket, coming back with wine and tomatoes and not much else. Her time at Abbeydore House had coddled her, made her incapable. It was right to have come to Paris, she thought, as the wine made her body heavy and soothed the edges of the nervousness that had sprung up at the sight of Laure. It felt grown up, an adventure. Something a proper writer would do.

They ordered artichokes and a green salad and flétan en papillote. It was not enough to soak up the wine, but by the time they were finished Erica was enjoying the detachment, and her cheeks ached from smiling. She'd forgotten Laure was funny, her humour dry as kindling. All her memories of Laure were intense, mostly sexual or overshadowed by their last, disastrous meeting, but now Erica remembered how much they'd laughed together. They talked about her department at the Sorbonne, overseen by a troutlipped man who only tolerated women on the staff if they were married or gay—"quite liberal, by accident"—and France's switch to proportional representation. Léa seemed determined to goad Laure into an argument about a recent poll suggesting thirty per cent of the National Front's current supporters voted for Mitterrand in 1981, but Laure was sanguine.

"Far left politics doesn't work for modern France," said Léa. "We need to accept we are a centrist country, or Le Pen's going to sweep it."

"We'll see," said Laure. It was not the superiority Erica remembered from seven years ago, but a considered confidence. Though Erica had not come to Paris for Laure, now the possibility of their friendship stretched out before her like a promised land. A friendship formed on conversations about art and films and politics, not babies and husbands. *That's not fair*, she thought. It made Emma and the others sound facile. They weren't, of course they weren't. But Emma did seem to always want to talk about either the past—their university days—or the future. No time or energy for the present.

Four hours into the evening, Léa finished her fifth cigarette and ordered a third bottle of wine.

"Oh, I'm not sure," said Erica. She was drunk, and she'd promised herself 9 a.m. starts during the week.

"I should probably go too," said Laure, checking her watch, a large, brown-strapped thing that served to make her wrist seem impossibly slender. "I have Michel tomorrow."

"He'd be here if he could!" said Léa. "How often do we get the gang back together. One more hour, OK?" She stood. "Need a piss. Don't leave, or I won't forgive you."

Laure gave Erica a sideways look, flaring her nostrils, and Erica snorted with laughter.

"Shall we run?"

"Run? Does Laure Boutin run?"

"Non. But I probably could."

"Ant runs," said Erica. "He says it's the best way to see a city." She felt suddenly a little melancholy. She missed Ant, and it was strange being somewhere that was not Abbeydore House without him.

"Where is he now?"

"Sweden, I think."

"Lovely this time of year."

"You've been?"

"Non."

Erica was drunk enough to look directly at Laure. Without her hands busy with a cigarette, she looked more vulnerable, open.

"You have a mark, there." Instinctively, Erica licked her finger, and rubbed the black smudge on Laure's nose. Laure flinched slightly and looked back at Erica, and Erica felt a charge pass between them, the electricity of a connection not fully burnt out. That Laure was still the sexiest person Erica had ever seen was not in doubt, but Erica hadn't expected to feel the aliveness of her effect on her.

Erica stood up as Léa came back. "I'm sorry," she said, with no thought other than escaping. "I've got to go."

She kissed Léa on both cheeks, and stooped to kiss Laure, her perfume filling her head.

"Petite joueuse!" Léa called after her, but Erica did not look back. She walked so fast she was two streets away before she realized she was going in the wrong direction. Towards Le Marais. She stopped and leant against a shadowy wall. Beside her was a line, people queuing outside a kebab shop hatch.

What the hell was wrong with her? She'd drunk too much, that was all. And it was a shock to see Laure, to remember how much she'd liked her. Loved her. But she was not a child any more, eighteen and dazzled by the world. She was married, happily so, here to write her novel until her successful, handsome husband came to meet her, and take her home, and get her pregnant, and—

Stop. She rubbed her chest. She'd not had an asthma attack in years, but now she felt the warning tickle at the edges of her lungs. As tourists and men in suits passed her, and the smell of frying onions filled her nostrils, Erica breathed until the danger receded. Next time, and she wanted there to be one, Erica would be prepared for Laure's effect on her. She would drink less, and not entertain any inappropriate thoughts. With this decided, she pushed herself upright, and joined the queue for a kebab.

Laure woke late, a rare occurrence of her sober life, but she and Léa had stayed at Café des Deux Magots until the early hours, fighting about Le Pen and worrying about Michel. She stayed because the café was not as tragic as she'd imagined—the food was rather good—and also she didn't want to go back to her bedsit and have time to do anything but fall asleep. No hours or minutes to fill with thoughts of Erica, her cheek plump against her own, her musk, the tickle of her long hair falling across Laure's ear as they kissed goodbye. The way she listened with her head slightly tilted, and truly listened, not affecting the pose of listening while actually thinking about what she wanted to say next. God but Laure had hated this in women she'd slept with—Hilde and Pauline especially—and now spotted it in some of her students. It was not that she wanted an audience, but to be heard was a privilege she no longer took for granted. For all her faults and madness, Gabrielle had heard her. Erica had heard her. Her father had, and Michel did. Precious few.

Her plan hadn't worked. She'd returned to the bedsit restless and unable to sleep. She finished her marking. She read *Villa Triste* again, one of the migrants from her father's collection. She put on the radio. Finally, she gave in and touched herself, thinking of Erica, and at last, as the sun started to rise, fell asleep.

But now she was late for Michel. Cursing, she dressed, calling Michel and hooking the receiver under her chin to speak as she did up her jeans.

"I'm so sorry, I'll be there by midday."

"Don't worry, little sister." His voice was hoarser even than usual. "I've only been sleeping anyway."

"You need anything? Fruit, bread?"

"Pack of Gauloises and a bottle of gin."

Laure smiled, sitting to slip on her boots. Between Barbara, Marie and Agnès, it had been decided Michel would be placed on a strict high-calorie, high-nutrition diet, and stop smoking and drinking. Two things that, in his words, made life worth living. "You and me both. Kisses."

She threw some magazines with articles she thought Michel would like into her bag, and hurried from her apartment. Michel was only an hour's walk away, and the metro was hell in summer, but since she was late she descended into the crush of Vavin and took the train to Montrouge. She passed the solemn graves of Cimetière de Bagneux to Rue Racine, stopping to buy a newspaper and a bunch of lily of the valley from the shop below his block, reduced and wilting but still fragrant.

She arrived sweating, a stitch in her side, letting herself in to the sound of Julie London and brandishing the flowers before her as an offering.

"Sorry, sorry," she said. "It's Léa's fault . . ."

She was brought up short. Michel was sitting in his usual spot on the sofa within reach of the record player, but he looked the worst she'd ever seen him. His skin was grey, a cold sore at the side of his mouth, his beard scrubby. He smiled wanly.

"Hi, little sister." He gestured at the record player, and Laure turned it down a bit, came to sit beside him.

"Don't look so dismayed. Am I that hideous?"

"Not hideous at all. You just look tired."

"Says you. Where were you? With a woman?"

"No. Well, Léa and I went for drinks. And . . . Erica was there."

"Ah." Michel smiled wickedly, and she allowed it because he looked himself, his old self, a moment. "Don't tell me."

"No! Fuck, Michel, she's married. And we're friends now."

"Mm." He coughed, covering his mouth with the crook of his elbow. Laure fetched him some tissues from the table, a cardboard box covered with a knitted doily. The doilies covered spare loo rolls, sat under vases, were everywhere in the apartment—each one made and sent by his mother, who couldn't visit as much as she'd like because of his father. Love notes in delicate crochet.

Michel nodded his thanks and clutched a fistful to his lips. Laure turned to hide her wince as she heard a painful rasp from somewhere deep in his chest, and went to the kitchen to fetch him a glass of water. Everything was neat and clean as it always was on Thursdays. Barbara had rearranged her entire teaching schedule to come at least twice a week, and she worked endlessly when she was here. She'd risen to the occasion of Michel's illness with a devotion unmatched by their closeness, and Laure felt another twinge of guilt that she was so late.

She carried the water back to Michel, who'd mastered his fit. He drank messily, water running down his chin, and the awful thought came to her that he'd been unable to fetch himself anything all morning, had been marooned on the sofa, perhaps since last night.

Wordlessly, she took his empty glass and refilled it, bringing through a jug left to dry on the draining board. Barbara or Marie would add mint, lemon, and so Laure brought a slice of lemon too, and dropped it into the jug. Michel raised his eyebrow.

"I could get used to this."

"Am I so useless usually?" said Laure, a little less lightly than she'd intended.

"Absolutely. But I don't look forward to seeing you for your domestic abilities. Come," he pulled her in to him, and she didn't resist. "Tell me about the tourist."

"Not much to tell. She's here to write her novel."

"Ah. How did she look?"

"Gorgeous."

"Oh no, do we have to have another talk?"

"Of course not," scoffed Laure. "She's married."

"To a man."

Laure nudged him. "You're impossible."

"But honestly, did you not feel anything?"

Laure hesitated a moment too long.

"Don't worry," said Michel. "I'm not going to lecture you. Lord knows I'd be one to talk."

Laure wrapped her arm around him, feeling his ribs. She'd hated Christophe for leaving him. It was the closest she'd come to understanding Michel's vitriol towards Erica.

"Will you see her again?"

"Maybe. She wanted to see you, actually."

"That would be nice. But not today, today is our day. Can you change the record? I couldn't fetch the Raffaella Carrà."

Laure stood and switched the vinyl. Disco beats filled the room and Michel reached up to her. She helped him to his feet. He felt lighter than last time they'd completed this motion, and he sighed with a small and uncommunicable pain. Laure bit her tongue. That was not her role either, to flap. Michel took his own weight and Laure walked him to the bathroom. It was a blessing it was so small, a wet room really, and Laure helped Michel to strip down to his underwear and left him seated on the closed toilet lid, the shower beating down on him. He used to grouse about this intrusion on his privacy, but lately it had become a necessity; sometimes he came over faint in the shower. Laure hovered near the door, her eyes sliding over the room. She felt there was something absent in her that other adults seemed to possess: to notice what needed doing. To her, the room seemed neat and orderly, but no doubt Barbara would spot its needs, anticipate what might come up later. She tried to look with Barbara's eyes, and took up the lily of the valley, cut the twine with scissors and propped them in a glass of water.

She sat on the sofa beside the blaring record player. God but she hated Raffaella Carrà. She stood again and opened the window. Another spring gone. Another summer in Paris. As Laure looked down into the narrow, shadowed street, she felt a wave of claustrophobia. She'd been considering leaving at the end of term, going to her father's house. But now Erica was here—and, she mentally chided herself, so was Michel.

The sound of the shower stopped, and Laure went through to the bedroom to fetch the clean towel she knew would be waiting on top of his chest of drawers. There was an unfamiliar smell: lavender layered over stale sweat, and she saw a half-burnt candle set on the bedside table beside a copy of *La Tempête*. She opened it and found the bookmark where she'd put it the Sunday before.

"I don't like anyone's reading voice but yours," said Michel. She jumped and turned. He was standing stooped in the doorway, the hand towel around his waist. It hid what needed to be hidden, but it was awful to see him naked, his bones jutting like a shipwreck from papery skin. "Agnès tries too hard and Barbara doesn't try at all."

She rushed forward with the towel and guided him to the bed. There, he directed her which underwear, shirt and trousers to fetch him, and she laid them out on the bed beside him before returning to the bathroom to collect his sodden underwear and wring it out, place it in the empty laundry basket, and use the mop to send the worst of the water down the unwilling drain. The record clunked and scratched, and in the silence she heard Michel coughing again. He stopped suddenly, and she hurried to turn the vinyl to give him privacy. As soon as "Mi sento bella" started up, Michel's coughs came again through the flimsy door.

Eventually it opened, and Michel walked in carefully, slumping once more on the sofa.

"Sorry," he said. "Today is a bad day, I think."

"No matter," said Laure. "I'll cancel the helicopter to Lac d'Annecy."

"And the reservations at Auberge du Père Bise? A shame."

"Next time." She held up the newspaper and he wrinkled his nose.

"Anything cheerful?"

Laure bent to pick out the magazines she'd kept for him. "Maybe you'd like to hear about Grace Depard's new hairstyle?"

"Absolutely."

Laure read to him for the better part of an hour, before making a cold bean salad topped with some of the powder Agnès said should be sprinkled on all his meals. They ate and then while Laure tidied up, Michel made his daily call to the café, checking all was well. She listened to him with his business voice on, and reflected that this was the closest she would get to being a wife, cleaning up after a man while he discussed funding shortfall and threatening letters. The letters had become common occurrences at the café. With the surge of the National Front people were becoming emboldened, scratching slurs into the windows and once posting an envelope of powder through the front door. It turned out to be talcum but caused a panic. Michel hated being away, but recently he was lucky to make it in once a week, and hadn't been at all in the last month.

She brought him a glass of water as he hung up and sighed.

"All OK?"

"The same. The rent keeps going up. I think they're trying to evict us. I'll get Marie to look into it."

"I could . . ."

"No offence, little sister, but I'll back the barrister over the art theorist."

"Your loss." Laure handed him the glass and sat back down beside him.

"How is work?"

"Good. They want to offer me more classes."

"Wonderful."

"Mm."

"No? What's up?"

Laure really did not want to talk about it.

"Is it Erica?"

"No. You've mentioned her more than me."

"Because I want the gossip! What was she like? When we used to talk on the phone she seemed quieter than during her time in Paris."

"She was probably scared of you."

"As she should be."

Laure thought. "Not quieter. More considered maybe. Her book sounds good."

This was true, but it had also sounded very un-Erica. Contained and posed, without passion. Laure would have imagined Erica writing an intense love story, or something Gothic, not a mannered family encounter. But maybe her tastes had changed. Maybe she had changed. Laure made a point of not reading Erica's husband's work, but from reviews knew it was very of the moment, biting and dark. Perhaps he'd influenced her in a different direction.

"Well, good for her. Where is she staying?"

"The seventeenth, not far from Marie and Agnès'."

"I'm sure Agnès loves that."

"I don't know why they never made up. She didn't do anything to her."

"No. She did it to you, which was much worse."

Laure looked at her friend. In his hollow face, his eyes were keen as ever. "How are you with everything?"

"Everything" meant drinking. "Fine. It's smoking I miss."

"Oh, I hear you." They both sighed, fists clenching around invisible cigarettes. "You know I worry."

"You shouldn't."

"I don't think anyone who saw you running towards them with bleeding feet wouldn't."

"That was years ago."

"Still—"

"Please. Let's not talk about Gabrielle." Even saying her name made Michel's face close. It was only at a distance Laure could see how close she'd come to losing everyone she cared about, to sacrificing herself on the altar of Gabrielle's fanaticism. But she did not want to go over it again.

"Music?" she asked.

"Television." But they were only five minutes into *Pierrot le Fou* when Michel said, "I think I would like to see her."

"Who?" said Laure, alarmed, the pall of Gabrielle's name still sitting on her.

"Erica. If that's OK with you."

"Oh." Laure collected herself. "Of course."

"I don't like how it was when I last saw her. And we've only spoken on the phone since."

"You don't need to explain. I can find her number for you."

"Thank you. Maybe we could see her on Sunday, if that's all right?"

"Of course," said Laure. She felt a small thrill that she would have a reason to call Erica, to see her again, for an innocent and unselfish reason.

They passed the rest of the afternoon in front of the television, old films showing on a loop, Michel dozing or passing comment on the luminosity of the lead actress's skin, the round ass of the actor. And though

Laure fetched water and snacks, helped him to the toilet and sat still as he slept with his head on her shoulder, in her mind she was already picking up the phone, already speaking to Erica, already watching her walk across the road towards her once more.

•

Work was going badly. Erica woke late with a headache and the smell of onions on her breath. It was past nine, and with a childish impulse she felt already that the day was ruined, that she wanted to throw the covers over her head and sleep the rest of it away. But then she thought of Ant, and she imagined telling him she was three days into her writing retreat in Paris without a single word to show for it. She brushed her teeth, brewed strong, sludgy coffee in the stovetop cafetière, and took a cup to the desk.

The light that had struck in all yesterday afternoon was now glossing the rooftops on the opposite side of the street. Erica looked at the title page she'd typed yesterday and hated her past self for not giving her something to start with. *Something is better than nothing*, that was Ant's mantra, and she repeated it to herself as she placed a fresh sheet of paper into the paper table. She thought of the black smudge on Laure's nose, her skin, slightly dry, under her fingertip.

That night, Ant called from his hotel room in Stockholm, and pulled Erica from a dinner scene she'd rewritten three times and still hated.

"Hello darling, how's Paris?"

Erica felt an unreasonable flicker of irritation. She was not in the mood for open-ended questions, for a chat. She was busy. But how many times had he been busy, and still made time for her? She gritted her teeth.

"Beautiful, of course. How's Stockholm?"

"Really lovely actually. The bridges are beautiful, and the food isn't as fermented as I'd assumed it would be. Lots of parks. Everyone's been very enthusiastic about the book."

"Of course," said Erica, a little briskly. He always seemed surprised that people fawned over him, over the books. Surely after three years it was old news?

"How's it been? Did you catch up with any friends?"

For a beat, Erica considered not telling him, but why? It was not a deceit: she hadn't known Laure would be there. And they were friends. Ant seemed not to take her romances with women entirely seriously, and if this bothered her she'd learned not to labour the point. "Léa," she said. "And Laure, last night. We went to Café des Deux Magots."

"Oh, I wanted to take you there! Writing the next *Les Mandarins*, are you?"

"Hope so." With a slightly uneasy sense of getting away with something, she diverted him. "What are you up to now?"

"Just been for a run," he said, and she heard a yawn in his voice. "Changing for this dinner at the National Opera House." She imagined him in his towel, wet from the shower, and felt a stirring of want.

"How's your book coming?"

"Well," said Erica, glancing at the desk, its small stack of papers. They looked pathetic suddenly, bald and fragile as a baby bird fallen from its nest. She wanted it to be done already, to see it encased in the protective validation of hardcovers, a spine. She wanted Ant to stop distracting her.

"Really? Great! What's happening—"

"I don't . . . I can't talk about it yet. I'm just in the middle of a scene."

"Amazing." Ant sounded so genuinely excited for her, she softened. "I'm desperate to hear more, but I'll let you go."

"I love you."

"I love you. I miss you, so much."

"Same. Enjoy dinner."

She put down the phone and returned to her desk, already a few lines ahead in her mind, and began typing to catch up. When the phone rang again ten minutes later, she answered it bad-temperedly.

"Ant, I'm trying to write—"

"It's Laure," said Laure, her voice apologetic. "Sorry, is now a bad time?"

"No," said Erica, and then less eagerly, "No. Sorry, I thought you were Ant. My husband."

"I got the number from Léa, I hope that's OK."

"Of course." Erica sat down in the hard little wooden chair beside the receiver.

"I was with Michel today, and he'd love to see you. He thought Sunday would work, if that suits you?"

"Yes," said Erica, wrapping the cord around her fingertip. "Oh, I'm glad. How was he."

"He's . . . you'll see. He's ill. Today wasn't so good. But he has better days."

"Should I bring him anything? What's his address?"

"He's on the Rue Racine in Montrouge. Ten o'clock?"

Erica's fingertip was turning white, she could feel her heartbeat pulsing in it. "Oh, yes. Lovely."

"It's easier if I'm there," said Laure.

"Yes," said Erica, realizing Laure thought she wasn't happy about her coming, and that it was maybe best if she wasn't corrected. "It'll be good to see him. And you. To see you both. Shall I bring . . ." she couldn't say wine, "some fruit?"

There was a smile in Laure's voice when she answered. "Fruit would be nice. He likes cherries."

"Great. OK. Bisous."

Did she imagine Laure's hesitation, the unnecessary weighting of the word as she replied, "Bisous," before she hung up?

Erica untangled her throbbing finger from the cord and replaced the receiver on its cradle. She felt faintly giddy, though maybe she was just hungry again. She glanced at the clock. Eight. She'd earned a dinner at the café on the corner. And then she could buy a bottle of wine, and keep writing until she got too tired. Her time here was her own, after all.

Sunday was blustery and bright. Erica wrote for an hour before showering and dressing with care, the same dress she'd worn to drinks with Léa and Laure, so Laure would know she'd not thought hard about it. She tied her hair back to save it from the wind, slung a net shopping bag over her shoulder, and left the apartment. Indecision once again seized her in the supermarket, even though she knew she was there for cherries. She kept picking up and putting down punnets, wondering whether to choose the vibrant red or the glossy purple, before the shop assistant gestured angrily at a dispenser of plastic gloves she'd never noticed before. She hastily put them on, picked up a punnet of each and some strawberries for good measure, a glass bottle of lemonade, paid and set off for the metro station.

Erica let her mind drift as the dark tunnels and bright stations rushed past. She thought of the brothers, now locked in an argument over their father's burial plot—he was still alive at this point—of Ant, who called every evening after his run, and of Laure, Michel. She'd not mentioned she was meeting them today. It hadn't come up, and he'd been unbothered by the fact she'd gone for a drink with Léa and Laure. He trusted her, and he was right to.

She changed at Châtelet, enjoying even the warren of the intersection. It was beautiful to be back in Paris. Maybe she could have felt so happy in Abbeydore House, if only the writing had gone as well there. But this city felt to her like it existed apart from anywhere else on earth. Only here did the life she dreamt of as a student seem possible. She needed to find a way to hold on to this sensation, when Ant arrived and the time came to leave. But she did not want to think about all that.

She emerged onto a street busy with buses, a high stone wall across the road, treetops visible over its expanse. Laure was not here yet, and so Erica shifted her shopping bag onto her other shoulder and crossed the road to the high wall, trying to find the name or entrance to the park. She walked back and forth along it, keeping the metro exit in view, but could find no break in the wall. Maybe it was a private garden, though she didn't think such large ones existed in Paris.

She waited to cross the road back to the metro, when between the passing of one bus and then another, she saw Laure turn a corner to stand beside the stairs. She had not yet spotted Erica, and Erica observed her, unseen. Her shirt, which although Laure wore sunglasses, Erica knew was the perfect shade to make her eyes bluer. Her thin leather belt, the trousers worn low on her hips. Her boots, which always made her look more substantial, grounded, than if she wore the ballet flats other woman as slim as her could get away with. Maybe she would be less intimidating in ballet flats. Erica sometimes listened to her friends talk about other women wearing things they wished they could get away with, and wondered if in fact their jealousy was desire. She certainly understood, looking at Laure, how the two could run close together, like electric wires sharing casing.

It was strange to watch her stand on the corner beneath the metro sign, no cigarette or tobacco tin in her hand, her head not downturned but raised to the sky. Erica longed to know what she was thinking. And then, as the traffic cleared and Erica began to cross, Laure saw her and her face, which Erica had not realized was hard and set, opened as clouds do.

"Hi," Laure said. "You didn't walk?"

"No, I just got here a little early. I was trying to get into this park."

"A cemetery," Laure explained. "The entrance is north." She gestured ahead of them. "Shall we go?"

Erica fell into step beside her. How often had they walked like this through Paris?

Laure nodded down at the shopping bag.

"You bought cherries."

"And strawberries."

They walked on in silence, until they reached Rue Racine. Laure slowed her step a bit and said, "You understand he is ill. I know you know, but it is another thing to see it."

Erica nodded, but still when Michel buzzed them up and Laure opened the door with her key, Erica had not been prepared to see him sitting on a low, plump sofa that seemed to swallow him up. Michel had been exceptionally beautiful, and now he was not. His face was cadaverous, and there was a cold sore beside his mouth, cracked and raw-looking. He did not stand up to greet them and as Erica bent to kiss his cheeks she realized he couldn't. He took her hands in his cool, thin ones and pulled her down beside him. He smelled of expensive perfume.

"Erica! You make corpses of us all. Have you aged at all? And that dress!"

"Bof," she said, embarrassed and thinking of something to compliment him on, but he saved her.

"Oh please, don't be Marie about it, and tell me I look good. I know I'm a fright. Dorian Gray's portrait, eh, Laure?"

"You're hideous," agreed Laure, stooping to kiss him. "But we love you anyway."

"I brought cherries," said Erica, pulling the bag onto her lap to show him. He exclaimed and thanked her, and Laure took the fruit to wash while he stayed holding her hand and looking into her eyes. His skin had a thin, crêpey quality that reminded her of an old person's, her grandmother who she remembered only on her deathbed. Erica felt a sudden and useless urge to cry.

"It's a lovely place," she said, glancing around. The apartment was full of books of course, and a movie poster for *La Cage aux Folles* was hung in a gilt frame on one wall, a large abstract painting in bruise-blues and purples on another.

"Just as well. A gilded prison! Laure must have told you I rarely get out the last few months. But they are angels about it, coming to keep me company every day, and Barbara is on the case—no doubt soon she will have harassed the doctors into finding out what is wrong with me."

"They have no idea?"

"They know what it isn't—no cancer, no fundamental deficiency." Michel shrugged as Laure came back in with the bowl of cherries and set them within reach. Wordlessly, showing it was habit to them both, Laure helped Michel to his feet and took him across the room, opened the door to a small bathroom and closed it behind him. Erica smiled sadly at Laure, but Laure refused to receive it, and instead frowned at the floor.

"I didn't know he—"

"It's not so bad," snapped Laure, though surely she knew it was. Erica swallowed, nodding, wanting to please her.

"I hope the cherries are good," she said. Laure said nothing. "You come every day?"

"No, Thursday and Sunday. Then Barbara twice, and Léa once, Agnès and Marie. Sometimes Christophe visits."

"It's nice they're still friends."

Laure nodded tightly, and Erica felt the familiar sensation of wondering how she'd said the wrong thing. The doorknob rattled and Michel came out, lightly leaning on Laure.

"Today is a good day," he said. "Laure did not have to wipe my shit."

Laure punched the air in mock triumph. Erica gave a shocked laugh.

"Such a good day," Michel went on, "I thought later we could go down to the café, and Erica could see what we have done there."

"Are you sure?" asked Laure.

"Certainly. But let's talk here for a while." He came unaided across the room, as though to prove how well he felt, and sat beside her once more. "Erica, tell me about your book!"

"There's not much to tell."

"You are writing it?"

"Yes."

"Well, that's better than many people do. People love to talk about writing but they never have time. Let me tell you, we all have time. It's desire only. And you are meeting that desire. I'm proud of you."

"Thank you."

"You still blush! How cute!" Michel tweaked her nose and she pushed him away, laughing with relief as much as anything. Here he was, still. She told him a little about the book—the title, the brothers ("Are they sexy?"), the father, the art.

"So you are picking Laure's brains?"

"Not yet," said Erica, glancing at where Laure had taken a seat in the only other place to sit in the room, the small dining table. "But I hope I might."

"Of course," said Laure. "So the youngest is a collector?"

"Gallerist. Their father is the collector."

"*The Collector* would be a good title," said Michel.

"That's a John Fowles book," said Erica. Did that mean he didn't like *Passing Rain*? Did she?

"The portrait, of their mother," said Laure. "The one that hangs over the fireplace. What style is it?"

"I was going to ask you," said Erica, inwardly thrilling at Laure talking about this detail as though it was real, alive for her. "You know the Picasso self-portrait, the one with blue? Like that. Naturalistic but mannered, a bit . . ."

"Expressionist?" Laure thought a moment. "It is on display at the Picasso Museum. We'll go and look at it."

"Perfect!" said Michel, and then in response to Laure's alarmed expression. "Not me, I know. I won't intrude on your date."

Erica snorted and pushed Michel gently, but Laure was quiet, her face closed as it had been before Erica walked across the road towards her.

"So how far through are you?" asked Michel.

"Barely anything. It'll be a novella, but still."

"You'll get there," said Michel bracingly. "I'm excited to read it. I keep telling Laure she should write a book, about art you know? The way she explains things is so clever and clear. I miss going to see art with her."

"I like your painting," she said, gesturing at the bruisey canvas on the wall.

Michel and Laure exchanged a look and Michel grinned. "I like it too. I bought it at a degree show, an artist called Frank Gregory. Laure hates it."

"It is unaccomplished," corrected Laure, "but I don't hate it. I feel nothing for it."

"Even worse," said Michel.

"Michel was infatuated with the artist," Laure explained. "He bought the painting so Gregory might think he was rich and sleep with him."

"It didn't work?" asked Erica.

"It worked too well," said Michel. "He made me pay for everything!"

They passed a few hours talking about Michel's early years in Paris, his brief time as a photographer's assistant and then a photographer's lover, the sponsorship of the café's first few months by another lover's wife, his work as an usher in the Opéra Garnier—phases of life that seemed fundamental to who he was but which they'd never discussed before. When Erica reflected on her own life, there seemed four clear stages: childhood, Laure, university and Ant. She glanced occasionally at Laure, who was listening delightedly to her friend, and wondered if she would feature so prominently for her.

At about one o'clock, Laure made a salad. They ate at the small table, Michel insisting on cloth napkins, "the good cutlery," which as far as Erica could tell just meant the forks with unbent tines.

"You're royalty now," said Michel.

"Is that what Léa said?"

"Absolument! The wedding sounded a spectacle."

"Is that a bad thing? In French it conjures guillotines."

"Oh, but we are all suckers for beauty. I'm sure you were a beautiful bride. And your groom." Michel fanned himself. "I have *Gargantuan* and I don't mind telling you the author photo would have decided me buying it even if he wasn't your husband."

Erica flushed. She didn't want to discuss Ant's good looks in front of Laure. But Michel gave her little choice.

"What's it like being married to Howard Keel?"

"Who?"

"Who!" Michel held his hand to his heart, mock wounded. "Gorgeous film star. *Oklahoma!*, *Calamity Jane!*"

"Oh."

"You have good taste," said Michel. Was he deliberately goading Laure, or was Erica only reading into things too much? "And rich is a bonus."

"It certainly makes life easier. That's partly why I am in Paris, to be a bit more independent. We were living at his parents' house, and it's very . . ." She searched for the word. "Comfortable."

"So you are playing at being poor?"

"No!" Though Michel's tone was unaccusatory, Erica felt defensive. "Just concentrating on what matters."

"Good," said Michel. His hand slipped on his glass and water spilt over the tablecloth. Laure covered the water with a napkin and looked pointedly at Michel.

"I'm fine," he said in French, "don't fuss."

"I didn't say anything," said Laure. "But maybe you could lie down."

Michel nodded, and said in English, "Nurse says I should rest. But in a bit, we can go to the café, OK? Don't go anywhere."

He refused Laure's help and crossed to his bedroom, closing the door behind him. Laure began clearing up, and Erica rose to help her. In the galley kitchen, Laure washed while Erica dried, as they used to after eating at Marie and Agnès'. It was easy to be quiet together during this task, but when everything was put away and they returned to the sitting room, Erica felt awkwardness settle between them, and cast around for something to say.

"Do you think you will write a book?" she asked. Laure looked slightly startled by the question.

"No," she said outright. "I don't have anything to say, really."

"I doubt that," said Erica, and this too made her feel defensive. Laure surely knew she was the cleverer of the two of them. If she felt she had nothing to say, what must she think of Erica's attempts? "But it's not only what you say, but how you say it. Michel is right, you have such a good way of making hard things seem simple." Laure raised her eyebrows. "Seriously. I've never met anyone who explains art the way you do."

Laure reached forward to the bowl of cherries, offered them to Erica, and put one in her mouth. Erica tried not to follow the cherry's progress from bowl to Laure's lips, her crooked teeth biting it from the stem, the muscle in her jaw as she chewed, the glimpse of her tongue as she pushed the stone out from between her teeth and placed it neatly next to Michel's on the table.

"Is this what you do when you come?" Erica asked. "Cook for him, tidy?"

"Usually we talk," she said. "But he's tired today. I don't think we will get to go to the café."

"That's fine," said Erica. And then, on a whim, "Maybe we could go to the Picasso Museum today?"

She'd made another mistake. It was barely perceptible, but she knew Laure's face, and caught the wrinkle of her nose.

"I stay with Michel on Sundays."

"Of course! I wasn't suggesting you leave him. Never mind, I'm sorry."

"Don't apologize." Laure took another cherry. "I didn't sleep well last night. It was so humid."

"Goodness yes," said Erica, thinking of her air conditioning and Michel's comment about playing at being poor. And then of Laure, sleeping naked as she always used to, the sheets thrown off.

"How is your apartment?" asked Laure.

"Fine. It has everything I need."

"And the writing is going well, as you say?"

"Yes. The first days weren't good, but now I feel in the flow."

"What else are you doing? Back in England, I mean."

Erica checked Laure's face but there was no barb there. Still, how to admit she did precisely nothing? The old desire to impress Laure remained, and she said the first thing that came to mind.

"I work in a library."

"Cool."

"How is your work going? I know we discussed it with Léa but . . ."

"I love it," said Laure simply. "I didn't expect to, but I do. I am finding it hard to be in Paris, though. I don't know. It feels . . . tight. Small. Maybe because I spent so much time in Bois-d'Ennebourg recently. My father's house."

"What's happening with the house?"

"I'm not sure yet. Maybe I'll sell it. Maybe I will live in it." Laure looked at her, fast and almost shyly. "I've not said that to anyone else."

"I won't say."

Laure nodded, glancing towards Michel's closed bedroom door. "And I couldn't with Michel so ill. But when he is better, and if I can consolidate my classes, maybe . . ."

She was putting these scenarios to herself for the first time, Erica could see, and Erica felt glad Laure could voice them to her, wanted to say something insightful.

"Sounds good." Ugh. She ate another cherry to avoid saying something else vapid.

"Maybe," said Laure again.

"Are you seeing anyone?" Erica meant it to sound like a follow-up question, but instead it seemed abrupt, out of place. Laure pursed her lips and shook her head.

"I know Léa said about my ex—"

"Gabrielle?"

Laure visibly flinched, and Erica wished she could snatch the name back out of the air.

"Yes. Well, after that I am in no rush."

"Of course." No rush. What a phrase. When had Erica last felt like she was in no rush? Stagnant, yes, but always self-chastising, urgent to reach the next stage as quickly as possible. And here was Laure, the elder of them, single with no possibility of marriage or children, and seemingly unconcerned about any of it. She absently rubbed the undersides of the rings on her left hand. "I didn't expect . . ." She too glanced at the door behind which Michel slept. "I know you warned me, but . . ."

"Yes. Even now, every time. He can't keep weight on. Barbara and Marie have him eating like an athlete, extra vitamins in everything. They have been wonderful to him."

"What's Barbara up to?"

Laure talked her through Barbara's lectureship, Agnès and Marie's new apartment, Claude's life as a functional alcoholic working in finance. They did not run out of things to talk about, and after another hour Laure checked her oversized watch and said, "I'm just going to check on him."

She rose and knocked softly on the bedroom door, going across the shadowed threshold and shutting the door behind her. Erica stood restlessly and scanned the bookshelves, her eyes snagging on a copy of Edwin Morgan's *The Second Life*. With a jolt, she realized it was her copy, the one she and Michel had swapped. Erica slid it carefully out and flipped through the pages, coming to a stop at "Strawberries"—

There were never strawberries / like the ones we had

And she was in the squat on Rue Charlot, feeding Laure strawberries from between her teeth, the strawberry cake of their last night together with their crossed forks on the table, Laure's nipples pink as the icing.

"He's still wanting to sleep."

Erica turned dazedly to see a fully clothed Laure, stepping from the bedroom.

"Should I go?" asked Erica. "I understand if—"

"He said we both can," said Laure, who sounded uncertain. "Usually I'd insist I stay but his mother arrives tonight. She comes when she can." Laure checked her watch again. "We will arrive at the Picasso Museum too late I think. Sunday hours. But we could walk a bit, if you like?"

Erica found there was nothing she wanted to do more in that moment.

•

Unconsciously, Laure took them her usual route home, bypassing the uninspiring Avenue Henri Ginoux and taking them through Cimetière Montrouge, past the unauthorized entrance to the catacombs where they'd once spent hours kissing. She was worried for Michel, and a little annoyed at him too, for his silly comments about dates and just then, as he'd told her to leave him in peace, saying, "I know you'd like time with the tourist, anyway." Why had he said it like that? Hadn't she made it clear she was fine being friends with Erica, seeing her and being in her company? He didn't need to be so insinuating. But then, the mentions of Ant had made Laure feel a bit unsteady, as though she was looking down from a high building. And the strawberries, still in their paper at Michel's. Laure had not eaten a strawberry since their final night of lovemaking: a pathetic truth that she kept to herself.

Pathetic, too, that when Erica's hand occasionally and accidentally skimmed hers, the urge to hold it was near-overwhelming. Two months, they'd shared a bed and a life, and all these years later the need to touch her burned as fiercely as ever. She felt the desire brush closer as they wound towards the Latin Quarter. Laure had masturbated twice last night, thinking of Erica's breasts, the soft part beneath her earlobes, her hair in her face.

"What are you thinking?" said Erica, and Laure startled, before realizing they'd come to a halt at Vavin, and were at the turn off to her street. For a wild moment, she thought of asking Erica to come up.

"We can keep walking. I mean, unless you'd like to go home?" She gestured at the metro. "I'm sure you miss your book."

Erica smiled. "It can wait a bit longer. What's new in Paris? The galleries?"

Grateful for a subject she could talk almost automatically about, Laure told her about the Musée d'Orsay, set to open the following year, the Pompidou's acquisition of some Kandinsky studies, the development of the Louvre. This took them past her area, out of danger, and brought them to the Pont Neuf. They were near Châtelet, so Erica could take the metro directly home. Would she realize, and peel away? They leaned against the railing between bouquinistes as they'd used to, and looked down into the glittering, stinking Seine.

"And L'Orangerie," said Erica, after a long silence. "That has re-opened too?"

It was as though she'd said, *kiss me*. An immediate line back to their past. She was surely inviting reminiscences, but when Laure looked at her Erica was still staring out over the river.

"Yes. The new layout is lovely. You should go."

"Maybe we could go together?"

This was too much. She was torturing her, surely she knew it. Yet when Erica looked at her, her gaze was unsure, but innocent. So it was not an invitation to what Laure hoped it might be. An invitation to an impossible want.

"Maybe you need a tour guide," joked Laure, but her voice was too sharp, as though she had slapped away Erica's offered hand.

"Of course, you are busy!" Erica said, a crease appearing between her eyebrows. Or maybe she wasn't hurt. Laure could no longer read her as she had been able to. The Erica she'd known was now another's domain. She thought of it as territory, and felt a childish urge to possess it as she once had.

Laure took a breath. "No, of course we can go. Term finishes next week, and after that I could stay awhile before I go to Bois-d'Ennebourg."

She'd said it as a test—of herself, and Erica.

"You're going to your father's?" Erica didn't hide her disappointment, and Laure felt relief, sour-sweet as sherbet.

"Thinking about it. But we can go to the museum, of course."

"Good. Week after next?"

"Exactly. Thursdays are good, before the tourists arrive."

"Oh, there's no escaping us." Erica smiled, and held out her hand. "Deal."

Of course, Laure realized the following Thursday that she'd organized their museum trip on a Michel day. She wanted to talk to him about it, but his mother was there, and her busy, slightly nervous energy filled the small flat and made proper conversation impossible. Laure left exhausted after prolonged questioning—about her work, her love life, what she thought was wrong with Michel—and didn't mention her plans to Michel until the following Sunday, when he sent his mother to the market.

"Honestly, if jail was not so dirty I wouldn't mind murdering her," said Michel, massaging his temples.

"She means well."

"She will not stop talking! And she wants me to call Christophe, like he would ever come back to me."

"She worries, that's all."

"I tell her not to. I have you all."

"Maybe that is why she is so worried."

"Ha!"

"But I meant to ask, do you mind if on Thursday Barbara comes instead? And I will come on Wednesday?"

"Fine by me," said Michel. "A class? But I thought term finished this week."

"Yes." Laure dithered a moment. "Erica and I are going to some museums."

"Ah." Michel looked at her, and Laure forced herself not to look away. "What did Barbara think of that?"

"It's none of Barbara's business."

"So you didn't tell her you are seeing the tourist?"

"I'm not seeing her."

"You quite literally are."

"Like you said, she needs help with some of the art theory in her book, and I haven't been to the rehang at L'Orangerie yet," and because he was still staring at her she said impatiently, "And anyway it's no big deal to go to a museum with a friend."

And yet she found herself phrasing it like a question, her intonation rising as she trailed off. Michel pulled her in to his side.

"Careful, little sister." He forestalled her protest. "Look both ways before crossing the road."

Michel's phrase echoed in Laure's mind as she and Erica crossed the Jardin des Tuileries from Rue de Rivoli the following Thursday. It was another sweltering day in a sweltering week, the grass dry, and Erica was wearing a sleeveless linen dress that showed the lightly tanned expanse of her décolletage and arms to such effect Laure felt a bit dizzy. She'd woken knowing this whole day was a bad idea, that tomorrow she would wake up emotionally hungover, but whatever pain was to come felt worth it when she saw Erica in this blue dress, her black bra straps misaligned and showing, her hair slightly wet from her morning shower. Laure had thought carefully about what to wear too, and chosen narrow jeans and a white tank top, the uniform of the unthinking dresser.

The night before they'd arranged by phone their itinerary, beginning at the furthest point from the seventeenth, the Musée Picasso. Though they'd never been there together before, the proximity to Rue Charlot was surely as unnerving for Erica as Laure, though both left it unremarked upon. The blue self-portrait Erica had been thinking of was on loan, but they'd found a beautiful engraving of Dora Maar, and Erica had asked Laure to talk to her about it while she took notes. It was like having a student with her. A student she wanted to see naked. Laure barely knew what she said, let alone if it was helpful, but while Erica was writing she wasn't looking at Laure with her large Laforêt eyes, and that made things easier.

They didn't linger in Le Marais. It was too full of ghosts, and they walked a different route to L'Orangerie than the one they'd taken along the river the first time Laure took Erica to see her favourite paintings. They chose a deliberately touristic café for coffee, the sort of place that was likely not even in business seven years ago. Laure felt her anticipation mounting as they joined the queue for L'Orangerie and were ushered inside. At least the layout was different, and they were not walking directly into their past, but as they moved silently through the museum, following the signs for *Les Nymphéas*, Laure felt a rising melancholy. Here they were once more, and never would be again.

At the entrance to the white, curved room, they paused waiting for a tour group to vacate the long wooden bench in the centre. It was still busy, but not unbearably so, many people having lunch before attacking their afternoon's sightseeing. When they stepped inside the room, there were only a dozen others in the space.

Laure was close enough to hear the small sigh escape Erica's lips as she walked towards *Les Nuages*. Laure felt a familiar, tangled rush of love that was for the paintings and also for Erica, for the girl she'd been when they first came here together. And a tenderness for Laure herself, that past girl who'd thought herself a woman, and stood before these paintings and seen death. She'd been wrong, she decided. The paintings might well be about time passing, but they were also so clearly about life to her now, defiant, cyclical, like movements in a musical composition, moving through the seasons and showing new beginning after new beginning. Darkness was not death, Laure understood this now, as someone who had walked through so much of it. While there was life, there was hope.

Erica was circling the room slowly, her head tilted in her usual way. Michel had been wrong: she had aged a bit, and it was beautiful, the light from the cupola window catching in the first wrinkle of her forehead. What would she look like in ten years, twenty, forty? In that moment, it was unbearable to Laure that she wouldn't be there to see her at every stage. That even if the best scenario happened, and they remained friends, Laure would not be the one to witness Erica age.

Laure sat on the bench when a space became free, and tried not to look at Erica. She wondered how Michel and Barbara were getting on. His cough seemed better to her yesterday, though she wondered if she was just used to it. This was the deception of long-term illness, she saw that now with her father's alcoholism, with her own to a certain extent. Things that once would not have been tolerated became normal. It was once inconceivable that Michel would not leave his house day to day, and now it was nearly three months since he'd done more than walk around the block and no one had an explanation. Laure realized she should be, could be, doing more. She'd been drifting in her duties, and leaving Barbara to deal with doctors, Agnès with his nutrition. She was like the fun aunt, swooping in, watching films, adding illicit sugar to his tea and bad-talking the strictness of the others. She needed to shoulder more of the burden.

A blue blur in her periphery, and Laure looked up in time to see Erica leaving the room at pace.

"Erica?"

She glanced back at her, and Laure saw she was crying. She hesitated, and then followed her, catching her easily and falling into step just behind her.

"Erica?"

"Sorry, it's nothing. God, how embarrassing. I just need . . ." She came to a halt in the next gallery. "Sorry, do you mind if I go outside? It's fine if you want to stay. I just want some air."

"I'll come," said Laure, confused, trailing Erica through the foyer and out into the heat once more. Erica weaved through the people cluttering the dirt paths and hurried towards the scant shelter of ornamental trees.

Many others were seeking shade, but Laure knew Erica was looking for privacy, to compose herself.

"Here," she murmured, and gently tugged on Erica's arm, leading her instead to the balustrade beside L'Orangerie. Erica crouched against the cool stone and shielded her face from view. Laure fought her instinct to rub her back. It was too intimate, she couldn't allow herself to offer that sort of comfort. She settled for crouching down beside her. Erica's breath was coming short, in little gulps.

"Are you having an asthma attack?"

Erica shook her head, gathering herself with a visible effort. She regained control of her breathing, wiped her face impatiently with the hem of her dress. "Sorry. I think I'm tired. I stayed up writing. And being in there was . . ."

She looked at Laure then, and in her face Laure saw desperation.

"It's impossible, isn't it?"

"I don't—"

"Never mind." Erica stood suddenly, dusting off her dress. "God, sorry. I must be due my period or something." Her cheeks were still shiny with tears.

"It's OK." Laure stood too, still not sure what exactly had happened. "Should we . . ."

"No, I can't go back in. I think I need to eat something, if you don't mind."

"Sure."

"Don't you ever get hungry?"

"Pardon?"

"I feel like I always suggest eating."

Laure didn't know what to say. Erica seemed to be spiralling, and she didn't have the energy to deal with it. "You want a café?"

"Anything." Now Erica seemed irritated, and Laure wished she was at Michel's, or at home, lying down in the dark. She led her across the Pont de la Concorde and into the first café they found. The pavement tables were full so they sat inside, the place feeling dingy after the midday sun.

Erica's silence had a snapped-shut quality, and Laure felt herself hardening in answer. This she had not missed, the sulks, the unreasonable anger that accompanied Erica's hunger. Erica even seemed irritated by Laure's order.

"You're only getting a starter?"

"Yes."

"Fine." Erica too ordered a starter and handed the menu to the waiter with ill grace.

"You can have two courses," said Laure.

"It's fine. I don't want to be eating while you're not."

Their meals arrived to a stony silence Laure couldn't wait to leave. At least Erica didn't try to force small talk. She drank two glasses of wine with the sort of grim determination Laure now found depressing, like someone taking medicine. Erica insisted on paying and both of them seemed relieved to reach the pavement.

"I think—" Laure began, ready to suggest they forget the Musée Rodin and call it a day, but Erica spoke over her.

"I know I'm being a brat. I was hungry. And maybe I've seen enough art today, if that's all right?"

Laure shrugged, wanting to convey it meant nothing to her either way.

"But if you have the afternoon, fancy being a tourist with me? I want to go to Shakespeare and Company. I never went before. Or is that too awful?"

"I can always wait outside." Laure smiled. "But seriously, it is a piece of Paris. The original Shakespeare and Company was for French writers as well as Ricans."

"Ricans." Erica snorted. "That sounds so seventies."

Their ease had returned, and it carried them all the way to the bookshop. Laure watched Erica among the shelves, her face rapturous as she exclaimed over different covers of her favourites, and strange little books she'd not read before.

"I love this one," she said, waving *The Hearing Trumpet* by Leonora Carrington at Laure. "Have you read it?"

"Yes." Laure had read it after Erica had sent her a postcard of one of Carrington's works, *The Old Maids*.

"Ant's book!" Erica exclaimed, snatching a hardcover off the shelf and holding it aloft like a trophy. "He'll be so excited to hear it's here. He's always wanted to be a Tumbleweed, you know, the writers who come and work and sleep here."

"I am familiar," said Laure crisply. It was stuffy in the bookshop, and the sight of Ant's book, Erica's pride, made her uncomfortable. "What about you?"

"Me?"

"You could apply. It is more for works in progress, not established writers."

"My apartment is fine."

Laure felt irritated with her. The point of the residency was not the accommodation, it was to read, to connect with other writers. How could Erica expect to write anything good in isolation? She followed her upstairs and back down, commenting distractedly on various books Erica waved under her nose.

"I think I'll buy these," said Erica, taking some slim volumes to the counter. Laure felt the day drifting to an end, relief commingled with disappointment. She was exhausted, and hot, and feeling guilty about Michel. Maybe if he was not too tired she would go and visit him, take him some more cherries.

"Laure?" She realized Erica had been talking to her. "Is that OK?"

"Yes, of course," said Laure, assuming Erica was about to leave.

"Great. It just feels weird not knowing where you live I suppose."

Laure stopped, ostensibly to allow Erica to pass through the door first, but as she followed her blinking into the afternoon sunlight she realized she must have just invited Erica to her place. Erica was smiling expectantly.

"To mine, yes?" Laure said, slowly.

"If it's not too strange. Obviously it's fine if you'd rather not."

It was strange, of course it was, but to admit that would be impossible. Erica clearly did not have a clear picture of what had happened to Laure.

How when they had parted, Laure, like a bee that had spent its sting, had unravelled. But she was through that now, sober, healthy, with a good job, an apartment. And maybe this could be more precious, more long-lasting. A friendship with the first woman she'd ever loved. They could go to the apartment, drink tea, and wave goodbye.

It was only half an hour's stroll to Rue Bréa, and Erica exclaimed delightedly about the genteel surroundings, how green it was, how close to the Sorbonne. As though in a trance Laure let herself be lulled by Erica's voice and she ushered her into her apartment without second-guessing. Erica stood in her small sitting room, staring at the wall. Laure realized she was looking at the poster that she had given Laure. The cheap reproduction of *Matin*, that Laure had thrown to the ground of her squat.

"Yes," said Laure. "I was a fool."

Erica looked at her, calculating. "I was too."

With the air of someone who had decided something long-considered, she closed the small distance between them, and kissed her.

Chapter Nine

It was a lie Erica would tell herself, later, so firmly and so frequently it almost became true, that she hadn't planned on kissing Laure in her apartment. But she had. From the moment she saw her outside the Musée Picasso—no, before then, as she walked through the familiar streets of Le Marais—no, before then, when she saw the paintings that had so transported her seven years ago—no, before then, when they made their arrangements the night before—no, before then, and before then, and before then. Maybe when she saw her at the café with Léa. Surely not when she decided to come to Paris, that was too deceitful, too awful. But all these thoughts would come after.

The fact remained that at some point Erica decided to kiss Laure, and so she kissed her. And Laure kissed her back. She took her to bed, the first time they'd made love in a bed, not just on a mattress on the floor, and afterwards they bathed together, the water run cool and shallow, air wicking sweat from their bodies. Erica would remember guilt arriving straight away, but in fact she did not think of her husband yet, though her ring clicked against the side of the bathtub as she ran her fingers over Laure's thighs, though she lay with Laure the same way she lay with Ant, between her legs, her head back against her chest, Laure's fingers stroking her hair, lingering over her nipples. The only difference in position was their knees bent double in the rowing boat of the bath, short compared to Abbeydore's tubs. It was Laure who first raised Ant, late that evening, after she brought them both glasses of water to bed, a bowl of sliced apple to share. They'd barely talked the past few hours, only in passion, smiling at each other with happiness, dazed by their want, their luck. But when she returned with the apple and the water, Laure said, "What now?"

Erica sat up, covering her breasts with the sheet. She looked at Laure, the naked glory of her. "I can think of a few things."

Laure frowned. "Seriously, Erica. Was that it? Are you getting it out of your system?"

"You? Of course not."

"Then? Are you leaving now?"

"Do you want me to leave?" Erica knew she was being obtuse, but she didn't want to have this conversation just yet. She thought she'd have one night at least.

"Erica."

"I know." Erica reached out for Laure, and she let her hold her hand. "This isn't just this. Sex. Fucking."

Laure laughed. "Don't you mean making love."

Erica covered her face. "God, I was such a prude!" But she wanted to say, *Yes, yes exactly*. She peered through her fingers at Laure, mock shy. "I mean, I missed you."

"I missed you too," said Laure. "For seven years I missed you. But so much has happened. You're married."

"I know." How else to answer that statement, but accept it? Erica had only ever believed in monogamy. She was too jealous for anything else. But this fact existed alongside another: she loved two people. How to explain that to Laure, without upsetting her, scandalizing her? "But today . . . today things changed. I've thought of you so much the past few years, but being here, being with you in those places we used to be. It made me realize how much I missed you. How much I don't want to be apart from you anymore."

Laure was looking at her own hands, sitting very still. "Do you understand I'm scared? What are you saying to me? What are you promising?"

"I don't know. I'm sorry, I don't. And I understand if that's not enough. But I don't want to leave."

Erica half hoped Laure would put a stop to this, right there and then. That she would be the strong one, the moral one, though she was not the adulteress here. But instead she nodded, and gave Erica that half smile, and they moved towards each other once again.

Here it was, at last. A life together, days then weeks, as adults. Time this summer was slower, and so too was their love. Not expressed in huge, earth-shaking moments of rupture, encounters of simmering tension, silent longing, but as a soft, continuous act, a daily, domestic making and remaking of a promise to each other. Safety in the mundane tasks of living. Devotion to everything they could be together.

Erica kept the flat in the seventeenth, but she rarely stayed there, only on the days Laure was with Michel. The deception felt louder there, the place Ant was paying for, but Ant's tour had taken him to Hong Kong, where the time difference made calls all but impossible. This neat inconvenience felt like permission to Erica, and she didn't waste time, just yet, on feeling bad for betraying him. At the back of her mind was the fact that her affair with Laure might not be an affair at all, that this might be the moment she leapt into a different sort of life.

In between working on *Passing Rain*, and walking through galleries, Erica would run the scenario where she stayed with Laure for ever. Where she phoned Ant, his parents, sorted the practicalities. Told the news to Barbara, Marie and Agnès. To Léa and Michel. It would not be easy. Nothing like the fantasy she'd imagined during their first summer together, when anyway she'd had no strings and no idea what true commitment was. They'd struggle, constantly, for money. They'd fight over where to live, Erica would battle guilt and isolation. Emma wouldn't forgive her. Elizabeth, of course, would hate her. Even in these imaginings, she had to place Ant in soft focus, so as not to see the hurt in his face. But he'd move on—a man like that, a beautiful, talented, kind man—

But how would she be changed by a life with Laure? Would she write all those novels she imagined? There would be fights, enormous fights, about money, about other women, other men, the spectre of infidelity looming over this relationship that had begun with it. No marriage, no children. Maybe she resisted the tidal heave of maternal instinct, as Agnès had for Marie, and they made a life of art: Laure's teaching on it, Erica writing. Maybe it would be a relief. Maybe she did not want children at all. Erica played versions of her life on fast forward, staying, not staying, but this was only possible when she was out of Laure's orbit. When Laure was there, there was only one choice.

They agreed early on that no one should know. Laure's friends no longer lived in each other's pockets anyway, and with Léa gone to Valencia, Michel trapped in his flat, Barbara busy with his care and summer schools and Marie and Agnès in the seventeenth, it seemed relatively easy to keep their own bubble protected. Laure regularly spoke with Barbara on the phone about Michel, and Erica took perverse pleasure in sitting in the background, listening in, a secret kept precious and safe.

The biggest test came a month into their affair, when all of them crowded into Michel's apartment for Laure's birthday. It was near-impossible not to kiss Laure's neck as she sat beside her on the sofa, or squeeze her hand as they passed each other in the kitchen. She felt Barbara looking at them both, and wondered if she could sense the tension between them, the old connection rekindled.

"Léa said you're here to write a book," said Barbara, in a tone that showed exactly what she thought of that. "How's it going?"

"Well," said Erica, and it was the truth. She'd written every day since she started sleeping with Laure, picking Laure's brains about this character's motivation, that character's views on art. She'd even modelled the older brother, an enigmatic professor of art theory, on her.

"Do you have friends in Paris?"

"Sorry?"

"Apart from us, of course." Barbara smiled insincerely.

"Not really. But I don't need the distraction."

"Very disciplined. And your husband doesn't mind you being here alone?"

"I know it's not your specialist subject, but wives aren't property any more." Erica wished there was alcohol at this party, though she'd barely drunk any the past month.

Barbara looked at her coolly. "You know it's a sore subject, that women cannot marry."

Erica bit back the impulse to apologize. "Ant's fine with me doing as I wish."

She'd always had the feeling Barbara didn't like her, or rather saw right through her, and when the pre-agreed time for them to leave came, Erica was relieved. She and Laure walked out with Marie between them.

"Are you coming back to the seventeenth?" asked Marie, and Erica made a show of checking her watch.

"I think I might wander around the Louvre a bit."

"I'll join you," said Laure, as though it had just occurred to her. Marie waved them off.

As they turned the corner of Michel's street, Erica turned to Laure. "Barbara knows."

"I doubt it."

"She was watching us all afternoon."

"She was watching Michel, he was sitting with us."

"She was rude."

"About what?"

"I think . . . do you think she's . . ."

"What?"

Jealous. Still in love with you. And under these silent worries, another, absurd fear: that Laure might feel something for Barbara. They spent so much time talking—yes, it was about Michel, but didn't people in situations like that often bind together? Barbara was beautiful, in her way, and fierce, and fiercely clever. But she was being silly. Laure was looking at her, waiting. Erica shook her head. "Nothing. What do you want to do? Go to the Louvre? I can buy you dinner."

"I would like to go to bed with you."

As though he'd heard Barbara's questions about him, Ant called the flat in the seventeenth that night. They'd managed to speak only twice since Laure and Erica's affair began, and Erica wished she'd found it harder. But the truth was she'd enjoyed their conversations, talking about how the interviewers always mangled his name, and how many times he'd been asked where he got his ideas from. He was flying to New Zealand soon, covering a couple of festivals, and then going on to Australia before beginning his return to Europe, so the time difference would continue to provide a useful buffer. But when Erica returned to the apartment the day after Laure's birthday, she found a message on the answering machine.

"Hi my love, sorry I missed you! I was worried I might wake you up. But I'm just getting in under the wire your time to wish you a happy anniversary. Paper, fittingly enough. I couldn't be more proud of you, and can't wait to hear how it's been going. I'm staying put in this hotel until Wednesday, so maybe you could give me a call when you get this? I miss your voice. I love you."

Erica sat, a little stunned. Their wedding anniversary. Their first wedding anniversary. She'd completely forgotten. She crouched down beside the phone. What was she *doing*? She had a beautiful man, a brilliant man who loved her, and here she was playing at lesbians with Laure—

But it was not just playing. She loved Laure, there'd been no equivocating about it. And she loved Ant. And life couldn't go on like this for ever. She would have to decide. The truth of that fact was like barbed wire snagging on the meat of her heart. *One day at a time*. Right now, she was in Paris. She was going to collect the books she needed, and then she was going back to Laure's.

But first, she would call Ant back.

* * *

Their affair took on a new intensity after Ant's message. Erica didn't relay it to Laure, nor her reply to his hotel's answering machine service, or her guilt at forgetting their anniversary, but instead clung tighter to her lover, hoping she would find a definitive answer to her impasse. It was not lost on Erica that she was not only choosing between Laure and Ant, but between a woman and a man and the attendant challenges of each. It was easy for now, because it was temporary, or at least they were transitioning towards a more permanent state of togetherness. Soon it would become tiresome, to not be able to be safely and openly affectionate in public. It would become a strain, to not marry, to not have children. She wanted it, she did not want it. When they were out at the Pompidou or the Louvre, Erica could well imagine a life without children, and saw how a life with them would therefore be without so many things she loved: sex, space, quiet. Less time for art, for reading, for writing. When they stood in front of *Saint Jérôme pénitent* and Laure told her how it was Titian's manifesto, a declaration of all he believed painting could do and be, Erica forgot she was listening for her characters, and just let Laure's words wash over her. A curiosity, a new way of seeing reawakening. Her sense of novelty at being so stimulated intrigued and dismayed her.

She wished she could see this relationship with Laure as what Laure had accused her of after they first slept together. *Getting it out of your system?* Like a holiday romance. But whatever happened, these days, weeks, months with Laure were an excavation of everything Erica thought she knew. The foundations of her marriage would not be left untouched. She wished she was more moral, and that her guilt would make going back to Ant impossible. She wished she was more moral, and had never started this.

"What are you thinking?" Laure would whisper into her hair at night. "I can hear your mind, so busy."

"Nothing. The book." *Everything.* She turned sometimes in her sleep, reaching for Laure in the dark, but Laure was so close by she must turn too, and they missed finding each other's faces, searched for each other's hands.

•

Here it was then. A love affair. Laure had never expected to find herself in one. The thing with Pauline, that was different. Laure was a girl, Pauline a seasoned cheat. There was never any thought of love. But Erica was married, and though even if she could Laure would never marry—she believed to her core that marriage was a prison, a trick—the word held enough weight to act as a boulder, pressing and pressing on her conscience. Why must her happiness come at the cost of someone else's? Why did she care? Erica did not seem to. But Erica seemed to be living in the moment so desperately it made Laure frightened to ask about the future. As days became weeks became a month and Erica stopped going back to her flat in the seventeenth, Laure began to wonder if maybe it really would be so easy. Maybe one day, Erica would say, "I have called Ant. I've told him it's over." And then they could go on as they were, for ever.

Erica called her husband on occasional Wednesday mornings, from a telephone box on the Boulevard du Montparnasse. Laure did not know how they agreed when to speak. They would pretend these hours didn't happen, never discussing them, but Laure would stand by the window, pressing her cheek against the glass so she could watch until Erica rounded the corner out of sight. She couldn't settle to anything while Erica was out. She'd thought to have escaped Paris by now, to have gone to Normandy, but she didn't want to suggest it to Erica in case she saw it as an opportunity to break off their affair.

She only sometimes wondered what Erica had told Ant, the lies she was having to layer like a house of cards. In general, there was too much bliss to dwell on these difficult contortions of her conscience. Their days took on a delicious rhythm, Laure waking first and working on her classes for next year, before brewing coffee and taking it to Erica at nine. They'd sometimes make love, or discuss their dreams—Erica had a recurring one where she flew, but badly, her feet bumping the stairs—and then both of them would work side by side on the sofa until lunch. In the afternoons they'd walk, or see an exhibition, shop for dinner. Easy days, simple days.

It was not perfect, and that was why Laure knew it could last. There were the small, domestic annoyances: Erica never rinsed out the bath after shaving her legs, and teased Laure when she chided her for it— "Says she of the squat! She of the Turkish toilet!"—and snored a little when she slept. She also showed no great interest in politics, and whatever brushes she'd had with socialism, let alone communism, had been left behind in her teens. But worse than any of this was her seemingly wilful misunderstanding of art, the way she'd sometimes cut Laure off mid-sentence to ask her to give the short version of her analysis, with no willingness to accept complexity. This was not the Erica Laure remembered, whose curiosity opened every question out like an origami fortune teller. Maybe it was an unfair thought, but it felt to Laure that Erica's time with Ant had closed her down, smoothed some of her rough edges. In her kinder moments, Laure understood Erica asked most of her questions as research—to flesh out her characters, and so she needed brevity from Laure, something that was distillable, but increasingly Laure felt her heartfelt ideas were window-dressing to the novel, and so too to Erica. When she read the pages Erica gave her at the end of each day before announcing she couldn't stand to watch her read them, flouncing off to leave stubble in the bath and coming back pink and gorgeous-smelling, Laure saw how Erica had often lifted, wholesale, her monologues, placing them into the least likeable characters' mouths.

There was a hollowness at the centre of the book. It was as if this was a story Erica felt she should be writing, rather than a story she needed to tell. At times it felt like a badly directed play, though the interactions between the oldest brother and his wife were wonderful. But Laure had read enough to know the best books felt like a compulsion to their authors, that they would write them whether they were going to be published or not. She made the mistake of saying this to Erica, attempting to reassure her it would be fine if *Passing Rain* didn't get published, but it backfired exceptionally.

"So it's shallow to want to be read? Great art can only be great if it's for the person writing it?" Her nostrils flared, a sure sign of trouble.

"I only mean it's not for someone out there. Not only for money."

"You know I'm not the rich one, right?" she snapped. "And if I—"

Erica stopped, panting, but Laure knew what she had been about to say. *If I leave him*. If she left, she would need to earn money. Laure felt a swelling joy. So she was thinking about the future, about their future.

"My point is," said Erica, "money matters, and no amount of communism is going to change that."

Laure resisted correcting her. "Can we talk about this?"

"About communism?"

"About this. Us."

Erica squeezed her eyes shut. "I'm sorry. It's so unfair. I don't know what to do, and I hate saying that to you. But I'm afraid, Laure."

"Afraid of what?"

But Erica refused to answer. Laure guessed she meant divorce, loving a woman, leaving the ease of an accepted, acceptable relationship. But couldn't she see it could work? It could be beautiful—that's what Michel had said to her about sobriety, and it changed her life.

"Don't be afraid," she said, and she said it to herself, for it felt as though she offered Erica her heart on a plate, bloody and beating, raw and precious meat. "There is nothing we could not do together."

Erica reached out, and Laure embraced her, trying to make her touch say everything she needed to say, to make Erica choose her. She was afraid, so awfully afraid, and she knew only one way to quiet her doubts. Later, as Erica lay beneath her, she wanted to ask between moans, *How is there a choice? How can you not want this?*

The phone rang early the next day, a Friday. Laure was reading on the sofa and snatched it up, not wanting it to wake Erica.

"Laure," said Barbara, without preamble. "Have you seen the papers?"

"Papers?" Her mind leapt, absurdly, to exams, the marking that would occupy her August. She heard Barbara's breath close to the phone, the rustle of a newspaper.

"Rock Hudson collapsed at the Ritz last weekend."

"Pardon?" Laure wondered if Barbara was drunk, though she sounded deadly serious.

"Rock Hudson, the movie star. He's in Paris, at the American Hospital. They said he had liver cancer. Did you see?"

Laure had heard something about it, on the radio. "So?"

"It's LAV. AIDS."

"Quoi?" said Laure, but she was playing for time. She'd heard it mentioned at the café, an ex-employee sick in hospital. She had a dark, rumbling feeling moving through her body.

"Lymphadenopathy associated virus. The Americans call it acquired immune deficiency disorder." Laure could tell Barbara was reading aloud from the paper. "It causes weight loss, illness, fatigue. Everything." And then, in case Laure did not know what she was getting at. "Michel."

"Michel."

"I've already called his doctor. They're not open yet, but we need to get him tested as soon as possible. I can't believe they didn't know."

"Had you thought of it?"

"Not really. I thought it was too rare."

"Isn't it?"

"Apparently not."

"But this is good, yes? They can treat it?"

Barbara was quiet a moment. "They're having to beg the president to let him fly back to America. Apparently there's no cure. There's awful talk on the radio, calling him all sorts of names. We have to make sure Michel doesn't hear. We have to tell him, take him to the hospital."

Laure glanced at the bedroom door, slightly ajar. She could see Erica's bare ankle. They had tickets for a late morning showing of *Cléo de 5 à 7*.

"I can be there in an hour."

Laure put down the phone and slid into the bedroom. Erica stirred as she opened her cupboard drawers, fetched underwear, a T-shirt, scooped her jeans from the floor.

"Laure?" Erica blinked up at her from under a shielding arm, her armpit stubbled with regrowth.

"I'm going to Michel's," said Laure, kneeling by the bed and stroking her hair off her face.

"Is he OK?"

"Fine, fine. I just . . . Barbara just called." Laure thought about telling her, about the Ritz, Rock Hudson. But that would make it more real, so instead she said, "Michel wants to see me."

"Is he all right?"

"Yes, probably just wants company. Sorry."

"Don't apologize. Shall I come?" She made to get out of bed, but Laure stayed her, a hand on her hip.

"Barbara is meeting me there."

"Oh. OK. Are you all right?"

"Fine." She gave what she knew was an unreassuringly tight smile.

Erica caught up Laure's hand and kissed it. "Will you be back for the cinema?"

"Maybe."

"Give him my love."

Rock Hudson's name and photograph were on the cover of every paper of every kiosk Laure passed, the headlines variously scathing, sympathetic, or scandalized. She paused to read a few lines of the articles: *an often deadly ailment . . . Asked what Hudson's chances of survival were, Miss Collart said only, "All that we can do is hope."*

Suddenly Laure felt very old, and very out of touch. If she'd kept her promise to Michel and visited the community café more often, no doubt she would have heard more about it. Maybe Barbara had suspected and not told her. If she'd been anywhere other than in bed with Erica, or at galleries with Erica, or walking around Paris with Erica . . .

She reached Michel's flat to find Barbara already waiting for her.

"You walked?" said Barbara. "No wonder it took you so long."

"There's no rush, is there? He won't be awake yet."

"Laure, we need to wake him. Don't you understand this is serious?"

"Please don't."

"Don't what?"

Laure got out her keys. As she opened the door she said, "I am here too. I understand."

"But you've not been here," said Barbara, pushing past her.

"Michel and I agreed—"

"I know where you are. Who you're with." She stomped up the narrow flight of stairs, and used her own set of keys to open Michel's door. Laure bit her tongue. There would be time later to argue, if that's what Barbara wanted to do.

Michel's apartment was dark. His mother had left a couple of days before and everything still smelt of lemons. Barbara nudged Laure ahead of her.

"You go," she said, drawing from her shoulder bag a copy of *Le Figaro*. "Show him this."

"You bought this rag?"

"It's the clearest report. Can you just get on with it." Barbara's voice broke, and she shoved the newspaper at Laure, turning away and into the kitchen. "I'll make coffee. The doctor's office opens in half an hour. We should go and queue in person."

Why did Laure feel such reluctance? She didn't want to cross into Michel's space with this fascist paper in her hand, with its brash headline and bad news story. But she pushed open his door. He looked small under his sheets, like a child. Laure woke him gently, and he started, his skin glossy with sweat. The room smelt fusty, though Laure knew his mother would have thoroughly aired and cleaned it.

"It's me."

"Laure? What the fuck? Is it Sunday?"

"No, Friday." She knelt beside his bed, as she had beside Erica. He shuffled upright.

"Can you open the curtains?" She did so. "Jesus, who's died?"

"No one." She gave an unconvincing laugh. Stupid Barbara, infecting her with her worry. It might not even be the same thing. "Barbara is here too. We're going to take you to the doctor."

"Why?" He frowned. "What's going on?"

Laure laid the paper on his bed. He read it, and his face slowly relaxed, exactly opposite to how she'd felt reading the words. *Incurable. Deadly. Poor prognosis.* When he looked up at her, his expression was as close to blank as she'd ever seen it.

"Can I have some water?"

"Of course. Barbara is making coffee."

Laure left him with the paper and fetched a glass of water. His reaction surprised her, or rather his lack of reaction. He seemed resigned. Barbara wiped her eyes with her sleeve when she came in. Laure softened.

"Barbara, you mustn't get upset. It will be all right."

"No, Laure," snapped Barbara. "I don't think it will be. And there's no one else I can cry in front of, so please just let me cry."

Laure thought briefly of hugging her. She would not have thought twice when they were younger, or even a year ago. But somehow Michel's illness, instead of binding them as she'd expected, had forced them into their own separate orbits.

"Here," said Barbara, thrusting a milky cup of coffee at her. "Tell him to hurry up."

They caught the bus to Michel's doctor. It was only one stop on the metro but Michel blanched at the sight of the stairs. They were the second in line when the surgery opened, and Laure left Barbara to argue with the receptionist while she and Michel sat in the small waiting room with an old man with visibly swollen ankles, and a child whimpering into her mother's bosom.

"Hey," said Michel, leaning in to whisper in Laure's ear. "You bring me to the coolest places."

Laure nudged him gently, nodding at the old man. "He's the right age for you, isn't he?"

"OK," said Barbara. "The nurse can do a blood draw. We'll take it to the hospital ourselves, so they don't have to wait for the deliveries on Monday."

Michel whooped softly. They waited another half an hour before Michel was called in by the nurse, and Barbara insisted on going in with him. While Laure waited, a song started going around and around in her head, the same few chords, and she couldn't get beyond them to the lyrics, to know what the song was. The child was called in by the doctor; she went unwillingly, clinging to her mother's hip. The old man shifted uncomfortably in the hard plastic chair. At last they came out, Michel very pale, Barbara clutching a clear plastic bag with a vial of dark blood inside.

"I'll drop this," she said. "Laure, you take Michel home. Wait with him until I'm back."

Laure made the mistake of checking her watch.

"Shit, Laure, can't you take a day off from the tourist?"

"I'm not—"

"Just take Michel home. I'm sure she can call her husband or something." Barbara stalked away, and Michel linked his arm through hers, leaning heavily on her as they began to walk. Laure waited for Michel to comment on Barbara's outburst, but he was panting by the time they reached the bus stop. It was busy with people commuting into the centre for work, and when the bus arrived there was no seat for Michel. She thought about asking someone to stand up—he was clearly perspiring, pale and so thin in this press of bodies, but he was keeping his head down, not wanting to draw attention.

She glared at anyone who stared. People used to stare because he was so beautiful, the handsomest man in any room. Now he looked like a bag of bones, bundled into the jumper so lovingly knitted by his mother. Words from the articles she'd read kept flashing across her vision. *Weight loss, fever, night sweats. Liver failure, kidney failure, heart failure.* They disembarked and Michel leant against the bus stop.

"Shit, I really am sick, aren't I?" He gave her a wobbly smile. "Shall we have a drink." He nodded at the café directly behind them. Laure settled him at an outside table and went to the toilet. When she washed her hands, they shook. She went back outside and sat down next to Michel. They ordered coffee and tartines, watched the traffic crawling by. At last, Michel said,

"The tourist, then?"

There was no point denying it. "Yes. But that's not why I stopped coming on Thursdays. I just wanted to give you and your mother more time—"

"I am not Barbara," said Michel. "You don't have to explain yourself to me." His eyes glittered. "OK, maybe a bit. When did it start?"

Laure sighed as though reluctant, but she wanted to give him pleasure. And she wanted to recount it, to remember the moments of drawing together, the agonizing unknowns, the blessed release as Erica put her lips on hers.

"All right, not too graphic," said Michel, mock-prudish. "So, is it another holiday?"

Laure wished she could say no. Instead she shrugged. Michel looked appalled. "You have asked her?"

"She doesn't know."

"Bullshit. And you are what? Just going to let her go back to the princeling?"

"It's not entirely my decision."

"I don't believe anyone could refuse you if you didn't want them to." He'd not referred to her *ravissement* in years. She'd not felt that power in years either.

"Erica did just that before."

"No. You didn't try to make her stay."

That was not how Laure remembered it, but something else was on her mind. "You think we are good together?"

"I always thought so."

"But you hated her!"

"No, I hated what she did to you. She's older now. I hope wiser. I hope she knows what a treasure she has." He squeezed her hand as their coffees and tartines arrived. "Above all I don't want you to get hurt. But

I know that is a useless hope. Look at me and Christophe. I am glad it happened, despite how it ended." A shadow crossed his face. "I should check on him."

"Ah." Laure hadn't considered this, even when she'd read the articles. *Homosexuals. Sexual contact. Sexual deviance.* "When you get the results?"

Michel looked at her, searching her face. She saw pity on his. "I know I have AIDS."

A stutter in her heartbeat. "What?"

The next words Michel delivered to his tartine, which sat untouched on its small plate. "Christophe was diagnosed at the beginning of the year. He's been in and out of hospital. Even saw the specialist they mentioned in that article you showed me."

Laure sat astonished. "What are you saying?"

"Laure, you lesbians have your heads in the sand. We've known about this for months. It was covered in our magazines."

"But why didn't you tell me? Tell Barbara?" Despite her annoyance with her this morning, Laure felt indignant on her behalf. "She's been killing herself trying to find a way to help."

He looked at her and his eyes pinned her down. "Barbara needs to feel helpful. She and Agnès with their powders and pills, they need a way to help. But there is no help for this, you understand?"

Laure's throat was closing around her words, but she forced them out. "I don't."

"I didn't want to tell you, because I didn't want you to look at me like this. I don't want you to look at me and see death. I've seen how people are, around Christophe."

"He is dying?"

"Aren't we all? But yes. He tells me, people are crying all the time, but it's not for him, it's for themselves."

"I don't understand."

"It doesn't matter. But how Barbara is reacting to me being sick is exactly what she'd want others to do for her. Agnès, the same. In these situations people give out what they would like to receive." He tucked her hair behind her ear, her meagre shelter from the world gone. "Not you, though. You listen to Raffaella Carrà and watch musicals with me." Dimly, Laure registered the song she'd not been able to name was Carrà's "A far l'amore comincia tu." "You don't clean or tidy or try to improve me. You let me be, and that is why I love you, little sister. And," he said briskly, changing the subject, "why I am worried about you and the tourist."

Laure felt she had whiplash. She was crying and there was no point trying to stop. "Michel—"

"I don't want to talk about it. I know what is coming, and I'm afraid, do you see? I'm afraid for us all. So please, can we sit here in the sun and talk about your love affair before I have to go back and start dying again."

"Surely there's something . . . if that actor was here, there must be experts in Paris."

"Experts in Paris who can't help him. Please," he said, and there was anger in his voice. "Enough. You are my safe place, Laure. I don't want to lose it."

They were still at the café when Barbara arrived on the bus from the hospital. She looked exhausted, and frowned when she spotted them waving her over.

"What are you doing here?"

"Having coffee," said Michel, and he and Laure giggled. They were on their third coffee, both of them wired and a little hysterical. "Did my blood arrive safely?"

"Of course," said Barbara, dragging a chair from the next table and sitting down hard. "Shouldn't you be in bed?"

"Barbara," said Michel, and he laid his hand over her hand, which was balled around her bag strap. "You have done your duty. You have done more than I could have asked for."

Barbara hung her head. "I should have done more. I should've realized before—"

"I forbid you from guilt. It is a useless emotion and this is not your fault." Michel's voice was still raspy, but firm. "Besides, Barbara, I am the one who should be sorry."

Laure kept her gaze fixed on Michel. She knew what was coming, and didn't want to see Barbara's reaction.

"I didn't tell you," continued Michel. "But I have just told Laure and you should know too. Christophe has AIDS."

A gasp. Laure watched Michel's pulse flickering beneath his ear.

"So you see, I must ask you to forgive me, for not telling you what I already knew. But I think a part of me did not want to see you look this way. To look at me like there is no hope." Michel leant forwards, and Laure traced the path of his arm to his hand, where it grasped Barbara's fingers, and up the sleeve of Barbara's jacket to her friend's face. She was stricken, barely breathing.

"But I will not feel guilty. And so, you must not either. Now please, relax. Sit with us in the sunshine."

He shut his eyes and tilted his head back. His Adam's apple stood proud from his throat, the bones of his chest like a ladder beneath the gaping neck of his T-shirt. Laure watched as Barbara's eyes filled with tears and she shut them too, tipping up her face. Laure gently took her other hand, unpeeling it from the bag, and laced her fingers through, both of them gripping tight.

•

After Laure woke her, Erica couldn't sleep. She considered going to the film alone. She'd never been to the cinema on her own before, but it seemed like something Laure would do without a second thought. But something like anxiety stopped her, and she watched the time she'd have to leave approach, arrive, and pass, and she was still in bed, watching the clock. As the hours ticked by, she felt a sense of failure that came just ahead of guilt. Her months in Paris to be alone and write, and her time was two-thirds gone. She was in love with a woman who was not her husband. She felt like a hollow person, paper mâché, and yet all her effort, all her energy, was spent keeping herself together. As she lay there at midday, hungry and bleak, she realized she was using them both—Laure and Ant—to fill herself, weight herself down. Where had it come from, this insecurity? She thought she would grow out of it, but here she was, twenty-five, living off her husband's family wealth, lying in her lover's bed. No wonder she felt hopeless. It was pathetic.

Her hunger finally got her up. She made the bed, determined Laure should not know she'd spent all morning sulking. She made herself sardines on toast, tinned fish being the only meat Laure could tolerate in the house, and opened the windows onto the street, looking down at Rue Bréa. It was a nice area, quiet but central. A far cry from Rue Charlot. But as she sat there, Erica felt a wave of—not nostalgia, it was too sharp for that—but remembrance. The wide, dusty floors, where Laure passed her books and played her music, talked to her about the speaking body and Julia Kristeva, terms and names she'd never heard of before, generally dazzling her in every possible way. What had Erica brought to those days? There must have been something, but she honestly couldn't remember.

This sense of her shortcomings stalked her still, across years and miles: that she was no match for Laure, could not give her all she deserved. Though Laure never commented, and Erica never asked, she wondered what she made of her using her insights in her novel. They were thoughts Erica couldn't have had without her. She didn't feel this insecurity with Ant—at least, not in the same way. Erica wondered if she could live with not feeling good enough, for the rest of her life.

There was still no word from Laure by mid-afternoon, and Erica began to feel nervous, and a little irritated. How hard was it to pick up the phone? And Erica couldn't call Laure at Michel's, because it might expose them. She tried to return to *Passing Rain*, but she was circling a climactic scene between the father and the eldest son's wife, and didn't have a reason for their argument yet. She stood restlessly. She had a spare key. She would go out—it's what Laure would do. There was that Lego Architecture exhibition at the Pompidou that Laure'd disdained. She'd go, and maybe even have a glass of wine. Erica scrawled Laure a short note, and left.

The exhibition was, after all, as facile as Laure had warned Erica it would be. It didn't help that out of habit Erica joined the queue for residents, and was turned back at the entrance when she could not produce proof of address. She had to join the tourist queue, and could feel her neck burning—she'd left without her hat. When finally she got inside, she realized the exhibition was aimed at children and spent twenty unhappy minutes surrounded by dozens of them and their tired-eyed parents. She left the museum without seeing anything else, and walked into the first restaurant she found. She ordered a glass of white wine and drank half of it in one gulp. She asked for another and to see the food menu. She ordered a plateau de fruits de mer though it was the sort of place where she'd never normally risk it, and a bottle of the white.

As she ate and drank diligently, as if it were a task given to her, she felt her thoughts crystallize into clear statements, so clear they were, with the ease introduced by alcohol and food, obvious. First, that her insecurity, her feelings of inadequacy over Laure—she could cope with them. After all, hadn't the exhibition just proved she was most often right? And maybe, once she too lived in Paris, with Laure, and was exposed to the same people and culture, she too would be brilliant. At least, she would be different, diverging from the groove she'd already begun to carve with Ant.

Erica fingered the ring that was so beautiful, and did not suit her. Her second conclusion was: she loved Ant. He was as close to perfect a man for her as she would ever come. But—and at last she had clarity on this—she could leave him. She couldn't imagine leaving Laure. She couldn't imagine leaving Paris and its galleries and restaurants, the quiet of Rue Bréa amid the glorious aliveness of the sixth, the parks and bakery and the library nearby. Her small desk by the window. Her pillow in Laure's bed. Her towels, which hung on the back of the door, where Laure put hers on the radiator. The radio, always on. The light falling just so through the bedroom window, and Laure's mouth on hers.

She'd decided. Erica's toes curled in delight. Her heart actually leapt, gave a small skip in her chest. She had *decided*.

And she knew that when these early days were behind her, and it had sunk in, and she had signed the divorce papers and had no money, for she would not ask anything of Ant, and summer was over and winter was here, she would not regret it. Even with the days short and cold, with no money for restaurant lunches, with—who knows—a novel rejected or published smally, she would still not regret it. Because she had Laure, and that was enough.

Before she began her walk back to the apartment, Erica called home—their home—from a telephone box. She didn't want to wait a moment longer to tell her. But the phone rang out, and she realized she hadn't put the answering machine on before leaving, and her good mood punctured slightly. If Laure had called, she wouldn't have been able to leave a message. She checked the time: four thirty. Surely Laure would be home by the time she was. She walked much slower when Laure wasn't there. She enjoyed how her legs felt stronger, her calves more shapely after two months walking everywhere. She'd gone soft in Surrey. The pool was drained in winter so her only exercise had been half-hearted tennis games with Elizabeth, who at sixty-something was still much better than her. God, how would she tell Elizabeth? Maybe she could be a coward, and let Ant do it. Let them say whatever they wanted about her.

It was boiling hot on the streets. Erica stopped at a café and had a beer. She had the leftover white wine in the bottle, warming, and thought she should throw it away. The café's television was on with the news, dominated by coverage about Rock Hudson, who had AIDS and was in Paris. Erica watched it for a while, and realized when she stood up that she was drunk. A man caught her elbow and said something suggestive as she brushed past him, and she barked as she and Laure had once barked at the man on the Sacré-Cœur steps. *Men.* They were all disgusting. She was glad she would never have to kiss a man again.

She arrived at the apartment parched, and was initially relieved to find it empty. She'd forgotten to discard the bottle of wine and so she put it in the fridge. She drank two glasses of water standing by the kitchen sink, refilled a third. There were no messages on the answering machine, and she was annoyed before she remembered about not turning it on. She poured the final, very large glass of wine, and sat down at her typewriter. *Make like Hemingway!* Emma would say.

It was past seven by the time the phone rang.

"Erica, there you are! I've been calling all afternoon."

"I've been out."

"Did you go to the film?"

"No, Pompidou."

"Ah. I'm glad you didn't wait for me all day."

"How's Michel?"

"Are you OK? Your voice is strange."

"Fine, tired. How's Michel?"

"Not so good." Erica heard a woman's voice.

"Who's that?"

"Barbara. It's OK, she knows about us. Michel too."

"You told them?"

"I hope you don't mind. Barbara had guessed, like you said."

"Nosy bitch."

"Pardon?"

Paranoia, like razor-limbed spiders, was scuttling through her brain. "She doesn't like me."

"She does. What's going on?"

"Nothing." A traitorous hiccup forced its way out. Laure went very quiet, her silence deeper.

"Are you drunk?" she said at last.

"No." But ugh, she was. The room was spinning.

"You sound drunk."

"What, I'm not allowed to drink?"

"Of course you are."

"Good." Why was Laure being like this? She was ruining it. Didn't she know Erica had good news?

"Listen, I'll be another couple of hours at least. I said I'd make Michel dinner." Erica heard Barbara laughing in the background. Why didn't Laure invite Erica to join them?

"Fine." Erica put the phone down on Laure's goodbye. She felt irrationally angry. She paced the apartment, a little unsteadily. She sat down at the desk again, and tried to write more, but Barbara's laugh was scratching at her. Erica gave up. If Laure was going to be hours yet, she certainly wasn't going to wait around here.

She went to the bar on the corner of Boulevard du Montparnasse, a dive really, and ordered a gin and tonic. She drank it at the bar and flirted a little with the bartender in the hope he would give her another for cheap, which he didn't, and scrounged a cigarette. This she took outside to sit and smoke on the pavement table. She felt her lungs cringe with every inhale, but smoking was a good distraction, and besides, she looked more local with a cigarette. She was drunker than she'd been in years, perhaps since the night she and Ant got together. But this might be the last time she ever drank so much, if she was going to spend her life with a recovering alcoholic.

She drank more, to shut up the voices, but they got louder. The street was orange with lamplight and she was tipping in her seat when she saw Laure waiting at the intersection of Montparnasse and Raspail. Erica waved, but Laure didn't see her. Erica stood unsteadily and squinted across the road. It was definitely Laure, and beside her, arm around her waist, resting her head on Laure's shoulder, was Barbara.

Jealousy splintered inside her like dropped glass. As the women began to cross towards her corner, Erica strode to meet them. Barbara saw her first, lifting her head and frowning. She pointed at her but Laure was already waving, confusion on her face. Erica stopped in front of them, others sidestepping to reach the pavement.

"What the hell, Laure?"

"What? I told you I would be late—"

"Why are you with her?"

"Erica," started Barbara, but Erica hissed incoherently into her face. Laure seemed to have frozen, but as Barbara stumbled she snapped back to herself. "Erica, arrête!"

She placed herself between them and Barbara threw up her hands. "Enfoirée. La touriste est folle!"

Incensed, Erica went for her again, but cars were honking now. Laure ushered them both across the street and began to drag Erica away. Erica struggled but they left Barbara behind, and when they reached Rue Bréa Laure pushed her against a closed shop front.

"Erica, merde! What's happened?"

"You tell me!" It had become real in Erica's mind. She could see Barbara's curly hair spread across Laure's thighs, Laure's long fingers clutching Barbara's shoulders.

"Calm down will you? Come inside."

Erica let Laure pull her to their apartment block, shoved ahead of her when they reached their landing and used her own spare key to open the door, which took her two attempts. She tumbled inside and whirled around to face her.

"You had your arms around each other! I heard her laughing on the phone."

"She was laughing at Michel." Laure was looking at her in a way that made Erica want to hide. "You're drunk."

"So what? You expect me not to have fun while you're out cheating on me? Fucking *Barbara*! What sort of name is that!"

"I am not a cheat," said Laure, and her voice was shaking. "And I do not have to listen to this."

"Where are you going?" Erica moved to block the door.

"Away from you."

"Back to Barbara?"

"Perhaps. She is not drunk out of her skull."

"Touriste, is it? Touriste, am I?"

Laure walked calmly into the kitchen and fetched a glass of water. Erica saw her spot the empty bottle of wine. She picked it up, and turned to face Erica, her face clenched with fury. "Did you drink in this flat?"

With the desperation of a child caught out, feeling nowhere to turn, Erica dived for the bottle. In her unsteady state, she knocked it from Laure's hand and sent it crashing to the floor.

Both of them watched it spin and smash, the floor covered in glass, the air filling with the smell of stale wine.

Laure looked from the bottle to Erica, and her expression was worse than anger. It was disgust.

"Laure, I'm sorry. I didn't mean—" She felt wretched, worse than she'd ever felt in her life.

"I would like you to go."

Erica swayed on the spot.

"What?"

"Take your typewriter, your clothes. I need some space."

Erica felt something inside her crumpling. "Is it Barbara?"

"Non." Laure's face was a snarl, an animal masking their fear. "It is you. You stinking drunk in my house, shouting in the street, bringing wine here when you know what I am. And I have spent all day with the most precious man in the world to me, a man who will die soon and there is nothing I can do about it, and you decided this was the day to lose your mind?"

"Die? What?"

"Michel," said Laure. "He has LAV. AIDS."

"AIDS?" Erica held onto the countertop, remembering the screen in the café. "Like Rock Hudson."

Laure sneered, and Erica recognized she was so furious she could not even shout. "Oui, Erica. Like Rock Hudson."

Erica tried to catch up. "But that's contagious, isn't it? Have you—"

She'd made a terrible mistake.

"That's your first question?" Laure turned away from her, unable to even look at her. "Non, Erica. You're safe, don't worry."

"I'm not . . . wait. I'm sorry." She combed through the tangle of her thoughts. The lunch, the decision, the celebratory wine. "Can I explain—"

"Not now. Now, I need you to leave. Pack, and I'll call you a taxi."

"Please, I love you—" She tried to take her hand but Laure recoiled and Erica saw no choice but to go, and make amends in the morning.

Meekly, she took her typewriter, dinging the keys as she slid it into its case alongside her manuscript. She heard Laure calling a taxi to the seventeenth with a feeling of unreality. How had the day slid so extraordinarily into disaster? She didn't know what else to take. A bra, two dresses. Shoes. She put these things into her canvas overnight bag. Her book, which was Laure's copy of *Gilles et Jeanne*. After hesitating, she took that too. It was like taking a key, or a ball of wool. She would be back to return it, of course she would. She soothed her mind with this thought as she would a frightened animal, and went back into the living room. Laure was sitting on the sofa, rigid.

"The taxi is here."

"OK." Erica glanced at the kitchen. "I'll just sweep that—"

"Go. Please." Laure's lip was wobbling. Erica suddenly felt very sober.

"Please, my love. I'm sorry, I'm so sorry."

"Do you even know what you are sorry for?"

All of it.

"Go." Laure did not shout, but there was such force behind the word it was like an incantation that sent Erica out of the door, down the stairs, and into the waiting car. She gave the address of the apartment her husband paid for. When they arrived, she tumbled from the taxi, and in the shadow of a broken streetlight she vomited, hard and until she was empty, onto the pavement.

•

Laure left almost immediately after Erica did. She left the smashed glass, fled her apartment like it was the scene of some terrible crime. The breaking of the bottle had ruptured the safe distance time had introduced between her and Gabrielle, and it was with the same adrenaline she moved through the dark streets, to the same person. She let herself into Michel's flat and crept into the living room, intending to sleep on the sofa.

"Who's there?" She heard the creak of bed springs, hurried to his door to reassure him.

"Sorry. It's me." She went to his doorway. Her eyes hadn't adjusted to the dark and she saw only the movement of his white sheets.

"What's happened?"

"Nothing." But Laure's voice broke on the word.

"Is it Erica?"

"It's late—"

"Tell me."

She sat beside him in the dark and told him.

He sighed. "A mess."

"A complete mess."

"You should call her."

Laure stared at the pale smudge of his face. "What?"

"She's been a brat, but she loves you. And you love her. And I don't want you to be alone, when—"

"Don't." Laure swallowed back a sob.

"Call her."

"Now?"

"I doubt she will be asleep. She is a kind person, she will be worried about you."

"I'm still angry."

"Fine. But tell her you will see her, call her tomorrow."

Laure went to the sitting room and dialled the apartment in the seventeenth. Erica answered after the second ring.

"Hello?" The desperate hope in her voice melted Laure's anger even more.

"Erica."

"Laure." Erica's voice was squeaky with tears. "I'm so sorry. I'm drunk and I didn't mean what I said, about Barbara and Michel."

"Let's not talk about it now," she said. "But I'll call you, OK? I'll call you tomorrow."

"Yes," said Erica, sounding giddy with relief. "Yes. Thank you. I love you."

"I did it," said Laure, going back through to the bedroom. She saw the dark gesture of Michel's hand. She went to him, and he put his arms around her, pressed her to his thin chest. She heard the knocking of his heart, his beautiful heart, the fucking miracle of him. He had to survive this. It was impossible he would not. Laure gripped tight to his pyjama jacket, and let him stroke her hair until she fell asleep.

She slept late for her—her father's watch told her it was eight thirty-five. Michel was still asleep beside her, the sheets soaked with his sweat. Laure moved carefully out from under his hand, and went to the bathroom to piss. She looked at herself in the mirror, and promised herself she would make good choices, even if they were hard. The smell of the wine on Erica's breath had tugged on the impulse that threaded under everything— to forget, to forget by drinking, to stop fighting and let herself just float. But it was not floating, it was sinking. It was drowning.

She was still furious with Erica: last night, she had come as close to hating her as she ever had. The drunkenness was one thing, but her reaction to Barbara, to Michel's illness—these were what sickened her. There could be no more drinking, not in her home. Not anywhere near her. Laure needed to focus: on Michel, on her future. If Erica wanted to be a part of that, she needed to make her decision. If it was Laure, things had to change.

She crept back out of the bathroom and into the kitchen to make coffee. Their dinner things were on the drying rack and she put them away. Saturday today. Marie and Agnès' day. They would be here about ten—all of them pushing their arrival times back over the last few weeks to allow Michel to sleep in. She wondered if Barbara had told them about the AIDS test. She wondered if Barbara had told them about Erica, drunk and shouting in the street. She took her coffee through to the living room. She'd never noticed how similar the layouts of her and Michel's flats were. His was larger, but there it was: a galley kitchen, a sitting room, a bathroom, a bedroom. More than many had, and yet lately she wondered if it was enough. Her father's house rose at her, tapped at the inside of her chest. The fields. The space. The luxury of stairs.

She imagined going with Erica, if that is what they decided. Stripping the wallpaper, throwing away that infamous hearth rug. She imagined going alone. Something like pleasure rubbed against her calves like a cat.

She heard Michel stir, murmur something, then call her name.

"I'm here," she said, and the house in Bois-d'Ennebourg slid back out of reach.

Marie and Agnès were delighted to see her.

"Where have you been? We thought you'd been kidnapped again," said Marie.

"Gabrielle didn't kidnap me."

"Close enough. Who is it this time?"

"No one." So Barbara hadn't told them. Good. She needed a clear head for whatever conversation she and Erica had, didn't need their opinions in her mind. "I was busy."

"We wondered if you'd been seeing the tourist," said Agnès, watching her carefully.

"Did Barbara tell you about my AIDS?" said Michel, rescuing her. The women turned to him in unison. He sat bundled on his sofa despite the heat, holding court.

"It's not funny, Michel," said Marie. "She called yesterday, after she dropped off your sample. When will you get the results?"

Michel glanced at Laure, and she knew he was about to tell them about Christophe. She went through to the kitchen to unpack the bags of shopping they'd brought. She didn't want to listen to it all again.

The day was almost joyful. A weight seemed to have been taken from Michel now the word was out there, alive between them all, and Laure felt bad he'd had to hold it alone so long. She remembered why she loved Marie and Agnès, how being around them made love seem possible and desirable, their comfort and slight smugness, their certainty that how they did things was the right way. It must be wonderful to be affirmed like that, to not have the sly undercut of self-doubt constantly stalk every statement. Laure thought she was meant to get wiser as she got older, but all she felt was there was less and less she knew. She used to believe her taste to be immaculate, her insights unique, but the more time she spent with the films and music and paintings she loved, the less she understood them. All day she thought of Erica, alone in the apartment in the seventeenth, and looked forward to and dreaded calling her in equal measure, about going in person to finally have the conversation that would decide their future. But the day galloped by, and it was late before Marie and Agnès left, after midnight when she reached home. No matter, Laure decided. Let Erica sit with it another day. She would call tomorrow.

•

By the time Laure called, it was already too late. When Erica woke the day after their fight to the phone ringing, the noise like a drill boring a hole into her temples, she was prepared to grovel, to do anything to make amends. But when she'd heaved herself to the phone and croaked, "Laure?" there was a crackle on the line, the unmistakeable pause of long distance.

"Erica! I'm at the airport. The final leg of the tour's cancelled, so I thought I'd come and see you."

It was a mark of her hangover that Ant's words took a moment to gain any sort of context in her foggy brain. "Airport?"

"Singapore." His words faded in and out of static. "I'm on the second stretch. I tried you yesterday but you were out."

"Coming here? To Paris."

"To where you are, my love. I land at Charles de Gaulle late tonight. I'll come straight to the apartment, I should be there by midnight. Wait up for me, won't you?"

He hung up, and Erica let the dial tone burrow into her skull. Tonight. She had to talk to Laure. Her watch told her it was only eight in the morning. Though she was exhausted, her headache almost blinding, she dialled Laure's number. It rang out. She called again. No answer.

Erica slumped by the phone. She was going to be sick. Or had she already been sick? Her mouth tasted awful. She thought she would have more time. But here it was. Why was Laure not answering? She needed somewhere to go, after she told Ant it was over. She wanted to start her life with Laure. The thought of his face as she told him caused another twist of physical pain. Only Laure could make her leave him. She stared at the receiver, dangling from its cord, and replaced it. Laure would call, and hearing her voice would make everything feel all right.

But Laure didn't call. Erica tried several times throughout the day, but there was no answer at the apartment. She considered calling Michel, but it felt trivial to trouble him after what they'd just found out. She napped all afternoon, waking thirsty and disorientated. In the bathroom mirror, she looked as though she'd been stung by something: bloated and awful. That would make it easier on Ant at least.

She tried, once more, to call Laure in the evening. Nine p.m. Ant would be landing in a few hours. The unreality of their reunion was already hitting her, the future tunnelling out from her like a fired bullet. But she knew what to do. She was resolved.

When he arrived in the early hours, rumpled and big and handsome, with a bottle in hand, she absorbed the initial shock of how good he looked, his tired eyes lending him an irresistible vulnerability. She'd practised what she was going to say, but he kissed her before she could speak. Immediately, Erica felt her body flood with relief, with gratitude. For his simplicity, or rather the simplicity of what they shared, which had a framework and a name, a contract they'd both signed willingly. For the safety of him, which was how much he loved her. It was as though she'd been waiting for permission to renege on all her high-minded resolve. On the braver choice.

"Nightcap?" he asked, and her stomach roiled at the thought.

"I've not been drinking," she said, and to her surprise his face lit up. He lifted her and kissed her, drawing back and beaming.

"I read that too. It makes it better, our chances."

"Oh," she said, feeling like the worst person in the world. He thought she'd been readying herself for pregnancy. "Yes."

She let him take her to bed and that was good too, and the shame and self-hatred she'd felt since last night sloughed off her like dead skin, and as he moved inside her Erica understood she was a coward, and could not take another, harder path. This was a betrayal of Laure, and so maybe enough to cancel them out. Maybe now, it could all be square.

The next morning he answered the phone before she could reach it, on his way out of the door in his running shorts, the Walkman he'd bought in Hong Kong clipped to his waistband. He frowned and said, "Hung up."

"Nuisance caller," said Erica, like it happened all the time. He accepted this and put his headphones over his ears, waved and closed the door a little too loudly after him. Erica counted to five, and called Laure back. She answered straight away but didn't speak. Erica could hear her shaky breath on the line.

"Hello?" She waited. "Laure?"

"He's there."

"Yes."

Another long silence. "Can you speak?"

"Yes. He's gone out."

"When did he arrive?"

"Last night. I didn't know until yesterday morning. I tried calling you."

"I was at Michel's."

Erica nodded. She should have tried his number. She understood now she didn't because she knew Laure would be there. "How is he?"

"He is himself."

Erica listened to Laure's breath. This moment felt like the moment of the kiss in reverse. If only she had spoken to Laure before Ant arrived. If only she had not smashed the bottle. If only she had not insulted Barbara. If only she had not got drunk. But Erica knew that all of this had happened because she could not hold her line, hold her nerve. The regret was a barb she would always carry, but she had betrayed Laure for the final time.

"I think it has to end," she said, calmer than she'd ever imagined. "Us."

Laure answered in a reflection of her voice, two glassy surfaces held up to each other, implacable. "I think so too."

The shock of it didn't hit Erica immediately. It was like a far-off flash of lightning, the roll of thunder coming later. Much later.

Laure spoke again. "I think I'm going to leave Paris."

"What, why?"

"I think it is over for me. Michel is dying. We are talking to a doctor but there will not be much help. When Michel is gone, I will go too."

"I'm so sorry." And she said it for everything, and it sounded as useless as it felt.

"I know. Me too."

She wanted to say "I love you," because of course it was still true, perhaps would always be true. They breathed together, and Erica imagined their breath travelling along the miles of telephone line across the city she'd thought to make her home, into each other's ears. It was over. How was it over, so suddenly? All of these hours, so easily unknotted.

"Goodbye," said Laure, awfully formal, final.

"Goodbye."

Laure hung up the phone, and Erica saw her in her mind's eye, standing in her small flat, and was glad she could not hurt her anymore.

Part Four

1993–2013

perhaps we shall never see each other again; perhaps we shall meet again but fail to recognize each other: our exposure to different seas and suns has changed us.

from *A Lover's Discourse* by Roland Barthes

Chapter Ten

Erica shielded her eyes, wishing she'd fetched her sunglasses from her handbag before it got wedged into the boot. The sun, combined with the wind whipping over the low windscreen, was making her eyes water, but she had been too busy making sure the girls were strapped in safely to stop Ant before he'd concertinaed their luggage into the trunk of the ludicrous car he'd hired, a 1991 Nissan Figaro with no leg room, in a shade of sage green that gave Erica flashbacks to the year they'd lived at his family home. National Trust property green, she'd come to think of it as. Rich-people green.

She was a rich person now too. She had no job, other than the girls, and next year Elinor would join her sister at school. And then what?

"We might have to put the hood up soon," frowned Ant, peering at the sky. "See that cloud? God I hope it doesn't rain the whole time, we might as well have stayed at home."

"It is quite like home," she agreed. "Fields and fields."

"More cows though. Doesn't Laure live next to a dairy farm?"

"Mm." Erica was still getting used to the idea of Laure in a setting like this. She was still getting used to the idea of seeing her at all. It wouldn't feel real until she actually did—but then, her last memory of her was seven years out of date. She'd not been invited to Michel's funeral, and though she knew it made sense it had smarted. She'd wanted to say goodbye, to make the fact of his death a reality. And if she was honest, she wanted to see Laure, to make amends with the safety of the baby who would be Elinor in her belly. But instead it was a wild coincidence that was drawing them back together after a lifetime. *Two lifetimes ago*, she thought, looking at her girls in the wing mirror.

Despite the wind flying into their faces, and the medieval mechanics of their car seats, the girls had somehow fallen asleep. Sylvia had her head thrown back, her mouth open, and Eli was drooping towards her big sister, dark head a halo of ringlets. It would be a nightmare to disentangle those when they arrived.

"Apples," said Ant thoughtfully. "Where are the apple trees?"

"Further south maybe? You know you won't be able to drink that calvados in front of Laure."

"I know, but I couldn't resist how cheap it was." He sighed. "A trip to France with no wine. It's sacrilege."

"Laure is a walking sacrilege. A French sober vegetarian."

"God help us."

"Maybe we'll be vegetarian after a fortnight next to a dairy farm. I can imagine you get attached." Erica half-hoped this would be the case. She had steadily gained weight since giving birth to Eli, and though Ant still told her she was beautiful multiple times a day, the magazines she subscribed to evinced the opposite. Kate Moss had been named "most beautiful woman in the world" in the edition of *The Face* Erica spotted in Ant's study, and though Erica knew it was absurd to be jealous of a sixteen-year-old, she was. Ant told her not to buy that trash, but it was easy to say when you were the one in the magazine, praised as much, by *The Observer*, for "ageing like fine wine" as well as writing era-defining books.

"Did you feel that?" Ant held out his palm. "I'm sure I felt a spot. We should cover the girls."

"It's warm, they'll be fine." Erica rested her hand on his knee. He was wearing his purple summer shorts. It amused her how Ant dressed on holiday, like a toddler allowed to choose their own clothes. All the shoots for newspapers had him in tasteful suits worn over acid wash T-shirts, or oversized coats with jeans. Ant despised the word "brand" but this was what his publishers had cultivated: a mix of old and new, traditional and avant-garde. He'd perfected his look in these photoshoots: a thoughtful smoulder, his hair swept off his forehead. Erica had learned not to tease him. Recently, the questions had turned increasingly to the new novel, which was still a work in progress and had been humbling him the past four years. He'd been on the phone to his editor the day before, talking through some plot point or another, Erica wasn't sure what exactly. Ant had long since stopped asking her opinion.

This was her fault, she knew. At first, they'd discussed everything, poring over each other's pages and marking them up as they had as students. *Gargantuan* was dedicated to her. She'd sent out her own novel—*An Inheritance*, it eventually was called—only when he'd assured her it was ready. An agent had picked it up straight away, but then struggled to place it, eventually selling for a low three-figure advance to a small press based out of the editor's Clerkenwell terrace. They'd not had the budget for a launch, and so to mark *An Inheritance*'s publication, Ant took her out to dinner with several of his novelist friends, her agent and her editor. The photograph of her, Ant, and his most famous friend had made it into the society pages of several newspapers. In it, Erica was holding a copy of her book and smiling, but the flash had obscured the jacket, and the captions made no mention of either her name or her novel's. *Anthony Cowper-Gray, Michael Ostler, and friend at The Ivy on Thursday night*. It sold too few copies for her publisher to bother telling her the numbers, and within a year she was pregnant, and she and her agent agreed to part ways.

Over and again, Erica tried to convince herself it didn't matter. She had finished a novel, a novel she cared deeply about and was quietly proud of. She had found an agent, a publisher, seen her book on the table at Foyles' flagship store. The fact the pile didn't diminish, and then vanished entirely, was something she could, if not forget, then not overanalyse. She had achieved the dream of being published, and if she had not seen what success looked like up close, maybe it would have been enough.

But if Ant's debut had done well, and *Excavations* even better, then *Marchmont* excelled. It became the hit of the spring, going into reprint twice before summer arrived. He was invited to every major literary festival, and Erica would accompany him, Sylvia in her arms, and sit trying to breastfeed in green rooms, change nappies in toilets with no facilities, attend afterparties where the toilet seats were dusted in white powder. She was almost relieved when she became pregnant with Elinor and the doctor told her not to travel. She was content to stay at their home in Burnham Overy Staithe, a converted mill with views over the water meadows and on to the sea. Erica dedicated herself to raising Sylvia, and painting the house, both of which appalled her mother-in-law.

"Why not hire a nanny?" Elizabeth would ask. "Why not employ a decorator? My dear, you have quite enough to be going on with."

But this was where Elizabeth was wrong. Erica had, at first, attempted to take Ant's advice and begin her second novel. But he didn't seem to understand that writing a book no one was waiting for was harder than writing one everyone was waiting for. That getting to think about nothing but writing was only a pleasure if you also got to talk about it with other novelists and interviewers and readers, so it became real and important. Otherwise, it was just lonely. Lonely and futile.

Erica immersed herself in motherhood. She loved Sylvia with a passion close to violence, and was content to sacrifice most everything else to become a Good Mother. So what if she was lonely, or bored, or perpetually so tired she could barely think straight. It was she who had wanted to come back to Norfolk, to buy a house by the sea miles from Ant's family. Her own were no use, and they barely saw them these days. She knew they would be alone, and here they were.

But it was only after Eli was born that Erica felt the last vestiges of her old self to be obliterated. She resented this tiny, mewling thing that had torn her open and cried ceaselessly. She was terrified of her own resentment, and frequently had to leave Eli crying in her cot and walk away to keep from shaking her. She had one, then two, then three bouts of mastitis, and everyone from Ant to her doctor told her to stop breastfeeding, but she knew if she could not do that one thing, the most natural thing, surely, after loving your child, then she would be nothing. A complete waste of skin.

Her worst thoughts were too ugly to voice to anyone, because she knew they made her a monster. If she told Ant, he would surely take the babies away, or at least hold these vile impulses over her for the rest of their lives. It did not help that her imagination was so vivid, everything from her sense of smell to her dreams dialled up a hundredfold since her pregnancies. She didn't blame her mother for only doing it once. It became clear there was something clinically wrong, and Ant proposed therapy, an appointment with a psychiatrist who could offer pills. But she declined, feeling that if she could not cope with this simple task, this thing billions of women had done before, she deserved everything she got. If her mother could do it, she surely could.

She got better. She came to love Eli, though she never admitted to anyone, even herself, that for many months she didn't. And now it was not in doubt that she loved her girls, but she wished someone had warned her how tiredness could become a boulder you heave around with you, or rather a boulder's worth of gravel, filling your hands and your head with sharp, grinding discomfort so there is no space, no time for anything but getting by.

Ant helped when he was home, but in that first year of her madness he was away for whole swathes of time promoting *Marchmont* in America, whole weeks that felt like years, when Erica would struggle from hour to hour, minute to minute, changing nappies, cleaning vomit, applying nappy cream to her chafed nipples and wetting herself just a little every time she sneezed. She'd shower with Sylvia asleep in her cot and Eli screaming on the bathmat, gingerly feeling her labia and perineum. Sex was like a laughable fiction, Eli conceived in the rush of hormones everyone warned her about that arrived when Sylvia was a year old.

Once, Emma brought her son Stephen to visit when Nicholas was away on a work trip, and it made Erica feel more than ever that she was failing. Stephen was a quiet, happy child, content to be put down in a corner with some blocks and sit watching Sylvia run around the flagstones, Eli crawling frustratedly after. Emma talked breezily about formula feeding and their sex life, how Stephen had started sleeping through, and though Erica knew she could break down and tell her friend everything, something—pride, embarrassment?—made her nod along while Eli yanked on her breast grunting "mik, mik."

"You're so lucky," Emma sighed, watching Eli chew Erica's nipple. "My supply was too low."

Stephen lay down and rested his beautiful head on his mother's bare feet.

It did get easier. Sylvia went to nursery, and then pre-school. Ant was home more to help with Eli, who remained wild and by four years old had still not slept through the night.

"She'll be big soon," he'd murmur over her head, as she starfished between them in bed. "We'll miss her needing us like this."

But though Erica had cooed and agreed, she could not wait for those days to pass. To have her bed back, her body, her husband, and even though the girls were older now, things were still not as they had been. She had still not made peace with the fact they never would be.

Paris was like a mirage, a fever dream she'd once—no, twice—had. She put it so firmly behind her sometimes she forgot it ever happened, any of it. When infidelity came up at rare dinner parties she attended, she was happy to tut along with the rest of them. She had a skill for self-deception. She'd believed she was a writer: she'd believed she would be a good mother: she believed she would never cheat on her husband. When Léa called to tell her Michel had died, she wondered if she could absolve herself of the last vestiges of memory and guilt by seeing Laure once more, severing the tie for ever. But that didn't happen, and instead Laure came bundling back into her life through, of all people, Ant.

In late 1992 he attended a day of lectures at the Sorbonne—his book in progress at the time was about a restoration expert, an idea since discarded—and came back to Norfolk raving about Laure Boutin and her analysis of mortality in Monet.

"She should write a book," he said. "I gave her my card."

Erica was cooking dinner with Eli hanging from her hip, and managed to say, "Laure Boutin? From the Sorbonne?"

"Well, she's based somewhere else now. Rouen or something."

Erica had experienced intense dizziness, and had to put down Eli, who wailed. She gripped the saucepan's handle until it burned. "I know her," she said.

"Oh!" Ant gasped. "Is she your Laure?"

Your Laure. He had no idea of the depths to which that phrase penetrated: to the tender spaces surrounding her viscera, betrayal and regret swimming around like parasites. She sometimes thought her madness was punishment, knew the secret was poisoning her from the inside, but there was no way she could tell him now.

"She said she knew me! I assumed she meant my books, and then she was gone, but wow. Your Laure. What a small world! I've emailed her already, asking if I can pick her brains."

"Has she replied?"

"Not yet, but gosh!"

When Laure did reply, it was with a polite explanation she was too busy to read his manuscript, but would be happy to answer some specific questions. These specific questions turned into a telephone call, and suddenly Ant seemed gripped by a desire to befriend his wife's ex-lover. Even though he could not possibly know she'd been, for a time, the other woman in their marriage, Erica found this impulse bizarre. He surely wouldn't be so comfortable if Laure were male. Ant frequently had passions though, for people or historical events or obscure Latvian composers. They came, they burned intensely, they passed. But his enthusiasm for Laure Boutin did not abate.

More surprising was that Laure relented. She and Ant became regular correspondents, and a few months into this unexpected arrangement, Laure invited the whole family to her farmhouse near Rouen. The moment Ant told Erica they'd been asked to spend August with Laure was so peculiar Erica wondered if she was dreaming, or if it was a prank. When Ant started discussing ferry timetables, she understood it was not, but she couldn't put up resistance without explaining that Laure was not a summer fling of fourteen years ago, but the person she'd nearly left him for only a year into their marriage.

So here they were, in the flatlands of Normandy, speeding towards the woman who she'd loved enough to imagine another sort of life. This other future, so long buried, nosed up in the weeks leading to their trip, like old bones uncovering themselves. Her pelvic floor wouldn't be decimated in that future, for one. But what else? Maybe she would have written another book, a better book, one she felt compelled to write rather than felt she should. Ant wouldn't admit it, but he had a bit of a bee in his bonnet about the success of women writers, especially lesbian fiction getting so much attention recently. She could have written one of those stories had she chosen the other path. Sometimes she opened the top drawer of her dressing table and took out the small jewellery box where she kept her talismans from Paris: the photograph of Laure; the cigarette she rolled her, the paper's gum undoing now, tobacco dry and shrunken; the spare key to Rue Bréa, which she found in her things months after their final awful scene. She should throw them away, but she never did.

Although, she thought, as they turned at the blue post box as instructed, an old farmhouse in the arse end of nowhere had not been in any of these versions. The house was slumped at the end of a potholed drive, a dusty pickup truck parked outside. Driving. Another thing Erica could not imagine Laure doing. She remembered her railing against the motor industry that had turned Paris into a city of cars.

"Is that it?" said Ant, a little apprehensively. "Lord, if it does rain, the girls are going to go stir crazy."

"A little rain never hurt anyone," said Erica. "Look at all this space for them."

"There's space at home."

"Yes, but you don't let them use it," teased Erica. "Worried about them drowning in the mill pond."

"It's the leading cause of accidental death in Australia. Swimming pools."

"I thought you were excited to come here."

"My mother will be scandalized we're taking the girls to stay with a lesbian."

"What nonsense, she's always telling us all her friends at the Boat Club are gay."

"Gay *men*, E," said Ant. "You know she's very Queen Victoria about these concepts. 'Ladies don't do that sort of thing.'"

Erica laughed despite herself.

They pulled up outside the farmhouse and the front door opened and there, without ceremony or warning, was Laure. Erica thought she'd have a moment to compose herself, fix her hair, check her lipstick. But Laure was already past the threshold, her hair now fully grey, her face lined, her body easeful and lithe. She looked so much older and more beautiful than Erica remembered.

Ant was already out of the car, slamming the door behind him. Eli woke with a start and began to wail, squirming to escape her car seat.

"Mama! Let me out!"

Ant and Laure embraced like old friends, kissing each other's cheeks. Erica busied herself with the girls, freeing Eli first while Sylvia sat rubbing her eyes. She lowered Eli onto the ground and she ran to Ant, hanging off his legs. He lifted her and introduced her to Laure: "Aunty Laure, like we told you, remember?"

Laure's eyes creased. "Aunty Laure, I like that. Though it should be *tante!*"

Eli burrowed her face in Ant's shoulder and Laure and Ant laughed. Sylvia hung back a little, and Erica crouched down beside her. "You all right, Goose? Nothing to be shy about. You hungry?"

Sylvia nodded. She was such a serious child, her rosebud mouth held in a stern pucker, her blue eyes dark-lashed. Erica hugged her, more because she needed it than anything, and then led her elder daughter to join the others.

"Erica." After a beat, Laure stepped forward and embraced her briefly. She smelt completely different, like lavender and fresh air.

"I'm hungry," Eli announced.

"Well," smiled Laure. "Let's go and eat."

Laure led them around the side of the house, where a picnic table was laid with wire cloches and a loaf of bread wrapped in paper.

"Do you want to lift them up?" asked Laure, and Sylvia looked to her parents for permission. Eli, though, climbed straight up onto the bench and began flinging aside the cloches to reveal boards of cheese and charcuterie, a peach salad with fromage blanc, and a lemon tart dotted with strawberries. Fucking strawberries.

"Come," said Laure. "Eat. What would you like to drink? Lemonade, grenadine, wine?"

"Wine?" said Ant hopefully. "I thought—"

"I don't mind," shrugged Laure. "I'd be a hermit if I minded people drinking around me."

Erica glanced at her. "I hope you didn't go to any trouble," she said.

"Would you like some?"

"Yes please," said Ant, as Erica said, "No, it's all right."

They exchanged a look and Ant, cowed, said, "Lemonade is fine."

Laure grinned and went inside.

"Hands, girls," said Erica, leading them to the outside trough beside the door and supervising the scrubbing of hands with a bar of lavender-scented soap. She'd smelt that scent on Laure's hair. She must wash with it. Laure returned with a bottle of white wine, glistening with condensation, and a jug of fresh lemonade for the girls. She poured them all drinks, and swung her long leg over the bench beside Erica.

"How was the journey?"

"Smooth. The drive from Le Havre was easy."

"Nice little car," said Ant, in the voice he used with his school friends. "A good runner."

Laure nodded politely.

"I didn't like it," said Sylvia quietly. "I like our car better."

"More space, isn't there, Goose?" said Erica.

Sylvia nodded and took another bite of bread. Eli was eating with gusto, and Ant contently sipped his wine and tilted his head back to the overcast sky.

"Nice place," he said. "Been in your family a long time, E said?"

"My great-great-grandfather built it."

"Himself?" said Sylvia.

"Yes, with his own hands."

Sylvia held up her hands. "Woah."

"That was a long time ago, so I've changed it a bit. But there's still a couple of rooms that need fixing up. I wondered if you might like to help me while you're here?"

Sylvia considered. "What sort of things?"

"Painting the walls, scraping off some old wallpaper. We also need to burn some furniture from the barn that has worms in it."

Eli and Sylvia squealed delightedly. "Fire!" shouted Eli. "Worms!" shrieked Sylvia.

"Child labour, is it?" smiled Ant. "I approve. I'm waiting until they can spell to get them to work as my typists."

"I can spell," said Sylvia, hurt.

"Me too," said Eli, standing on the bench and puffing out her belly.

"What is your favourite word to spell?" asked Laure.

"Pool!"

Erica snorted. "Eli . . ."

"Spell it?"

"Puh-ooh!"

"Very good," said Laure seriously.

"Words aren't my favourite," said Sylvia. "I like painting."

"Laure likes painting too," said Erica. "She's a professor in art theory."

"What's that?"

"I teach people what to think about paintings."

"How are you finding it after Paris?" said Ant. "Erica had you pegged as a hardcore Parisienne."

"I love Paris," said Laure, sipping her lemonade. "But Paris did not love me."

"Done!" announced Eli, hopping down from the bench.

"The field there has crickets. Hundreds of them." Laure pointed. "Want a jar to catch some in?"

"Yeah!" Eli followed Laure inside, and Ant leaned into Erica.

"Do you think it's safe?"

"There's no one for miles around."

"Snakes? Cows?"

"I think the snakes might hear Eli coming. And we'll ask about the cows."

Eli came back outside, clutching two old jam jars. She passed one to Sylvia. "Come on!"

"One moment, girls," said Erica. "Stay away from the cows."

"They're fenced in," said Laure. "We can go and see them tomorrow if you like, fetch some fresh milk."

Sylvia and Eli looked at each other, awestruck, then took off for the fields.

"You're good with them," said Erica.

"Léa brings her little boy sometimes. You know she lives in Le Mans now?"

Erica nodded, though in truth she hadn't kept up with Léa since hearing about Michel. Her world had shrunk to the girls, to Ant.

"I did a reading there once," said Ant thoughtfully. "And Rouen, come to think of it."

"Who publishes you here?"

"Laffont," said Ant, and no one but Erica would be able to read his slight affront that Laure didn't know this, and so presumably didn't own his books.

"And yours was Minuit, wasn't it?" Laure asked Erica. "You must sign it for me."

"You read it?"

"Of course I read it. It was so sad, so clever."

Erica chewed slowly. Her cheeks were flushing, she could feel them. Of course Laure would know she'd taken, wholesale, her words about art for the book.

"See?" said Ant, smiling at her across the table. "You should be proud, E."

"You're not proud?" said Laure.

"No, I am. It's just, the book didn't do anything."

"How do you mean."

"Didn't sell."

"And?" said Laure dismissively. "What do the public know."

"Wasn't reviewed either."

"Critics only write reviews they can make about themselves, everyone knows this." Laure topped up her and Ant's glasses. "Are you working on anything new?"

"No," said Erica, sobering up immediately. "I haven't written in years."

"Why?"

"She's lost her confidence," said Ant. "Though I tell her she's bloody brilliant."

"I'm not," said Erica, blushing harder. "I don't have anything to write about. Or at least, no good words to say it with. And even if I did, I'm busy with the girls, the house."

"You must come, Laure," said Ant. "It's right on the water meadows. Have you been to Norfolk?"

"Non, never," said Laure. Her hands were held perfectly still in her lap, palms upwards, like she was waiting to receive something. "Strange where life takes you. Sometimes right back to where you start."

"Yes," said Erica, looking out over the fields, her girls two bright blots, blue and green, their dark heads a smear of movement, their pale limbs shining. She should have put more sun cream on them. They should be wearing their hats. Their joyful shouts bounced off the house behind them and vanished.

"Well, you must come and visit," said Ant. "We've room, and the sea is on our doorstep, practically."

"Oui," said Laure. "Thank you."

She began to stack the plates, and Erica stood hurriedly. "Let me."

"You are my guest, please. Sit, have more wine."

Erica did as she was told, and Ant refilled her wine glass. When Laure had disappeared inside he leant across the table and reached for her hand. "You seem awfully on edge, my love."

"Do I? I suppose it's just strange being here, seeing her. Seeing her here."

"Not your typical country bumpkin, is she?"

"Says you."

"Definitely rain coming," said Ant, frowning up at the grey sky, pressing lower over their heads. "Do the girls have shoes on?"

"I think so," said Erica, squinting at their forms. She wanted, suddenly, to be away from him, from Laure and the house. "I'll go and check."

She started out across the fields, the ground baked hard and unyielding, the cropped harvest crispy under her sandals. A piece of grass, or hay, or whatever it was poked into the soft skin beneath her toes and she yelped, stopping briefly to remove it.

"You're all red, Mummy," announced Eli when she arrived, and Sylvia went to Erica and put her arms around her.

"Are you OK, Mummy?"

"Fine. I'm fine, Goose." She forced herself to smile, and gestured Eli to join the hug. Eli came and almost immediately wriggled free.

"All sweaty."

"And you are all grassy." Erica began to pluck trimmings from Eli's green dress. "Have you turned into a hill? Oh no! My daughter is a hill! Help! Help!"

And as the girls screeched and laughed, Erica promised herself she would have a good time, make sure the girls enjoyed themselves. They were here now, so best to make the most of it.

•

Laure squinted at the figures rolling about in the distance through the kitchen window. Erica, a mother. How strange. How beautiful. And something, Laure noted with a dull twinge of pain, she could never have given her. It suited her, the extra weight, the unbrushed hair, the slight hollows beneath her eyes. She wore motherhood well. She hoped her husband told her so. He seemed harmless enough, sitting with his head tipped back, regarding the sky. She had read his book of course, ready to hate it. It was no classic, but it was better than she'd wanted it to be. It had been on the shortlist for the Prix Femina étranger. She'd known him the moment she saw him at the lecture last year, been dismayed when he approached her. And now, here they were.

She lifted the plates from the soapy water and began to scrub. She'd become almost fanatical about hygiene since Michel was officially diagnosed, and they understood the repercussions of bringing illness or germs into his orbit. As much as anything, she was conscious of her hands, the bitten tips and yellowed skin reminders of her past life. Better to keep them scrupulously clean, or busy in the action of cleaning other things. The farmhouse was a godsend for this—when she moved in she doubted it had seen so much as a duster for decades. The kitchen cupboards were not, as she'd always assumed from the colour, oak, but a far lighter shade of pine. The kitchen linoleum had been beyond saving, so she'd lifted it to find wide, handsome floorboards mostly untouched by woodworm. She'd beaten out the rugs and paid for an expensive hire of a carpet-cleaning contraption, using it until the water ran clear and then once more for good measure. She'd polished all the windows, the smell of vinegar and lemons transporting her to her squat, to Erica and the lit candles, the first moment she knew she wanted her to stay.

She'd hired help from the farm next door, a boy who assisted her in patching up the barn roof so Laure could sleep there whilst they stayed, giving her room to Erica and Ant, and the girls were in her childhood bedroom in bunkbeds she'd sourced from a family in nearby Montmain. The farmer himself had driven her to collect them in his pickup, helped her disassemble the beds and then heaved them up into the bedroom at the farmhouse, left her to puzzle them back together.

As she prepared for her first proper visitors, Laure convinced herself that she'd done nothing more than she would for Léa's overnights with her son. But now she knew that wasn't true. She'd wanted to impress Erica, and to prove to herself, once again, she'd done the right thing leaving Paris. Still, after five years, she wasn't entirely sure. She'd stayed through Erica leaving, through the attacks of '85 and '86, though they'd sent her into a state of fear she couldn't reason away. She stayed through Christophe dying, and when Michel was moved into hospital. It was one of the greatest regrets of her life that she wasn't there when he died, had gone home for a change of clothes, some more books. Barbara had called her.

"Michel's gone."

Laure had slid to the floor, the receiver cord stretching from its spiral, the plastic case of the telephone hot against her ear.

"Barbara?"

"Michel's dead." Barbara's voice was thick with tears, a whisper. "Will you come?"

"I'm coming."

Barbara made a small noise, something like assent, something like a gasp, a stifled howl, cut short as she hung up. Laure sat on the scrubbed linoleum of her flat on Rue Bréa. She knew it was coming, of course she did. There was no one who didn't know about the plague by now. The testimonies arrived that year too, Simonin's *Danger de Vie* passed from friend to friend with the fearful reverence of a sacred text and black spot. Even in Laure's circles, only a couple of steps removed from the younger and more active crowd, they hadn't realized how long and how close the disease had been stalking until those first stories circulated, and by then it was much too late.

But still she'd not been prepared. How could she be, after all their history? All those nights, smoking in her squat, in his community café, their plans and high-minded hopes. Their heartbreaks. Their triumphs. Weren't they going to change things, she and him? Weren't they at the least going to make each other's lives better? She knew she should get up and go to the hospital, but along her arm shot sudden pain, as though the receiver had delivered an electric shock. Then a terrible numbness, and the telephone dropped from her sensationless fingers. It was as it had been in Gabrielle's flat, when she felt certain that sobriety would kill her, the angel and the demon struggling for her soul. But this was worse. Michel was dead. And all the weight of what could not be undone folded in on her like a black hole, a fathomless mass, annihilating.

She felt the urge to drink drag at her like an anchor around her ankle.

As soon as the funeral was done, she gave up the lease on her flat and left Paris. What had once felt a safe place was dangerous, not only because of the disease but because of the reaction to it. She saw how hated they were, still, even here. Section 28 had been watched at first with ridicule, and then concern. *But it couldn't happen here* became a plea rather than fact. Laure had seen the ugliness felt towards people like her and the way they lived. The death of her most-loved friend only solidified the rot. She'd left Bois-d'Ennebourg to seek a broader church, and then felt the city squeezing her out.

"You're jumping ship," said Barbara coldly, when she told her. "I didn't think you were that sort, Laure."

"What sort?"

"A coward."

A coward. Until Barbara said it, Laure didn't know it was the thing she most dreaded being.

"Can I help?"

Laure jumped at the sound of Ant's voice. He stood in the doorway, a little hesitant, like a child summoned to the headteacher's office.

"You can dry, thank you."

They stood shoulder to shoulder at the sink. He was only a head taller than her, but so broad he seemed much bigger.

"Amazing view," he said, and she inwardly sighed. Not someone comfortable with silences.

"Not much to see." He laughed, at nothing so far as she could tell. Taking pity, she went on, "When the flax is in flower the colour is extraordinary."

"Oh, I'd have liked to see that. Sorry we couldn't come earlier, I was in Germany all June."

He spoke as though she'd invited him. The way she remembered it, he'd invited himself. She'd wondered if Erica was at work behind this, but her reticence said otherwise.

"This suits me fine. Term doesn't start until September." She put the final plate on the rack for him to dry and got started on the cutlery. Did he know about them, their affair? She studied him and decided definitely not.

"Well, it's very kind of you to have us. We're all in need of a holiday."

"Does Erica have much help, at home?" She didn't know if that was too direct a question, but as Ant seemed keen for her to know he travelled a lot, she was interested in their arrangements.

"A cleaner. And Sylvia's at school, so it's mostly her and Eli now. I don't know how she managed without a nanny, she's superwoman. But you know that."

"How do you mean?"

"I know it was a long time ago. Hell, I had a first love too. Patricia. Horrible girl." He gave an uncomfortable laugh. "Erica clearly has better taste. I suppose it's strange for you too?"

Laure's hand tightened on the sponge. "Mm. Not really."

"I suspect I sound stupid. I mean, she's married to me, isn't she? It's a bit confusing."

She's bisexual, Laure imagined saying. *It's not difficult. She loved me, and she loves you.* But instead she pulled the plug, emptied the catcher into the bin.

"Lesbian literature is very popular now," he went on. "Jeanette Winterson does very well."

"Good," said Laure briskly.

"Have you ever wanted to write a book?"

"What, because I'm a lesbian?" She smiled to soften it, though she didn't want to.

"Ha! No. Because . . . you talk very well about art. Erica says you changed the way she looked at it."

"That is why I am a teacher." Laure dried her hands on a fresh tea towel.

Ant finished drying and leaned against the counter. He was trying to look relaxed, but she could see that he didn't know what to do with his hands, putting them in his pockets, tapping the surface behind him, and finally crossing his arms. "You've never wanted to write?"

"No," she said. "I'm content to be a reader."

"Well, we need more of those!"

Something about his delivery told her he'd said this line before to a rapturous audience. He was fine. Nice, even. She resolved to be less prickly.

He glanced out of the window. "Ah, they're coming back."

Erica was carrying Eli, her hip thrust out to support her weight, an arm caught under her legs, Sylvia walking alongside. Her hair was even more tousled, full of dried stalks, and the crimson blush was spread over her neck and chest.

Laure felt a pang of nostalgia.

She had spent her whole life knowing she didn't want children. But since Léa started bringing her son around, she wondered more and more if that was a defence mechanism, a stifling of a longing before it could take root.

She watched Erica and her girls, saw how Eli was almost her mirror image, Sylvia more her father's child, and wondered what their faces would have made together. Erica's hair and lips, Laure's eyes and nose. Erica's passion, Laure's obstinacy. Sylvia was a name she liked, and then? Maybe Rose. Sylvia and Rose. This would be a good place to raise a family—she had often been happy here as a child, even if over the years she had sometimes chosen to forget that.

Laure stood tangled in her fantasy until Ant broke into the frame, Eli squirming to be put down and running, headlong, into her father's arms, waving her jar in which crickets were leaping. Erica shielded her eyes and caught sight of her through the window. Laure waved and felt stupid, but Erica smiled, and waved back.

The next morning, Laure took the girls and Erica for a walk while Ant went for a run. They saw him off, his minute neon shorts making him visible for miles, and then took the desire line Laure had cut across the cropped fields, a route she'd walked since she was a girl. Eli unselfconsciously held Laure's hand and tugged her down at every opportunity to stare at beak-broken snail shells and worms brought to the surface by overnight rain.

"I've never seen Eli so focused," Erica murmured as Eli held a translucent dragonfly wing up to the sun.

"You do not have the space at home?"

"We do, but we mainly walk to the beach. The fields are for cows. Ant has a terror of them."

"Does he not like animals?"

"Only eating them. Sorry, crass."

Laure waved her apology away. "Please, remember I am Marie's friend."

"Oh, steak for breakfast!"

"Sometimes, still."

Eli dropped the wing and she and Sylvia walked ahead. They'd reached the edge of the field, where hedgerows were full of birds and the girls delighted in the flung shapes of chiffchaffs and dunnocks spilling from the leaves.

"Have you seen her recently? Marie."

"No." Laure felt the familiar lump in her throat, which swelled like a boil whenever she thought of Paris and the friends she'd left behind. Marie and Agnès had been more understanding than Barbara, but still she knew they missed her, that things would have been easier if she'd waited a bit longer after Michel died, kept their group together until they all found their feet again.

"I don't think I ever said. I know I didn't say . . ." Erica hesitated, her eyes on the girls walking just ahead now, and Laure wanted to ask her to please, not apologize. Not for how they ended, not for Michel. Laure didn't want to talk about it. "I know how much Michel loved you, and how much you loved each other. It must be a very big hole."

Hole was wrong. It was more active than that, extra newtons of gravity exerted on her body. Sometimes people talked as though it was a relief, to see him out of suffering. Maybe it made Laure selfish, but she did not agree that death was better. Not where Michel was concerned.

"But good to have this place, maybe?" Erica continued timidly, into Laure's silence. "Something to focus on."

Laure took pity. "Yes. There's plenty to do." Barbara's voice in her head again. *Running away, playing at farms.*

Erica was gone, her focus pulled back to the children. "We should eat something soon, or they'll go feral."

"There's a copse just ahead," Laure pointed. "It's cooler there."

"Girls, head that way," called Erica. "We're going to eat."

"Petit dayjunenay!" shouted Eli.

They sat in the shade and ate torn-off sections of baguettes and whipped butter so fresh it seemed to evaporate in their mouths. Erica moaned softly at the taste of it and Laure tried to pretend she hadn't heard. The girls asked Erica what the French names of everything on the picnic cloth were, and Erica answered hesitantly, deferring to Laure, apologizing and blushing at every mistake. Laure hated seeing her this way, hated how she had once mocked her attempts. As they walked back to her house, the girls running in a criss-cross ahead, she said, "Your French is good. You should speak it more, speak it with me."

"It's terrible. I stopped completely after . . . I don't even read it anymore."

"It's a shame," said Laure.

"Well, you all speak English anyway. The language of the oppressor."

"Oh yes." A shameful fluttering of glee at this reminiscence, both of them skirting around their last encounter in favour of their first. It was safer.

Ant came into view, stretching outside the back door.

"Good timing," called Erica, waving.

"I've been back ages," he said. "I'm parched."

"The door is unlocked," said Laure. Ant tried the handle as though not believing her.

"Oh. Yes." He grinned. "Sorry, forgot you can do that here."

They went inside, the kitchen filling with the smell of his sweat. Laure set the kettle on the hob while the girls hung off their father and told him about the cows.

"I found a dead dragonfly!" said Eli. "And loads of snails." She emptied her pockets, showing him the shells.

"You need to wash your hands before we eat. Shall I make breakfast?"

"We had something already," said Erica, a little anxiously. "Shall I make you eggs?"

"No, no, cereal is fine." Ant began opening cupboards. There was tension in the room suddenly, a zing like electricity.

"Here," said Laure, fetching down some cornflakes.

"Thanks." Ant filled a soup bowl and fetched the milk from the fridge.

"Don't use it all," said Erica.

"I'll eat it dry shall I?" Ant splashed a tiny amount into his bowl and snatched up a spoon, pushing outside. Eli went to follow him and Erica said, "Let Daddy eat, sweet." And then, to Laure, "He's hungry after his run."

She shrugged. "He could take an apple next time."

"Good idea. I'll suggest it." Erica's fingers were twisting in her hair.

When he was done, Ant came in and apologized, kissing Erica on the forehead. Laure saw her melt against him, and wondered how her skin felt now, no longer smooth and unwrinkled. There were fine hairs along her jawline, light creases across her breastbone, her roots brassy with dye.

"Sorry," he said directly to Laure. "I'm awful when I haven't eaten. When have you booked Giverny?"

"Next week," she said. "It's busy."

"Perfect. Maybe we could visit Rouen? The Musée des Beaux-Arts has a Caravaggio I'd love to see. I'm a great fan of the Baroque."

Of course you are. "Yes, they have Velázquez too."

"And I want to see where they burned the girl!" said Eli.

"Elinor," said Ant, repressively.

"Jeanne d'Arc?" Laure nodded. "We can go there too. Today, if you like. The buses run every half an hour."

"Yeah!" Eli punched the air.

"Ah," said Ant, "today won't work. I have to write, get some pages ready to post to my editor tomorrow."

"I could take the girls," said Erica. "We could go to the museum again with you tomorrow, take the pages to post in Rouen."

"I'd like us to go together," he said. "I'd like to be with them."

"But you'll be writing," said Erica, and then, as though he'd admonished her, "But yes, tomorrow. Of course."

Ant finished his cereal and rinsed his bowl, Laure trying not to notice how he didn't use washing-up liquid, how the water ran a little milky as he placed it on the rack.

"I'll go and shower." He planted another kiss on Erica's forehead. "And girls? Excellent shells. We'll clean them up and take them home for our collection, shall we?"

When he'd shut himself in the bathroom off the kitchen they moved into the sitting room.

"Do you still want to go to Rouen today?" asked Laure. "We could just walk around, there's plenty to see."

"No, I think Ant wants us to go together, if that's all right. Maybe we could do something to help with the house today?"

"Yes, though I am happy to take the girls. Are you happy to paint with me, girls?"

"Yeah," said Sylvia.

"Can I burn the worms?" said Eli.

"We could sort the woodworm," nodded Laure. "They'll be fine with me. You can work if you want."

"Oh, I don't."

"Maybe you could start here. Something new."

"No," said Erica firmly. "Thank you."

Laure didn't know how she'd misstepped, or overstepped, but clearly she had. She nodded and went into the kitchen, re-washing up Ant's bowl and spoon and pretending not to hear the shout as the water went cold next door.

"Sorry." Erica stood in the doorway. "I'm tired."

"Then sleep," said Laure, turning to face her as she dried the bowl and spoon and put them away. "Let me help you, Erica."

"I'm fine." She smiled, and the strain was clear on her face. "I, too, want to burn some worms."

"Want to choose some music for the murder?"

"Lovely idea, I'll ask the girls—"

"Why don't you choose," said Laure. "Though don't mock how much Raffaella Carrà I have."

"Who?"

Laure staggered as though she'd been shot, affecting Michel's overt shock. "Ah, woman! And you call yourself bisexual?"

An awkward silence. Erica looked at her, and then at her feet.

"Sorry," said Laure.

"No," Erica forced another smile, "I'm sorry."

"For what?"

"Not knowing who Raffaella Carrà is."

"You should be."

They worked outside, retrieving pieces of furniture one by one from the barn and either breaking them down for burning or spraying them with vinegar, their faces wrapped in old scarves. The girls shrieked with disgusted delight as the larvae wiggled to the surface, Eli squashing them with aplomb and Sylvia crying until Erica assured her they didn't have feelings.

"They don't, do they, Laure?"

As a matter of fact, Laure was sure they must in order to react to the vinegar, but she looked into Sylvia's tearful face and understood why people lied to children.

They made steady progress, the girls turned serious with a task to do, to a soundtrack of Pearl Jam, R.E.M., and Raffaella Carrà, the latter summoning Ant downstairs to complain. Giggling, they moved to the barn, taking Laure's portable radio. The girls tuned in to random local stations and danced, their bodies moving in sexless imitations of Erica's familiar sway as they sprayed the pockmarked chairs and tables, the ancient milking stool left over from when this land too had been for cows. It was the most fun Laure had had in a very long time. When they piled into the kitchen for lunch, Ant appeared rubbing his eyes.

"How's it going?" asked Erica.

"Not well," he sighed. "I think I pushed too hard on the run. I feel all . . ."

"Maybe open a window?"

"The music—" He stopped himself and shook his head. "I sound like a misery! How did you do?"

"We are worm-slayers," said Sylvia.

"I killed a million jillion worms!" said Eli. "What's for lunch?"

They were not allowed to go to Rouen the next day either, and the day after that the Musée des Beaux-Arts was closed and so they delayed further. Laure didn't understand why they couldn't go into the city anyway, but she didn't want to get into it. Besides, there was a lot to be getting on with at the house.

So long as they were fed and watered at regular intervals, the girls were determined little workers, happy to be set to any task Erica deemed safe enough. After the woodworm, they helped Laure scrape the wallpaper from the hallway walls, Ant banished to work outside, out of the way, until the heavens opened. Laure preferred when it was just the four of them, though Ant was strong and helpful, willing to take direction. But Erica changed around him, becoming deferential, more self-conscious in her parenting.

It was worse still in Rouen, when they finally made it one overcast morning. Ant had insisted on driving, though the car could barely comfortably seat four. Laure warned him it was a market day, and so there'd be nowhere to park, but he said brightly, "Somewhere will open up! It's a numbers game."

They spent a miserable twenty-five minutes circling the square, Erica crammed in the back with the girls, before Ant announced it was a stupid city that did not have enough parking, and allowed Laure to direct him to a large, unmanned car park on the outskirts.

"We're bloody miles away," he grumbled, as they walked through a residential district towards the centre. Erica caught Laure's eyes and rolled her own, Laure passing off her laugh as a sneeze. After fifteen minutes Eli wanted to be carried, and Erica offered so Ant would not have to let go of his typed pages, packaged carefully and clutched to his chest. Laure and Erica took turns carrying Eli, and Laure was surprised how her body responded to two thin, strong arms around her throat, bony legs wrapped around her waist. It felt wonderful, and her body experienced the sort of rush she used to have from the first waking sip of wine, or lying in Erica's arms. A peace that settled into her bones.

When they found a post office and sent Ant's package, he relaxed considerably, stopping at the next café to buy them all ice creams, which fuelled them for the final push into the city centre. They joined the queue for the museum, Erica fussing for the girls to wear their hats and making everyone, Laure included, reapply sun cream. Laure didn't know how Erica held it all in her head, everyone's wellbeing, everyone's whereabouts, needs and wants. It was like watching a hostage negotiator at work.

Finally, they reached the museum, and Laure led them straight to the gallery where Caravaggio's *Flagellation of Christ* was installed. Eli took one look and announced, "Don't like it!"

"You haven't looked at it yet," said Erica.

"Don't want to. Can we see something else?"

"I would quite like to look at it."

"I can take her," said Laure. "We can meet you in an hour at the café?"

"Oh, no. It's all right."

"I want to go with Tanty Laure," said Eli, hanging off Laure's hand. "I want to see some horses."

"I know just the place," said Laure, checking with Erica.

"Can I go too?" asked Sylvia.

"I think both of you is too much—"

"I can manage," said Laure.

"Let her take them, love," said Ant, settling back on a bench with his legs extended before him. "Come, sit with me."

"If you're sure."

"I'm sure."

•

Erica watched them go with a feeling of trepidation and longing. She didn't much care for this painting either. She always found Caravaggio too theatrical, the artifice too pronounced for her to access any sort of feeling. In her less kind moments, she suspected that Ant liked Caravaggio because of the emphasis on brutality and difference—he claimed it was a very masculine sort of painting. She knew Ant prided himself on being a feminist, raised by strong women. That she had once called *Salome Receives the Head of St John the Baptist* "camp" following a trip to the National Gallery had produced a sulk lasting a whole train ride home was not worth dwelling on, and she hadn't even got started on *Boy Bitten by a Lizard*.

But she had to admit it was good to sit beside her husband, to feel his large, firm arm around her, inhale his scent. They'd made love the night before, for the first time in . . . she didn't care to count. Too long. It was good, if a little clumsy, his elbow catching and pulling her hair, but there had never been another man who fitted her so well, who understood so absolutely how to read her pleasure and respond to it. They'd kept the lights off at her request, and she could almost forget her sagging breasts, her loose belly, the slight pain as he entered her, and imagine herself desirable again. She hadn't come, too much in her head, stopping Ant from going down on her in case she tasted strange or looked wrong. Ant telling her to *let go* hadn't helped. But it was a start, and she leaned into him with a frisson of excitement at the thought that tonight they could do it again. Maybe this trip would be exactly what they needed after all.

"Remarkable," said Ant, after a further few minutes of silent contemplation. "My love, I long to take you to Naples. There's nothing like a Caravaggio in situ. I'm sure you'd change your mind if you saw his altarpiece."

"We can go to Naples," she said. "I never said we couldn't."

"But let's just us go, no kids. You and me."

He kissed her neck, and she pushed him gently off. "Not in public."

"Oh please, we're in France!" He tried again. "We could fly into Naples, drive down to Sorrento. Lie on the beach in the sun."

"We live near a beach." Erica was bored just listening to herself. Why was she like this? She was thirty-two, not a hundred. She had a husband who loved her, and moreover desired her, who was talented and kind and wanted to take her to Italy. The girls loved going to stay with their grandparents, with cooks who would prepare them whatever they wanted, and a heated pool, and their cousins on the next road over. Why couldn't she just say yes? Why couldn't she just *let go*?

"Erica? Are you listening?"

"Yes, sorry. What?"

"Never mind." Ant sighed. "Why don't we go and see something you want to look at."

He offered her the floorplan, and Erica looked at it blankly. What did she want to look at? Lately her tastes were more defined by what she didn't like, didn't want. She scanned the pages for a familiar name, and without thinking about it answered, "Monet."

They walked hand in hand to the gallery, finding the painting in a room with Pissaros and a gaudy Renoir. While Ant peeled off to examine a seascape, Erica came to rest before *La Seine à Port-Villez*. A grey, gauzy scene viewed from a curious elevation. A tree breaking the right picture plane, forcing the viewer further back: a play between being drawn towards and pushed away. Muted colours that in fact were multi-colours: pink and yellow and blue and sun-touched green. It was smaller than she'd been expecting, but still she could fall into it, the boundaries between her and the painting as blurred as the rendering of the river.

"Mummy!"

Eli charged up to her, nearly taking out her knees. Erica caught herself and turned to see Sylvia and Laure following, holding hands and talking. Laure smiled at Erica, and then noticed the painting behind her. Erica felt the heat starting. Why did she feel as though she'd been caught in the act of doing something indecent? She ducked to Eli to hide her blushes.

"Did you find a horse, sweet?"

"Yeah, it was sad."

"The horse was sad?"

"Géricault," said Laure, "a study. The face is in the *écorché* style."

"Écorché?"

"Flayed. To show the anatomical detail."

"Ah."

"But then we found murder horses!" said Sylvia.

"*Diomède Dévoré par ses Chevaux*," clarified Laure.

"They were *cool*," emphasized Sylvia. "Did you see the murder horses, Mummy?"

"No, but I'd like to."

"You can always find Erica by the Monets," said Ant, slinging his arm around her shoulders. Erica could feel Laure looking at her, but stayed focused on her youngest, shrugging off his embrace.

"Are you thirsty? Shall we go to the café?"

"Orange juice!"

"With water. How about you, Sylvia?"

"Yes!" Sylvia took her other hand. It was still hot from Laure's. She let her girls pull her away, the others following behind. Why was she being so weird? It was fine to like Monet. Fine, even, that the reason she did was because Laure had introduced her to it. Ant loved the Eagles because Patricia had. Lovers left impressions on each other, parts of themselves that would never be exorcised. So why did it feel illicit for Laure to know she sought Monet's paintings out?

The girls talked a mile a minute while they sat with their juice boxes, an apple each untouched on the plates in front of them.

"Jerrycold kept body parts in his studio. They rotted and rats came."

"His paintings are being eaten by the paint!"

"Jerrycold?" frowned Ant.

"Géricault," clarified Laure.

"Sounds a character." Ant downed his espresso. "What else shall we see?"

"There's plenty," said Laure. "Some beautiful still-lifes."

Ant mimed a yawn, and Erica nudged him.

"Sorry," he grinned. "Never understood the appeal."

"Want me to change your mind?" said Laure.

Ant raised his eyebrows delightedly. "Absolutely."

Erica walked behind them. She should be relieved they were getting on. That was why they were here, after all. They were both interesting, interested people. But instead she resented the ease she saw between them. Even when it was only her, Laure, and the girls, Erica felt there was someone, something standing in the way. Of course there was Ant, their past, but she'd nurtured the desire for a friendship with Laure through so many moments when it would have been easier to let it fade, and now here she was, happily married with her beautiful family, staying at Laure's house. She'd got what she'd wanted in so many ways. So why did it not feel enough?

This feeling of insatiability marked Erica's following days. Her appetite increased: for food, which was always fresh and colourful, even the girls eating the salads and most pungent of the blue cheeses; for wine—having got over the fact Laure didn't mind, she and Ant would drink a bottle between them at lunchtime, and nearly one each at dinner; and for sex, which delighted and amused Ant in equal measure. Apart from the trip to Rouen, Ant was mostly shut in their bedroom typing, driving to the local post office to send off pages every other day, so their only time alone was spent in bed. Erica didn't want to talk, only to feel him inside her, the wine fug melting their edges together, their bodies flowing into and out of each other as they used to. She wanted to know she was loved, desired, safe. Something inside her that had been untethered a long time was drifting further out, and she longed to come back to herself, to feel like a whole person.

"Are you all right?" he'd whisper afterwards, his arm wrapped around her, his body pressed into the length of hers, sweat cooling in the breeze from the open window, and Erica would nuzzle back into him, holding on tight, watching the light from the barn leaking through the parted curtains and knowing Laure was still awake. Probably reading, or listening to her radio, in her makeshift bedroom in the barn, while she and Ant sweated into her mattress.

Laure's set up in there was ramshackle and sweet, her childhood truckle bed, a bedside table fashioned from a crate, a lamp and a bowl Erica eyed with suspicion until Laure said, "It's for brushing my teeth."

The girls thought it was marvellous. They thought Laure was marvellous, and the farmhouse, the fields. Sylvia didn't fuss about the rain, about her hair getting wet, the mud splattering her ankles. They found an abandoned dormouse nest and Eli carried it carefully to show Erica, tiny dried flowers woven into grass stalks, moss and feathers, like something from a picture book. Her younger child seemed mellower, or maybe the landscape was large enough to contain her. Why did it feel so different to Norfolk? They had space there too. And she was not left alone so much here. She had Laure.

The day of the visit to Monet's gardens at Giverny dawned overcast. Ant decided to stay behind to work, make the most of the quiet. His agent had called with new thoughts and he was in a bad mood.

"Not so much of a carrot man, is Charles."

"What did he say?"

"Doesn't matter. I'll sort through it, get something down and be in a better mood this evening."

He kissed her softly and smiled, pressing his forehead down to hers. "I'm sure you'll help cheer me up."

She smiled and moved away. "Maybe you could get the house straightened out a bit? We've rather taken over."

Ant rolled his eyes. "It was hardly pristine when we arrived."

Erica's palms felt itchy. The pressure in the air was giving her a headache, and she hoped it wouldn't rain before they arrived at the gardens. "Please. If you have time."

"I probably won't," he said, "but I'll see."

"Maybe you could tidy instead of going for a run?"

"I need my run. You know it's how I keep my head on straight."

Erica chewed her tongue. She didn't want to pick a fight. "Good luck then."

Throughout the bus ride, her stomach did somersaults. It was like she was going to meet an illicit lover, or sit an exam. In her year of madness, when her brain had felt on fire or suspended in some thick, viscous liquid, she'd grown used to the dulling lows of depression, almost comforted by the numb exhaustion. Worse by far was the anxiety, the jolting, sour racing of blood through her veins, her body bolting like a wild horse at the slightest stimulation. She used to drink Rescue Remedy like water, and wished she had some now, the comforting grape sting of it, the quaint glass dropper.

"Are you all right?" said Laure. She was sitting in the seats in front on the near-empty bus, the girls up with the driver, singing along to his radio. Erica recognized "Tandem" by Vanessa Paradis, Sylvia doing her unnervingly sultry nonsense French while Eli flicked her hair around.

"Fine."

Laure smiled and swung herself around to sit beside Erica. The warmth of her leg pressed against Erica's, and Erica wondered how she could bear it, how she could bear to sit so close and so casually. It made Erica's skin tingle, heightened the prickling chase of her blood.

"What is wrong? You don't feel well? I can take the girls alone."

"No, I want to go. It's what I've looked forward to most all trip."

She had given herself away, and looked out of the window to hide her blush.

"It is a special place." Laure gave her hand a brisk squeeze. "You won't be disappointed."

The radio cranked jerkily into France Gall and the girls cheered. "Laure, Laure!"

Laure grinned and swung her way down the aisle, shimmying her shoulders. The girls laughed as Laure mimed along, jutting out her chin and throwing her hands about exaggeratedly. Erica tried to smile when Sylvia looked over to check, but her lip was wobbling. What *was* wrong? What was wrong with her? She was almost relieved when Eli complained of feeling sick half an hour into the journey and she could lose herself in caring for her, accepting a plastic bag from a previously dour-faced old woman who turned out to have perfect English and not be half as fierce as the marionette lines alongside her mouth suggested.

"Look at a fixed point," she advised Eli. "The horizon."

Eli, pale and tearful, nodded, and threw up into the plastic bag. It mercifully only had one hole in it, and the bus driver pulled over to let Erica throw it away and clean up Eli with water from bottles offered by the passengers. She sat up front with her youngest's head burrowed into her armpit, trying to soothe her own breathing, to guide Eli into calmness.

Sylvia and Laure sat at the back, and occasionally Erica would shift to look at them, their heads close together, talking. Laure was so good with them both, but Sylvia in particular seemed mesmerized by her. The grey light, which drained the interior of the bus to a noirish foreboding, sat well on them, two lovely faces, faces she knew so well.

What would Laure's children look like? The thought arrived from nowhere, peculiar and bittersweet. Her straight nose set between plump cheeks, her long fingers brushing back those perfect ringlets that still sprang against Sylvia's nape when she climbed from the bath. Laure with a white towel, wrapping her child's stretching body, arms with little bangles of fat at the wrists, clinging around Laure's elegant neck. Laure turning to Erica and a small body between them, a body they created together.

Impossible. Stupid. A betrayal to even think it. Erica breathed in Eli's scalp, her smell still strong under the lingering sweet-sour of vomit. This was real, her daughter sleeping against her, her daughter with her husband's lips and hair, her own eyes.

"We're here! Look!" Sylvia's shout jerked Eli awake, and she scrambled to see the sign for Giverny as it passed by. Erica listed into the space where her daughter had been, like another tether had been cut. She righted herself and looked out of the grimy bus window. The village was like something from a Disney film, half-timbered frontages and thatched roofs, climbing roses and blue-painted shutters peeping through thick growths of ivy. But it was not sleepy or inanimate, the roads lined as they were with tourists and hawkers selling postcards, and Eli and Sylvia pressed their noses against the glass to exclaim at the beautiful buildings, the lampposts curved like snowdrops, the fields of wild poppies tangled in the gaps between houses.

The bus driver dropped them at the house's austere frontage even though it was far past the allotted stop. As they stepped directly onto the narrow road, the girls blew exaggerated kisses, and Erica felt her anxiety increase. The line stretched alongside the tarmac, and her headache pressed sharply against her temple. But before she could start along the queue, Laure touched her shoulder.

"We have tickets. Come."

She led them to the front of the line. They moved through the security check and into a vast gift shop. The girls tugged at Laure's hands, cooing at key rings and brightly coloured shawls printed with Monet's paintings, but Laure shook her head sternly.

"Non. Later, if you must. The real treasure is ahead. We'll go directly to the gardens. Do not look outside the windows, OK, girls? See it first when you are among it."

It reminded Erica viscerally of the day they went to L'Orangerie, Laure coaching her on where to stand, how to look. She, too, resisted looking out of the windows as they walked through the crowded house, arranged as it would have been in Monet's time, with replica paintings hanging on the walls, straw hats on the coat pegs, copper pans above the vast range, blue and white tiles buffed to a shine. Had Erica been in a different frame of mind, she would have loved to linger, taking in the details as though standing in a giant doll's house: the shells on the windowsills, the brushes standing in paint-stained water. But even these large, lovely rooms felt claustrophobic, and she moved past her dawdling girls to regain the fresh air, stumbling down a couple of stone steps and onto a lightly gravelled pathway. She had the impression of green before closing her eyes and inhaling, grounding herself before Laure or her daughters caught up. She could smell fragrant, humid sweetness, and she gulped it down greedily. She must not panic, not ruin the day.

Erica opened her eyes. The gravel crunched as people moved past her, but she stood still, transfixed. The green lapped at her, and from its lushness sprang purple lavender, lion-faced dahlias, the high golden clocks of sunflowers. Beyond, trees screened the borders, giving the impression she stood at the flower-drenched edge of a forest.

"Wow!" Eli's sticky hand clutched at hers, and tugged her forwards. Erica went willingly, pulled into the magic of the garden. Everywhere was a new joy, a bee alighting on honeysuckle, butterflies drowsing across the radiant pokers of lupins, paths obscured by spreading salvia and the blousy explosion of hydrangeas.

Erica walked dazed where she was bid, lifting Eli to the clematis growing up trellises, rubbing lavender between her fingers for her daughters to smell. Her anxiety faded the further they moved from the house, people dispersed among the foliage until they found themselves in a pocket of isolated movement, their rhythm breaking them away from the other visitors so it was as though only they walked in Monet's garden. She and Laure spoke not a word to each other, but Erica felt her close behind, answering Sylvia's questions in a low voice, as though they walked through a cathedral and she spoke a catechism of petals: *delphinium, marigold, nasturtium.*

At last they reached the place Erica had not known she'd been waiting to see. The lake arrived from behind a curtain of willows, its first glimpse like a mirror of the sky spread with flowers. Erica stopped dead as the midday sun broke through the grey hanging clouds, and as though in a moment of divine intercedence, the waterlilies shivered in a breath of wind, their waxy petals like palms upturned in pink and white supplication. Eli let go of her hand and ran to cross the bridge, Sylvia overtaking her, their feet slapping on the wood. They were a perfect photograph, her girls, the stuff of round robins and framed mantelpiece focus, but she didn't reach for the camera in her bag. All Erica could do was stand, and wait.

A cool, soft hand brushed against her loosely curled fingers. Her little finger extended, found Laure's. They twisted around each other, small vines, and held on tight.

•

It was only a minute point of contact. An inch or two of her skin, pressed against her skin. But Laure felt herself flayed. She knew as they stood beneath the willows that Erica felt what she felt. Saw what she saw. Not only what was before them, the lake and its abandoned boat, the waterlilies putting on a show, the girls waving at their reflections through the wooden bones of the bridge, scuffing their shoes across the slippery moss. Not only what was behind them, the bare floorboards of her squat, the grey-pink light of Paris dawning over their entwined limbs, the walks along another bank. But the other existence, laid over this like something thinner than skin: like gossamer, like breath.

Only a breath away, this other truth existed, where she and Erica were. Had been, for all these years. The fights, the kisses, the walks and the embraces. The words, whole libraries of them, spoken to each other, words weighed and thrown, exchanged and given. The looking, the learning of each other's changing faces, so slow it was never a change at all but one continual thread of mutual recognition, in step. She remembered learning how Rembrandt's paintings glowed with light caught in the layers of oil and varnish, ancient light trapped there the day he made the very first marks. This is how Erica was to her: shining with the light that fell upon her on the steps of the Sacré-Cœur over a decade ago. All that history. All that possibility. And somewhere, a version of Laure—a better, braver version—had seized it, and never let go.

Laure stood very still, balanced like a pond skater, not wanting to be the one to break the surface. Their breathing was in sync, so what Erica exhaled, Laure inhaled, the closed loop of them working in a lemniscate; infinity snagged around their intertwined fingers, and Laure knew if she turned her head, Erica would mirror her. If she bent her head forward, Erica would follow. In this other reality, she kissed her beneath the willows, and time bent back like a dancer to the room in L'Orangerie, and Laure asked Erica to stay, that first time together in Paris, and Erica did.

And then Eli, evidence of the version of events they'd lived, they'd *chosen*, for Laure knew she was equally culpable in this, was pelting back across the bridge, shouting, "Mama! There's fish!" and Erica's finger twitched and released, and Laure watched Erica move away from her, towards her daughters, Monet's waterlilies open-faced, aghast beyond her, beneath this version of the sky.

"I'm cooking!" Ant announced as he threw open the kitchen door, the eye-watering waft of garlic and chilli chasing him out onto the path. "Pasta alla norma!"

Laure felt as though she was caught behind a veil, or a Vaseline-smeared lens. She had slipped into another reality and was finding it hard to re-emerge.

"How was the writing?" asked Erica.

"Terrible." Ant kissed Erica on the lips. "Why do you think it's so tidy in here?"

Ant had indeed tidied, and cleaned, and to Laure's chagrin seemed to have done a great job of it. Aside from the counter and the stove, the kitchen was spotless.

"How was the garden?"

Laure felt Erica glance at her, and smiled brightly. "I'll let Erica and the girls tell you. I'll just have a little walk, I think."

"Great idea," said Ant. "But don't be too long, the tomatoes need fifteen minutes tops."

Laure left them to it, stepping into the purplish dusk. It had rained on the bus ride back, and the ground smelt grassy and expansive. She breathed it in, trying to ground herself, trying to push back the scream that had been building in her throat since Erica let go of her finger in the garden. Instead she counted, in two three four, out two three four, like the therapist she saw before leaving Paris taught her. The therapist who told her she should wait a bit longer, see, and so Laure stopped attending their sessions. *Coward.*

There was a heaviness in her chest, an ache. She knew it was heartbreak, and hated herself for it. But that moment in Giverny had given her something far more painful to hold. Hope. When Erica had held her hand, Laure felt the old recognition pass between them, the synchronicity they'd found that last summer in Paris, when it was as though their hearts beat to the same rhythm. But the girls were there. The girls were here. And her husband, in her father's kitchen—her kitchen—cooking Italian food. She wanted to cry, to stamp her feet like a child, and instead she laughed into the gathering dark. She felt a snail shell crunch beneath her shoe and lifted her foot to find a sticky, still-retracting mess.

What she wanted with Erica, she could never have. That way was closed. They'd missed their chance, their chances. Even if Laure did tell her how she felt, and Erica felt the same, what would they do? Erica, live here? Bring the girls? The courts would never allow it. And Erica would not choose her, just as she hadn't the last time, or the time before that. She chose marriage, children. And Laure could give her neither.

No. Erica would leave with her family. Laure looked out over the fields, in the direction of her father's house. Her home. She had survived heartbreak before and again. But even when she slept beside Erica every night in the flat on Rue Bréa, knowing as she did that their hoped-for future together might yet slip away, she'd not felt this desolation. All her chances were spent. And now she lived in a different world: where Erica had children, and Michel was dead, and her friends in Paris felt she'd abandoned them. She scraped the oozing, dying creature off her shoe. It would be all right, she told herself. It would be OK.

How many times had Laure told herself this? Enough to know it was true, and not at all.

Laure could have guessed what the goodbye would feel like. She longed for a fever to confine her to bed, for Ant's cooking to give her the shits, but the food at dinner was good. Their final day was a clear one, untroubled and easy. The girls were so sweet she could not even summon a little resentment for them.

"You will come and visit, won't you, Laure?" asked Sylvia anxiously. "Maybe for my birthday in September?"

"Come to mine, in May!" said Eli.

"September is sooner," said Sylvia. "And Christmas maybe?"

"We go to Grandma's and she makes baked ham and turkey and beef ribs—"

"Laure doesn't eat animals, Eli," said Sylvia, scandalized. "And I think I won't either, anymore."

She looked at Laure, who smiled and said, "That's exciting," and Sylvia beamed.

The girls babbled on and on about Laure visiting and presented her solemnly with cards they'd made with pressed flowers held onto paper with Sellotape, Sylvia's careful writing proclaiming their thanks and love. Ant deigned to leave his typewriter alone for the final morning, and Laure wished he wouldn't, wished she could have had these final hours alone with Erica, or alone with Erica and the girls, sustain her fantasy a few moments longer.

While the car was loaded with the last of the bags, Erica lingered in the kitchen, washing up their mugs. Laure watched with regret as she cleaned her lipstick off a shell-imprinted cup, thinking she could have kept it, pressed her lips to it. She took up a position beside Erica, and dried.

"It's been a wonderful trip," said Erica at last. "The girls want to stay for ever."

Stay for ever. Laure imagined herself saying it aloud.

"And it's been just what Ant needed. He's made such progress here. I can't thank you enough for having us."

Laure's fingers brushed Erica's as she took the final mug from her hand. Did she imagine Erica's intake of breath, that spark she'd felt by the waterlily lake springing up once more?

"Erica!" Ant, calling from outside. They were ready to go. They were leaving.

"You'll come and stay? We've plenty of room, and it will motivate me to finish decorating the guest bedroom."

Erica was watching her, a frown pinching her brows, her lips slightly parted, pink and cream, slightly dry from her time in the sun. Freckles across her collarbones.

"Yes," said Laure, without fully knowing what she was agreeing to.

"Good." The dart of her tongue, a nervous smile. "Well."

Laure could not have sworn it happened, even in the moment. But Erica leaned in, and brushed her lips against Laure's neck, just below the ear, the place where her pulse was drumming hard against the thin skin. Where she had kissed her before she got on the bus home, when they were young and in love for the first time. And then she was gone, walking fast away. Laure followed, dazed, into the sunlight.

Smile, she told herself. Laure smiled. *Wave*, she told herself. Laure waved. The sage-green car drove off down the dirt track, small hands waving madly from the open back windows, the low sun glancing off the glass of the windscreen, so inside was opaque, inscrutable. Laure touched her neck, felt the thudding of her blood.

Chapter Eleven

TO BE OPENED ON THE 27th of July!!!!!

The Mill House
Burnham Overy Staithe
Norfolk
England
The World
The Galaxy
The Universe!!!

2nd July 1995

Dear Laure,

HAPPY BIRTHDAY! We hope you have THE BEST DAY EVER and DANCE even though you are OLD NOW! We miss you and hope to see you soon. PLEASE KISS THE CAT FOR US!

Love,
Sylvia and Elinor xxxxxxxxxxxxxxxxxxxxxxxxxxxxxxxxxxxxxx xxxxx

Dear Laure,

Happy 40th Birthday! How has so much time passed since our visit! I hope we can organise a date to meet soon. I hope you received the flowers we sent on publication day. Will it be translated into English? We hope so.

Love to Barbara, and to Lapin.

Love,
Ant and Erica

Dear Laure,

We went to this exhibition last week, and I thought of you. Ant says you have converted him regarding Still Life artworks, and add to the mix Velázquez and Goya he was beside himself with joy. Anyway, I hope you like the catalogue, and hope it reaches you in time.

I know I've said it on the phone, but I was so, so glad to hear about you and Barbara. Michel would be happy, he loved you both so much.

How are you? From my bad French, it seems your book is a triumph amongst readers and critics alike. I so hope to read it—once I could have, but now I'll have to wait for the translation which I'm sure is coming. The years seem to slip by so easily. My girls are growing up, becoming little women. Sylvia is a great beauty, and a deep thinker. Elinor is wild and clever, and only sits still to read. The photographs can't really capture them. They are both very proud of their Aunty Laure.

Erica hesitated. What she wanted to write, she could not. That hearing the news Laure and Barbara were living together was like walking across glass. That when she heard about the book she felt not joy, but a deep, abrading jealousy. That what she felt for Laure herself was not pride or even simple jealousy, but a sense of ownership, a ravening desire for possession. For her, and for what she had.

Erica had spent too much time in therapy not to recognize this was not about Laure at all, not really. These feelings had come afterwards, she knew that logically if not actually, like looking at a photograph of a treasured memory until you cease to be able to see the moment as it was, but only as it was held in that snapshot. It wasn't about her marriage, which was happier than most despite Ant's travelling and her madness. It wasn't about the miscarriage, though that had felt like being adrift in an endless and freezing sea. It was about herself. It was always about herself. She was so tangled in her self-indulgent, stupid fantasies, her plots for revenge against everyone from her parents to the man who cut her up on the school run, it was hard to feel much about reality that was not a mirror angled back at herself, her feelings, her bitterness and regrets. Her psychiatrist said this was paranoia masquerading as narcissism, that she wasn't really selfish, only sick. She'd been prescribed pills, but she sometimes forgot to take them, and preferred it that way. The pills flattened her out, made her forget things, like she was living life through fog.

The trigger for this episode—lasting two years and counting, so when did it stop being an episode and start being who she was rather than something she had?—had been the loss of their third child at fourteen weeks. The doctors offered to investigate but Erica couldn't stand the idea. They had him cremated and scattered him at sea before Erica felt ready, because she was worried if she kept him in his little wooden box she would never be able to let go. Though everyone from Elizabeth to the doctor told her it was best she lost him so early, she felt she'd loved him a lifetime, and could not imagine the future without him. She named him Gabriel, an angel's name, her favourite author's name, and dreamt of him for a time, except he was never a child, he was always a man, Ant's double, patting her gently on the shoulder and saying *It's all right, Mama*. The grief rolled her further out than she'd been even after Eli's birth, though she knew that too was part of it. That she'd seen this third child as a third chance, a chance to get it right, to finally be a Good Mother. And wasn't that monstrous? She hated the way her therapist Jan left silences, her pen tapping lightly on her notebook, as though keeping time. She tapped the pen against her letter, to be tucked into the catalogue and posted alongside the girls' handmade card and her and Ant's impersonal Clintons offering, to Laure's farmhouse in Bois-d'Ennebourg. Laure and Barbara's. Erica swallowed, and finished.

And we are proud too. Happy birthday, and give the waterlilies my love.

Bisous,
Erica

X

It was childish, but she hoped the mention of Monet's garden, which was one of the subjects of Laure's *Le Pont* and which she visited every year, would spirit her back to their visit together, the touch of their fingers amidst the gentle breeze. She hoped Laure would think of it, and long for her, as Erica longed for Laure when she held the box containing the cigarette and photograph. What did it say about her, that she scattered Gabriel's ashes within days but had not thrown this box of keepsakes away? It was not a loving desire, to wish this pain on another, but she willed it anyway as she folded the paper, and pushed it into its envelope, tasting the glue bitter on her tongue.

•

The Farmhouse
Bois-d'Ennebourg

12th August 1995

Dear Erica,

You catch me between trips. You will know all about this, but the publishers have been merciless, sending me to every book club and shop in France it seems. But good news! "Le Pont" comes out as "Reflections" (not my choice) in England in September, and Barbara and I shall come over for a small tour and holiday. We hoped, in fact, to spend some time with your family in Norfolk, if you are around? Our phone calls and letters have so painted a picture in my mind, and I long to see if it is accurate. Perhaps we could be there for Sylvia's birthday? The 17th? Looking at the diary it is a Sunday.

I would call more but Barbara's online all the time at the moment, thesis season! Do tell the girls I will call soon, and let me know by phone or letter (or email, if you have it? Barbara's email on card enclosed) if a September trip would suit. Come to the launch event, if you like. It's at Hatchard's on the 9th of September, and then I'll be touring and we could come to the Mill on the 16th for a few days.

Laure x

Laure put down her pen and flexed her right hand, staring out over the fields. The flax was in its final bloom, and the colours were sun-faded and gentle. Erica's letter was still unfolded beside her on the desk, and she traced the paper. Odd how they had, in these times of computers and printers, cheaper phone calls and the slow encroachment of the internet, fallen back on exchanging handwritten missives, like teenage pen pals. Erica sounded happy, she sounded sane, but Laure knew her friend had been ill for a very long time. Friend. That was what they were, now. A brush of hands, a brief kiss on the neck. For a long time, Laure obsessed over them, and over how a person can, in a single action, a moment, promise something to the other they did not intend to offer.

But so much had happened these past two years. Her book, pouring out like a fever dream in the weeks after the Cowper-Grays' car left her dusty drive. And Erica's miscarriage, of a pregnancy conceived in Laure's own bed. Erica's madness. Laure had talked to Ant, and he said recently Erica seemed better. He spoke of her illness in the overly bright tone of someone who had worried, deeply and for a long time, that they might lose the one they loved. She hoped he was right about her recovery, that he would be around a bit more. It was clear how much he loved Erica, yet still he seemed to tour constantly. They'd met on his tour in Paris last

September, her there to deliver a lecture, and he'd loved the novelty of the bar she chose.

"A proper bar," he exclaimed at the paper tablecloths, the wine-glass-ringed counter. Being there with lesbians only heightened his delight. Agnès had taken to him instantly, which later caused a fight with Marie, but all were charmed by his endless buying of drinks, his easy repartee, the photograph of Erica and the girls in his wallet. He talked of his pride for them all, about Laure's book, recently published, and his tour, the characters he'd met. He moved Agnès to tears when he insisted on visiting Michel's grave on the outskirts. They went early the next morning, before his train to Le Mans, and he laid hothouse lily of the valley on the simple slab.

A brush of hands, a brief kiss on the neck. Nothing in Erica's phone calls or letters hinted she'd thought anything of these gestures. So when Barbara kissed Laure on her final night in Paris, it felt right. The forgiveness felt as good as the kiss. They'd dated tentatively for a few months, before finally admitting they loved each other. It had been full immersion ever since, Barbara quitting her job at the Paris Descartes, and taking a position at Université de Rouen and moving in. At Marie and Agnès' twenty-fifth-anniversary party, they'd watched as their friends exchanged rings and vows and kisses, celebrating their unmarriage, and Barbara had rested her head on Laure's shoulder, and Laure had thought *Yes. Maybe. Yes.*

She was happy. Her book had been released in the Rentrée Littéraire, and made several libraries' lists, a Parisian bookstore's prize shortlist. It did better than anyone expected it to, and rights had sold in five countries so far. She'd had enough money from the lease of her land to the farmer next door, but this was now comfortable living, easy living, of a kind no one in her family had ever experienced. She wished her father could see her, could see how settled she was, how centred. And sober, still, though the smoking crept back in as she searched for ways to make the book launches and events bearable. It was just easier to have something to do with her hands.

She lit up now, a Gauloise Blondes—she no longer resisted the fact she was a walking cliché, and she could afford it—and tapped the cigarette on the tin ashtray she'd carried faithfully from the bar where she'd stolen it to Michel's, to her squat to her bedsit on Rue Bréa, and finally here. She would not move again, she knew. This was life as it now was, with Barbara and her books, her cigarettes and, in ultimate deference to parody, their cat, Lapin. Laure had wanted to keep all five of the small, squirming kittens the farmer's cat bore shortly after Barbara moved in, but Barbara put her foot down.

"It's me who'll have to clear up the shit while you're on tour," she pointed out. "One cat, one girlfriend, one vice. You're a one-woman woman now, Laure, let's stick to what works."

Lapin was a long-haired tortoiseshell with amber eyes, and the most beautiful cat Laure had ever known, though it did give her a twinge of regret to think of the kittens all those years ago that she never fed. She wrote about this moment in *Le Pont*, a memoir-cum-art-theory book of her relationship with Monet and his work, from her visits to the overgrown gardens at Giverny to her pilgrimages to *Les Nymphéas* and beyond. Critics had praised its innovation, its honesty, though at the heart of the book was the conceit that Monet drew a line between her and her father and no further. The fact that it coiled around her addictions, her lovers, her sexual identity, was omitted, and so it was a fraud of sorts. A fiction. But she hadn't wanted to open those boxes, to let the reading masses perceive her fully. Some critics noted a certain bloodlessness in the writing, an obfuscation of her private life where she was open and excoriating about the theories and analysis of Monet's work. *One gets the sense we read only the reflection*, wrote *Le Monde*, *and never grip the root*. Those voices were mostly drowned out, and still Laure was glad she wrote the book she did. Her only misgiving was that soon it would be released in English, and Erica would see into the heart of her deceit.

She folded the letter and put it in the envelope, peeling off the adhesive strip and sealing it. Let Erica think what she wanted. She'd not said a bad word about *An Inheritance*, how Erica had quoted Laure almost word for word, in the father's monologues. They were both entitled to their stories, after all.

•

The green frontage of Hatchard's framed the display as though it'd been specially painted. Erica had waited to buy her copy of *Reflections* at the launch, knowing this was what authors and publishers preferred, and now wished she hadn't. Maybe it would be less of a shock to see the jacket, an extreme close-up of Monet's *Reflets Verts* so you could see the texture of the brush, reflections in contrasting pink across it, LAURE BOUTIN in smaller type below. It looked like a real book, an important book, weighty and relevant, as her own never had. Sometimes she felt *An Inheritance* was another figment of her imagination, that her memory of being published was a manifestation of her madness. She certainly never saw it in a window.

Erica hesitated, and Ant squeezed her elbow. "Come on," he said gently. "I can see Micky. You'll know loads of people."

Inside, people were stacked against the bookshelves, the central staircase blocked by another display of Laure's books. And there was Laure herself, dressed in a crisp black suit, black brogues, a white shirt. She looked louche, effortless. Erica would never understand how she did it. And there, right beside her, was Barbara, also in a suit, dark green with a rollneck knit underneath. Her hair was brushed out but it didn't look frizzy as Erica's did, only voluminous, making her narrow face seem like a Klimt. They were holding hands, smile lines etched around their eyes as they talked to a man Erica vaguely recognized as someone important, an agent or a critic. It was a room full of someones, and she wished she hadn't come.

Ant, who'd promised not to leave her side, dropped her hand in order to embrace his friend Michael Ostler. Erica and Ostler's second wife Victoria smiled tightly at each other. Victoria was young, in her early twenties still, a photographer of some talent, and possessed of very thin arms. She reminded Erica of Patricia, that long-ago fragment of Ant's past, but she was all right really. Just a bit clipped, a bit performative, the hand on Michael's shoulder (she was a head taller than him even without heels), the camera slung around her neck.

"How are you, Erica?" she asked, in the voice she'd adopted since the miscarriage, shared against Erica's will in a thinly fictionalized story that Ant had published in *The New Yorker*.

"Fine, thank you."

"Have you read it yet?" She pointed at the piles of *Reflections* heaped on the table.

"No," said Erica, reaching across Victoria for a glass of lukewarm white wine.

"Oh," Victoria's spidery hand touched her elegantly protruding clavicle, "it's *beautiful*. When Michael told me what it was about, I thought yawn, you know. Monet's not really my thing. But actually, he was revolutionary, ushered in this whole new phase of painting. Radical. And the stuff about her father!" Her hand fluttered, a racing heartbeat. "Just so tender. Really special."

"I'm looking forward to it," said Erica, sipping.

"Ant met her in Paris, is that right?"

"Yes, but I met her first."

"Really? When?"

"In Paris, years ago. 1978."

Victoria's eyes boggled. Erica couldn't be bothered to do the maths, but Victoria might have just started school. "Wow. What was she like?"

She hadn't been expecting the question. "She was . . . you know." *Everything. She was everything. Dirty and beautiful and clever and rude.* "French."

Victoria laughed, and Erica took another glass of wine. Ant had moved out of her orbit, she could see his broad shoulders, thick hair as he stood talking to a group of women. Publicists, probably. Fans, certainly. Laure was still caught in a circle of people and hadn't noticed her. She could slip out now, go to the pub around the corner, come back in an hour to fetch Ant. She missed her girls, wanted to be home with them. Maybe she could find a phone box and call them. Lately London felt too loud, too grimy, the escalators on the Tube death traps, the trains themselves receptacles for filth. And the lighting was awful. They could afford taxis, and Ant even offered to have them chauffeured from home, but that seemed an abominable waste. Besides, she was better now, wasn't she. And a little low-level suffering, like a splinter, did her good.

"Excuse me," she said to Victoria, who was already casting around for someone more interesting to talk to. But as she downed her wine and moved towards the door, a hush fell over the crowd, and she knew she'd missed her window. Resigned, she scooped up a third wine, they were measly pours after all, and turned to the staircase where, sure enough, a man was standing with a glass of wine in one hand, a sheaf of papers in the other, and a copy of Laure's book tucked under his arm.

"Good evening, everyone, I'm Simon Merrister and I've the honour of being Laure's UK editor. We're delighted to welcome Laure to her first event here in London, and—"

Erica tuned out. She'd become adept at this, the engaged expression, hitching onto other people's laughter, throwing little glances and smiles around the room, raising her eyebrows and her glass at the right moments. But from the corner of her eye, she watched Laure. Barbara's arm was wrapped around her waist, her head tipped onto her shoulder. It looked a little awkward, not like when Erica had stood pressed against her. They'd fitted so beautifully.

The editor droned on, and whatever he said extracted more laughs and emotion from the crowd than a standard speech. Perhaps it was a good one, but no matter. Erica had heard it all before in one form or another. She'd attended five launches for the books that would define their generation that year alone. By the time he gestured Laure onto the staircase, clinking their glasses—his of red wine, hers of water—against each other, Erica needed the toilet. But she couldn't move, pressed into a corner, and didn't want to attract attention. She just hoped Laure would keep it brief.

"Thank you, Simon. That was so generous and so indicative of how you've held my work. The translation by Lucy Cafferty is similarly generous, genius really, and I am so glad I didn't let you talk me into translating it myself, or I doubt we'd be having such a lavish launch." A ripple of laughter. They were so easily amused, book people. "But seriously, thank you to you and the team at Century for your diligence, care, and pride in this work. It is no small thing to publish a book, and I am very grateful. Just a couple more thank yous, to my friends Erica and Anthony Cowper-Gray, who I hope are here . . ." She looked around, and Ant, who stood a head taller than anyone else, waved, said loudly, "We're here!" and then pointed to Erica. Erica, who was experiencing pins and needles of shock at the mention, managed to keep her face arranged in a gentle smile as people nearby turned to look at her.

"Yes," smiled Laure. "There you are. Ant first encouraged me to write a book. I believe he said, 'Lesbian books are all the rage,' or words to that effect." Another, bigger laugh at that. "And I must say I'm pleasantly surprised that even books by lesbians about art and dead fathers have a shot, no doubt in part due to Anthony's kind words, which now appear on the back jacket." A smattering of applause. "And Erica." Laure looked directly at her. God, but she was so beautiful. Beyond beautiful. Handsome, radiant.

"There is little to say because sometimes words are so small. But thank you. You have inspired me more than I can explain."

Erica's knees were weak. She leaned back against the bookshelves, feeling the wood poking into her back, her legs. The beam of Laure's attention moved on to Barbara, like a lighthouse, plunging Erica once more into dark.

"Barbara, I know living with a writer is like living with a vampire. We come out only at night and suck all the life from the room. But you have been my champion since we were girls, and I'm so grateful. To love you, and to be yours." Sighs of indulgent delight. "And finally, to Michel de Benoît. This book is dedicated to him, because my father gets enough of a look in the story itself. Michel could have done anything, and he chose to run a safe space, a place where gay men and women, transsexuals and everyone between were welcome. This is not a book about that part of my life, but it is about how to be quietly radical is to be wildly radical. That when we touch one life, save one life, we save all of humanity. In this book I argue art can change the world—you may not believe it, but know at least the world is changed for the better for having had these three men in it: Claude Monet, Phillipe Boutin, and Michel de Benoît. Now please, enjoy the famously warm wine and please buy a book!"

Laure raised her glass, and the room broke into applause. In the ensuing rush for the staircase, Erica dislodged herself and hurried to the toilet, a single cubicle set through a stock room. Her chest felt tight, and she wished the doctor had allowed her to keep her inhaler. Her asthma had turned out to be panic attacks, and she was expected to manage them with breathing. She was tired, so tired of everything coming from her. She wanted the reassuring blue tube, the cool puff hitting the back of her throat. She wanted something to fix her. She rested her head against the cool plaster as she pissed, and forced herself not to cry.

•

Laure tried to peel herself away from the latest effusive author/editor/critic introducing themselves, but it was like fighting the hydra: no sooner did she manage to extract herself than another popped up. Barbara had escaped and was standing with Ant, but Laure wanted to find Erica.

When at last she caught sight of Erica's wavy auburn hair moving across the room, she cut a man off mid-sentence with a smiling "Excuse me." Head down, she forced her way through the crowd and squeezed Erica's shoulder.

"There you are!" Erica looked up at her, and Laure felt her smile falter. Erica looked awful, glassy-eyed and pale beneath too much make-up, her hair badly coloured, harsh against her skin. The corners of her mouth were turned down, and the only line on her face was between her brows, a worried furrow. All this Laure absorbed in an instant, before Erica's face changed with such rapidity Laure knew it was practised. She smiled up at her, her beauty shielding the terrible sadness Laure had seen there a moment before.

"Hi, Laure!" she said brightly, pulling her into a hug. "Congratulations! I was about to buy your book, try and fight my way into the queue to get it signed."

Erica snatched up a copy from the table beside them and pressed it into Laure's fingers.

"You don't have to buy it," said Laure, weighing the hardback in her hands. "I'll send you a copy."

"Don't be silly. Ant reckons you're on track for a *Sunday Times* listing, is that right?"

"I don't like to know the numbers."

"That's so chic," laughed Erica. "Ant practically has his publisher on speed dial during publication month. I can't wait to read it."

Laure felt herself relax a little. So Erica's dismay wasn't at the contents of the book. It was likely nothing to do with her at all.

"And I can't wait to come and stay. Have some proper time with you all, finally see where you live." Barbara appeared at her side, kissed Erica's cheeks and snaked her arm through Laure's. Was that a hint of possessiveness in how tight she held her? Laure couldn't deny it made her feel good. "We're excited, aren't we, Barbara?"

"For Norfolk? Can't wait." Barbara smiled at Erica with genuine warmth. "Laure talks of nothing but how much she loves your girls. Two of the best people in existence."

"Of course, with such parents," said Laure, cringing a little at herself. The atmosphere, the heat in the airless room, made her feel a little giddy, a bit drunk almost.

"They're excited to see you. But we've got to get back to them, unfortunately." Erica's tone was brisk, brittle. "Thank you so much for having us."

"So soon?" Laure frowned. "Ant mentioned you might stay in town."

"Sylvia's having a hard time at school. They're already on at them about exams," said Erica. "It's nicer for her if we're home."

"Isn't it a long way?"

"Train to King's Lynn, an hour's drive at most," shrugged Erica. "We do it a lot."

"You didn't have to come," said Laure. "Though I'm glad you did. I'm sorry you have to rush off."

"The things you do as a parent. But we couldn't miss this. We're really proud of you, Laure."

But the sadness was creeping back into her face. Laure wished she could draw her aside into a quiet corner, ask her what was wrong, but there was no quiet corner to be had. Erica embraced them both briefly, and then was pushing towards Ant, holding court. Laure tried to keep an eye on their conversation, but she was spun away into another introduction, another overly intimate confession, and when she next scanned the room Ant and Erica were gone.

The coming week was a whirl of readings and interviews and trains, Laure expertly shuttled from one town to the next, often only knowing which when she caught sight of the signs on train platforms. Thank goodness Barbara was there, making sure she drank enough water, ate, ran to the chemist's for throat lozenges and running her baths in the few hotel rooms that had one. She'd massage her hands and kiss her neck, and they'd sleep curled like question marks on comfortable and uncomfortable beds, a piece of home with her wherever she went. The events themselves were a success, well attended, and on Tuesday she learned she'd entered the *Sunday Times* non-fiction chart at number eight. Her publicist ordered champagne and drank it with Barbara while Laure sipped her sparkling spring water from a champagne flute.

The only blight was Erica. The sadness Laure had seen in her face. She thought of calling, but it was ridiculous when she'd see her at the end of the week. It bothered her most of all because she recognized it, had herself felt that sort of despair.

At last it was Saturday, and they arrived at King's Lynn station to find Ant waiting for them in his silver Jaguar, a handwritten sign saying "LAURE BOUTIN SUNDAY TIMES BESTSELLING AUTHOR" in Sylvia's careful lettering held up in front of him. He smiled.

"The girls were desperate to come, but it would have been a squeeze for both of them with your luggage and they couldn't choose between them."

Laure gestured for Barbara to ride in front and slumped in the leather seats behind, closing her eyes just for a moment, and waking an hour later to find them pulling onto a gravel drive in front of the most charming house she'd ever seen. Set in an L, the Old Mill House was built of orangey brick, topped with matching clay tiles that glowed in the September sunshine. The mill pond stretched silver and blazing to its front, a small bridge set over it.

"It's beautiful!" exclaimed Barbara, climbing out of the car. Laure followed, shielding her eyes from the glancing sun. The front door set directly onto the bridge opened, and Sylvia and Eli tumbled out, so impossibly tall and lovely, barefoot and dressed in dungarees. Laure felt a disarming rush of love for these creatures who seemed to love her so much and dropped into a crouch to receive their flattening hugs.

"Careful!" called Ant, unloading their cases from the boot. "Come on, Mummy wants us in position for the sunset."

"It's my birthday tomorrow!" said Sylvia. She was, as Erica had said, a little woman. Small breasts budded under her T-shirt, her teeth were encased in braces, but still the familiar serious scrutiny. Eli was even more transformed, almost as tall as her sister and her dark hair lightening to a sandy brown, freckles across her nose after a summer outside.

"Who are you?" Eli asked Barbara directly.

"Barbara," said Barbara. "I'm Laure's friend."

"Girlfriend," Eli nodded. "You're pretty."

"Thanks."

"Are you French?"

"Oui."

"Je m'appelle Elinor. J'ai sept ans."

"Bravo."

Sylvia pulled Laure through the low, wide front door. Ant must have to bend double. Inside the ceiling was beamed, light pouring in from large modern windows that showed a breathtaking view of the wetlands beyond. Laure stood a moment, arrested by the colours: blue blue sky reflected in a wide, slow river, the glitter of the sea beyond and a green-and-gorse tangle of vegetation clinging to the horizon.

"And that," smiled Ant, coming to a halt behind her, "is why I let Erica talk me into living in Norfolk."

"Hush, you love it." Erica moved into the kitchen, smiling broadly. Laure was relieved to see it reached her eyes. She was dressed in a Laura Ashley print, her hair loose, the artificial colour less troubling in the flat afternoon light. She hugged Barbara and then Laure, and Laure sensed no fizzing energy this time, no sucking sadness. She seemed calm, composed. Of course she was, she was home, in her element. This was the life she wanted, with her handsome husband and beautiful children, in her lovely home. Laure could never have given any of this to her. The thought slunk like an assassin into her mind before she could stop it.

"Journey OK? I can't wait to hear about the tour."

"Laure was magnificent," said Barbara, and there was the same possessive tightening of her grip.

"I don't doubt it. Have you put the cases in the room?" That to Ant, who had just re-emerged behind her.

"Yep." He rubbed his palms together. "Now, what can I get you? Gin and tonic, Barbara? Tonic and lime, Laure?"

"Perfect."

"I'll bring them out."

Erica led them through the galley kitchen, into a generously sized sitting room. This too was backed by plate glass, and Erica slid the doors open, so there was no divide between outside and in.

"It's great for parties," she said. "If we ever hosted any. Though Ant's school friends would likely get drunk and fall into the estuary."

She showed them onto a wooden deck that overhung the river. A skein of geese flew like flung silk across the clear sky. The girls pulled Laure down onto one of the rattan sofas surrounding a matching table, and Barbara sat beside Erica.

"It's Grade Two listed," she said, "but there was a loophole, or Ant's father created one, I rather think." Laure watched her closely, now. Her phrasing was odd, overly formal. Was she nervous, or maybe drunk already? "Anyway, this back wall was in a terrible state of damp, so we redesigned it."

"Bloody fortune," said Ant, emerging with their drinks on a lacquered tray. "For some glass. But we love it."

"I love it," said Laure. "This view! I want to fall into it."

"I thought you'd like it," said Ant. "Plenty of reflections around."

"I bet you write like a dream here."

"I've had to get good at writing anywhere, but this is the best possible place. Reminds me of writing by the lake at UEA." He kissed Erica on the cheek as he passed her her drink, and then sat down on a single chair. "We used to write together, didn't we, E?"

"A thousand years ago."

"I remember it like yesterday," he smiled. Laure felt a little tug in her chest. She too remembered it like yesterday, every moment with Erica. Amazing how the mind could hold so much history.

"How did you two meet?" Ant went on. "I don't think I've ever heard the story. Originally I mean."

"At Michel's café," said Barbara. "What Laure said at her launch was right. He made a little corner of heaven. Paris was so wild, so dirty."

"It was wonderful," protested Laure.

"Don't be defensive, you're the one who ended up leaving! But Paris, it suited you then. You were wild and dirty too." Barbara glanced at the girls, but they were occupied with collecting feathers trapped in the rattan. It looked like a pigeon had been got by a gull. "But I grew up near Versailles. Things were quieter there."

"Barbara's parents had a flat in Paris too," said Erica, a little over-loud, inserting herself. Laure glanced at her, wondered if she was recalling the kiss in the stairwell, all the nights spent drinking there. She definitely seemed tipsy, what Laure had mistaken for calm only the quiet consideration of the drunk.

Barbara flushed. "Yes. They bought that as an investment. They wanted me to have somewhere to go, if I needed it."

Erica laughed. "All that socialist stuff you all spouted, and your parents were second-home owners."

"Erica," said Ant, gently. "Steady on."

"Sorry." But Erica had the giggles. "Sorry. But you remember Donna? Turns out her parents owned a mill in Birmingham. Way back, they owned slaves. And you," Erica laughed even harder as she pointed at Laure. "You inherited a house! Didn't you believe in a hundred per cent inheritance tax?"

"Erica, stop," warned Ant. The girls were watching them now, wary as little fox cubs peeking from their hide.

"Just hypocrisy," said Erica, shaking her head. Laure felt suddenly furious. How could she be like this, when time together was so rare and precious?

"We can't all marry money," she said in French. Barbara shushed her, and Erica looked at her squarely.

"No," she answered, also in French. "You can't marry at all."

If she'd thought it was a trump card, she was wrong. It only made Laure feel deeply, irreparably angry. She got to her feet, the exhaustion of the week and disappointment of this encounter buzzing around her like a cloud of biting midges.

"What the fuck, Erica." She stormed across the platform and down the steps set into its side, striding out across the marshy field, feeling water seep into her shoes.

"Laure!" She heard Sylvia's shout, but was glad, when she heard someone coming after her, that it was not one of the girls, or Erica or Barbara, but Ant. She needed someone she could vent against, someone who could take it.

"What is wrong with her?" she said. "She's being a bitch."

Ant looked defeated. "I've sent her to bed. She's like this since . . . you know. Her meds make her strange."

"Make her rude?"

"Sometimes. What did she say to you? My French is rusty."

"It doesn't matter."

"It wasn't anything . . ." Ant shifted, the ground squelching beneath his shoes. "It wasn't about you?"

"How do you mean?"

"About you two."

"Oh," Laure fought the urge to laugh. "No. Nothing like that."

Relief crossed Ant's face. She longed to ask him why he'd asked such a thing. He'd never so much as alluded to what Erica and her had once been to each other before. She got the impression he hadn't taken it seriously, or that Erica had downplayed it, but maybe she was wrong.

"We should rescue Barbara," said Ant, glancing back at the platform. Laure had walked further than she realized. "And ah, look. The sun's setting."

Laure turned to see the world ablaze. Pink and gold danced across the sodden ground, stretching long-legged wader birds into elegant sculptures that flickered between abstraction and reality. It was exquisite. Laure looked back to the house, to Barbara exclaiming over Eli's feathers, Sylvia sitting chewing her nails. And in the window above, a face bronzed by the sunset, haloed in the ending day.

•

Erica woke in the early hours. She could tell it was before six, because the room was still blue-dark, and it became light so soon here, even in winter. She used to hate it when the girls were young, the light flooding in around the binbags she taped onto their windows in an effort to snatch an extra half an hour's sleep, but now she loved the gentle wake-up.

Ant was fast asleep, and she gently removed his arm from her side. She felt a rush of love and guilt, for his instant forgiveness, for her behaviour yesterday. She hadn't thought she'd feel so raw about seeing Laure with Barbara, but she'd been more than hurt, she'd been angry. A ridiculous reaction. She would do better today.

She slipped into the bathroom and took two paracetamols, her Pill, her meds, regarded herself in the mirror. Thirty-five. Her best years were yet to come according to *Cosmopolitan*, though in the same edition were stories from Hollywood of women her age being rejected for jobs playing mothers in favour of twenty-year-olds. *Keep young and beautiful if you want to be loved*, said the subtitle. And here she was. Dyeing her hair, doing Pilates. In the same issue was an item about affairs, how flings can keep your marriage fresh. She'd read it with detached interest. She was all but certain Ant had affairs. He was away so much, readers saw him as a sort of god, and she was mostly frigid since the miscarriage. Her jealousy used to be a wild animal tethered to her chest, but now she only wanted not to be left. And not to know. Don't ask, don't tell. She washed her face, applied eye serum, cream to her neck and décolletage, her perfume over the top.

She'd had a good week, since the low of the launch. She'd taken her medication, done therapy, cycled to collect the girls from school. She'd swum every day off the Cley beach, the water long-summer warm and the pebbles swirling around her ankles. Ant stayed home on Wednesday, and they'd made love, the windows open, curlews calling on the flats.

So why did she still feel tipped off balance by Laure's presence? She'd never had to see her with someone else, but wasn't time meant to have smoothed the edges of her emotions? It was like being caught in a riptide back to her past, endlessly carried towards the currents of teenage angst. She was bored of it, bored of herself. *Enough*.

Today was her daughter's ninth birthday. Her kind, thoughtful, serious daughter. She would not ruin it for her. Erica slicked on some lip balm and mascara, finger-combed her hair so she would look as though she just woke up refreshed and put together. Her hand shook as she applied her mascara, a knot in her hair pulled and made her want to cry all over again. *No*.

She crept back past Ant's sleeping form and onto the landing. All was quiet and still, the girls' doors pulled to, and the guest room door closed. Erica wondered if Laure still slept with her limbs flung wide, like a starfish. She padded down the stairs, hugging the side near the wall so they wouldn't creak. In half an hour Eli would be awake and want to help with birthday pancakes, but she would get ahead with decorating the sitting room for the party that afternoon.

The back doors were open, light and birdsong flooding inside. Erica saw the back of a head poking over the rattan sofa, blotted into black by the sun. She knew it was Laure. She watched her hair move in the breeze, her hand lift a mug to her lips. Glancing into the kitchen, she saw the kettle still steaming, the cafetière missing from its place, a tea towel folded neatly on the countertop.

Laure still hadn't noticed her standing there. She tipped her head back, and sighed audibly. Erica wondered if she should slip back upstairs, unnoticed, leave Laure to her peace, but then Laure rolled her shoulders and turned her head, stretching, catching sight of Erica in the process. She smiled, and Erica rushed to cover her embarrassment at being caught staring.

"Morning," she said, smiling back.

"You caught me." Laure held up a lit cigarette. "Ant said it was fine so long as the girls didn't see."

"Of course!" Erica suppressed an instinctive cough. "It's nice out there, isn't it."

"Beautiful. So calm, and alive with all the birds."

"Have you spotted the marsh harrier? He's magnificent."

"Ah." Laure looked back over the river, the tide out so the marshland was lilac and pink with sea lavender, the sky brightening to pure blue. "Not yet."

"He'll be around. Can I get you anything?"

"Non. Come, sit with me."

Erica went obediently, sat in the single chair, her back to the sun. She watched Laure's profile as she poured another cup of coffee from the cafetière. "Want one? Sorry, strange to offer in your own home."

"No, thank you. I'll have tea later." Coffee had started to make her feel sick, a shortcut to anxiety.

"What are those?" Laure was pointing at a couple of birds, toddling across the sand.

"Plovers. You know the name for a group of those is a ponderance."

"Ponderance. I like it."

Erica pulled her robe closer around her body. Laure was dressed in navy cotton pyjamas, austere and unfashionable. She looked wonderful, her skin clear and lined around the mouth, her hair silver. And cigarettes may be bad for you, but she looked so cool, like Lauren Bacall or Joan Didion. Timeless. Erica rubbed the lip balm deeper into her lips. It would be obvious she was wearing mascara in such direct sunlight. She felt clownlike and childish.

Laure was looking at her strangely, and she realized she'd asked her a question.

"Sorry?"

"I asked if you were all right."

"Oh, yes, fine, thank you. Sorry about yesterday, I was tired. Drank a bit much."

"Mm." Laure nodded slowly, bending to tap ash from her cigarette into the dish Ant had supplied for this purpose. "I call bullshit."

"Sorry?"

Laure crooked her elbow, her cigarette at right angles to her cheek. It was a pose Erica had seen her adopt so often, the familiarity of it almost made her smile.

"I said, I call bullshit."

"I heard you."

"You're not fine. At the launch you were not fine. Yesterday you were not fine. And now, you are not fine. You don't want to talk to me about it?"

"Not really."

"OK." Laure let the silence stretch. Erica trained her gaze out at the marsh, the tide on the turn, the water lapping over the mud and sand. Laure must have had therapy, to be able to play such long chicken over the silence. Erica caved.

"No. I'm not fine." In her periphery she saw Laure set down her cigarette, lean forward to listen. "I'm tired, all the time. Even when I sleep enough, I'm tired. I'm bored but that's terrible, because I have my girls, I have this house, I have Ant. But I'm bored. I can feel my brain going . . . mushy. Off. And all my friends are Ant's friends. Emma and Nicholas are living some perfect life in Kent, and I'm just here. Which would be fine if I was a good mother, but I'm not."

Laure made a noise of protest and Erica squeezed her eyes tightly shut. "If you knew. If you knew half of what I thought. You'd think I was detestable. Though maybe you already think so."

Laure laughed, a short, mirthless chuckle. "Erica, please. Why would I possibly think that?"

Erica swallowed what she wanted to say. How when she really wanted to punish herself, she thought of how she behaved in the flat on Rue Bréa, the smashed bottle. Instead she said, "I sound ridiculous, don't I?"

"Not at all. I know many mothers feel this way." Erica chewed her tongue. "What do you do for you? Do you write?"

"You know I don't."

"Have you considered—"

"I don't write. I don't want to." *It isn't so easy*, she wanted to shout. *Not all of us can just do it, and be published, and have launches in other countries.*

"All right, then what?"

Erica searched for something. "I swim. In the sea, most days."

"That's good. And you drink?"

"Yes." Erica jutted out her chin. "So?"

"I am just saying, be careful."

"I'm not an alcoholic!" snapped Erica. "I'm just unhappy."

Laure looked so terribly sad for her Erica wished she hadn't said it. "And what I said yesterday was so stupid. I'm sorry."

"It was stupid," agreed Laure. "Barbara was very hurt by it. She's been campaigning for marriage equality for years now."

"Really?"

"Yes." Laure shrugged. "Plenty think marriage is a trap, and straight people are welcome to it, but others think we need it to be seen as valid."

"And you?"

"I think I would marry Barbara. She wants to."

Erica absorbed this blow, her skin feeling very hot. "I'm sorry," she repeated.

"But never mind that. I'm worried about you." Laure laid her hand on Erica's arm. Her palm was warm and dry, rough. Her nails were still bitten stumps. Erica felt the familiar charge run through her pelvis.

"It's all right. I'll be all right."

"You're still having therapy? Good. Me too." She picked up her cigarette and relit it with a small silver lighter. "It's important. You matter, Erica."

"Who are you and what have you done to Laure?"

"I know. Soft soft soft. Being in love does this to you, non? You know I have a cat now. All I mean is, if you needed to talk, you could talk to me."

Erica stood up rather than say what she wanted to. "I should start decorating. I hope you're ready for thirty nine-year-olds."

"Is there a name for that?"

"Hell?"

Laure snorted and stubbed out her cigarette. "I'll help."

•

There was a point, an hour into the birthday party, that Laure leaned over to Barbara and said, "I need a drink," and for the first time in a long time, meant it. Barbara snorted and pressed another mini-pizza into her hand. In her desperation, Laure ate it.

The morning had been bucolically lovely. The girls came down about seven and Sylvia cried at the sight of the sitting room covered in floral banners, purple and gold balloons rolling over the furniture. She hugged her mother and then Laure, whispering "Thank you," and Laure thought again of the other life where she had a child, and decorated their house with balloons for their birthday. They made pancakes; the smell drew down Ant and Barbara, and all of them sat down to eat, passing the lemon and sugar, Nutella and sliced banana, until the girls were high on sugar.

Sylvia opened her presents, a small bottle of perfume from her grandmother Elizabeth, who was taking her to the ballet the following weekend. Sylvia spritzed it everywhere, spreading the over-sweet musk just like the one Erica wore when they first met. Eli gave her an album by a band called Boyzone, and from her parents came a small book locket, which opened to reveal pages engraved with a message. Laure handed over her own gift, carefully wrapped by Barbara and bought at an independent bookshop in Cheltenham.

"Jacqueline Wilson!" Sylvia gasped. "I haven't got this one!"

"It's signed," said Laure. "She was in town for a festival."

"I love it," said Sylvia, and burst into tears again.

Ant put on M People and they danced around the living room while Erica started the party food, refusing help and pulling from the oven tray after tray of mini-pizzas and chips and chicken nuggets. She arranged them on platters with token lettuce and cucumber slices, and Laure watched her, checking her face for signs of sadness or strain.

The thirty schoolmates descended early that afternoon.

Laure had assumed that because they weren't young children the noise would be tolerable, but the girls scream-sang along to every song, and the boys charged about screeching, and Laure saw why Erica had cleared every surface. The organized fun section of the party, where the children raced to eat a doughnut dangling from a string attached to the ceiling, was the only moment of respite. Erica spent most of her time in the kitchen, fetching napkins or beers, pouring wine for the mothers who stayed, or for herself. Whenever Laure caught sight of her she seemed to be sipping from a freshly topped-up glass.

After a couple of hours, Barbara went upstairs, complaining of a migraine and insisting Laure stay behind. One of the mothers approached her and engaged her in conversation about her book. It turned out a couple of them had read it already, and Ant, mock-offended, said, "None of you have read *my* books," to which the parents laughed and one of the fathers, ensconced on the deck with a beer, called, "I did, Ant! Bloody hard work!"

Amidst a ripple of laughter the mother said, "And is that your girlfriend?"

"Yes," said Laure, as repressively as she could. She tried to escape upstairs, but Barbara was asleep, the room as dark as she could get it, so Laure fetched her a glass of water and returned to the fray, dodging questions about her book and her sexuality as best she could. Luckily, after a Tracy Beaker–themed cake and more dancing, the sugar crash hit the party hard. With efficiency unmatched by any military, parents departed in a great rush and crunching of car tyres on gravel, leaving the house looking like a tornado had ripped through, the remains of balloons and doughnuts and crumpled napkins everywhere. Sylvia was tearful, and Eli wild, jumping on the sofa cushions.

"God," said Erica, her hair in disarray, a smear of icing down her button-fronted tea dress. She stood over the sink, scraping bits of mini-pizza out of the strainer. "Why don't we learn?"

Ant chuckled, his spirits clearly buoyed by company and the beers he'd drunk on the terrace. "Leave that. I'll do it."

"It's all right—"

"Let me," he insisted, taking the strainer from her hand.

"All right. Thank you." Erica looked out of the window. The day was still splendid. "I think I need some fresh air. Girls? Do you want to go for a swim?"

"The sea is the fishes' toilet," said Eli, solemnly.

"We could go to the beach then, have a kick about?"

But the girls, it turned out, wanted to watch a film called *Andre*, about a girl who befriends a seal.

"We could go and see a real seal," said Erica, trying once more.

"I'd like to see a real seal," said Laure.

"Oh! Well it's not a guarantee. But sometimes they're hauled up on the sandbanks at Wells. It's only a ten-minute drive."

"Why don't you walk?" suggested Ant. "It's a beautiful route through the marshes, past Holkham. Catch the bus back."

"It'll take a couple of hours. I don't want to be away from Sylvia."

"I think it might be bedtime after the film. I can do it. You don't mind do you, Sylv?"

Sylvia waved distractedly, focused on the VHS being extracted from its case by Eli.

"See? Take some time for yourself."

"It's OK if you don't want to go," said Laure.

"No, tomorrow is rain," said Erica. "A walk would be nice if you're up for it."

"Sure. I'll ask Barbara."

But Barbara was in the grips of a painkiller-induced stupor. "Go," she insisted. "Please, close the door."

"Does she need anything?" asked Ant, when Laure reported back downstairs.

"Just rest," said Laure. "I've taken her more water. She gets them sometimes. I think the tour was tiring, looking after me."

"It's always harder on the partner," said Ant, hugging his wife. Erica smiled tightly and asked if Laure had walking boots, a swimsuit.

They loaded a rucksack with a thermos, leftover cake, thin towels and swimming costumes. Laure pulled on a thick pair of socks Erica lent her, and laced up a pair of Ant's boots, only a little too big. Ant waved them off cheerfully, beer in hand, and Laure suspected they'd find the house no more tidy when they returned. The girls were entranced by their seal film, and didn't even look up to wave them off.

Erica led her directly off the deck, onto the marshy land Laure had stormed onto the previous day. In a few minutes they reached a wooden gate, and Erica ushered Laure through. A slightly raised track rode a spine of grassy land, alongside the river-sea, high now, but flowing outwards. Laure could see the swaying of seaweed and sea lavender beneath the water, through to the deep reflection of the high blue sky. Ahead, sand dunes towered like hills.

"I'm sorry Barbara isn't feeling well," said Erica. She was still dressed in her tea dress, the green like something from a Tamara de Lempicka painting. Combined with the boots she looked like an idealized version of a farmer's wife. "I'm sure the party didn't help. I don't know how you got through it without a drink."

"She loves parties. Just tired, as I said."

"And you?"

"Tired too. But I'm so glad to be here, in this place. You told me I'd love it." Laure filled her lungs, felt the familiar squeeze at the edges. In some ways she wished she'd never stopped smoking, and so would not miss the expansiveness when she inhaled. But who was she kidding, she thought, pulling one out from the packet. She fucking loved it.

"How is your asthma?" she asked.

"I never told you. It wasn't asthma, in the end. It was anxiety attacks. Panic attacks." Erica smiled weakly. "I know. I was having them before it was fashionable. I rarely have them now. Never, really."

"Good." Laure shuddered. "It was awful, that time in Paris. Seeing you unable to breathe."

Erica kept walking, but her body lost some of its ease. "That was a bad trip."

"It was all right. I liked . . . Donna?" Laure remembered her name perfectly.

"Poor Donna. I treated her so badly."

"Are you still in touch?"

Erica laughed. "No. I'm not in touch with any of my exes. Apart from you."

They walked on. "How is Hilde?" asked Erica.

"Good. Living with a woman in Burgundy somewhere. They have a kid."

"Wow. Hilde's?"

"Yes, and some guy. We have our ways." Laure wriggled her eyebrows, but Erica didn't laugh. They walked side by side where the path was wide enough, Erica slipping ahead when it narrowed. After a long silence that brought Laure to her filter and them to the end of the path, onto a wooden slatted route that climbed amid the dunes, Erica said,

"Did you ever want to?"

Laure stubbed her cigarette out in the loose sand beside them.

"Sorry if that's too personal. Never mind." But Erica sounded testy, almost irritated. Laure wondered if she felt she owed her something, after her confidences of the morning. The truth was Laure had wanted children, and never more than with Sylvia and Eli around. When she was with Erica, at her father's house, in the garden at Giverny, and could imagine that version of the world rising to the surface, so close she could cup it in her hands. But no, that wasn't for now.

"No. Barbara did, once, but I'm happy with the cat."

"I'd love a cat," said Erica. "But Ant's allergic."

Laure stopped, arrested by the sweep of dune rising thirty, forty feet to her right, a steep incline of grass on one side, the other a near-sheer cliff of white-gold sand.

"Want to run down?" asked Erica, and Laure shrugged.

"Sure."

Erica looked amazed. "I didn't think you'd say yes."

"That looks worth doing."

They clambered to the top of the dune. The sea was revealed, miles of glittering grey-blue. "The skies here are enormous!"

"You sound like the tourist board. Do you want to go first?"

It seemed very high up now Laure was here, the scoop of the slope almost concave beneath them.

"Here, I will." Erica leapt down into the basin of the sand, throwing her weight back and windmilling her arms, her boots sinking deep into the sand, which slid alongside her as she ran, almost falling, all the way to the bottom and up the gentle incline opposite, collapsing onto all fours and panting with laughter.

"Come on!" she shouted. "Allez!"

Laure secured her cigarettes and lighter, and leapt down too, immediately lost her footing, and tumbled shoulder over knee over head over arse all the way to the bottom. It felt like being inside a washing machine. Sand flicked into her eyes, up her nose, inside her shirt, abrading her back and pouring liberally into her socks. She came to a spluttering halt, and felt Erica's hand turning her over.

"God, Laure! Are you OK?"

"That was amazing!" she shouted, feeling in her stomach the late surge of adrenaline, like a shot of cold vodka. She sat up, wincing, and felt beneath her hand something hard and metallic. She thought it was her lighter, but when she raised it she saw it was a bullet casing, familiar from the fields around her father's house.

"Oh!" said Erica. "You found one! Ant's been looking for years."

Laure held it out to her, and Erica shook her head. "You keep it. This whole area was used for training in the wars."

Laure slipped the casing into her pocket, though her house was lined with them. She knew she'd want to remember this dune, this moment. She began to brush sand from her hair and clothes. Erica knelt in front of her. The run had disarrayed her dress, and her cleavage showed deeply as she reached forward and helped Laure de-sand herself. Laure looked surreptitiously from beneath her hair, the light stretch marks, the creamy skin pressing against the black bra.

"There," said Erica, sitting back on her heels. "I think that's the best we can do."

"I'll shake them out when we swim."

She took Erica's offered hand and let her haul her to her feet.

They scrambled out of the dune's shallow basin and re-joined the wooden path. Things felt easier now she'd made a fool of herself. The silence was less charged. The sea too, that helped. The dunes tumbled them onto a wide, golden beach, the water going out noticeably fast. Aside from a far-off dog walker, and a train of distant horses, there was no one around.

"We've not timed this very well," said Erica, shielding her eyes. "We'll have to walk out to swim. But there'll be more sand for the seals, so." She held up crossed fingers. Laure returned the gesture instinctively, and Erica raised her eyebrows.

"Getting superstitious in your old age?"

"Barbara's influence. I salute magpies and no longer walk under ladders."

"Wise."

"How is it so empty?"

"Only really busy in school holidays. There's so much space here. Wells will be busier. There's an amazing fish and chip shop. I'll get you chips after our swim."

"It's like a permanent holiday," sighed Laure.

"Well, it's different when you live here. A lot of deprivation. And if you aren't born here, it's not always friendly."

"You were born here."

"Ant wasn't. They see him like an invader almost. The mill, it was split into three houses before we bought it. People were angry about smaller homes being taken away."

Laure chewed her tongue. After Erica's comments about Barbara's flat yesterday, she was well placed to tell her what she thought of that. But in the spirit of friendship she said, "I guess like Paris, a tourist can see only the good bits."

"How was it going back?"

"Not good, but the publisher insisted. I kept seeing Michel everywhere."

"Ah, I'm sorry."

Laure flinched, as she always did when someone gave her sympathy she didn't deserve. "His café is still there, still running. We did an event there. So many young people, staring at me like they had no idea what I was on about."

"I'm sure they found you inspirational."

"Ha! Can you remember seeing a forty-year-old when you were in your twenties?"

"Not really. I'm pretty sure anyone over thirty was invisible to me."

"We're worse than invisible to these people. The young gays—queers, they call themselves—they find us contemptible. The elders. Why have we let the world get worse, not better? Why are there not equal marriage laws, blanket abortion rights, easier legislation around transitioning, adoption." Laure remembered one attendee, blue hair, piercings, a doll-like face, chiding her for assuming she was—they were—a girl. She hadn't meant anything by it, and then felt angry a child was telling her off. *You weren't there*, she wanted to say, *you weren't there when things were really bad*. But she'd been furious too, when she was young. Even at people who didn't deserve it. "Maybe that's too harsh. Not all of them. Some of them were sweet, and interested. It's so easy to say they are all this or that, no?"

They walked on, the dunes falling away and replaced by a forest, which ran along the edge of the beach like a wall.

"Pines," said Erica, pointing. "Want to walk through?"

Laure followed Erica into the forest. It was hushed and cool, the floor carpeted in needles, the trunks curiously bare before flaring into lush green above them, as though they walked between matchsticks.

"How old are these trees?"

Erica looked up. "Not sure. Sorry, Ant's the good guide."

Laure wondered what had happened to Erica, to her curiosity. The hunger with which she examined the world, asking questions, none too stupid, nothing too insignificant to escape her notice.

"He'd have told you about Burnham Thorpe," Erica went on, gesturing vaguely back the way they'd come. "It's where Lord Admiral Nelson was born. Or Admiral Lord?"

"Who?"

"He helped Britain win the Battle of Trafalgar."

"Ah," said Laure. "That did not turn out so well for us."

"Oh! Was that you? France, I mean? I thought it was Spain."

"Easy mistake. Both, I believe. But we're friends now, aren't we?"

"Sorry?"

"France and Britain."

"Oh, yes."

•

Erica didn't know what to say, or even what she wanted to say. Why did she not know what she wanted anymore? Every decision felt at once meaningless and overwhelming. She'd felt relieved when Ant pushed her out of the house, and hugely guilty for leaving Sylvia on her birthday. Resentful her daughter didn't plead with her to stay, and grateful she could be alone with Laure. She hated that she needed it, this time with her. She needed her arms around her. She needed her, and that was worst of all. She struggled with her tears, but they came anyway, the warm breeze stinging her eyes.

"Erica?" Laure touched her shoulder. How could she touch her so easily? Why didn't she feel what Erica felt, that electricity, the static that made her ears buzz and the hairs on her arms stand up? Her despair found the easier course, channelling into anger as it so often did.

"Are we?"

"Quoi?"

"Friends?" Erica faced her. Laure swam in her tear-filled vision, her silver hair alight against the dark pines. "We've never been able to be friends."

"We are friends." Laure frowned. "The past couple of years. We've been friends."

"Friends on the phone. Friends when we write. But when I came to your father's house, what then?"

"Erica," she said warningly. "Please. Nothing happened."

"No. But I wanted it to." The truth, a living thing in the air between them.

"You don't know what you're saying. Your husband is waiting for us, your children."

"Barbara."

"Yes, Barbara."

"Her waiting paid off, didn't it."

Laure sneered and turned away, started to stride back through the trees. "I'm not listening to this."

Erica yanked her wrist, hard. Laure hissed and spun to look at her. "Don't touch me like that."

"I know you loved me, but did you like me? Do you like me now?"

"I'm here, aren't I?"

Erica could tell Laure was bewildered, as well as angry. She tried to funnel her tangled thoughts into a simple line she could deliver.

"I don't think we can ever be friends. Because I'm still in love with you."

The rustle of the trees suddenly fell away. All Erica could hear was the rushing of blood in her head, like someone shushing her to sleep. Laure was caught in her contrapposto turn, half towards, half away from her. She looked in that moment the physical embodiment of those moments Erica played in her mind, over and over. Approaching her on the steps of the Sacré-Cœur, pressing their bodies together on the stairwell at Barbara's, turning up to her birthday trip with Donna, kissing her in her flat on Rue Bréa, watching the girls on the bridge at Giverny, brushing her lips against her neck in her father's house. All those letters she didn't send, before Ant. And after their affair, all those times she felt her life was a bolting horse and she was losing control of it, her panic feeding the chaos, when all that could soothe her was imagining the other life, the other path, where she and Laure were together and never parted. The books she would have written, the choices taken away—like marriage, like children—that shackled her to domesticity. She loved her girls, she loved the baby she'd lost, she loved Ant, but she was lost and lonely, and she needed something to cling to. And here was Laure, again, halfway gone, halfway here.

Slowly, Laure turned towards her. Her mouth was held in a thin, pale line, all colour drained from her face. In her expression, Erica could read her reply, and it was as though a trapdoor opened under her feet, plunging her beneath the dropped needles into the stifling dark of the earth.

"Erica, I—"

Erica tried to speak, but there was a lump in her throat. She shook her head, stumbled backwards, away from Laure.

"Wait."

"Please, don't," Erica managed, walking fast through the trees. She did not want to cry, but she was, her whole head pounding.

"Erica, you have to listen!" Laure slipped by her, blocking her path between two trunks. "Please, listen to me."

But Erica knew she wouldn't hear anything she wanted to. She sidestepped, her hip catching painfully on a snapped-off branch. She welcomed the pain, the punishment of it, hated her lumbering body, her stupid mouth, her exhausting brain. She wanted to slip from her skin and dive into the water, become nothing, foam on the waves.

She broke through the tree line and started to run across the beach. She never ran, only walked fast on the treadmill Ant kept in his study, but despair and mortification drove her on. Sound rushed back in, the wind, her own breath, Laure's shout. She didn't stop until she reached the water, warm as a bath, waded until it covered her calves, sticking her dress to her thighs, her stinging hip. Once she was waist deep, the current tugging gently at her dress, she ducked beneath the surface and screamed, bubbles breaking against her cheeks and nose.

She screamed until she was empty, and then she was yanked above the surface, and Laure was there, also fully clothed and up to her waist in water, shouting in her face.

"Putain de bordel de merde! What the fuck! C'est quoi, ce bordel!" Erica stood limply as Laure shook her. "You want to kill yourself, hein? You want to die? What the fuck!"

Erica couldn't get a word in. The bag was soaked through, it felt full of rocks. She didn't want to kill herself. She just wanted to not exist for a while.

"Of all the selfish . . . what about your girls?"

"Shut up about my girls!" Erica was angry now too. Laure had no idea. Laure didn't have a clue. "I wasn't trying to kill myself. Did that look like a suicide attempt?"

She gestured at herself. Laure's face twisted, and suddenly she was laughing. Erica stood dumbstruck as Laure collapsed onto her knees in the water, her shirt billowing out around her, laughing and laughing.

"Merde!" she panted. "Merde!"

"What's wrong with you?" But Erica felt her hysteria bubbling up to meet Laure's. Her lips twitched. *No.* She might not be able to control her tears, but she would not laugh.

"Pardon . . . pardon. You just . . . putain! You look ridiculous. We look ridiculous."

Erica looked down at her dress stuck to her body, the rucksack still on her back, her walking boots still on her feet. She did look absurd, like she'd fallen off a boat. "It's not funny," she started, but she caught Laure's laugh, both of them shaking and snorting.

"Stop!" Erica begged. "Stop, I'll wet myself!"

"So wet yourself," gasped Laure. "It's the sea! It's the fishes' toilet!"

Erica collapsed back onto her knees, giving up the contents of the rucksack as doomed, howling with laughter. The current pulled at them and she gripped Laure's hand for balance, and Laure clutched back. Erica could barely breathe. The current tugged at them and that made them laugh harder. Erica pissed and Laure shouted, "Beurk! It went warm!" and they became helpless, spluttering and splashing. Finally, Erica mastered herself and sat hiccupping on her haunches.

"God."

Slowly, Laure struggled into silence. With her free hand she rubbed her face, still wheezing and shaking her head. "Quelle andouille."

"You're the andouille."

"Oui. And you. Both of us."

Laure clambered gracelessly onto her knees, still holding Erica's hand, so they faced each other, bobbing slightly in the rhythm of the waves. Behind her the empty beach, the dunes, the forest. Her face was lined and after the exertion of her laughter, drained. She looked deadly serious.

"Did you mean it?"

Erica felt the plummeting once more. "Of course I meant it."

"Have you always felt this way?"

"I think so. Yes. I don't know."

Laure laughed again, but sadly. She looked defeated. "We tried. We tried once, twice. And both times you left."

"I know. I regret it."

"Erica, have you seen where you live? Have you seen your children, your husband? I mean, he's not my type but I have it on good authority he's handsome."

"I love them. But I miss myself. And I miss you."

"It sounds like you miss being young."

"Maybe. But I do miss you, now. As I am now."

The sea had retreated inches, so what once covered her waist was now only lapping her thighs. The breeze ran chill across her body, and she shivered. Her teeth started chattering.

"Allez," said Laure. Erica let her help her to her feet and they waded out of the water. Erica dropped the rucksack onto the wave-moulded sand and rooted through it. The towels were soaked, but the tea in the thermos was warm and she poured Laure a cup. She insisted Erica have the first. She drank, and her teeth stopped clattering. She refilled it and Laure stood with her hands wrapped around the metal lid, blowing on the steaming liquid with a faraway expression in her eyes. Erica pulled her sopping swimsuit from the bag.

"I'm going to swim," she said, and Laure nodded mutely, turning to give her privacy. The beach was still deserted and Erica changed briskly, stripping off her dress and underwear, pulling on her ancient black Marks and Spencer swimming costume. If she were really serious about seducing Laure, this would not have been the outfit she chose.

It was already receding, the past twenty minutes, like a car crash glimpsed in the rear-view mirror. She walked past Laure and into the sea, her body cold and then, almost immediately after she began to swim, warm. Her pulse began to regulate, her breath coming deeper, the unbearable tension in her fingers and toes unfurling. The water took her weight and she felt everything else drop away. So it was over, done. She had spoken her truth, as the magazines told her to, and she'd been rejected. Laure loved Barbara, and now Erica would accept it.

She was relieved, in a way. She would not have to betray a good man again, nor embarrass the girls by dragging them off to live in France, or moving Laure into their home. Her girls. How could she have explained the mess of it, the failures and weaknesses of her heart. She would have to work on the grief, the guilt, but she would survive it. This was another fork in the road, and the way was clear.

She ceased her breaststroke and floated on her back, in the act of turning catching sight of Laure on the beach, completely naked. Her skin was so white, no tan lines, her pubic hair as silver as her head so she seemed to shine, featureless as an airbrushed figure in a magazine, only the dark pink of her nipples breaking the white. It was only a glimpse, and then Erica forced herself to stop looking. When the slow rotation of her float brought her back around, she saw Laure was dressed in Erica's spare swimsuit, wading to meet her. The tide had carried her further out, but she checked she could still touch the sand below her. This flat place had once stood proud of a prehistoric sea, connecting Britain to Scandinavia. Doggerland, this upland was called, and Ant was dismayed when his editor made him cut all mention of it from *Excavations*. A departure too far, he said. Erica felt these passages were the most tender in the book, and still thought Ant should do something with them, short stories perhaps.

Laure came to stand beside her, the water up to her chest. Fine, downy hairs furred her underarms as she swept her hair up, exposing her long neck, her collarbones, the xylophone of her ribs. Erica's suit hung baggy from her, a loose second skin. She crouched and came to float beside Erica, her hand brushing hers. Erica felt the dull ache of desire, its companion sting of loss. Laure's hair fanned out around her, silver strands like the fronds of a jellyfish, tickling Erica's shoulder. Erica closed her eyes against the blue sky and inhaled deeply. She felt the water respond to the movement of Laure beside her, lift and lower her, lift again, and then she felt a shadow across her face, and then Laure's lips on hers.

•

In the end, Laure kissed Erica because she wanted to. It was that base, that unwarranted. Hadn't she, for more than a decade now, resisted the urge to drink, and a thousand other sordid impulses? So why, when she had already moved past the danger, forborne Erica's entreaties, her outright declaration, did she look down at Erica, floating on the warm English sea, and give in? Because it was impossible not to.

So she kissed her, for the first time in a decade, and it was as though time collapsed and she found her mouth as she'd found it that first time, a stolen kiss on the Rue Asseline, or the last, in her apartment in Rue Bréa. She kissed her, and Erica kissed her back. And as though they danced, she rose to her knees, and they pressed their bodies against each other, and pulled down the straps of their suits, and kissed each other's breasts, Erica rolling her nipple between her finger and thumb and squeezing just so, and then Laure's hands moved beneath the elastic of Erica's costume, into the tangle of her hair, and against the hard nut of her clit. Erica moaned into her mouth, spreading her legs wider in the shallow water, and Laure slipped one finger inside as she'd always liked, just one, bringing her own body to grind against Erica's hip. All was warm, and wet, and they worked on each other slowly, heads on each other's shoulders like they did indeed dance, or lips on each other's ears, each other's lips, and Erica slid her own hand over Laure's and showed her how she had changed, what she liked now, and when she came the sound was like a jolt of electricity directly to Laure's core. Erica slid her fingers into Laure; though Laure had long since stopped enjoying being penetrated she liked it now, and they looked at each other as they used to, and it was as much the sight of Erica's mouth, her tongue, as it was the feel of her fingers that pulled Laure into ecstasy.

The water had moved them further out, the rucksack and their clothes dark blots on the white-gold sand, Erica's tea dress like a patch of emerald field. The edges of Laure's vision began to sharpen, the pleasure radiating slowly from her like scent. Erica pulled her fingers away and looked into her face. Laure could feel reality sneaking back up on them, but she held it at bay awhile longer in order to look at Erica, frankly and without apology or guilt. The world held them in stillness, the pause between heartbeats, and there was only the two of them balanced on this patch of earth, like the bright dress against the sand.

Then Erica raised her straps over her shoulders to hide her breasts, and Laure mirrored her. Laure's hair had come loose, and she swept it back, tucking it behind her ears, and Erica did the same to hers. They embraced, each moving to meet the other, and both of them understood what it was, and now, after all they'd said and done, all the people they loved and betrayed, all they'd learned and left behind, what it could never be.

Barbara could tell something had happened, Laure knew. Laure felt it was a red smear across her face, vivid as blood. And anyway, they had been friends too long.

Ant laughed at their wet clothes, seemingly guilelessly accepting Erica's explanation they blew into the sea. Barbara didn't say anything. Not when Laure announced the publisher needed her in London for an interview, and that they would have to leave the next morning, or when they went to the guest room to pack. She simply folded their clothes, Laure's and her own, into their separate bags, and lamented with the girls they had to go so soon, and made small talk with Ant at the dinner table.

The tension that usually fizzed between Laure and Erica was gone, spent in the waves. Though it was the end of it, and the end too perhaps of her and Barbara, Laure felt an abiding sense of calm. That night, Barbara rolled away from Laure on the expensive sheets, and Laure suspected that, unlike her, she didn't sleep at all. Was she a terrible person, for feeling that it would all be all right?

Both rose tired-eyed and early the next day. The taxi Ant had somehow wrangled late last night appeared as planned, like a miracle from the dark, and they packed their bags into the boot, leaving a note thanking the girls, making no promise to return. No one waved them off, the curtains of Ant and Erica's room remaining tightly closed. The beautiful mill receded behind them, unseen.

On the long train ride to London, Barbara read her book though her eyes didn't move, flicking through the pages with deliberate force, and Laure looked out of the window and grieved for the grief she was not allowed, the second great grief of her life that she did not deserve. When she told Barbara what she already knew, she might lose her, but if Barbara stayed it would mean a lifetime of repentance. That was fine by her. She didn't practise what to say, how to convince her, or paint herself in the best possible light. She would tell it unvarnished and straight, as Barbara had always told her things. She owed her that at least.

In the lovely, velvet-and-lined-curtain quiet of a hotel in Bloomsbury, Laure laid it out. Barbara sat on the edge of the king-size bed and listened with her head bowed. She barely moved, only a slight slump of the shoulders when Laure told her she'd kissed Erica first. When Laure was finished she said,

"Is it done? For good?"

"For ever." For the first time, it was utterly true.

"Do you want me?"

"Yes. Only you." This too was the truth. She could be alone, deserved to be. But she wanted Barbara, her kindness, her steadiness, her utter knowing of Laure. Her care of Michel, the fact she'd been the one with him when he died, that too conferred a preciousness. It was perhaps Laure's greatest regret that she'd not been there, but proximity to Barbara allowed a connection to that moment. Their shared history, an amount of time that could never be built again. A life without her would be less, and after the absolute reign of fire with which Erica tore through her life, she understood it to be a better one. It was love, what she had felt for Erica, and it was not. Not the sort of love she needed.

Barbara nodded. "I need time to think. Can you stay somewhere else?"

Without argument, Laure picked up her bag, and left.

She walked through London's mid-afternoon drizzle, her crumpled suit jacket scant protection against the chill. She walked aimlessly, her bag cutting into her shoulder. She passed the Great Ormond Street Hospital and the grey colonnades of the British Museum, the beautiful brick and balconied mansions of Russell Square. She dawdled in a second-hand bookshop, and did not, as she usually did, search for signs: Barthes, or García Márquez, or another marker of shared history.

She crossed the Bloomsbury Group's hallowed Gordon Square and into the area of a university, students nursing cigarettes outside their lecture halls. She should feel anxious, or awful, but she felt calm. It was out of her hands. She had closed a chapter of her life, and her only regret was hurting Barbara in the process. If she lost her, that would be another regret, but she understood she was not deserving of her forgiveness and could do no more than meet Barbara where she wanted to meet her. It was in the hands of the most capable person Laure knew, and she trusted her to make the decision that was best for her. How awful, to be capable. For people to believe you can handle more than anyone should.

She continued into the rain, which began to fall in earnest as she reached the Seven Dials of Covent Garden, near where her publisher had taken her to lunch at a fancy Italian restaurant, and plunged across the garish grind of Leicester Square, following the crush of umbrellas and damp-coated commuters along the channel of Charing Cross Road. She bypassed the station, breaking away from the flow towards Trafalgar Square like a lone fish, and crossed the Strand into a narrow park to the river. The Brutalist box of South Bank's National Theatre rose monolithic across the water, the rain falling so hard it smeared the grey into grey. She stood leaning against the river wall, watching the rain fall, pummelling the surface of the Thames, feeling as though it washed the last remnants of Erica from her skin. It had been an exorcism, their lovemaking in the sea, a release, and she was ready at last to move on.

She turned her back on the river, and loosely retraced her steps north, past restaurants opening for dinner service, resisting the pubs and bars lit like lighthouses along the cloud-darkened roads. Her shoulder was aching, her skin numb with cold, but it felt like old times, when her body was bruised after a night's ill-conceived fucking and walking was the only way to soothe her. She followed her instinct, seeing few landmarks but knowing with an ancient sense she moved north, away from the river.

Finally she found herself back in the genteel residential surrounds of Bloomsbury, and kept going, past the hotel Barbara was staying in, and onwards to the neighbouring scruff and dinge of King's Cross. As she approached the edge of the Euston Road, a crossing into less salubrious streets, she recognized a name: Marchmont Street. She stood, arrested, trying to remember where she knew the name from. Then, as it so often did, Michel's voice slipped into her mind.

"In London you know, they are opening a bookshop, only for gay literature. On Marchmont Street."

Laure walked as though in a dream down the road, a nondescript street of estate agents and newsagents and dry cleaners, coming to a halt outside a white-fronted shop. There it was, painted in black on white: GAY'S THE WORD. In the window, *Love Bites* by Della Grace, *Tales of the City* by Armistead Maupin, *Sexing the Cherry* by Jeanette Winterson, *Ceremonies* by Essex Hemphill. And there, face out beside *A Boy's Own Story* by Edmund White, was *Reflections*. Laure's throat tightened. She had not expected it to be there, but here she was alongside her brethren, her people, her heroes and the writers Michel loved, or never lived long enough to read. She knew she should go in, but she felt oddly afraid. At certain points in her life since Michel's death she'd felt his presence as a tangible thing, not a spirit but a physical will, and now he arrived beside her, as he never would, and pressed his hand to the small of her back.

The shop was larger than she'd been expecting, and closing. The bookseller looked up when she entered and smiled. He was ringing up the till, but gestured at the shelves and said, "Go ahead, I'll be a few minutes. Maths isn't my strong point."

Laure smiled and walked past him, past fiction and memoir, where she noticed two more copies of her book face out, to poetry. This was where Michel would have come, would have stood, greedy to find more words, more men and women who understood him, could voice his griefs and ardours better than he ever could. Laure picked a book at random, a cover Michel would like, two men in bed, the buttocks of one exposed. She flicked through the pages then picked up its neighbour, a slight navy volume with a central image of a skeletal statue gesturing at the sky. *The Man with Night Sweats*. Laure felt a chill run over her own flesh. She opened it, again at random, and found herself reading a poem about a man regarding another on his death bed. "Still Life." She turned a few more pages, and found another, "Memory Unsettled." *When near your* death a friend / Asked you what he could do, / "Remember me," you said. / We will remember you.

Hands shaking, Laure approached the counter.

"Oh no! You aren't going to give me more money, are you?" said the bookseller.

Laure smiled back. "I'm afraid so."

"Ah, an accent! Where are you from?"

Laure still had an instinct to say *Paris*, but she answered, "Rouen."

"Amazing," he said, and Laure had the sense he didn't know where it was. Then he said, "Joan of Arc, right? An icon if I ever knew one. Have you read *Margery Kempe*?"

Feeling embarrassed by her presumption, Laure shook her head.

"Have a look. It's deeply sexy." He plucked a book off the counter and pressed it at her. "Margery Kempe was this Norfolk mystic, hence Joan of Arc. She spoke to God, and in this, Glück imagines her having a sexual relationship with Him."

Laure flicked through, finding the language rich and strange, and added it to the Thom Gunn.

"Every book in here is brilliant, really," said the bookseller, ringing them up. "Our manager has great taste."

"I'm glad I found you late, or I think I'd have spent all day here."

"You're welcome to." As he rung her up, Laure saw her book was on the counter too. If Michel were there he'd announce her as the author, tease her for being embarrassed. She paid, waving away his offer of change, and left the shop.

The rain had stopped, and Laure slipped the books into her jacket pocket, holding their slim spines as she crossed the Euston Road. King's Cross was coming alive again after the rain, sex workers talking on corners, men picking fights with the air. It was dirty and vibrant, shining with wet, and it felt like Paris after rain, her Paris, Le Marais as it had once been.

Her stomach gave a treacherous rumble. The appetite she'd gained after quitting drinking remained even after taking up smoking once more, and she ducked into a café. It was warm, the window steamed up, and her order was taken by an unsmiling Polish woman. She ate a cheese sandwich, smoked a cigarette, drank a black coffee and enquired about the rooms upstairs.

Her room in fact was downstairs, in a basement with a barred window at eye level with the pavement. The single bed was narrow, the toilet shared. It reminded her of Erica's room in the pension in Paris, the one they were chased out of, except it smelled of cigarettes and the sheets were spotlessly clean. The window frames rattled when a Tube trundled by. Laure kicked off her shoes, peeled off her wet clothes, and lay naked on the pristine bed, springs sagging beneath her as she lit a cigarette and blew smoke at the stained ceiling. She could read shapes into them: clouds and stars, like the ones her father painted on her childhood bedroom.

Laure rolled over and picked out the novel the bookseller had recommended. *Margery Kempe* had a cover of fierce purple and green, like a schlocky horror novel, but inside the words were rich and pillowy, outrageously sexy. The sacred and the profane, one and the same. Reading some of the passages she remembered the orgasm of the previous afternoon. It had been her first in some time. She and Barbara rarely had sex, but if Barbara took her back Laure would try to remedy that. There was time. She had time.

She set the book aside and turned off the light. It was dark outside, the orange glow of streetlamps leaking around the thin curtains. Exhaustion tugged at her. She pulled the book of poetry from her jacket pocket and slid it under her pillow, hoping, that night, to dream of Michel.

•

Erica heard the taxi leave before sunrise with a sense of relief and resolution. She felt she'd taken a cure for a sickness long rooted. It took the feel of Laure's wetness on her fingers, the taste of her in her mouth, to finally cement for her the unreality of her fantasy. It was because Laure felt exactly the same, tasted as good as she remembered, that Erica realized even this was not real. Even as she lost herself to sensation, she knew she had wasted so much time in this other life, and needed to return for good.

She went downstairs in the blue light of pre-dawn, and began to tidy. She was grateful for the task while also knowing this era of her life was at an end. She was tired of wasting her luck. She would hire a cleaner. Eli and Sylvia didn't need her home all the time. What would she do instead? One of the mothers yesterday mentioned the need for reading monitors at the girls' school. Maybe she could apply to work in a bookshop, or a library. A librarian. Were there degrees for those? Undoubtedly, which would horrify Ant's father, God rest him. Horrify Laure.

"How do you always beat me to the dishwasher?" Ant was in the doorway, his boxer shorts rucked up, hair tousled. She could see the shine of his scalp through thinning hair, and knew he would hate it, going bald. Ageing. She smiled, pressed start on the dishwasher.

"They're gone," she said, gesturing at the note on the table. She hadn't bothered to read it, there would be nothing of consequence. Ant nodded, picking up the paper.

"Shame they had to go so suddenly."

Erica busied herself with the tea towels. They had dozens now, from school, given to them, arrayed across two drawers. It was ridiculous really. She must free up some space—

"Erica." Ant was standing beside her, very close. His face was still heavy with tiredness. She felt the warmth of his body against hers. "You know I love you, don't you?"

She wondered if he was about to confess something: an affair, a terrible illness. She turned to look at him, and found he was searching her face.

"I love you too," she said. He seemed to be waiting for something, as though she were about to offer him a confession. But Erica had already decided she would not tell him about Laure. She would simply be a better wife. "I've decided I want to start working again."

He looked amazed, and then so happy she laughed. "E! Do you know how long I've waited to hear you say that? We can set up a desk in my office, write together like old times—"

"Not writing. I don't want to write." It was true, now she said it. "I think I want to do something with books though."

"Something with books!" Ant whooped. "We'll work it out. You're feeling better, aren't you? I can see it."

She kissed his mouth, and pressed herself against him. She felt rather than heard his murmur of surprise. It had been years since she initiated anything, but something was awake in her now, a clarity. She wanted this life. She chose him.

Chapter Twelve

For all its long-awaited joys, the one part of being a school librarian Erica could not accept was the fact the computers lived in the library now. It meant constant tapping, constant update dings, constant monitoring to make sure the Year 9s were not trying to access unsuitable websites, or the Year 7s crashing the system trying to download Mario Kart or The Sims. She wanted to think and talk about books, and though she understood she needed to undergo safeguarding training regularly, and file reports about loan numbers, and design herself the posters comparing books to films in an effort to get the kids to believe her constant refrain "Reading is cool!," it was intolerable to her that she was expected to know how to restart Paint or unjam a printer.

Still, at least she knew Eli wasn't one of the students typing www.blue.com in an attempt to bypass the intranet's security. She was still so mortified her mum worked at her school she barely came to the library at all. Her youngest would eventually come back to her—it had already happened to Sylvia, now in Year 12 and unashamed to hug her on sight—but she couldn't help feeling hurt that Eli found her presence so excruciating.

Erica stifled a yawn and checked her phone surreptitiously. Ant was in charge of dinner that night and she was anxious for him to confirm he'd taken the lamb chops out of the freezer. That, and to know what his agent Charles thought of his new pages. After the triumph of his fourth novel, Ant had been struggling, circling around an idea for six years now—a record even for him. Erica told him selling on an idea to an editor he'd not worked with before was a bad move, but he'd been blinded by the publisher's excitement and sold for a "major" pre-empt. That editor had left soon after and Ant was adrift on the quickly changing tides of staffing. Thank goodness for Charles, who despite encouraging Ant to take the money was now proving himself an invaluable buffer against the publisher's desire to see a return and put out any old crap. They'd have published his shopping list in hardback if they could. Time and again Erica told him to give the money back and return to his old publisher, his old editor, who would soon set him straight, but he refused. No messages, so Erica texted again: *Anything from C? Lamb chops out?*

As she pressed send, her phone buzzed with an incoming message from an unfamiliar number, a French code. Her ears began to ring. She opened it, and read: *Hi Erica, it's Léa from Paris. Can you call me on this number?*

Léa. They hadn't spoken since Michel died. What was it? Ten years ago, twelve? The bell rang for end of lunch, and once Erica had ushered the final stragglers from the computers and bean bags, placed the monitors on standby and replaced any stray books, she locked the library door behind her and went to the staff room. It was deserted after lunch, that distinctive sandwich-and-soup aroma haunting the foam-stuffed chairs, and she sat in the prized corner seat and pulled out her mobile again. She should wait to get home to call. But curiosity triumphed, and before she could find reasons not to, she typed the number into her keypad and pressed the call button.

Léa answered so quickly Erica knew she must have been staring at it. "Oui?"

"Léa. It's Erica."

"Ah." A long exhale. The line was crackly. "Pardon, my head . . . I've spoken to so many people today. Erica, hello. I'm sorry for the message. How are you?"

"Fine." Erica was confused. "How are you?"

"Not so great. Um. I contacted your husband's agent because I didn't know your number. I hope this is OK."

Erica waited for her to reach her point. She was not used to people going through Ant to get to her when it was so often the other way around.

"Laure is ill. She is in hospital. She had a . . . how do you say . . . pardon, I should have looked it up."

"French is fine," Erica said. Everything in her body was clenched.

"We say AVC . . . I think it stands for accident vasculaire cérébral."

"A brain accident? A haemorrhage?"

"Her right side is stuck. Paralysée."

"Paralysed," repeated Erica. "A stroke?"

"Oui, oui. A stroke."

But Laure was only in her forties.

"I don't know," said Léa, as though answering an unheard question. "Barbara said to call anyone who might want to see her. I know things . . . how do you say. But I know she loved you."

Erica's throat was tight. There was sudden heat behind her eyes, the ringing in her ears getting louder.

"Where is she?"

"Sainte-Anne in Paris. She's been awake two days, we weren't sure—" A catch in Léa's voice, a stifled sob. "But she is awake. She cannot move her right side. We want her to have visitors, to remember."

"She doesn't remember?"

"We don't know. She doesn't talk."

"Will she . . . is she . . . will she live?"

"She is alive."

When she got home the house was full of Brahms, so she knew Ant must be writing. His phone was on the counter, the lamb chops beside it, juices leaking all over the stone. She hastily wiped the counter, placed the chops on a plate, scooped up his phone and hurried to his study.

The door was ajar, the music loud. She peered inside and saw Ant was not at his desk at all, but sitting in the chair he read in. She could see one long leg, his hand resting on his thigh. Not reading, either. Erica pushed the door open.

"Ant?"

He looked up at her, his eyes glassy, the skin around them tight and red. Erica rushed to him and crouched in front of the chair, heart stuttering at the thought of more bad news. "What's happened?"

"Did Léa call you?"

"Yes." Erica frowned. Was he crying about Laure? She had not allowed herself tears yet. "Did you hear about Laure?"

"Yes. I thought you'd want her to tell you."

"Oh, Ant. It's going to be all right. They work wonders now." Erica felt her mother's brain take over, her shock pushed aside to make room for solution-finding, comforting.

"Are you going?"

"I don't know." Erica stood up and pressed pause. The Brahms ceased.

"I think you should." Ant was regarding his hands. His hair was recently cropped short to defy the thinning, and she was still unused to the shape of his ears, their bareness. "I think she'd want to see you."

"Maybe. I don't know. It's been so long. Would you want to go?"

Ant gave a hollow, hiccupping laugh. "No." A long pause. "I know, you know."

Erica stopped stroking his hand. "Know what?" But from the look he gave her, sorrowful, slightly desperate, she suddenly understood.

"I know what she was to you. I know it wasn't only that one summer in Paris before we met. I could tell when I got back from tour, met you in Paris." He checked her face, and she couldn't deny it. "You kissed me differently. Wanted other things in bed. Your book was full of a voice that wasn't yours. When I realized it was her—"

"How?"

"You talked about her. A lot. I'm not stupid. I worked it out. But then we had our girls, and I thought that was it, I thought it was enough for you."

His lip was trembling. Erica's head felt like it was floating away from her body, an absurd balloon. She wanted to reassure him, but she was in shock. He'd known. He'd known, and carried it all these years.

"But then I saw her name on the lecture list, and I went only to see her. I thought I could confront her. I knew I could never tell you. I didn't want to lose you." He shook his head. "But I liked her. And there was something in me that wanted to test you. I know it's cruel, but maybe I wanted to show her how beautiful our life together was, and how nothing could break it.

"But I was wrong, wasn't I?" He looked at her, and she saw in his eyes the last glimmer of desperate hope that all of what he was saying was fiction. "I knew since Normandy."

"Nothing happened," said Erica. "Nothing happened there."

"Maybe not what happened here." He swallowed, wincing. She didn't know what to do. The beach, the sea. He'd known, he'd known. "But something happened. It was between you. I couldn't stand to see it. Didn't want to be around it. I know I was a prat, that trip."

"You weren't."

"But I was jealous. And insecure. And the book was so hard and my wife was so obviously in love with someone else. A woman!" He laughed again, a sob. "But what kind of man can admit that?"

"You should have told me—"

"You should have told me!" It was not a shout, but the force of it sent Erica shuffling back on her knees, pushing herself up into his desk chair.

"I didn't know what to tell you," she said at last. "I didn't know myself."

"Really?"

"I know it sounds stupid." Erica looked out of the window, at the marshlands shining pewter in the brisk spring sunlight. She could have denied it. But she wanted to tell him the truth, even if the lies felt kinder. "But especially after all the stuff with Eli, with me I mean. I didn't know what I was."

"I knew you were ill," said Ant. This was a conversation they'd had before, but she didn't stop him. Let him say whatever he wanted to. "I told you. I offered you all the help you could have needed. Why didn't you let me help you?"

"I thought I deserved it. But that doesn't excuse . . . I didn't know. Nothing happened in Normandy." This was a lie, but how to explain the touches, the fantasies of Laure and her children running in Monet's garden? It was worse, almost, than what happened here: the thinking of it, the not telling him.

"But you loved her. And you were together, in Paris?"

"Yes."

"And here?"

The guilt was a noose. "Yes."

He nodded. "I knew. I knew and I waited for you to tell me. But you didn't and you didn't and then things were so good with us, maybe even because of that? I don't know." He cradled his head and spoke to his lap. "Don't answer that. I don't want to know."

"There's been nothing since then. No contact at all. And it was so stupid, so awful. I'm so sorry." Erica felt tears starting though she didn't deserve them. "I'm so sorry. I didn't know how to . . . I love you. I really do love you."

"You know, I never once thought of leaving you. Even after I realized. Does that make me pathetic?" He looked like a lost boy, a lost child dazed by the enormity of the world, the unfamiliarity of its extent.

"I'm sorry. I love you."

He searched her face. "Do you?"

"Yes. More than anything."

"I don't understand." His voice cracked, his eyes filling once more with tears.

"I'm sorry." She went to him, and he let her hold him, his head pressed into her middle, shoulders shaking. How to explain she once loved Laure more than him, or rather the idea of her. That many times she wished she hadn't left Paris, and never met him, had their girls. Loved Laure the rest of her life. That sometimes, she understood that a whisper away from this world, that was how it was.

At last, his sobs receded. He sat back, looking exhausted. "Are you going?"

"No. I don't know."

"I think you should go. If it were me, I would want you there."

Erica looked out again at the marshes, the far-off sea. Somewhere in Paris, Laure was afraid, in pain. She remembered Léa's words. *Stuck. Doesn't talk. She loved you.* The man in front of her loved her too, loved her constantly, kindly, passionately and actively. He was offering her forgiveness, although it hurt. He was letting her go to her ex-lover with his blessing, putting aside his own feelings as he had so many times before. What was it about a man's sacrifice that made it so much more moving? Perhaps because she didn't expect it, and neither did anyone else.

But Erica didn't want to go. She didn't want to endure Barbara's pointed looks, or leave her girls before exams. Most of all, she didn't want to see Laure like that. Stuck. Mute.

"It's the right thing to do," said Ant, his voice a little more level. Erica nodded.

It was Erica's first time on the Eurostar. She fell asleep in England and woke an hour later to the brightening French countryside whipping by. The train delivered her into the heart of Paris, and as she descended into the metro she realized she hadn't had to check the map.

She disembarked at Glacière in the fourteenth, not far from where Barbara's parents' apartment was. She hadn't thought to ask why Laure was in Paris, and now realized it was likely because she and Barbara had moved back. Until she spoke with Léa, she didn't even know if they were still together, but now she had a vision of them living in the small apartment, cooking in the kitchen where they used to smoke and kiss, sleeping in the bed where Claude and Léa used to sneak off to fuck. Laure, back in Paris. She wondered what had led to that happening.

The hospital was once an asylum. Ant had fallen down a Yahoo hole researching it while Erica packed, reading facts about its past and current speciality as a psychiatric hospital, its recent expertise in neurology.

"They have state of the art facilities. She's in good hands." Erica wondered when the hospital would crop up in one of his short stories. It was beautiful, designed in an elegant colonial style, but her directions for the neurology unit led her around to a modern glass extension. Laure would hate it.

She signed in at reception, and was directed to a ward on the second floor. She took a brightly lit lift and the doors opened to reveal a long corridor, broken only by a brace of chairs. On one, sitting bolt upright, was Barbara. Erica walked towards her as quietly as she could, practising what she could say, but when Barbara saw her, she only stood up and embraced her.

"Barbara, I—"

"Not now. I'm glad you came," she whispered. "She's awake."

Laure was in a room on her own. It was white, all as white as a cloud. A radio was playing a familiar song. Laure was propped up on pillows, and she turned her head to look at Erica. Erica stood arrested in the doorway, by her beauty, her movement. It had been so long, and Laure looked so much older.

"Ravie," she said.

"Ravie."

Her voice was slow and careful, but when she smiled, both sides of her mouth turned up. Erica crossed to her, bent down and kissed her forehead, cool and lined. She smelled as she always did, the hospital stink not permeating her.

"You came," she whispered. "Thank you."

"Of course." Erica took her rough hand, mindful of the cannula. They sat quietly, the only sound that song on the radio. Was it usual for a hospital to be so quiet?

"How are the girls?"

"They're fine. They send their love. How are you feeling?"

"Shit." Laure swallowed, her throat clicking. Erica poured water from the jug into a paper cup and held it to Laure's lips. Laure sipped, gestured for more.

"But you'll recover," said Erica, knowing she was doing what you were not meant to do to ill people, making promises, moving them on. "Ant said this place is specialized."

"In addiction too." Laure smiled again, so small. "I think we are all surprised I'm in the neurology department. How is Ant?"

"Good. Fine. Worried about you. And . . . he knows about us. About . . . Paris. About the beach."

"Mm. Barbara too. That is the problem with good partners, no getting around them." Laure shifted, and Erica helped her rearrange herself on her pillows. She looked at Erica, as though her face were a hard sum. "Do you think we could have been that? Good partners?"

"Yes," she said. "I think so."

Laure smiled, a painful wince. "I think so too."

And then what? Erica sat across from her husband as the other future unspooled before her, the one she was too scared to set into motion. Even as she imagined it, she winced at its childish whimsy, its simplicity.

"I don't want to go," said Erica, in a small voice, and Ant's relieved exhale told her it was what he hoped she'd say.

Erica texted Léa, a message she agonized over, explaining she couldn't come, and Léa texted back: *OK*. It was an anti-climactic end to the matter, and Erica thought often of how Laure's recovery was progressing in the coming weeks, months. She didn't allow herself to regret it, but she returned to the fantasy of going, replaying scenarios where she saw Laure again.

A year or so after news of the stroke reached her, Erica did what she promised herself she would never do and Yahoo'd Laure's name. The top results were for *Reflections*, but Erica scrolled until she found a more recent hit, an article in the *LiRE*, a French books magazine, about a book called *L'Abîme*—The Abyss. She clicked through, and a photograph of a woman bloomed on screen.

Were it not for the caption, Erica would not have recognized Laure. The right side of her face was sagging down, like some awful special effect in a film. Her eyelid drooped, her mouth hung slightly open, and the crease of her lip was shiny with saliva. But her gaze was steady and defiant, an invitation to look and to see, and on the heels of Erica's instinctive repulsion chased an instant guilt. Was she so shallow, still? Laure's silver hair was brutally cropped, close to her scalp. The background was blurred but she was arranged against grey, a city setting. So, she was still in Paris.

Erica hesitated and scrolled down. *L'Abîme* was to be released next month, and was about her alcoholism, her encounters with paintings in Paris, her finding of love. There was Barbara's name, and Erica saw she was now a practising clinical psychologist. Or maybe she had always been. Had Erica even asked her what she did when they visited? So it was a book about addiction, and art, and Barbara. The cover was abstract, and scrutiny of the caption revealed it to be a slick close-up of a still life by Edouard Manet, *Anguille et rouget*. Spitefully, Erica wondered who of Laure and Barbara was the eel, and who the red mullet.

She navigated back to Yahoo and typed *The Abyss*, receiving only hits for the 1989 film she'd gone to see at the cinema with Emma. It had been her first night away from the girls, and Emma's first from Stephen. They'd drunk a bottle of wine and Erica fell asleep halfway through. She added "book" and scrolled down two more pages before concluding it had not yet found an English publisher. She was sure Ant would hear about it if it did.

She closed the page. She was more shaken than if she'd discovered Laure was dead, and she hated herself for that. That her love for Laure was so closely entangled with resentment. She pictured Laure's face, all her faces, her face in anger and ecstasy and now, half-frozen in a disappointed slide. She could yet see her. Could yet reach out and say: *Congratulations on the book. I'm glad you're alive. I miss you.* A few moments would throw up some email address or other. Erica closed the tab.

Chapter Thirteen

Death came slowly, politely, almost apologetic, with a warning knock. Another AVC a week ago, her fifth all in all, after two episodes in her youth were found to have been consistent with symptoms of stroke. Her youth. Laure faltered over the word. She was young when Gabrielle disappeared her from her life, young even when she heard Michel had died. It seemed to her she would still be young, if these periods did not keep dragging her back, dragging her forwards into old age. Fifty-four. Surely she would outlive her father, who never stopped drinking or smoking for longer than a month. The disbelief that it could be otherwise was perhaps what kept her alive so long.

But as she sat bundled warmly in her newly essential wheelchair on their small balcony, in the apartment Barbara kept insisting they should give up due to the lack of a lift, and felt the now-familiar and no-less-terrifying beginnings of pain in her temple, the pins and needles buzz along her right side, she understood it was ending. It was a shame, to die on such a miserable day, in the most miserable month. Barbara was resting in their bedroom, and Laure could not call for her. She hadn't been able to talk clearly for some time, the slurring causing her such embarrassment she eventually gave it up entirely, though Barbara told her not to be so stupid. A shame not to have used her voice when she could, for something so petty as pride, not to have said *I love you* one last time. She tried to say it now, into the grim late afternoon darkness, but her tongue might as well have been a pebble in her mouth. Saliva was beginning to gather at the back of her throat, but she couldn't swallow.

The fog was coming now, closing over her vision. She would miss the particular light of Paris, its blue, its grime, the narrow pavements and dog shit, the smell of Gauloises, even the traffic. Not the tourists though, it could keep those. She was lucky to have had a great love affair with the city that so many people left with bitterness: she'd found her way back, and their second love had been sweeter. So too with Barbara. She wished she could tell Barbara not to be too sad. Tell her she wasn't afraid. They'd exchanged rings only last year, when the latest attempt to legalize gay marriage was thrown out. She was sorry she couldn't give Barbara this thing she so wanted, hoped she'd done enough to show she would have, if she could. The freckles on her chest. The soft give of her waist. Her thoughtful consideration of what to have for dinner, like it must be special, every night: a legacy of Michel. These were things she was sad to leave behind.

As the fog thickened, she tried to summon the other people she loved to her: Léa and her son Luc, Marie and Agnès, dyke dowagers of the Left Bank. Her agent Francine. Alors, it was like a speech at a launch. Who was she forgetting? Her newer friends too, Samuel and Laurent, Sophie and Manon. Her father—no. He was ahead.

The pain in her temple ratcheted, and she felt warmth spilling through her trousers. No good death for a whale, wasn't that the saying? No, that was the title of the short story collection she was working on. It wouldn't be published now, and maybe that was good. She'd never wanted to write it in the first place, though dying was perhaps an overreaction. What else would she miss? Music. Art. *Les Nymphéas*. How strange she thought it was about death when she was young, when recently it was all life to her. Life held exactly as it was, a shimmering surface stretched over everything that mattered, illusory and no less beautiful for it. She would miss Giverny, though she imagined where she was going, if not oblivion, was a garden. A garden with willows over a lake, and a bridge where her father would be standing. Michel, holding Lapin. Her mother a little behind, blurred as in a slow-capture photograph.

And then, of course, she thought of Erica. She thought of the letter she imagined writing her so many times, but there was never the right moment, or maybe she kept hoping she wouldn't have to send it, because she wouldn't die before they saw each other again. It ended thus: *There will be a day you will regret not coming. Probably you already do. But I want to tell you two things: I understand, because I regretted not being with Michel, in the end. And because I never got his forgiveness, and so never forgave myself, I forgive you. I will miss you.*

And then she could no longer breathe, but the pain had peaked and she was over the other side. She didn't feel hot, or cold. But nor did she feel, how goes the fairytale, just right. Her heart stopped, and her mind remained for the length of several heartbeats. Impossible, she decided, that there is nothing. A garden, yes. There may be a garden. And then Laure died, and everything she was, was no more.

•

Erica was watching the ten o'clock news alone, Ant working upstairs with his music blaring—Richter, his new obsession—her nightly phone calls with Sylvia in London and Elinor in Sheffield done. She sat scrolling through Facebook until she heard Fiona Bruce's voice announcing a segment on gay marriage becoming legal in France. Erica set down her phone and looked at the television. A challenge to the change in law had been overcome, and as of today, 18 May 2013, the amendment was constitutional. People of the same sex could get married in France.

Erica leaned forward. The screen was full of images of men kissing men and women kissing women, people of all sexes in suits and wedding dresses, drinking and cheering. Erica scanned the backgrounds for slices of Paris she might recognize, but there was nothing. The Paris of her memory was only that, had likely never existed. She picked up her phone again, and on a whim, typed *Laure Boutin* into Facebook's search bar. It returned dozens of results, and Erica began to skim the faces, clicking through pet photos and sunsets to scan the information, but none of it fitted. Erica inwardly cringed. Of course Laure would not have Facebook.

She hesitated, knowing to take another step could not be dismissed as a whim. *Leave it*, she said, in the same stern tone she used with Bluebell, the terrier Elinor made them get though she left for university the following year. *I'll take her with me!* Bluebell, currently suffering from an acute bout of flatulence, was snoring by Erica's feet. She needed to take her out once more before bed. She needed to leave it alone. But she opened the web browser and re-typed the name.

There was no need to scroll. It was the first item. An obituary in *Le Monde*. Erica's fingers felt numb as she tapped the link. There was a photo of Laure, the same one she'd seen the last time she'd searched her name. It was Laure. Her Laure. Laure was dead. Erica checked the date. 16 February 2010. Three years ago.

Her breathing became shallow. Laure had died three years ago, and she hadn't known. No one had told her. She hadn't known. Hadn't felt some cosmic tug on the cord that once bound them, no rippling of reality to let her know the other life was spent. She turned off the television and stood up, climbing the stairs.

"Ant?" she said, loudly to be heard over the music.

"Mm." He was elsewhere.

"I'm going for a walk, with Bluebell."

"OK."

He probably hadn't noticed it getting dark, was in that flow state where time and space acted outside the bubble of his writing, untroubling and unimportant. He could write till the early hours, like that. She wouldn't tell him just yet. Tears were coming, and she needed to be outside. She went to her dressing table and opened the top drawer, taking out the jewellery box she'd often thought of destroying, or throwing away. Her hands shaking now, she opened it. The photograph, Laure on the steps of the Sacré-Cœur, unbearably young and beautiful, serious face, serious book, hand a blur, bringing her cigarette up to her mouth. Erica left it where it was. Perhaps she could get it to Barbara somehow. Strange to keep it after all these years, especially after their betrayal. Best to let it go.

The cigarette though. Erica lifted it out of the box like a relic. She slipped it into the pocket of her dress, a floaty, shapeless affair Ant called her "tent," and picked up a box of matches beside her scented candle.

Bluebell sensed a walk even before she put her shoes on, darting to and fro, fetching her favourite ball, a stick rescued from the mud on their last walk. She was too soft on her, too soft on any dog. A cat would have suited her better, but she never convinced Ant he might have grown out of his allergies.

Bluebell tugged her out into the darkness, sniffing around her favourite patch of lawn and squatting to pee. When Erica led her out of the gate, she let out a whine of delight and strained on her lead, pulling her out along the winding path between the marshes, and on to the sea. The dunes were shadows of their former selves, the storm that killed a season's seal pups cutting metres and centuries off their height, but still they arrived like slow hills in the chill May air. Erica let Bluebell loose and the dog ran ahead, her fluorescent collar shining. The tide was in, the beach reduced to a few feet of white sand. Erica sat on the sloping butt of a dune and stared out into the darkness. The sea hush-hushed against the sand. Bluebell splashed in and out, delighted and snapping at the waves.

Erica pulled cigarette and matches from her pocket. Her flesh was goosepimpled in the breeze as she clenched the roll-up between her lips and cupped a struck match in her hands. The cigarette drooped, tobacco spilling from its unravelling paper, and as the tip lit, the entire thing came apart.

"Shit!" shouted Erica, as an ember fell into her lap, the elastic band twang of a small burn on her thigh. She patted it out, and began to laugh. How stupid. How apt. The perfect tribute. Tears were falling freely down her face, and Bluebell came helter-skeltering back, leaping and licking, her awful breath hot in Erica's face.

Erica scooped the tobacco, pieces of paper, dust of ash into her hands and clambered to her feet. She kicked off her sandals, awful orthopaedic things that she could walk for miles in, and waded, Bluebell leaping for joy alongside her, into the frigid sea. Was Laure cremated, she wondered, or buried? She would send Barbara the photograph, and if she wanted to get in touch, she could. Eventually, if it was appropriate, she could ask where she was, if there was a grave or a tree. Barbara owed her nothing, and she must expect nothing of her.

She looked down at the remnants of the roll-up. Stupid to have kept it all this time, and yet she was glad. She let go of the fragments, taken quickly by the easterly breeze. In her mind, she walked towards Laure on the right-hand steps of the Sacré-Cœur, exactly as she had. She smiled into the face of a person she would come to love. She opened her mouth, and in her best bad French said, "Bonjour."